PRAISE FOR JACK D. HUNTER

"Well researched, and the character developement is first rate. . . ."
—*Register, Mobile Alabama* on *Slingshot*

"The story grabs you from the start and the plot twists keep it continuously intriguing. . . . Hunter is at the top of his form in the genre he knows best: international intrigue."
—*Wilmington News-Journal* on *Slingshot*

"Smart and amusing . . . an extremely clever plot and dazzling characters. . . . Very well done."
—*Kirkus Reviews* on *The Potsdam Bluff*

"Enough twists and turns to keep you on your toes. Just when you think it's all over, Hunter grabs you with a hammerhead stall leading into a spinning spiral before landing solidly on the last page."
—*Compass* on *Sweeney's Run*

Slingshot

Jack D. Hunter

A TOM DOHERTY ASSOCIATES BOOK
NEW YORK

SLINGSHOT

Cover art by Alan Ayres

A Forge Book
Published by Tom Doherty Associates, Inc.
175 Fifth Avenue
New York, N.Y. 10010

Forge® is a registered trademark of Tom Doherty Associates, Inc.

ISBN: 0-812-52457-8
Library of Congress Card Catalog Number: 94-37834

First edition: January 1995
First mass market edition: April 1996

Printed in the United States of America

0 9 8 7 6 5 4 3 2 1

To Tommy
Many are the miracles we have shared.

(And, of course, to Jill, who knows what
Tina's all about.)

A special note of thanks to a very special attorney
DAVID E. HUDSON
who gave so generously of his time and savvy.

The best political community is formed by citizens of the middle class. Those states are likely to be well administered in which the middle class is large. . . . for the addition of the middle class turns the scale and prevents either of the extremes from being dominant. . . . Revolutions break out when opposite parties, the rich and the poor, are equally balanced, and there is little or nothing between them.

—Aristotle
384–322 B.C.

Has not [the tyrant] another object, which is that [the people] may be impoverished by the payment of taxes and thus compelled to devote themselves to their daily wants and therefore less likely to conspire against him?

—Plato
427–347 B.C.

A great fortune is a great slavery.

—Seneca
8 B.C.–A.D. 65

CHAUNCEY, VT (USP)— The mayor and four selectmen of this Green Mountain village were slain tonight when a masked trio burst into a meeting hall and swept the platform with machine-gun fire.

The attack, thought to have been the work of so-called Middies protesting the proposed 20 percent universal consumer tax on coffee, wounded a fifth member of the board and terrorized villagers packing the room.

Killed were Gladys Macfarland, 62, mayor for 17 years, and selectmen William Holly, 45; Thomas Cooch, 50; Daniel Lewis, 38; and Richard Holt, 53. Selectwoman Victoria Swanson, 46, was in intensive care at Brattleboro Hospital.

According to State Police Capt. Robert Dinswood, witnesses said one of the gunmen shouted, ''This is what happens to stooges of the tax tyrants in Montpelier and Washington.''

Dinswood said the meeting was called to explain how the coffee tax—a joint federal-state move to finance repairs to U.S. secondary highways, rural state roads and small-town infrastructures—would benefit the Chauncey area.

(Note to desk eds: Folo, with quotes from Vt. governor, others, is in prep for A Wire distrib.)

BULLETIN **BULLETIN** **BULLETIN**

Prologue

Ordinarily Ludwig took much pleasure in the ride to Schloss Donnerberg, especially on a day like this, with a fresh-fallen snow sparkling under a brilliant sun. But today, with the news he bore, enjoyment was hard to come by.

Of all the populated regions of the world—and he had a veteran traveler's appreciation of each—none offered a greater variety of beauty and surprises than his beloved Bavaria. He loved to ride through it, stroll through it, ski through it, drive through it. And it seemed never to change, despite two world wars and the schizoid national rot that had ensued. Rolling hills and expansive meadows in countless shades of green and purple; towering crags crowned by perpetual snow; lakes so deep they were black; monumental forests; and the epic juxtaposition of medieval hamlets and futuristic cities, wandering lanes and autobahns, bucolic stillness and urban clamor—an amalgam to be found nowhere else on Earth. And high on an eminence overlooking a hundred square miles of it all was Donnerberg—itself an incredible yet tasteful conjugation of crenelated castle and Malibu modern. Ludwig's capacity for envy had long ago been sated by his own success, but if there had been anyone left to envy, it would be Anton Rettung for his ownership of this extraordinary place.

As the Mercedes nosed under the mile-long canopy of snow-lacy chestnuts leading to the summit, Ludwig instructed, "Take this slowly, Heinz. These trees date from Charlemagne, and I want to savor them."

"As you wish, sir," the driver said.

In the backseat, deep in a womb of fragrant leather, sipping brandy from a silver cup, Ludwig gazed at the trees, but his mind was examining his anxiety. There was no little irony in the mix: Things had been going rather well this past week, and by all rights he should be calm, satisfied. But beyond the obvious concerns something subtle, indefinable, nagged—an ambiguity that lurked somewhere beyond thought.

The meeting, for all its momentous implications, could turn out only one of two ways, and if Rettung rejected the idea, they'd simply find another way to make it all happen. Rettung represented a difficult obstacle, to be sure, but the worst he could do would be to cause further delay.

It's the Cooper thing. Rettung is a formality. Cooper is a disaster. And I'm fretting about how to break the news to Takai. Yes, that's it. I'm dealing with cowardice here.

He waited for his mind to reassure him. (*Poppycock. You're no coward.*) But there was only the motor's soft purring, the tires crunching on snow.

And then there was another question, imprecise, bipartite: *Just why are we doing this? And having done it, what will we have accomplished?* He heard his own voice: "The game for the game's sake. Is that it?"

Takai stirred and gave him a sidelong glance. "Are you nervous?"

Ludwig pressed the button that closed the glass partition between them and Heinz. "Uneasy, yes."

"Relax, my friend. If Rettung says yes, we can proceed at once. If he says no, we'll find another way."

"I have unhappy news."

"Oh?"

"Frank Cooper is proving to be a heavy problem. He has discerned our intentions, and he's gone ballistic."

"Damn."

"Yes."

"How did he find out?"

"I don't think he 'found out' in the normal sense of the term. He's a very perceptive, intuitive type, and I think he saw the pattern of activity and made an educated guess. He happened to be right on the money, because in a very hot call yesterday he sketched out the basic scheme right on the phone. One, two, three."

"So what does he propose to do about it?"

"That's what bothers me most. He didn't say."

"I don't follow you."

"Frank's a writer. And it's my experience that when Frank's very angry and says nothing, that means he's about to write a fiery letter to somebody."

"In this case, which somebody?"

"My guess is the FBI. The FBI has jurisdiction in things like this, I believe."

"Does Tremaine know of this development?"

"Not yet. I've said nothing to anybody. Only you."

They fell into a prolonged pause, each staring at the passing snowscape as if hypnotized by its majestic silence.

Takai said then, "So that gives us two problem people now: Rettung and Cooper."

"I'm afraid so."

"The first need is to persuade Rettung, and we're handling that today. But we must negate Cooper at the earliest moment. He's a chronic, do-gooding zealot with a word processor and a huge audience. We can't tolerate that."

Ludwig said, "Frank will call for very special handling. He's an extremely difficult man to persuade or influence. Particularly when he's on his idealism horse. Just look at what he did with Martin's Six-Twenty. And I assure you, in this situation, he's feeling even more self-righteous."

Takai considered that. After a time he said, "The first need is to forestall any letter-writing by Cooper. Inform Tremaine of this development at once and tell him to apply whatever muscle he has at the FBI. If a letter arrives there, it must be intercepted and destroyed before it arrives on the desk of the director, who can't yet be counted among our friends—and is most unlikely ever to be. As usual, though, tell Tremaine only what he must know. As Cooper's longtime friend, we can't be sure where his logic ends and his emotion begins. So 'wary' is the word there.''

"And Cooper himself?''

"My people will handle him.''

They met in the Great Room, dwarfed by the lofty, vaulted ceiling, the colossal fireplace, the steppe of lushly carpeted floor, the wall of soaring windows and their view of the Tyrolean Alps. Rettung had placed his wheelchair so that he sat with his back to the windows, possibly because there was nothing they displayed he hadn't long since considered, but more likely because, by presenting him in silhouette, the placement gave him the advantage over his visitors. Seated on the arc of sofas, Ludwig and Takai faced the titanic scene, subdued and squinting against the glare, like spectators at the Creation.

As usual, Rettung gave no time to pleasantries, choosing instead to get right to business. "So then: Why have you requested this meeting, Ludwig?'' he asked in his reedy, old man's voice.

Ludwig, because he knew that Rettung placed a premium on brevity, was equally terse. "Mr. Takai wishes to establish a new foundation under the Rettung Internationale umbrella. He proposes the George Washington Fund for Political Research, which will open with a base grant of ten million dollars from Takai Electronics Industries of Kyoto.''

Rettung's watery, grapelike eyes turned slowly to regard the diminutive Japanese. "What would be the purpose of this fund?''

Takai nodded his head in a courtesy bow before answering, and the reflected snow glare on his sleek black hair, his round, soft-looking face, created an effect that suggested an illuminated ceramic figurine. His German, while faultless in construction, was weighted with Japanese pacing and inflections.

"May I say again, Herr Rettung, how honored I am to have been appointed to the board of your—"

Rettung held up a translucent hand. "Please, Mr. Takai, the point. I am an old man, and I have no wish to spend what remains of my life listening to obsequious presentations. What will your foundation do?"

If Takai had been offended, there was no sign. "The United States is generally accepted to be the linchpin of the world's political, economic, and social machinery. How fares the United States, so fares the world, so to speak. But today there are indications that the United States has become too large and too heavily laden with ethnic and geopolitical divisiveness to be effectively governed. In earlier times it thrived under its unique form of representative democracy, but today there are signs of serious disablements, decay—most of it due to the personal venality and lust for power of individuals in high places. The George Washington Fund proposes to offer grants to unpublished and generally unrecognized scholars, political scientists, sociologists, and economists, with a view toward precisely defining the American problem and offering—and testing—entirely new approaches to its solution. The need for new ideas is—"

Rettung broke in, "Certainly you can't be serious, Mr. Takai. What you are saying sounds absurdly similar to the catalog description of an American arts-college course in problems of democracy. With the kind of money you are making available, it seems that much more could be achieved than a mere reinvention of the wheel by the freshman class."

Takai, Ludwig saw, again gave no indication that he considered the old man's sarcasm to be an affront. He simply persisted. "Beyond the paralysis caused by its own greed and institutional egocentrism, the American government suffers from unprecedented economic pressures and cataclysmic collisions of rival cultures and ethnic vainglory that accelerate the overall degeneration. Seething discontent, verging on open rebellion, rages among huge blocks of the overtaxed, much-abused middle class. Ways must be found to inspire new thought, new inventiveness, that will, by stabilizing this wobbling of the American form of democracy, eventually bring stability to a world still groping through the smoke left by the Cold War. It's our opinion that—''

''Mr. Takai, let's cut this short. While I share your concern over the incipient American collapse and its effect on the world order, and while I respect you and your vast accomplishments, not only in industry but in sociological and philanthropic fields as well, and finally, while I most sincerely welcome your presence on the board of Rettung Internationale, I must reject your proposal. The—what is it? the George Washington Fund?—might well be a worthy project for a foundation. But I believe that it is too far removed from the basic raison d'être of Rettung and its subsidiary networks. Rettung is purely philanthropic. It is designed, first, to bring creature comforts to the world's needy and suffering, and, second, to inaugurate and support research and development that will enable needy peoples and nations to lift themselves out of the international slum. The foundation you propose deals with politics and political machinery, which, while part and parcel of crisis management, are of little practical assistance in providing better agricultural yields, water distribution, sanitation and hygiene, homemaking, rudimentary industry, and the like. Rettung and every one of its subsidiaries are devoted to pragmatism—community-level practicality. Your fund is academic, theoretical, and, therefore, categorically outside the Rettung definition. I'm sorry, but that's my position.''

The Japanese said, ''I am sorry, too. I was hoping that the Rettung umbrella might be broadened to include new areas of activity.''

Rettung turned his wheelchair, making ready to leave the room. ''Your George Washington Fund might indeed be viable. But not with us. Now, if you will excuse me, I'm tired and in need of medication. You gentlemen will be served luncheon in the veranda room, and you are invited to enjoy the handball court and swimming pool, if you care to stay awhile. Good day.''

Takai's opaque black eyes turned to regard Ludwig, but the German's gaze was oblique, and his face was pale. The five-minute meeting had been a catastrophe, and Ludwig was struggling to accept that reality.

As Rettung wheeled past the divan, Takai reached out with his right hand and, with a touch so light, so delicate it seemed almost affectionate, pressed his thumb against the old man's nape.

The chair faltered in its roll, and Rettung's faded eyes widened slightly, as if something extraordinary and not unpleasant had suddenly appeared before him. Then with a small sigh, the old man folded in on himself.

After a time, Takai said quietly, "Please call the butler, Edmund, and ask him to phone for a physician."

Ludwig, his eyes glazed and averted, dabbed at his mouth with a snowy handkerchief. He was unable to speak.

"Please," Takai said, "pull yourself together. Our host has suffered a fatal heart attack, and there are many things to attend to. And first among them is Frank Cooper."

One

Matt Cooper had adored his alcoholic, melancholic mother. She'd been loving, loyal, smart, and sort of cute beneath all the boozy Cassandra crap. It was this last, her claim to have the "gift of second sight"—always voiced in a whisper, eyes darting from side to side as if the devil himself might be listening—that gave him the only reason ever to be truly annoyed with her. The drinking he could almost understand, considering her apologia: "If you were always lonely the way I'm always lonely, you'd drink, too." But he could see no justification for the grim pleasure she derived from her so-called capacity for divination and prognostication. Obviously it was no gift; it was a thousand-horsepower curse. She had never foreseen positives or gain; her visions were always bleak and negative. And usually unrealized. The slamming of a door, the ringing of a phone, the fall of a leaf, for that matter, could send the dear woman into a week of despair over some impending disaster which hardly ever, as far as he could tell, came about. And finally, when borne over the years as a component of her burdensome marriage to Frank Cooper—Mr. Wonderful Himself—the "gift" had accelerated her trip down the flume of gin and left her beloved son with a recoil determination never to believe anything unless it could be seen, touched, smelled, heard, tasted, or explained.

Yet for all this determination to the contrary, and despite a profession rooted in pragmatism, there were times when he was oppressed by the spooky possibility that his mother had not been pipe-dreaming and might actually have passed along to him an ability to perceive bits of the unknowable and unseeable. Now, at this very moment, for instance, there was a kind of unspecific, indefinable weight on him—a physical thing. Staring into the misty night, listening to the moisture dripping from the eaves, he tried to analyze the sensation, to see its meaning. What he got instead was a glimpse of oncoming evil.

He didn't see evil, exactly. He felt it. Yet he *did* see it. A fleeting shadow, crossing his mind. More than a hunch, less than a vision.

Trouble, big-time, was on the way, sure as hell.

He simply *knew* it.

Maybe it was his world: everything a downer. Nothing was given his professional attention unless it spoke of calamity, corruption, rage, slaughter, envy, protest, vanity, material poverty, and the poverty of mind, body, and spirit that destroyed minds, bodies, and spirits. Or dealt with self-serving, self-perpetuating governments whose satraps at all levels were increasingly despised, feared, and violently resisted because they seemed unable to divest themselves of the idea that the populace was no more than a huge, undefended feeding ground.

What's the good word? There ain't no good word.

Ah, well. He who lives by the word shall die by the word, eh?

The waiter brought the bread and wine, an intrusion that broke the spell and turned Cooper's attention from himself to the candlelit procession below.

At Christmastime, the Chamber of Commerce and its tourism auxiliaries would go into a swoon over Watch Night. "A centuries-old Yuletide celebration— quaint, lighthearted, and guaranteed to delight the visitor,'' rhapsodized their brochures and promo sheets. ''Hundreds of candle-bearing townspeople in medieval garb parade through the narrow streets of St. Augustine's Spanish Quarter, first to the old city gates and a ritual posting of guards, then back to the plaza for a blessing by assembled ecclesiastical leaders.''

Cooper, thanks to his journalist's perception of the hustle as America's national sport, accepted this wryly as simply one more example of the local passion for hyperbole and its concomitant distortion of history into a dollar sign. Parades gather crowds, and crowds buy things, and if an ancient religious rite is expropriated by those who traffic in rubber alligators, silly hats, and raunchy T-shirts, who's to be surprised? Certainly not Matthew L. Cooper.

Because tonight was the night and the hoopla would make parking impossible anywhere in the historic preservation district, he had left his car on San Marco, in a spot roughly midway between his father's house on Water Street and Luigi's, an aromatic little restaurant on both floors of a restored English-Period house on St. George Street, where he had come for a late supper of chicken parmigiana. He ate in solitude beside an upstairs window, giving occasional consideration to the eerily lit parade as it shuffled northward on the street below.

There was a stir at the landing, a quick, soft-spoken consultation between the hostess and a new arrival. A young woman appeared in the archway, a camera slung on a shoulder, a bulging tote bag on the other. She wasn't tall, but her figure was trim and sturdy, suggesting energy and resilience. Her hair was dark, cut short in a boyish way, and her brown eyes were large and amiable. He guessed she was in her early twenties.

Their gazes met.

''Hi, there,'' she said, showing pleased surprise.

''Hi.''

''You're Matthew Cooper, of the *Times-Union,* right?''

He felt the mild panic that comes with being recognized by a stranger. ''Well, yes—''

She came to his table, hand outstretched. ''There's no way

you'd remember me. I'm Tina Mennen. I attended the seminar you led at the press association meeting in Orlando last year.''

He pushed back his chair and rose to shake her hand. Her grip was firm and warm. "Nice to see you," he parried.

"You're called Coop, right?"

"By everybody but the IRS."

"I really liked your piece last Sunday—the one on the double-dipping legislators. Great stuff."

"Thanks," he said, still at a loss, still embarrassed and uncomfortable. He glanced at her camera gear. "What are you up to these days?"

"Got hired finally."

"Oh?" He groped for a clue as to how he might avoid sounding like the village idiot.

"Yep. I was one of the wannabes in your audience. Now I'm in the trade. I'm a reporter on the St. Augustine *Record.* They've given me purely entry-level stuff, but I'm working."

"How about that."

He felt the gathering of resentment. This meal had a special purpose that was now being derailed. Most times he preferred to eat alone because he found it impossible to enjoy food and talk at the same time. But it was a special pleasure to mess his way privately through a late-night pile of pasta and sidebars; the combination of wee hours and dilatory chowing down was a kind of spiritual thing, a rite with which to restore sensibilities rubbled by the day's assorted poundings. So he had entered the restaurant with the hope that this therapeutic ritual would come through again and brace him for tonight's duty call. No chance of that now; his upbringing required that he invite her to join him.

"Sit down, maybe?"

"Oh, I shouldn't, Coop. I just came in for coffee, and I don't want to butt in any more than I already have."

"Well, whatever pleasures you—"

His lack of enthusiasm obviously didn't diminish her own. She slid into a chair and motioned to the waiter, a teenager wearing a smile stiffened by ten hours of sucking up to credit-card autocrats from Buffalo and Chicago and other winter wonderlands. "Coffee, eh, buddy?"

The boy ambled off, scribbling on his check pad.

Unslinging her gear and adjusting herself to the chair, the girl said, "Don't tell me that you're down here because you've heard that the Watch Night parade is really a protest march by Middies."

He assembled an expression that acknowledged her little joke. "If you take a look at the marchers you'll see a few of St. Augustine's Leets in there, too."

"Then they're taking their lives in their hands. Did you see that story on the A-wire tonight? The one on how a gang of Middie coffee-tax protestors machine-gunned the whole town council in that burg up in Vermont? I mean, there's a real revolution stirring up, wouldn't you say?"

" 'Thought to be Middies' was the operating phrase in that story. Whether they were Middies or just a bunch of punks is up for grabs."

"What crap. Why would punks wipe out a village government, especially these days, when governments lean over backward to kiss their behinds? It's Last-straw City with the Middies, pal. Confiscation of income, inflation, corrupt politicians, runaway crime, unemployment are bad enough. But when you screw around with their coffee—watch out."

He held up a hand. "Please. I've had enough business for the day. I just don't want to talk about the middle class and its fight with The Elite. I don't want to talk about the news business, period."

"So why are you here, then?"

The question, asked by anyone else, would have been no more than a conversational gambit. Coming from her, it was presumptuous, intrusive. Too tired to fence, he gave her a straight answer. "I'm catching a late supper before a visit with my old man."

"I hope you have better luck at seeing him than I have. I've been trying for a month to interview him for a book-page feature. I can't get past that secretary of his."

"Oh? You know who he is?"

"Of course. That was one of the reasons your seminar was so well attended. Everybody knew that you're the son of Frank Cooper, the famous author."

He tried to smile, but it didn't work. "The sins of the father are visited on the son, eh?"

"Hey, I certainly don't mean to downsize your own rep, seeing as how you're one of the hottest investigative reporters in the South and all. But your daddy is my special hero—always has been since I began to read English—and I'll tell you here and now: He has a powerful draw, not only on me, but on all mortals who yearn to write for a living." She paused, smiling. "Anybody ever tell you how much you look like your father?"

"It would be easier to count those who haven't told me."

"He's really a super writer. Plain super."

"I suppose so."

She gave him that quick glance. "Suppose? Don't you know?"

"Well—"

Amused disbelief was on her face. "Do you mean to tell me that you, the son of Frank Cooper, haven't read Frank Cooper's novels?"

"Not all of them. The earlier ones. Part of the others. Not all of them."

"How come?"

"It's hard to say—"

She laughed softly. "I bet I know why. You're a writer, too. You're jealous of him. Of his success. Am I right, or am I right?"

He felt heat rising in his face. "You're all kinds of cheeky, aren't you."

"Not really. I just say what I think. Usually."

"That's going to get you kicked all the way to Uranus someday, pal."

"I suppose you're right. My father's warned me about that more than once."

"You should listen to him."

"Hey," she said, suddenly apologetic, "I didn't mean to

come across smart-ass. Honest. It's just that I've seen this before. In me. I had a classmate in college who got her first novel published. A real coup for a woman only twenty or so. I was so madly jealous I never did read her book. Sort of like, if I didn't read it it would go away, you know?''

Cooper, working to maintain his cool, dabbed at his lips with his napkin, then made a business of consulting his wristwatch.

She was unabashed. ''How come you're going to visit him so late?''

''For my father, it isn't late. It's the middle of his workday. He does his thing between ten at night and two in the A.M.''

''The eccentric writer, eh?''

''His secretary covers the daytime traffic while he goes underground. Then, like Dracula, he comes up when the sun goes down. He claims he gets more done at night. No phones, no interruptions.''

The waiter brought the girl's coffee, and, after a trial sip, she said, ''That's why I have trouble getting past the secretary, obviously.''

Still struggling inwardly with the stab she had delivered, he was determined to show outward cool. ''One of the ironies of fame is that people work their buns off for years to get public attention, then, once they've got it, work their buns off to maintain their privacy. Since Mr. Wonderful is superfamous, he's superprivate.''

''Don't you like him?''

His persistent irritability rose another notch. ''What kind of question is that?''

''Well, I mean some people love their parents but don't like them. You sound sort of—The Old Man, Dracula, Mr. Wonderful—you know: sarcasm. Dislike.''

In a kind of reflex, he came back at her. ''How about you?'' he snapped. ''Do you like your old man?''

''I idolize him.''

''What's he do for a living?''

''He owns and operates a travel agency in Philly.''

''Is he successful?''

''You bet your katooty he is. Actually, he was successful

before he came to the States. He was a lawyer in Bonn, but the call of the States was loud in his ears. He brought us—Mama and my sister Lori and me—to Boston when I was eight. But there isn't a lot of call for German lawyers in Boston—or anywhere else, for that matter—so he used his savings to buy the agency from a friend who was retiring. He's made a beeg thing of it, and I'm proud as hell of him.''

"So how come you aren't into travel agentry?"

"Same reason you don't write fiction. I don't want to be known as Karl Mennen's daughter—I want him to be known as Tina Mennen's pop. It's trying to get out from somebody else's shadow. Wanting your own identity, and like that.''

Cooper pretended to stifle a yawn. "I'm not into that psychological stuff.''

She laughed softly. "Then you surely don't believe in fate, in predestination, eh?''

"Nope.''

"Well, take another look: Reporter struggles unsuccessfully for days to land an interview with a famous dude. She drops into a restaurant for coffee and, *shazam,* said famous dude's son is sitting there, alone, lonely, and dying for some conversation.'' She laughed again. "Fate, see? Even predestination, maybe.''

The annoyance shifted into a higher gear. "I wasn't alone and lonely and dying for a conversation. Nor do I see what your struggles have to do with my having a late supper, and coincidence and shazam, and like that.''

She shrugged, and sipped at her coffee again. Then, winking at him across the rim of her cup, she said smoothly, "I think it's sort of obvious. Fate brought me here so that you could learn of my problem and offer to intercede—to persuade your daddy to grant me an interview.''

Her presumptuousness was annoying enough, but now she had introduced an element that raised the octane to pure anger. During Cooper's eleven years of front-line duty as a correspondent in civilization's war to contain its own chronic savagery, he had learned never to be without his full metal jacket of aloof self-interest. Journalists are among the world's most competitive creatures, and, since none of them had ever given him a break, it had become his abiding policy to return in kind. "Sorry," he grated. "I don't do that kind of window."

The pretty eyes blinked. "Oh?"

He decided to spell it out for her. "I'd been a reporter for only six months when I learned not to get involved with other news people. A cub for another paper was working the same turf I was assigned to. We got sort of friendly, and I soon saw that he was a pilot fish—the half-trained product of a cookie-cutter journalism school who, to survive, would swim in the wake of some pro, snapping up the crumbs the pro dropped. Which was okay with me, because the system in those days allowed no better way for a marginal greenhorn to learn the ropes. But which was sort of dumb of me, too, since I could see how the guy tended to pass up the crumbs and use his cutes to gain access to the pro's main meal, if you know what I mean. He would use the aw-shucks-poor-little-me act and, because news people are suckers for the underdog, the pro would get suckered. So I should have known better. But one day I got to feeling sorry for the dude and I tipped him to a feature story that was tangential to the mainliner I'd been developing for weeks. He not only picked up on the feature but also broke an embargo date and pirated enough of the mainliner data to effectively preempt my exclusive. So I don't help any news people do anything anymore."

Her amiability faded, and the soft brown eyes took on a glint. "What did you do to the pilot fish?"

"I'd like to say I punched him in the nose. But I didn't, because all I'd have gotten out of that would be a minute's satisfaction, a lawsuit, and a pink slip. I subscribe to the philosophy that getting even is better than getting violent."

She placed her cup on its saucer, carefully, tidily. "So what you're saying is, you won't put in a word for me with your dad."

"You got it."

She began to gather her things. "Well, I certainly didn't mean to hit your hot button, but it seems I have. There's no room at your inn for a bedraggled beginner who just happened by, eh?" Her face was pink.

"Give me a break, pal. You didn't just happen by. I heard you talking to the hostess. I heard you use my name. You knew I was here before you came into this restaurant. I don't know how you knew, but you knew."

The pink became red. "I happened by, believe me. I was walking through the garden from the parking lot and I just happened to see you up here in the window."

After a taut interval, she rose from her chair, gathering her things. "Well, thanks for the coffee."

She turned and strode into collision with the waiter, who, retreating in a mad parody of a soft-shoe dance, kept his tray of wine glasses miraculously horizontal.

Cooper, unamused by the slapstick, watched somberly as she disappeared down the stairs.

He returned to his meal, finding that it had cooled. He ate it anyhow.

It was close to eleven when he left the restaurant. The parade crowds had disbanded and gone home to bed, yielding the district to its late-night cadre of drunken brats squalling their way to ignominious adulthood. He made for the Avenida at the bay-front end of Hypolita Street.

Beyond the fort and its seawall, the black expanse of the Matanzas was restless in the freshening wind. Farther out, east of the inlet and Anastasia Island's concrete-and-palmetto suburbia, was the ocean. Thundering. Infinite. Smelling of vastness and eons. Remote, invisible, and unrelated to the midnight streets, yet an abiding presence, oddly intimate, oppressive.

No, more than that.

Malevolent.

Cooper felt this, and he hunched into his raincoat, an instinctive move to reduce the bulk he presented to the chill blowing in from the north. As he walked, he felt, too, the special spookiness of St. Augustine, an ancient harbor town rooted in savage religiosity and contention. And for a moment he thought he heard footsteps on the promenade behind him. But a glance showed him only that the seawall walkways and the Avenida itself, where traffic usually murmured through the night, were lifeless, empty. Then he tried to define sounds that seemed to drift down from the five-hundred-year-old fort, long since secured for the night by its federal custodians. The uneasy river and its inlet? The distant booming of the sea? Ghosts from the town's iniquitous past? Maybe one, maybe all—

He came to a halt and stood in the darkness, staring at the fort. His voice, low and filled with self-contempt, broke the silence. "God, Cooper. Are you ever a mama's boy."

He continued on to his beat-up red Ford and, as he stood at the driver's door, fumbling with his key ring, Tina Mennen racketed past in a prehistoric VW. Their glances met, then she looked away.

He shook his head, angered still again, this time by everything—by his ambivalence regarding his father; by his stagnating career; by a moment of privacy shattered by a presumptuous, angle-shooting jerk; by the raw night and the murky town; by the romantics who would abandon armchairs and TV for a cold and soggy shamble down Saint Boosterism Boulevard.

By everything he was, wasn't, could be, and wouldn't be.

The house was a Victorian mountain of clapboard and slate and stained glass, dappled by the restive shadows of wind-stirred oaks and Spanish moss. It sat between the street and the marshfront, stern behind stucco walls and wrought-iron gates, chalky in the reflected glow of garden lights. It had eighteen rooms, servants' quarters over the carriage house, and an in-ground pool and a dock and boathouse. It had been built as a vacation cottage for one of Henry Flagler's oil-baron buddies before Flagler had invented Palm Beach. Frank Cooper loved it "because it's big and fancy—but not so big and fancy that it invites rubbernecks and burglars." Coop despised it because his mother had been so unhappy there.

He punched the electronic gate-opener his father had given him for use on occasions like this, then, when the way was clear, drove to the parking pad beside the gazebo. At the side door he remembered that it was Manfred's night off, so he stood in the wind, fussing with his key ring, and it was only after he'd found the key that he realized the door was ajar. Not merely unlocked. Open and free-swinging.

He knew at once what he'd find.

He even knew where.

Frank Cooper was in the kitchen.

On the floor, surrounded by Christmas wrappings.

A bullet hole in his chest.

Two

The 911 call brought a squad car and a young, solemn patrolman who, after checking the body for a pulse, told Cooper to stand aside and touch nothing. Glancing at his watch, the cop wrote a note on his pad, then began to mutter importantly into the tiny radio on his left shoulder, all the while sending his gaze from the body to the table, the paper clutter, the walls, the ceiling, the countertops, and the appliances. Report finished, he instructed Cooper to come along while he looked around the house. After what seemed to be thirty hours, police were suddenly everywhere, the whirling lights on their car roofs sending shards of alarming brilliance through the neighborhood, their voices abrupt and harsh, their flashlight beams probing the night. Cooper and the patrolman returned to the kitchen just as a squat man in a rumpled brown suit came through the side door, blinking and blowing on his hands.

"Florida in winter," the squat man said to no one in particular.

The young cop's earnestness went up a notch. "Sergeant,

this here gentleman''—he nodded toward Cooper—''says he's the one that called. Says he's Matthew L. Cooper, son of the victim, Frank J. Cooper, resident of this house.''

''Anybody else around?''

''No, sir. I checked.''

''This is a helluva big place. Eighty-three people could have been jumping out the windows while you were checking. Somebody could have rearranged the downstairs furniture while you were checking the upstairs. Right?''

The patrolman looked unhappy. ''I followed procedure, Sergeant. I did the best I could.''

''The medical examiner's been called?''

''Dispatch says he's on the way.''

The squat man stifled a yawn and, for the first time since his arrival, directed his faded blue eyes at Cooper. ''My condolences. I read a couple of your daddy's books. He wrote good stories.''

''Thank you.''

''I'm Sergeant Nickerson, Homicide. Stand by. I'll need to ask you some questions.''

''Sure.''

Nickerson turned to examine the scene, seeming to enter a trancelike withdrawal from the surrounding busy-ness. Like the patrolman before him, he looked at everything, his gaze moving from side to side, up and down, a radarlike scanning of the terrain where some kind of hell had come and gone and left its litter. After a time he stirred; stepping slowly, carefully, a halfback learning the gavotte, he approached the body. Kneeling, he peered at the bloody shirtfront, tested the pale neck with the back of his hand, and then, resting on his haunches, took a notebook and ballpoint pen from his jacket pocket and began to write.

Cooper stood in stony isolation, dealing with an astonishingly painful, kaleidoscopic replay of his life with that inert lump on the floor. Frank, the enigmatic omnipresence. Frank, indifferent and taciturn one moment, sentimental and garrulous the next. Frank, brilliant and witty and unaware and dull, all in a single package. Frank, a man of driving passion and lazy indifference, and never a clue as to which would be dominant at any given time. Gone now. Reduced to an incredibly inert—what? Trash heap?

Standing there, struggling, he felt the return of an old familiar—the imp of outrage that had ridden his shoulder since boyhood.

When he was in grammar school, he had saved for months to buy an electric train. Frank would have bought him one, of course, because Frank had been a generous man, all his faults and foolishness notwithstanding. But a father's gift would not have satisfied a youngster's need to establish the dimensions of his self-sufficiency. He knew exactly which train he wanted; he had seen it running on a fancy table in the toy department of McCrory's big store downtown. A nickel here, a dime there, three pennies and a quarter—he finally amassed the twenty-eight bucks, which, on the Big Day, he put in his lunch pail, planning to make the buy after school. The money was stolen during the morning recess, and his disappointment and rage became everlasting, actually leading him in later years to consider a career in law enforcement.

It now settled its focus on the lump on the floor.

He had been introduced to sudden, violent death as a Marine in the Balkan Intervention. Despite the desensitizing he'd undergone there, he remained fascinated by the mysterious process that enabled a compound of common chemicals to think, to move about, to invent, to have a conscience. To his mind, if there was such a thing as a miracle, humankind was it. Yet he had difficulty with the idea of built-in death; it seemed reasonable to expect that such a marvelous creation would be programmed to endure, not inevitably to die. But he also had a deep appreciation of order and tidiness, characteristics that most surely would be among the many intrinsic to whatever power was in charge of creating universes. And so, by these lights, he'd decided that death must be respected simply as that half of the life cycle which remained to be explained and that the need for those operating in the comprehensible half was to be useful and caring while waiting for the unfathomable half to come into full illumination. No big deal.

Except, that is, when somebody butted in and knocked another's cycle out of sync. That was quintessential thievery. Anybody who would cut short another person's life merely to meet a current need or convenience would steal electric train money, by God.

And now here it was again. Like Bosnia. He'd had an awful time with all of this in Bosnia.

Soldiers' bodies there, Frank's body here: Litter left by The Ultimate Thief.

Viewed—in Bosnia, and in this kitchen—with that special anger.

Outside there was a slamming of car doors, and, in crazy contradiction, a rescue wagon arrived with much warbling and hooting and blinking, even though there was no traffic on the streets and, indeed, nobody to be rescued.

Nickerson closed his notebook and stood up. "Okay," he told the patrolman, "that'll be Doc Lewis. All the lights and hooting will bring in the neighbors. Hold Randall on the door and have O'Toole keep the people from trampling the lawn. The walls and gates will serve as a cordon, but in any case I don't want any unauthorized folks on the grounds before we do a daylight walk-through inspection. Put ribbons across the entrance and driveway gates, hear?"

"You got it, Sergeant."

"And I want the FDLE Mobile Crime Lab from Jax down here as soon as. Have Dispatch find out just where the hell it is. Meanwhile, tell Goodman to do his EDU stuff. Make sketches, take measurements. I want the whole goddamn kitchen dusted and fumed as quick as possible, because Doc Lewis is going to want to get in on the body right off. And I want stills and videos here and on the grounds. Look for footprints. The dirt's still soft from Tuesday's rain, and we might get lucky. But first off, I want a Polaroid of that package the victim was working on. The one on the table. I want a clear shot of that doodling that's on the paper, on top there. See it?"

"Sure do, Sergeant."

Nickerson turned to give Cooper an inquisitive glance. "Meantime, let's you and me go into the dining room there and have a chat. Okay?"

* * *

They sat in the high-back chairs at the mahogany table, and Nickerson pushed aside the bowl of fake fruit to make room for his notebook. He gave Cooper a pseudo-amiable inspection. His voice had lost some of its previous harshness. "Are you all right?"

"Still trying to handle the shock."

"Need a smoke, or a drink, or anything?"

"No."

"All right, then," Nickerson said, consulting the wad of papers before him. "Your driver's license says you are Matthew L. Cooper and that you live in Jacksonville."

"In the Riverside section. The old part of town."

"You rent? Own?"

"I inherited the place from a newspaper pal, Allen Drumm—everybody called him 'Bongo'—who died of an overdose several years ago. He had no family."

Nickerson made a note. "He must have liked you a lot to leave you a house."

"I helped with a couple of his problems, and he was grateful, I guess. It's not much of a house, really. A 1920s thing, held together by termites. But it suits me."

"Your occupation is—?"

"I'm an investigative reporter for the *Florida Times-Union*. I'm supposed to dig out the significant dirt that clogs life in North Florida and nearby Georgia."

"That makes you a tall horse, eh?"

"Surely you jest. It's a good job, as newspaper jobs go, but I'm not exactly one of the giants of journalism."

"Only one guy to cover two states? You must be busier than a one-legged ballet dancer."

"I'm backstopped when necessary." After a pause, he said, "I'm surprised you haven't seen my byline, my photo."

Nickerson shrugged. "I don't read the *T-U*. I read the *Record*. So tell me: what were you doing here tonight?"

"I've made a thing of visiting Dad at Christmastime. A little ritual, sort of. It was about the only time we had a chance to talk, the two of us being so busy and all."

"You came directly here from Jax?"

"No. I had a late supper at Luigi's on St. George Street. My father worked at night. So I planned a late arrival. I got here around eleven-fifteen."

Nickerson scribbled some more in his book. "When I was on car duty I used to see his lights burning at one, two in the A.M. He called Dispatch a couple of times in the wee hours to ask about police procedures. A real night owl."

"I take it you never met him."

"Not directly. I knew him by reputation, naturally. Read a couple of his books. But never shook hands." Nickerson jotted another note. "Can anybody else place you at Luigi's tonight?"

Cooper gave the detective a moment of study. "You mean I need an alibi?"

"Hey, I'm just gathering facts. Trying to hang faces and names on them. No offense."

"The waiter. I don't know his name. Teddy, or something. And Tina Mennen, the *Record* reporter. I bought her a cup of coffee."

"Is she a good friend of yours?"

"I've never had even a conversation with her before tonight. She said she attended a seminar I led in Orlando last year. She recognized me in the restaurant, then introduced herself."

"Did she leave the restaurant with you?"

"No. She was working on a story."

"What time did you leave?"

"A little after eleven, I think. I'd parked on San Marco because of the parade. I walked to the car and drove directly here. The side door was swinging open. I looked in the kitchen and found—I saw the—"

"So you dialed nine-one-one right away. Right?"

"Your nine-one-one board will show you exactly when I called."

"Did you shoot your daddy?"

"No."

"I had to ask."

"Of course."

"Would you agree to a GSR test?"

"A what?"

"A gunshot residue test. We dab your hands for traces of barium and antimony left on the skin when an ammo primer goes off. It tells us whether you've fired a gun in the past six hours."

"Or whether I washed my hands after shooting, right?"

The detective shrugged. "Touché. You had plenty of time to wash your hands before we got here."

"So much for your GSR test, then."

"Yeah. So: Did your pappy have any enemies?"

The question sent Cooper's mind to Tina Mennen, and he felt a twinge of guilt. "A thousand or two."

"I'm serious."

"So am I. Dad was a successful writer, so unsuccessful writers hated him. He was a thinker and a nose-thumber, so the Leets and the Intelligentsia hated him. He was a free spirit, so the Establishment drones hated him. Jealousy and resentment go with the business he was in."

"Can you be more specific?"

"Nothing current, because we haven't been seeing much of each other in recent years. But he told me once it was a miracle that he sold as many books as he did, because a lot of the stuff in them was politically incorrect in the eyes of the mainline critics. And he said he used to have a lot of buddies—you know, golf partners, fishing pals, guys to do lunch with—but when his books began to sell and the movies began to buy and he got his name in the papers, almost all of them disappeared. I asked him why, and he said he thought it was because his few real friends didn't want him to think they were moths crowding his limelight and the others were choking on their envy."

"He didn't have any close friends, then?"

"My mother. His lawyer. His agent. A few other guys rich and clouty enough not to be threatened by him."

"Sounds sort of dreary."

"Dad was a lonely, defiant man."

"How about the rest of the family? Do you have any brothers or sisters?"

"No. I'm it."

"Where's your mother?"

"She died seven years ago."

"So did your daddy have any current, ah, relationships?"

"I have no idea. He dated a few women, I understand. Dinners, theater. That kind of thing. But was he sleeping around, I don't think so."

"Why?"

"He was still carrying the torch for Mom. Last Christmas Eve he got a little drunk, and he assured me—flat-out, and with considerable pride—that my mother had been the only loving, unselfish, intellectual sex-machine in the world and that, just by having existed, she made every other woman a monumental bore."

"That must have embarrassed you."

"Did it ever."

"Did you like your father?"

Cooper gave the detective a lingering glance. For the second time in a single lousy night, a stranger had blurted the troubling question. And again, as if a tape had been triggered, the vignettes scrolled in his mind: Frank Cooper, laughing uproariously over a stupid newspaper editorial; frowning angrily over a checkmated board; slumping pensively in his big old chair, caught up in Mozart; pounding away at his primeval Underwood, a pencil in his teeth, eyes hot with inspiration; squinting among the sun-brilliant sand dunes, orating on the incredible pelican; halting Mom in her kitchen bustling to hold her close and kiss the top of her head; leaning over his boy's bed, tucking in the blankets, wordless, tender.

There was a sudden surge behind Cooper's ribs, a thickness in his throat, and he recognized the fact of his grief.

Nickerson rephrased the question. "You said you hadn't been seeing much of each other recently. Why was that? Didn't you like him?"

"I don't know." The words sounded strangled.

"What does that mean? How can you not know?"

"I've always had trouble figuring out what I thought of my father," Cooper managed. "He could be so great, and then be such a pain in the ass."

"In what way?"

"When we were together he would rag me about my career choice. He was disappointed in my becoming a journalist. He said I was squandering whatever writing talent I might have on media formula stuff.''

''And what did you say to that?''

''I said it was the pot calling the kettle black—that there's nothing more 'formula' than the genre fiction he'd been turning out over the years.''

Nickerson turned a page in his notebook and continued his careful writing. ''So you argued, then. Did these arguments ever get nasty?''

''Not really. Mom would usually step in and keep things from getting out of hand.''

''How did she feel about all this?''

''She wanted the best for both of us, and she said we each were operating according to the way the good Lord had set our dials and we should just shut up.''

''What do you think the argument was really about, Mr. Cooper?''

Again Cooper considered the detective with a contemplative stare. After an interval he said, ''I've often asked myself that question. And I think my mother came closest to it. She said she believed that Dad and I saw in each other a symbol of our personal limitations.''

''Explain that.''

''She said Dad considered my talent superior to his own, and he writhed under that perception.''

''And what was your perception?''

''I've always known that I could never muster the single-minded self-discipline and feral persistence that enabled Dad to excel in the freelance jungle for thirty years. I need a solid base. Predictability. Stability. He was in show biz, in a manner of speaking.''

Nickerson made another note. ''So all this boils down to the fact that you and your pappy didn't get along so hot.''

''We just went different ways, that's all.''

''Anybody else I can talk to about what went on in the family?''

''Manfred Kohlmann, maybe. He's been on Dad's payroll for years as a combination butler-housekeeper-gardener-chauffeur sort of guy. He's been around when the family's had some of its blunter discussions. This is the day he takes off to visit an old friend in Daytona Beach. But he'll be here in the morning.''

''You say your father had a secretary?''

''Louise Farman. She's worked for him for ages. A nice old gal. Her number's beside the wall phone in the kitchen.''

Nickerson was about to ask another question when the man with the camera pack came through the archway, brandishing a Polaroid print. ''Hey, Sarge, here's that shot you wanted. The one of the doodle on the package.''

The detective's serious eyes studied the photo for a full minute. Then he turned it in his hands, cocking his head like a curious dog's. Eventually he handed the picture to Cooper. ''What do you make of that?''

''It looks like a doodle, or something. Or maybe it's some kind of insignia, or an emblem, maybe. Whatever, it looks like a Y with a U superimposed on it.''

''Mean anything to you?''

''Not a thing. Looks sort of like a slingshot, wouldn't you say?''

''Your father scrawled it on the package wrapping before he died. The Christmas package he'd addressed to you.''

''How can you be sure? Maybe the sketch was made by somebody else at some other time.''

Nickerson smiled faintly. ''Another touché. Maybe you're right. But the ink on his other gifts and cards on the table came from the ballpoint pen beside his hand. And the sketch was made with the same ink.''

''It appears.''

The detective nodded. ''Right. It appears. Want to lay a bet on what the lab says?''

Cooper shrugged. ''No. I think you're on target. But the sketch beats me. I couldn't even guess what it means.''

''Do you own a firearm? A revolver, maybe?''

''Of course not. I gave up guns when I left Bosnia.''

''How about a rifle? For hunting, like.''

''Not even a water pistol.''

Nickerson snapped his notebook shut. ''Oka-a-ay. That'll do for now. Sure hope you'll be available for a while, Mr.

Cooper. There'll be more questions, obviously.''

"I'll ask my boss for a couple of days off. I'll stay here at the house. I've got a lot of things to take care of. Lots to worry about.''

Nickerson nodded somberly. "Yes, Mr. Cooper, I'd say you do indeed.''

The detective was turning to leave when the young cop came in with Manfred in tow. "Sir, this man came through the cordon. Says he's the deceased's house and property manager. Name of Kohlmann. Manfred Kohlmann.''

Manfred stood in the archway, straight as a cue stick, shoulders back, face pale and expressionless, eyes like old dimes. Nickerson gave him a lingering, silent inspection before speaking. "I thought you were in Daytona on your day off.''

"I was, sir,'' the old man said quietly. "But, as you see, I have returned.''

"You've heard what happened here?''

Manfred's ancient eyes seemed to dim. "I have, sir. When I arrived and saw the police vehicles, I—I asked one of your men, and he told me.''

Nickerson opened his notebook again. "Let me have your driver's license, please.''

The detective took the card, noted the vital statistics recorded there. "How long have you been working for Mr. Cooper?''

"Since October 23, 1946. Mr. Cooper and I became friends during the last days of World War Two. He sponsored my entry to the United States.''

"How and where did you meet?''

"I was an infantryman in the Wehrmacht. I had been taken prisoner. Mr. Cooper, who was an officer in the American army, interrogated me. He discovered I am quite fluent in English. He removed me from the prison camp to do chores in his office and we eventually became friends. Soon after he returned to civilian life here in the United States, he sponsored my immigration and citizenship. I have been in his employ ever since.''

"Did you shoot Mr. Cooper?''

Manfred blinked. "Most certainly not, sir.''

Nickerson closed his book again. "Okay, that'll do for now. But stay close, Mr., ah, Kohlmann." As he made for the door, he laughed softly. "We all know the butler can't have done it. Right?"

Cooper thought it odd that a policeman would joke at a time like this. If nothing else, it was in rotten taste.

Kohlmann stood in the darkness, beyond the knots of police and their darting flashlights, staring back at the main house, his heart beating rapidly, heavily.

After a time, he sighed deeply, then turned and slowly made his way to the door of his quarters in the south ell. He said aloud, softly, in his native German, "So at last it comes to this. After all these years, I'm in the killing business again."

Three

Congressman J. Fenimore Quigg had become acquainted with the reporter, Matt Cooper, at the Tri-County Labor Day Exhibition at the Bensonville Memorial Fairgrounds. And, because it was his nature, he began at once to consider ways to turn the encounter into a financial advantage.

The exhibition, an annual event heavily attended by the farmers, shopkeepers, and skilled tradesmen who composed the bedrock population of three abutting Midwest counties, was traditionally a family day, with patriotic speeches, band concerts, baseball, and fireworks. It was also a day of importance to politicians; the fairgrounds would fairly teem with party workers and officeholders—from ward heelers to U.S. senators—come to dandle tots and toss horseshoes and make ecstatic faces over home-baked pies.

This year's theme was "Hi-Tech Agriculture," and the pièce de résistance was a huge demonstration of farm equipment. Here on ten acres were displayed the current products of most of the nation's manufacturers, a panoply of state-of-the-art diggers, planters, reapers, packagers, and all the doodads between. The perimeter of the vast array was marked by a rectangle of booths peopled by spokesmen for the industry's legions of suppliers and their ancillaries. And Matt Cooper, rumpled and handsome and insistent, had appeared out of nowhere to ask quiet, outrageously penetrating questions of George Thorson, the fertilizer magnate, who was currently under investigation in connection with the Iowa corn production scandal. The congressman had been sipping whiskey with some of the Thorson people behind a tent flap at the rear of the booth and, along with the rest of them, had overheard most of the interrogation. He'd been chilled by Cooper's performance and had promised himself that, whatever the cost, he would never—ever—allow himself to get on that young man's shit list.

Wherever power and influence throbbed, Quigg would be inexorably drawn there. And young Cooper represented a form of power, which, if properly exploited, might someday serve as an important source of relief for the congressman's chronic fiscal exigencies. More than the cliché "power of the press" was implicit here; it was Cooper's laid-back magnetism, which was akin to the cool, focused, and insuperable power enjoyed by the extortionist who acquires knowledge of a target individual's specific vulnerabilities. If Cooper could be harnessed, shaped, put to work in the special interests of Congressman Quigg, well, next stop, the Senate.

Maybe even the presidency, eh?

After a decent interval, Quigg had said good-bye to the shaken Thorson and carried his plate of fried chicken, baked ham, potato salad, and roasted corn to the table beside the lake occupied by the banker Oswald Franklin and family. There, eating hungrily, he fondly patted Oswald Franklin's shoulder, flirted with Oswald Franklin's wife, chucked Oswald Franklin's fat little brat under his several sweaty chins, and surreptitiously squeezed the knee of Oswald Franklin's nubile, hot-pants daughter—all the while keeping a furtive watch on the lakeside boathouse.

Exhibits and hand-shaking aside, Quigg had attended for a single compelling reason: to identify the guest speaker invited by the Ringmasters, the six-member cadre of the national power elite that jerked political chains from town halls to the White House itself. A Capitol Hill informant had advised him that the Bensonville picnic was to be the site of a secret meeting at which the Ringmasters would decide what to do about Thomas Wilson Fogarty's bid for reelection next year as president of the United States.

The election would, of course, be a dilly.

Gridlock—the chronic, inalterable, and inevitably fatal malignancy—had brought the nation to what Quigg, borrowing from Bunyan, liked to call "the slough of despond." Thanks to the popular outrage over the general economic torpor, rapacious taxation levels, and a federal government woodenly heedless of any issue unrelated to its own perpetuation, there were widespread cries for the recall of unresponsive legislators, for a national referendum on how to rid the political process of "the tyranny of the electoral college system," and for money donations to support a movement, newly organized on the West Coast, to impeach Fogarty.

The fact that both parties were driven by ego, greed, and insatiable hunger for political immortality played directly to Quigg's hand, since nobody was more egocentric and avaricious than he and no one could exceed his capacity for side-changing. Gridlock, voter outrage, and the concomitant national chaos were what Congressman J. Fenimore Quigg was all about, by God. Quigg was an independent, a maverick; who occupied the White House mattered little to him. His sole ambition, party platforms and national issues notwithstanding, was to retain his House seat long enough to become a senator.

He was doing pretty well, all things considered.

The same outspokenness of the old salesman-saloon days, the same fearlessness in the face of crushing opposition, the open contempt for The National Establishment, and his unrelenting drumfire of CNN-covered House floor speeches in which he championed the Middies—the middle-class taxpayers and their support groups of the elderly—had brought an extraordinary notoriety for a lowly three-term congressman. He was much sought-after for speaking dates, for talk-show appearances, for think pieces in the snootier magazines, for ribbon cuttings and contest judgings. What his notoriety had not yet brought were the huge sums of seed money needed for a successful Senate race. So, next to the primary need of re-election itself, the feeding of a chronic money-hunger was his transcendent preoccupation, and fundamental to both was a casting of the Bensonville runes.

The contemporary Ringmasters were Sam Goodman, the New York television and movie poobah and West Coast commercial real estate magnate; Lou Pizarro, the internationally renowned Washington lawyer; Barney Griswold, the Chicago banker; Steven Bartlett, the New York financier; Pat Tinker, CEO of the Chronos newspaper and magazine chain; and Eleanor Roman, Boston academician and gadabout political philosopher. And a tall, elegantly dressed old man Quigg later identified as Stanley M. Tremaine, a Jacksonville, Florida, attorney, was their guest speaker.

Quigg's early years had been virtually apolitical; he considered party organizations and their raucous hypocrisies a monumental bore. But here, once again, coincidence—a peculiarly strong force in his life since boyhood—had presented him with a major opportunity.

A decade ago, while traveling the territory as an insurance salesman, he had observed that although registrations in Emory County, the geopolitical epicenter of the Fourteenth Congressional District, were split forty-nine percent Republican, forty-eight percent Democrat, and three percent Independent Progressive, the electorate there was in reality almost one hundred percent seething with inarticulate, unorganized rebellion against the excesses and indifference of central government. The discontent ranged much farther than Emory County, of course; anger over the superfluities and the self-perpetuating connivances of the entrenched ''Elitists''—the moniker ''Leets'' had been coined by Doug Toohey, the talk-show host, and had almost overnight become part of the language—was becoming transcontinental and incendiary. Particularly resented were the apocryphal tyrannies of the legendary Ringmasters.

From nation to hamlets, street talk had it, elections had

become mere stage business whose slates and results were preordained by money or favors. Businesses couldn't open, buildings couldn't be built, land couldn't be drained or tilled—even a house couldn't be painted—without the approval of the Ringmasters and their legions of well-heeled toadies. It was they who decided what the nation was and would be. Period.

For the pure hell of it, Quigg had begun to taunt them. In saloons and fast-food joints and airport waiting rooms, it had amused him to make little speeches about "the snobby few who dictate how we all live around these parts." He would lay outlandish charges against the Ringmasters, challenging them to refute his slanders. One night (here was that coincidence again) he'd had a few too many at Andy Tutweiler's Pub and announced to the swillers there that he would file for the seat soon to be vacated by Elmer J. Latimore, the Fourteenth District's Republican congressman, who would not be seeking re-election due to poor health. He'd climaxed the spiel with a promise: "By God, I'll vote as one independent sumbish who won't kowtow to any goddamn political party or kiss any asses. It's time we Middies take this wonderful district back from the frigging goddamn Ringmasters and their manipulating Leets." With astonishing speed, word of mouth cleaned up the speech and equated it to the Declaration of Independence. In a matter of days, a grassroots organization had formed around him and he'd found himself fulminating at churches and granges and fire halls and dinner meetings from one end of the district to the other.

All this had vastly amused the professional pols, of course; but by dismissing him as "an unsophisticated and hopelessly uninformed street-corner windbag," they virtually guaranteed the defiant landslide crossover that gave Quigg the primary and eventually handed him the congressional seat he had now held for three terms.

Nobody but the Middies liked Quigg.

Nothing but money controlled him.

Quigg leaned forward and, pressing the button, spoke into the intercom.

"Brad, are you there?"

"Yes, Congressman."

"I'd like you to do something for me."

"Of course, sir. You want me in your office?"

"Please."

Waiting, he turned in his high-backed leather swivel chair to consider the beauty beyond the tall windows. Despite his independence and his relatively modest tenure—a three-termer was considered a newcomer by Capitol Hill's ruling patriarchs—he possessed one of the more pleasant suites in the Cannon Office Building. And the view from it this day was especially nice, with the Capitol and its surrounding parklands sparkling white after last night's dusting of snow.

The office stemmed from a coincidence, too. On a Saturday afternoon early in his first term, he had been the only other person on the Rotunda stairway when Deke Finnegan, the antediluvian vice chairman of the Ways and Means Committee, had suffered his painful and debilitating tumble. Quigg had used his own shirt to slow the bleeding, and had ridden with the old man to the hospital in the Capitol Hill ambulance. Deke was very powerful, of course, and upon recovery had suggested to the appropriate fixers that there was no real reason why Congressman Quigg had to be officed in those miserable two rooms in an HOB loft. So now Quigg could turn from a regal window and regard his executive secretary, Bradford Willoughby, from a massive chair behind a massive desk framed by flags, book-lined walls, and velvet drapes.

"Did you watch the noon news on the nets, Brad?"

The young man nodded, his eyeglasses sparkling with reflected light from the window. "Just turned it off, sir."

"You saw the segment on the Frank Cooper murder?"

"Sad. Cooper was one of my favorite novelists."

"Mm. I want to get a line on him and his son, Matthew, who, it appears, is his only heir. Not just the usual bio stuff, but Standard and Poors—the good stuff."

"Yes, sir."

"But I want even more—a very deep-dish profile—on that guy who's been doing the talking for them. That Jacksonville lawyer. Tremaine."

"Stanley M. Tremaine. He's a very big gear in the South-

east, sir. He's a media expert and represents the Rettung Fund
and several of its subsidiary foundations.''

"He was also guest speaker at last fall's meeting of the
Ringmasters. That, my boy, impresses the hell out of me.''

"Judy Lincoln, of the Florida Press Service, says he was a
state legislator at one time, too. He's very widely known and
importantly connected.''

"So tie a line on him for me by way of an investigation. Call
our eye in Towson. But tell him we don't want to spend more
than I can comfortably voucher.''

"He did pretty well by you on that Chalmers thing.''

"Indeed he did. Those pictures of Chalmers and the girl in
the shower were a real bonus. I own Chalmers now.''

"Is there anything else, sir?''

"That's it for now, Brad. Just tell our man to get somebody
down to Florida as soon as. I'd like to own Cooper and Tremaine, too.''

"Federal Bureau of Investigation.''

"Mr. Gilchrist, please.''

"One moment. I'll connect you.''

"Gilchrist speaking.''

"Brad Willoughby.''

"Hi. What's up?''

"He's asked me to have a private investigator look into Tremaine and that reporter in Florida—Cooper. Matthew
Cooper.''

"Did he specify which PI?''

"The one he uses in Towson.''

"All right. Thanks for the call.''

WASHINGTON (USP) — Lou Pizarro, confidant of presidents and Cabinet officers and attorney famed for his successful defense of corporations charged with violations of environmental laws, was shot to death by a sniper tonight as he dined at his suburban Virginia mansion.

Fairfax County Sheriff Fred Zimmer says, "It looks like the work of a sniper. A single high-powered rifle shot, fired from the garden outside the Pizarro home's dining room, came through a window and struck the victim in the chest. We have no suspects at this time."

A spokesman for the Benning Clinic, where Pizarro was taken by ambulance, said death was instantaneous.

(Desk eds please note: Since Pizarro was a member of "The Ringmasters," reactions of government leaders and corporate CEOs, as well as an updated backgrounder and obit, are in prep for A wire distrib.)

Four

The day before he was to return to work, Cooper got a call from Stan Tremaine, who invited him to lunch at the Jackson Club, a members-only penthouse eatery Frank Cooper once derided as "the place where the city's Rolls roll in for rolls."

Cooper was glad to find something to do on this, the last day of the so-called death-in-the-family leave granted by the paper.

Despite his carefully constructed facade of coolness, the aftershock persisted, effectively disrupting the rhythm of what he had come to regard as normal living. Free time, formerly a cherished asset to be protected by any means from any encroachment, had become a kind of black hole in his personal universe, and he found that it could be dealt with—make that "tolerated"—only by way of activity, the more physical and mindless the better. Lunch with Stan required getting out of bed, bathing, shaving, dressing, reading the paper. Breakfast at one of those rattling, plastic places, where cute little uniformed girls waggle their cute little uniformed rumps and pretend to be interested in what you plan to set sailing along your alimentary canal. Then chores. The business of coping. Laundry. Dry cleaning. Gasoline, and a check of the Ford's bilges. Then the tribal rite of lunch, no doubt to be devoted to Stan Tremaine's report on the Cooper estate's legal status—the scoop d'jura over the soup d'jour, so to speak.

Because Frank Cooper had been such a private person, and because he himself really didn't give a good damn about any of it, Coop had only the skimpiest knowledge of his father's business affairs. As the clichéd kid at the top of the stairs, he'd listened to late-night discussions—sometimes arguments— between his parents, and in later years there had been frequent mention of Stan Tremaine. It had been vaguely understood that law firms retained by Charlotte Davis, his agent, and Obelisk, Inc., his publishers, kept protective eyes on Frank's works insofar as their own proprietary interests were concerned. But it became obvious, even to Matt's uneducated eye, that the barristerial legions encircling Manhattan's publishing Caesars offered precious little protection to the plebs toiling, alone and vulnerable, in a literary outland teeming with litigious Huns. So for the past twenty years Frank had retained Stan—a tall, graying, bespectacled, and exquisitely attired senior member of Tremaine, Perkins & Rowe, and sometime politician—as his personal courthouse paladin.

Not that Frank had been heavily involved in lawsuits. On the contrary; except for a few smart-ass letters—read and razzed at family dinners—from readers who appeared to hold him personally responsible for printing errors and ink ruboff on dust jackets, his career had been generally free of acrimony, legal or otherwise. Thus Stan had become less the defending champion and more the fishing buddy who oversaw routine real estate settlements, will revisions, trust management, and copyright renewals.

Stan was A Major Force, though, as far as Rudy, starched and shiny and daintily coiffed maître d' of the lofty Jackson Club, was concerned. On this day, Rudy all but genuflected.

"Mr. Tremaine, how very nice to see you. We have your favorite table in the southeast corner."

"Thanks, Rudy. I'm taking no calls, by the way."

"Of course, sir," Rudy said, giving Cooper a fleeting, side-long glance. Rudy didn't approve of any newspaperman unless he owned the newspaper, but in Matt Cooper's case, the disapproval had long since escalated into open dislike. The reasons: (1) Frank Cooper had declined the board's invitation to join the club, and (2) Matt Cooper persisted in dressing casually whenever he showed up as a guest (which was often, since his main job was to skewer errant pharisees of The Church of the Holy Profit, a species whose standard first line of defense against awkward questions was to beguile the questioner with an expensive lunch at an exclusive club). Clearing his throat gently and managing to avoid Cooper's eyes, Rudy added, "I might mention, Mr. Tremaine, that guests are to be suitably dressed. As usual, Mr. Cooper is not wearing a necktie."

Most journalists, spectacularly relaxed in their attire, carry clip-on ties in the event the news chase leads through rigidly formal turfs, like funerals or senior proms. Now, nailing Rudy with a glare, Cooper produced a ready-tied four-in-hand of vomitous pattern and hung it on the breast pocket of his blazer. "The hell I ain't, Rudy-baga. See?"

"Mr. Tremaine, would you please tell your guest that ties must be worn in the conventional manner?"

Tremaine, grinning, said, "Come on, Coop. Stop screwing around. I'm hungry."

"Nothing in the Constitution of the United States says a newsman can't wear his necktie on his chest. Or hanging from his dingus, for that matter."

Tremaine's amusement segued into a mock courtroom frown. "Mr. Cooper has a point, Rudy. The Supreme Court, ruling on Schmuck versus Freebs in 1908, found that the Constitution specifically allows a man to wear his tie on whatever part of his body he might choose."

Rudy's face clouded, suggesting that he took this news badly. After an interval, he snapped his fingers at a nearby waiter. "Show these gentlemen to table ten."

When they were finally seated and had ordered, Tremaine sent an amiable, evaluating stare across the snowy linen and glittering silverware. "Sometimes you're more like your old man than your old man was."

Cooper shrugged. "Rudy's a squid."

"Indeed he is."

There followed an awkward pause in which they each pretended to listen to the polite tinkling of Charlie Lang's roll-around studio piano, now located in the southwest corner. Charlie grinned across the room and mouthed, "Hi, Coop." Cooper saluted him with his glass.

"Speaking of your old man, I want you to know how very sorry I am about what happened. I haven't had any real chance—personally—privately—to—Then all that rotten publicity, the media circus over the murder—"

"No need, Stan. I know how this has stung you. Hell, you were closer to him than anyone. I think you and Louise Farman are the only people anywhere he really trusted. And I want to tell you again how much I appreciate your taking charge— fighting off the media, consoling Mrs. Farman, the arrangements with the mortician, and all that."

"There wasn't all that much to arrange."

"Why do you think Dad was so set against a funeral?"

Tremaine sighed. "He told me why. He said he didn't want a funeral because he was afraid nobody would come."

"Oh, God."

"A lonely man, with a lousy self-image."

"I didn't realize it was that bad."

"He was quite a man in all respects. And he was about the only one who didn't know it. His death was a terrible waste. Some junkie breaks in, looking for silverware and videos to feed his habit, and takes away a damn exceptional human being instead."

"You think that's what it was? A burglary gone wrong?"

"What else? Who else? An irate reader? His readers liked him. A jealous husband? Frank long ago stopped playing around—especially with other men's women. A gambling debt? Frank wouldn't even buy a lottery ticket, for God's sake."

Cooper stared at the clouds, which, at this height, seemed to be touchable. "Well, I'm not so sure, Stan. I mean, something strange must have happened there that night. Burglars rarely carry guns, and the soft-nosed bullet, distorted, unreadable, suggests premeditation. The room: nothing broken or stolen, nothing out of place. And Dad had time to draw a little something, a logo or insignia of some kind, on a scrap of package wrapper.''

Tremaine's eyes showed sudden curiosity. "Insignia? What kind of insignia?''

"It was done with the ballpoint pen found beside him. It looked sort of like a slingshot—a Y with a U superimposed on it.''

"Any idea what it meant?''

"Not the faintest. But if, as the police say, Dad died instantly from a dumdum through the heart, he must have had time before the shot to make the sketch—to, well, doodle. Which means he must also have recognized the shootist. Maybe even have had a conversation with him. Right?''

"Maybe. What do the police say about the doodle?''

"Nothing. They expect me to tell them what it means.''

Tremaine coughed gently, sipped some wine, then dabbed with his napkin again. "Strange is the word. But not so strange to those who knew your pappy best. His sense of humor was huge, but usually guarded, private.''

"You mean the doodle might have been one last little private joke? Or some kind of defiant raspberry?''

"Who can say? Certainly I can't—and I knew him as well as anybody ever did.''

There was another stilted, wordless interval.

Cooper, seated next to the floor-to-ceiling window, struggled briefly with vertigo—a sickening awareness that the sheet of plate glass was all that separated him from a thirty-four-story fall into eternity. But then, as it always had, the sensation shifted into something akin to exhilaration; from the rim of infinity, the view of the finite was awesome, with the city and its glistening towers all around, with the sparkling river arcing into the green sweeps of Riverside and Ortega and Orange Park, with the nameless, other-world hues at the sun-hazed horizon.

And then, finally, as always when he visited this room, his mind echoed the relentless question: *What am I doing in this Here, when there are so many Theres out there?*

It was more than a poor man's discomfort at being in the company of rich men. To be sure, the six one-dollar bills in his plastic wallet did little to engender a sense of belonging in an assembly of Acapulco suntans, thousand-dollar suits, diamond-studded wristwatches, and pretentious drawlings about stock options and takeovers and the crowd at Zermatt, or Cannes, or The Springs. But this economic apartheid, for all its inconveniences and humiliations, was nowhere near as onerous for him as the lifelong, unanswered questions as to why he was who he was, why he was doing what he was doing, and why he was doing it in a civilization designed and supervised by twenty thousand generations of assholes.

"How are you making out, Coop? Really, I mean."

"All right."

"How's the police investigation going?"

"The cops are still hassling me a bit. You know: 'Where did your father get his laundry done?' 'Who did your father have lunch with on July 22, 1991?' Then questions about the doodle, repeated, over and over. But, for all that, I get more trouble from the flakes. Souvenir hunters tearing off chunks of the Water Street property. Calls from seers and mediums. Requests for interviews from supermarket tabloids. Proposals from"—he made quote marks in the air with his fingers— " 'attractive, wealthy widows who like skinny-dipping in the moonlight or are available for sensual fun while skydiving.' "

Tremaine sniffed. "The world is filled with cashews."

"You've noticed, eh?"

The salad and rolls arrived and they were into the preliminary munching when Tremaine said casually, "I didn't ask you to lunch just to be sociable, Coop."

"I never thought for a minute that you had. I like you and, I think, you like me. But you're first and always a working lawyer. And working lawyers never do anything without premeditation or practical reason—especially when socializing."

"God, you sound like my ex-wife."

Cooper smiled. "So what's on your alleged mind?"

"Did your father ever discuss his writing with you, his research, his investments—the workaday details of his career? His will, maybe?"

"My father never discussed anything with me. He made speeches, to which I listened." He laughed softly. "Come to think of it, though, they were usually pretty good."

"I wonder especially if he ever mentioned his involvement with Rettung Internationale, the charitable fund he had been associated with since 1952. The nature of his work there, the people he worked with, that kind of thing."

"Rettung—that fund to benefit war orphans?"

"Well, it's considerably larger and more comprehensive now. Kids are still a concern, but the base foundation has since developed almost a dozen subsidiary foundations."

"He never said boo about Rettung to me. Why do you ask?"

"There were many facets of Frank's life that he kept entirely private. I knew basically that he was president of the base foundation, and I did some of his Rettung paperwork—mainly IRS stuff—now and then. But right now I foresee a lot of questions from the executor that I won't be able to answer without documents I don't have."

"Mrs. Farman showed me your list. Maybe she'll find stuff that will tidy things up for you."

"Maybe. I just thought I'd touch base with you, too."

"I mean it, Stan. With me, Frank Cooper was as silent as a sphinx's sphincter."

Tremaine smiled wryly. "That's the kind of thing Frank would have said. He, too, had a fondness for hyperbole, for elaborate overstatement—"

"Well, he had no particular fondness for me. So he didn't talk to me much. About Rettung or anything else."

"Hold on, Coop. Your pappy had a deep and abiding affection for you. He used to tell me that his major curse was his inexplicable inability to let you know that."

Cooper gave the lawyer a quick, doubting glance. "You're kidding, of course."

"No."

"Well, if he was able to tell you, why wasn't he able to tell me?"

"You're too sensitive and worldly-wise not to know how silly that question is."

Cooper put down his fork and sat back in his chair. "What

the hell is this all about, Stan? Did you ask me to lunch so you could lecture me on how wonderful my father was? I know how wonderful he was. The big trouble was that he never took the trouble to find out how wonderful I am.''

Tremaine held up a peacemaker's hand. "Steady, boy. Steady. I am not about to lecture you on anything. I am, though, about to let you know how much Frank really did care about you.''

"Come on, Stan. Talk straight.''

"He left you an estate whose after-tax value is slightly more than two hundred and twenty-three million dollars. Is that straight enough?''

A moment of dizziness persuaded Cooper that he had indeed passed through the plate glass and was en route to the pavement thirty-four stories below. He was dropping like a stone, turning and twisting as he went, numb and without a breath in him anywhere. He was watching, yet couldn't see; he was being consumed by feelings that had no names, yet he couldn't feel. All the while Stan Tremaine was prattling on about living trusts and irrevocable *inter vivos* trusts; about trustors and trustees and estate management and CPAs and insurance policies and real estate and stock holdings and specific legacies versus general legacies and how really very goddamn lucky he was to have had a father who had spent a very high percentage of his life making sure that Matthew Cooper, his only issue and sole survivor, would get the best possible deal in every possible way.

"So how does that grab you?'' Stan summarized, his blue eyes showing wry amusement behind his sensible lawyer's eyeglasses.

"He drove a three-year-old Dodge.''

"Come again?''

"I knew he was well off, but, my God, I didn't know he was—well *off*.''

"I don't know what your definitions are, Coop, but today ten million makes a man rich. You've been left twenty-two times that. By all measures, your pappy wasn't well off, he was into stinking-richhood. And now you are. You're not truly superrich, but you are more than comfortable.''

"But he never showed—I mean—his lifestyle—''

"That was one of the many things I liked about him. His great good fortune never made him arrogant. He drove a Dodge around town and a Jeep on fishing trips because they were safe, tough, and appealed to his sense of utility and economy. He chose to live in the Water Street house because he was a small-town man at heart, and because he had such enormous contempt for those he called—with that alliteration he was so godawful fond of—'nouveau-riche rednecks in their palatial plastic playpens.' And he kept a low profile out of plain modesty. Many rich men keep low profiles in the interest of personal safety, or as a means of avoiding all those people who come with their hands out. Frank Cooper kept a low profile because he hated show-offs and didn't want to be accused of being one.''

Cooper shook his head in wonder. "God, I never realized there was so much money in books. I knew he sold a lot of them, but my aching adenoids—''

Tremaine humphed, his long, manicured fingers deftly checking the fold of the hundred-dollar silk handkerchief in the breast pocket of his hand-tailored English jacket. Frank Cooper had once jokingly characterized Stan as "what you'd get by crossing Beau Brummell with Clarence Darrow,'' and the fondling of the lapel led Coop once again to recognize how unlikely had been the longtime friendship between this jurisprudential fashion plate and his old man, the paradigmatic rumpled man of letters.

"Books were the smallest part of it. Books got him started, but he played the money he got from them wisely. I should know. I'm the one who played it for him.''

"You?''

Tremaine nodded, his good-natured, well-barbered face a parody of self-satisfaction. "I can say in all modesty that my investment and foundation savvy, along with some adroit exploitation of tax laws, made you what you are today.''

"Don't brag. I don't look so hot today.''

"True. You need a haircut, and your collar's frayed.''

"What kind of investments?"

"Foundation stuff, primarily. Also common and preferred stocks, state and municipal bonds, a bunch of real estate, both urban and rural, some high-risk, high-return venture stuff—commodity futures, oil exploration, movies, TV productions, that sort of thing—plus some muscular pieces of banks, domestic and international. It's pretty involved."

Cooper stated the obvious: "If you made my father's fortune, you took your cut. No doubt about that, eh?"

"That's also true. But my cut derived from a flat retainer, paid to me annually so that Frank, utterly bored by money matters, could be liberated from the direct management of his fortune. And that's the other reason I want to talk with you. Your father's will appoints his bank to serve as executor, which means the bank will formally settle the estate in the interest of any and all claimants. He named me to continue as administrator of the trust, under which you own the fortune but I—with the bank monitoring my performance so as to be sure I don't rip you off or turn in a lousy performance—will oversee the nuts and bolts and try to make you even richer. If you prefer to manage things yourself, or—and this is even more important—if you and the bank don't like the way I perform, you can vote to fire me outright and appoint a new administrator."

"What's your retainer?"

"The executor's fee is set by the state: two and a half percent of the total estate value, plus expenses. As trust manager, I've been temporarily authorized the same amount I received from Frank while he was living: five hundred and fifty thousand a year, plus expenses, accountable monthly."

"You're an expensive wretch, ain't you?"

"For managing an estate that size, I'm cheap."

"Am I allowed to give you a raise?"

Tremaine gave him a quizzical look. "Raise? Why?"

"I'm a believer in the good old incentive system. What if I pay you, say, the five-fifty and expenses but also award you a flat ten percent of any increase you bring to the estate's net value—a figure confirmed annually by a CPA and a second bank as impartial referee?"

The question in Tremaine's eyes became amused admiration. "Ah. That would make you a very dear boy indeed, dear boy."

"The richer I get, the richer you get. Right?"

"The cleanest incentive there is," Tremaine said, testing his handkerchief again. "And I appreciate your gesture—your kind and generous consideration. But it really isn't necessary, Coop. I have enough money already—more, actually, than any reasonable man could want. The business of being wealthy, you'll find, becomes more than the mere amassing of more wealth. It is that, of course, but the psychic reward comes from the amassing itself—the game of amassing. Once a man has gathered to himself enormous assets, vast acreages, gorgeous homes, splendid automobiles, and other such creature comforts, he finds little excitement in acquiring another house, another car, another racehorse, or whatever. The only adventure, the only thrill, left to him is derived from the planning, the scheming, the angle-shooting, the Machiavellian cruise along the boundaries of law and respectability. Which means networking his wealth, intertwining his power and influence with those of his peers toward ever-larger spreads of power and influence. And, on the flip side, you'll learn very quickly that, while you might have a six-figure checking account, the preponderance of your wealth is in investments, and cannot, without considerable difficulty, be turned into cash. You are worth two hundred and twenty-three million dollars, sure, but it would be a major undertaking to convert that worth into walking-around money. I'm in somewhat the same shape. I have more than enough to meet my needs and most of my wants. One thing you can be sure of, though, is that I'll be giving you maximum effort, because I'm one of those men who thrill to the game itself."

"Well, maybe so. But the raise stands."

"And I thank you. Meanwhile, in the next several weeks we will be having tons of lawyer-talk. And there'll be conferences with the CPAs. I'll update you daily."

"I'll call Jim Thwaite at my bank. He'll do whatever papers we need to make him your raise referee. Okay?"

"Fine. Is Thwaite competent at this kind of thing?"

"Beats me. All I know is, he always covers me when my checks bounce. A guy like that just has to be a wonderful person—a great judge of character."

Tremaine's expression was that of a headmaster who hears wind breaking during chapel hour. "You actually *bounce* checks?"

"With a balance that cruises at an average of fifty bucks, bounced checks become a way of life."

"Well," Tremaine said evenly, "those days are gone for good. An interim money-market account containing two hundred thousand dollars has been opened in your name at Republic National. To write checks on it, you need only to stop by the bank and sign the necessary cards. Meanwhile, I urge you to take off for a week, maybe two. Take a trip. Pull yourself together in the great American Outback while the CPAs and I do our things."

"I can't do that. I'm right in the middle of an industrial-strength flush-out. My boss would kill me."

Stan smiled faintly. "Boss?"

"Yeah. Gert Shaw, at the paper."

"You're not being serious, are you?"

"Of course I'm serious. Gert would tear my ass off."

Stan, amused, sank back in his chair. "This is why you need some time away from here, Coop. You need a pause for priority identification. To come to grips with the reality of your drastically altered situation. To understand that your life has been forever changed and to make some basic decisions as to how you will cope with that truth. Gert Shaw is already part of your unrecoverable past."

"You're saying that just because I'm rich I can't work on a newspaper? Come on—"

"Certainly you can work on a newspaper. But you'll quickly discover that you won't enjoy it. Not at all."

"Give me one good why."

"I'll give you the Big Four: One, you'll never know whether your progress is due to skill and hard work or to suck-ups, pushing you along in an effort to curry your favor and largess. Or two, whether your failures are—or are not—due to the machinations of the envious. Or three: your own impatience with troublesome people—your readiness to punish those who annoy you. And—''

Cooper broke in. ''What the hell does that mean?''

Stan turned the wine glass in his long fingers, holding its contents to the light. ''I'll illustrate. There was a very rich Texas oil man who loved to go on site and watch his wells produce. One day he left the field to take a room at a hotel in Houston so that he might clean up for lunch with an associate. None of the hotel people recognized him. The doorman, eyeing his grimy face and oil-spattered overalls and caked boots, tried to turn him away. The desk man, the bellhops, were sour and rude, but he finally succeeded in renting a tiny back room. The next day, the rich man bought the hotel and fired everybody on the payroll.''

''So what are you saying? That if I don't like the way an editor changes a lead on me I'll buy the *Times-Union* and fire everybody?''

''Of course not. I'm saying that your tendency will be to solve all your problems, cure all your vexations, with money. And, when you discover that such solutions bring you no lasting satisfaction, the frustration increases.''

''So what's number four?''

''Ah, yes. The big one, the most oppressive of all. The one I call 'the withdrawal from the human race.' Thanks to your major wealth and the consequent notoriety, you will never again be able, alone, blithely and with impunity, to do so much—or so little—as hop in the car and buzz on down to McDonald's for a burger and fries. Someone will always recognize you. Someone will always make a fuss over you. And then the stares begin, the word spreads— 'Hey, guess who's in the corner booth, for chrissake'—and you realize that every crumb you drop, every smear on your lip is being scrutinized by a sea of judgmental, envious jerks. 'He don't look like nuthin' special to me, godammit. The sumbish can't even eat a burger without gettin' catsup all over his fuggin' face.' No matter where you go, what you do, you become the immediate target of every con man, favor-seeker, and incipient kidnapper between here and Mars. So to beat the rap, you go underground. You travel with an escort. You hang out only with those who share your problems because they, too, are very rich. And they'll probably bore the living crap out of you, and you'll stop wondering why so many of them drop into booze and drugs or high-risk sports—auto-racing, stunt flying, politics.'' Tremaine paused for a sip of wine.

"Jesus. You're just full of sunshine, aren't you."

"Take it from me. I've watched it all."

"Dad seemed to make out okay. He'd eat burgers and fries downtown—"

"Of course. Very few knew how rich he was. He acquired his wealth over decades, and without publicity. He was not a member of a family whose wealth makes its name a household word. His celebrity came from public performance of his art, not from the amassing or inheritance of money per se. But you're different. Tomorrow the media will be alive with reports of your inheritance, and from tomorrow on, your life will no longer be entirely your own. And that, my dear friend, is why you will not enjoy working on a daily newspaper."

Cooper was silent, staring out at the world and listening to Charlie Lang's piano. He sighed finally and said, "Well, one good thing about all this: I can afford to have my house tented and debugged. The cockroaches are eating what the termites can't get at."

"You're not going to continue to live in that rat-trap, are you?"

"It's an okay place—handy to everything. It just needs pest control, big-time."

Tremaine shook his head in exasperation. "Do yourself a favor, Coop. Give me the key to your dad's office and access to his files. Take a long vacation. Get lost. When you come back, I'll have everything ready for you to sign and take over. I'll have some nice houses for you to look at. A tailor to put the right clothes on you. Some—"

"Whoa. The key and access you got. The rest of it I'll have to think about."

Five

The firm's headquarters building was in Jacksonville's Southside, a parklike vastness in which glittering castles of glass and steel—erected by microchip lords and worked by yuppie serfs—exemplified feudalism in the current idiom. Tremaine hated both the building and its phony rurality, since he was an arrant metropolitan who associated the business of law with the clamor and variegated stinks of skyscraper canyons. He was hating it especially much this day, regarding the chirping birds, the sparkling lake, and the breeze-stirred palms outside his office window as taunting reminders of how far he'd been spun off from the center of the juridical universe.

There had been a time when, with the mere raising of a monarchical eyebrow, he could have moved the offices and everybody in them from Independence Square to Pluto between breakfast and lunch on any given Thursday. No longer; his seventy-fifth birthday last June had formally corroborated the de facto dethronement that had begun a decade ago.

Standing by the sheet of glass, only partly aware of the distant warbling of phones, the muted sounds of office equipment, the regulated voices, he peered out at the afternoon, struggling to jettison his resentment, the unhappy reliving of the life and times of Stanley M. Tremaine, Esq. The hardscrabble boyhood in Palatka; the pennilessness and the being outside of everything, brought to exquisite intensity by the Big War and its whimsical separations and deaths. The GI Bill, prelaw at Cornell, then beyond it, Harvard and the shingle, hung in newlywed desperation on the storefront in Tallahassee. The networking: from legislative assistant to Senator Boyd to a junior spot in Boyd's law firm, then on to the hire by Old Sam Riggles, ruler of the Jacksonville legal cosmos, and the eventual partnership and specialization in protecting Amos Carr, the firebrand North Florida publisher, from the wrath stirred by his acidulous newspapers. Appointment by the governor to complete the term of Senator Morgan, dead in the saddle at Maxine's whorehouse one chilly night in Tampa. The thumping defeat in his run for a full term, his two failed runs for the State House. His partnership with Bill Perkins and Clarence Rowe and its guarantee of heavy-duty money. Perkins was dead now, and Rowe languished in an Ocala nursing home, and the firm was in its fifteenth year of occupation by a small army of Ambitious Andys who wore Italian neckties and smelled of expensive cologne and spoke with arrogant glibness through clenched jaws. And who had voted to relegate him to a limited partnership, wherein his name would remain in the logo and he could tenant an office so long as he carried a lion's share of the overhead, stayed out of management, and limited his practice to oddball clients, like that Bohemian scribbler, Frank Cooper.

They never said he was too old. That would have been discrimination, and actionable. But their eyes condemned him for having allowed himself to become so old.

And, in truth, there were times when he felt his age. Like today. Lunch with young Matt Cooper, dredging through Frank's past, had brought back the war, and Chevrolet-Coupe, France, Sauerkraut am Rhine, Germany, and all such craphouse burgs where his youth had gone rancid, then rotted away forever.

Speaking of which.

He turned, crossed the plastic carpet to his plastic desk, lifted the plastic phone, and direct-dialed the plastic towers in Munich's plastic resurrection.

The ethereal, faraway clicking as the receiving phone computed and identified the call's country of origin. The recorded woman's voice, its cultivated English throaty and somehow sensual: "You have reached the main offices of Rettung Internationale. We are closed until tomorrow at nine hundred hours. Please try us then. Thank you for calling."

Damn. He checked his watch. It was almost eleven P.M. over there. *I'm not old, I'm senile, for chrissake.*

He hung up and tried Ludwig's home phone.

"Hier Ludwigheim," Leopold, that stuffy horse's ass of a butler, intoned. *"Wer dort, bitte?"*

"Stanley Tremaine calling. Is Ludwig there?"

Leopold switched to his stuffy English. "I'm sorry, sir, he and Frau Ludwig are attending the opera this evening."

"Well, have him call me when he comes in. Either my car phone or the Ponte Vedra number. No matter what time it is."

"Very well, sir. I'll—" A pause, in which Leopold did some international breathing. Then: "Excuse me, sir, but they have just returned. Hold for a moment, please; I'll switch your call to the library."

After another interval, Ludwig's cool voice came on. "Good evening, Stan."

"Sorry to call so late."

"We came home early, actually. You can't imagine how boring it is to sit through *Tosca* for the four-hundredth time. The Takais felt the same, so they are joining us for a late supper."

"Takai's there already?"

"He has some business in Zurich, so he flew in early from Kyoto. He'll finish up by the day after tomorrow—plenty of time for the Rettung board meeting."

"What's his mood?"

"Cool. Japanese are known for their patience. But I know he's anxious for you to come up with something."

"I'm working on it."

"So how did your luncheon with young Cooper go?"

"Disturbingly, I'm afraid. The good news is that Coop has only the most superficial interest in Frank's business and wants me to continue as manager. The bad news is that Frank managed to draw the Slingshot insignia on a package he was wrapping at the time of his—ah—death."

Ludwig said nothing for a full ten seconds. Then: "That's disturbing news indeed. Did Coop show any sign of understanding its significance?"

"None."

"You're sure?"

"I've been a lawyer long enough to know playacting when I see it. No, he's truly mystified—as are the police."

"Oh, God. The police saw the drawing?"

"Of course. They see everything at a homicide scene."

"Do they have any idea who did the killing?"

"Apparently not. My sources at City Hall, the media, Coop himself, indicate there are no leads."

There was another pause while Ludwig considered all this. "Coop," he said at last, "worries me. He's a news reporter, filled with curiosity."

"He worries me, too, and for a larger reason. He's very much like his old man. Tenacious. Cynical. Iconoclastic. Cavalier. You should see him taunt snooty maître d's. He's Frank all over."

"One Frank's enough for any thousand years. We cannot afford another one on the Rettung board. Absolutely cannot."

Tremaine made an impatient sound. "Hell, Ludwig, we might be getting our bowels in an uproar over nothing. Coop is very well off at this point. Once he digests that fact, he'll start having a lot of ideas as to how he will spend his time. It's my guess that he won't even want to take his father's seat on the board. For one thing, he's a good newspaperman, and good newspapermen rarely join organizations or groups that generate news. It's a matter of ethics—the need to avoid the perception of bias, or serving two masters. For another thing, I get the clear idea that just about everything his father did bores the crap out of him. So it doesn't make much sense to expect him to get knee-deep in the affairs of Rettung, the one big thing, aside from novels, that Frank's identified with.''

Ludwig was skeptical. "We don't know that for certain, do we. If Coop is as much like his father as you say he is, he's got a wide streak of the quixotic in him—the stuff of starry-eyed reformers. And this is precisely what we've got to guard against. He could, simply by being true to his character, choose to become active in Rettung and eventually learn enough to destroy our years of careful work.''

"So what do you recommend?''

Ludwig was silent for a time. Then he cleared his throat delicately and said, "Exactly how you deal with Coop is your business. All I ask is that, whatever you do, you maintain absolute secrecy—don't tell him a thing.''

"Well, thanks a whole hell of a lot for nothing. Not only am I expected to find Takai's political lever, but now I'm also expected to mother-hen a rich kid.''

"I don't mean to sound indifferent—you know very well how concerned I am about all this, what with so many people and such a huge sum of money and the future of our whole undertaking at stake. But the facts are simple: we have no more than three months to find and destroy any of Frank's records and correspondence that might, if discovered by his son, blow Rettung Internationale and Yankee Doodle sky-high. It's up to you, and you alone, to find the means by which we can avoid such a disaster. And also, unfortunately, you are the only one among us who can keep young Cooper preoccupied and governable while the search goes on.''

"Still—''

Ludwig broke in, his tone suddenly brittle. "The Takais are waiting. Before I go, let me assure you, Stanley, that if you show the slightest ineptitude in this matter, Takai most certainly will step in and deal directly with Cooper—and with you, as well. You and Allen are already on probation, thanks to that ill-timed, misbegotten massacre of the town council in Vermont. Another sign of loose management, and Takai will come down on you, severely. Please don't let that happen. I'm too fond of you to lose you to Takai's anger.''

The dial tone sounded.

* * *

That was one of the toughest loads to carry in this thing—the need to go gingerly, often grovel, when communicating with Ludwig and so many other foreign egomaniacs. The only thing going for the sons of bitches was their money, amassed over generations of international thievery or cornered by corruption; but their control of these vast, ill-gotten, and mostly inherited sums had somehow persuaded them that they were demigods and that Tremaine and other mortals were to be tolerated and channeled, like the animals that raced for them or worked their farms or provided passing amusement (when properly broken of willfulness or other bad habits) in private locales.

His irritation with all this, compounded by his irritation with himself, moved Tremaine to pick up the phone and call Harry Allen, who, as national military coordinator for Yankee Doodle and therefore his direct subordinate, was somebody who would listen politely, for a change.

Allen typified the Middie (or what the Leets' more acerbic pundits liked to call "the Midiot"): despite his qualities and achievements, he had constantly to fight a tendency to think of himself as a jerk because he was widely and importantly portrayed as being precisely that.

Allen had retired in anger from the U.S. Army when he was passed over for appointment to the Joint Chiefs. He was a thoroughly experienced soldier, having risen in a span of nearly four decades from recruit to lieutenant general. He was smart, tough, gutsy—his ribbons ran from shoulder to navel—and he was highly popular, not only in the military but also among those great hordes of Middies who appreciated his stand-up opposition to the atrociously expensive U.S. involvement in the Balkans. But among the Leets and other members of The Establishment he was considered a loose cannon and, worst of all, deficient in the diplomatic graces, a character trait unacceptable to the Beltway Chic and other members of the government intelligentsia. Which, happily, turned out to be a divine gift to Yankee Doodle. Allen was a world-class expert on guerrilla warfare and, now that he was properly incandescent over what he called "the willful destruction of a goddamn wonderful nation by three generations of self-adoring, onanistic shits,'' precisely what was needed to organize and arm those middle-class legions whose antigovernment fulminations crammed the pages of *Sour-Grapevine* and other unlicensed, nationally circulated protest publications.

As usual, Allen answered his own phone. ''Acme Sporting Goods Corporation. Allen speaking.''

''Tremaine here. Call me back on your scrambler.''

''Yes, sir.''

Tremaine hung up and waited until the phone in his desk drawer sounded its muted purr.

''Hello, Harry. Is everything all right with you?''

''Yes, sir. How about you?''

''All right. Have you heard anything from Seattle?''

''I just received an overnight from Bill Perkins out there. He reports that he was invited to speak at a meeting of the Middies for Tax Reform—held in an abandoned warehouse, of all places—and by the time he left he'd signed up forty-seven guys willing to give space to weapons storage. Twelve of them are ex-service people who agreed to form a militia training cadre for the Seattle area. Bill says that this bunch is the maddest and most militant he's run across since the church rally in Dallas.''

''Any problem in getting guns to Seattle?''

''Don't see any. Abner tells me that the people in Miami have organized a shipment via a daisy chain of private planes that don't have to file cargo data with the feds. It takes longer than moving them up there in disguised commercial packages, but, what the hell, they aren't exactly going to be used in any big hurry.''

''That's what I called about. We're accelerating. Topside wants you to hurry.''

There was a moment of silence at the other end. Then: ''Hoo-boy. What means hurry? I've already caught blue hell about that Vermont thing—which, as you know, was uncontrollable because the perpetrators were hotheaded teenage assholes. Now they want me to *unleash* that kind of thing, for chrissake?''

''We're both on probation for that one, Harry. But that was an aberration—one of those things that comes with an operation this size. What I want now is evidence that we're truly organized and that we can live down the aberrations. I want you to send me by next Friday an updated master plan for the conversion of untrained, disorganized groups of dissidents into a clandestine militia. I want to know also how you expect to tap into and exploit the discontent among members of the regular armed forces—how these individuals and units can be encouraged to serve covertly, first, as training cadres for guerrilla operations, and then as field-command entities when operations are formally launched.''

Allen sniffed. "Tono, that squid Takai sent over to advise me, says we should use the regulars to convert our forces into conventional armies that can eventually fight the central government's loyalist conventional forces."

"Well," Tremaine said, "just ignore him. We want to avoid conventional warfare altogether, maintaining only that amount of organized hell-raising that will erode the national political base and force a mass resignation and subsequent reformation of the national government. Takai himself insists on that."

"I'll ignore Tono with pleasure."

"When can I expect your update?"

"Tomorrow, by overnight express."

"Include a rundown on weapons inventory. Sites, just what and how much is stored at each—that kind of thing."

"You bet, sir. I think you and Topside will be very happy with what I have to report."

"Good."

"I hope you don't mind my asking, sir, but is there any word yet on who will be the big front man in this gig?"

The question was presumptuous, because, intentionally or no, it tacitly needled Tremaine, the individual responsible, for having failed to cast Yankee Doodle's starring role. But it was also a question to be expected from a pragmatist like Allen, and so he took no offense. Allen was simply being Allen.

"Yankee Doodle's political side is not quite so easy to slap into shape. You, for instance, are blessed by recruits who make no secret of their indignation, their belief that they have nothing to lose and much to gain by armed resistance. I must penetrate to the personal cores of people who make an art of hiding their true feelings. You deal with charts and logistics and edicts. I deal with psyches, which can't be pinned to a wall and studied.''

"Sure, sir. I understand. I'm just anxious to get the good word.''

"Of course you are, Harry, and so are all of us. I hope we can pick our front man and send the announcement along the chain before the end of this month.''

"That would be great, sir.''

Another pause followed, this one peculiarly more tense.

"Anything else on your mind, Harry?''

"Nothing specific, sir. It's just—''

"Just what?''

"I find myself wondering whether he'll be a Democrat or a Republican. Isn't that nuts? What the hell difference does it make?''

"That's the whole point of Yankee Doodle, Harry. The political forces that bore those names no longer exist. They're simply labels adopted by the two groups of Old Boys who have divvied up the power and have sent the rest of us down the toilet.''

"I know. But—''

"You're troubled by nostalgia. Memories. We all get those whim-whams now and then. Forget the past. It's gone, unchangeable. We can't handle tomorrow until it gets here. So that leaves only today. Concentrate on today, and the whim-whams go away.''

"You're right, of course, sir. It always helps to talk to you. I can handle anything I can see or touch. I'm good at dealing with the real. It's the intangible, psychological stuff that wears heavily sometimes. You're great at pulling those things into plumb for me.''

"Pragmatism is your strength, Harry. We have too many woolgatherers and entrails readers as it is. That's a good bit of what got us into trouble in the first place. Now we need people like you, who can look at things and say, 'Hell, this sucker's broke, and here's how we get it running again.' Remember, none of this would be happening if the nation had remained healthy. But it's sick, mortally sick, and the people who are running it don't give a little damn because they caused the sickness—to them the sickness is good for what ails us. So somebody has to take hold and rassle the country into Surgery. That's you and I and all the others who are as angry as we are.''

''I suppose. You know something else that pisses me off big-time? It's when some punk tourist sidles into my headquarters and announces that Takai has sent him to train a special squad of snipers. What the hell do we need with special snipers? All my militiamen will be expert marksmen by the time I'm finished.''

''Takai, all his employees, are indeed arrogant jerks. Hell, Harry, just indulge the bastards. Takai wants to train some snipers? Let him train some snipers. Takai's the source of many big bucks, and we've got to stroke him.''

''You know you can count on me. But I don't have to like some of the things you want me to do.''

''Right as rain, Harry. I long ago learned never to entirely trust a soldier who doesn't bitch.'' He laughed, and, after a moment, Allen did, too.

''I'll be expecting your update in tomorrow's mail.''

Tremaine hung up, then sank back in his huge chair to watch the palm trees wave and rustle in the brassy evening.

He was suddenly very lonely.

Six

The morning after Cooper's lunch with Stan Tremaine, the *Times-Union* ran a ten-inch story below the fold on the business section front. It had head-and-shoulders cuts of his father and himself and what seemed to be a carefully neutral headline announcing the bequest.

That things had changed was apparent from the moment he arrived for work.

The day-shift gate guard, an ex-cop who was normally as cordial as a dyspeptic storm trooper, actually called out, "Good morning, Mr. Cooper," and waved him into the parking lot with the hope that he would have a good day, hear?

Lucy-Something, the loquacious, irrepressible mail girl, rode up with him on the elevator, red-faced and mute.

Bill Ramsey, the day copy desk honcho, made way for him in the corridor, nodding politely and, for the first time in history, failing to pass along the joke of the day.

And Dusty Rhodes, the music columnist and a renowned kidder, whistled the oldie, "Brother, Can You Spare a Dime."

Willing away these ominous omens, he went directly to his cubicle and gave the prenoon hours to chores—phoning sources, reviewing yesterday's notes, and organizing his gun-running file. He skipped lunch and began to frame a letter to the FBI's Washington headquarters.

According to whispers on the street, Abner Hefflefinger, a Duval County district judge, had become a multimillionaire via his collusion with that portion of the Miami mob which busied itself with the import and interstate distribution of illegal weapons. The FBI had investigated, rumors had it, but the probe had squizzed, thanks to the judge's close ties to big shots in the Administration in general and the Department of Justice in particular. With so much smoke rising, Cooper had decided to use the Freedom of Information Act to suck out whatever files the FBI had on the matter. This letter, the fourth, was a tricky write, a fact which, when combined with his lingering emotional hangover, made for arduous going.

He was into midafternoon and the tenth rewrite when his VDT screen blinked the message that Gert Shaw, his supervising editor, wanted to see him.

Most of the cityside reporters were out on their beats, and the evening copydesk crew had only begun to drift in, so Cooper's progress across the huge, windowless newsroom was mercifully free of encounters. En route he hastily devised a little speech, because Gert would most certainly mention his new status.

Gert was a tallish, angular woman with graying blond hair and half-glasses that sat near the end of her nose. Her husband, a freelance photographer, had died years ago in a Central American plane crash. Even so, she had managed to bring their three kids into educated and useful adulthood while making her own agonized climb from copy girl to newsroom administration. Cooper admired the hell out of her, not only for her triumph over single-parenthood and venomous male chauvinism but for being one of those rarest of birds—a boss who led by pulling instead of pushing. He considered it important to show good form in the presence of one who had weathered everything.

"Hi, Coop. Close the door and take a seat."

With the newsroom buzzing shut away and the tin desk between them, Gert took a moment to appraise him. Characteristically, she began at the top. "I don't know whether to congratulate you or to commiserate."

"I don't know what to say myself."

"The money's changed your whole life overnight."

"So I've been told."

"What are your plans?"

"I'm not sure I have any yet. It's all come down so fast. My father's lawyer wants me to take a couple weeks off, to sort things out in my mind—that kind of thing."

"Is that what you're going to do?"

"Well, I'm only midway in the Hefflefinger thing. I've got to keep going on that."

"So how's your day going?"

So much for prepared speeches, eh, Coop? "Okay. I'm drafting still another letter to the feds."

"What's the hang-up?"

"To get information out of the FBI, you have to know the FBI name for what you're looking for. I'm pretty sure that Hefflefinger is gunrunning and that the feds have run a check on him. But I don't know what they call their file."

"Can't you simply ask for it generically?"

"Sure, but it's unlikely we'd get anywhere for our trouble. We could ask, say, for the 'Hefflefinger File,' and the FBI could answer, 'No records.' But sitting right on the same shelf under the title, 'Illegal Weapons Traffic—Miami and Jax,' there could be a file containing seventeen hundred documents deriving from their look at the judge."

"So what to do, then?"

"We ask for the FBI search slip. That's the paper the FBI employees use to map the route taken in the records search prompted by our original request. It lists the search prompts, the records actually found, and those not found. It'll give us an assist in deciding what to ask for next."

Gert considered that for a moment. Then: "I still have trouble understanding why a guy like the judge would get himself tangled up in such a goofy, high-risk business. Money just doesn't hack it. He's already rich. His family was rich when it buddied around with George Washington and Thomas Jefferson.''

''Kicks, I'd say. Or maybe political fanaticism. He might be collaborating with the lunatic fringe that's been holding rallies and yelling about the second Boston Tea Party—that kind of thing.''

''Any way you look at it,'' Gert said, ''he's a freaking hypocrite, a lousy run-of-the-street crook. Is there anything else we can be doing to get documents help?''

''Sure. Now that the Bureau has assigned our request a research analyst—a woman name of Elliot—we can call her personally and ask if there's anything more we can do to help her search. When we get to talking with a warm body a lot of unexpected stuff comes out. It's chemistry or something. Right now, though, I'm writing a letter to Elliot as a kind of prefatory move, a courtesy, so that our phone call won't tighten her buns.''

Gert gave him a wry look. ''You keep saying 'we,' and 'our,' and 'you'—as if you're not the only guy working on Hefflefinger. As if you're cranking up to shift the load.''

A momentary pause, the tiny interval theatrical people call ''a beat,'' hung between them. Then Cooper, feeling an absolute need to be utterly candid with this compelling woman, said, ''Sorry, Gert. I have to lay it out. Even while I was telling you what I was going to do, I knew it was crap. Right now, I can no more chase down a decayed judge than I can sing soprano. My old man was murdered, and that makes me very goddamn angry. And now that I'm a half-assed suspect, I'm even madder. I've got to work on that. I've got to find out who killed Dad and why. So newspapering seems sort of irrelevant.''

Gert readjusted her glasses and sighed. ''Why is it that I'm so unsurprised?''

''I'll have to resign, you know. It's going to take all my time.''

''The police aren't exactly inactive in the case. Why don't you let them handle it?''

"The police aren't doing squat, Gert. They have one detective on it, and he spends most of his time trying to hang the whole thing on me."

"People will say that you've resigned because you're a fat cat now. That you're giving up a calling to play in the sun with naked babes. They'll say a lot of rotten things."

"I have a lot of faults, Gert. But worrying about what a bunch of assholes say about me is not one of them."

"Well, I have to try to keep you aboard, you know. So I'm using the only ammo I have."

He gave her a small smile. "You don't need ammo. I can't think of a job I'd rather have than this one. And, God knows, I can't think of a boss I'd rather work for. It's just that some son of a bitch stole my pappy, and I'm going to find that son of a bitch and tear his gender off."

"Do you need anything from me?"

"Just more of your patience until I sort things out."

"Take the time you need. I'll assign Cohen to the Hefflefinger thing. I want to fry that bastard's ass. I want headlines that say he's off the bench and in a cell."

"You'll nail him, Gert. Like all criminals, he thinks he's smarter than the rest of the world. But he ain't. And that's what'll finish him off."

The phone rang, and Gert, after a glance at her watch, lifted it from its cradle. "Be with you in a moment," she told the mouthpiece, which she then covered with her hand. Giving Cooper a wink, she said, "Okay, have at it, soldier. And let me know if I can help."

He pushed himself from the chair and, turning, opened the door.

"Coop?"

"Yo." He glanced back at her.

Her eyes, showing ice-blue above the half-glasses, were level and pensive. "I've learned that the pain eases up. It never goes away, but in time it becomes manageable. When you get your teeth knocked out, you learn to chew another way if you want to survive."

"I guess so."

"Your father was one hell of a writer."

"Yes. Yes, he was."

"And he was a hell of a man."

"You knew him?"

"I interviewed him when I was a reporter."

"How about that."

"And we went out a couple of times after your mama died. Nothing big-time. Just a couple of lonelies, sharing their lonelies."

"I'm glad. That proves he had good taste, good sense."

"I wanted you to know that. In case you picked up on it somewhere and got some wrong ideas."

"Appreciate it."

"Now get out of here. I've got a newspaper waiting." She lifted her hand from the phone. "Shaw speaking. Hey, Charlie—I've been trying to get you all day—"

Cooper let himself out and closed the door behind him.

Evening, and elevators everywhere sighed under their burdens of cocktail-bound humanity. Cooper rode his all the way to the basement bowels, where he retrieved the Ford and climbed the curving drive into The Outside. The twilight sky made great lavender slashes among the glassy towers, and in the dusky canyons a pleasant breeze dissipated the fumes and blatterings of the traffic that clotted between red lights. He concentrated on driving for driving's sake, a mechanism meant to help him deal with the day's confirmation of Stan Tremaine's preposterous presentations.

Fitzgerald's melancholy aphorism—". . . the very rich . . . are different from you and me . . . even when they enter deep into our world or sink below us, they still think that they are better than we are . . ."—refused to leave his mind. Both as college boy and professional journalist, on those occasions when he had experienced put-downs in close encounters of the megabucks kind, F. Scott's words had somehow served to assure him that superciliousness has a way of eventually biting its owner in the ass. But now he himself was one of the truly rich, and it was dismaying to realize that society would now summarily convict him—on circumstantial evidence alone—for having the kind of patronizing arrogance he had learned to detest in those others.

Sic semper stiffus luckius.

Nobody likes a loser and everybody hates a winner.

Shee-it-oh-dear.

The lights were on when he arrived at the Water Street house, and he found Mrs. Farman still at work in her office. Her gentle face, the archetypal representation of Old South refinement, was pale in the glow of the desk lamp. She attempted a smile, but it fell apart and became a discernible trembling of the lips.

"Well—Mr. Matt," she managed. "I—I didn't expect to see you this evening."

"I came for the briefcase I left here Tuesday." He examined her more closely, then shook his head, concerned. "You really ought to knock off, Mrs. Farman. You look economy-sized zonked."

"The day's been awful. You wouldn't believe the number of phone calls. All of them wanting to talk to you about 'propositions' and 'ideas' and heaven knows what else."

"So call the phone company and unlist the number."

"Thank you. I'll do that with great pleasure." She nodded at the papers piled on her desk. "So much to do. A quiet phone should help with this."

"Vot's dot?"

"Mr. Tremaine has given me a list of the things that are needed for estate settlement. It's quite extensive, and he needs them as fast as I can get them together."

"All lawyers want everything yesterday. Why don't you tell him that your *per stirpes* is on the blink and won't writ a single *certiorari?* That your corpus needs to rest its habeas, or something."

"Well—" The lip-quivering became more pronounced.

"That was a joke, Mrs. Farman. I popped a funny, and you're supposed to laugh."

She removed her pince-nez and, taking a tissue from a box on the credenza, dabbed at her eyes. "I don't think I'll ever laugh again, Mr. Matt. I was so terribly fond of your daddy, and it seems so—impossible—that he won't ever again walk through that door there, making jokes like you do, grumping about some file or other, or wanting to know where the newspaper went. All because a thief—"

He reached across the desk and patted her hand. "Hey," he said softly, "lighten up. Let him go."

"He was so good to me. So like a son—"

"Now it's my turn, dear lady. And I'm ordering you, as Frank Two and Honcho Designate, to take off a couple of days. Go plant a magnolia, or fry up some grits. This probate stuff will wait."

She shook her snowy head. "Mr. Tremaine was quite clear. He needs everything on this list no later than Friday evening."

"Tell you what: You knock off until Monday and I'll handle the list. The paper owes me a couple of days of comp time, and I'll take them and get at this pile."

"Lordy, Mr. Matt, you wouldn't even know where to look for things. I hardly know where to begin myself."

"All the more reason. You get some rest and I'll be confused for both of us. Being confused is my main thing."

"Mr. Tremaine—"

"And I'll handle him, too."

BOSTON (USP) —Eleanor Roman, internationally renowned academician and counselor to some of the nation's most powerful political leaders, was slain by a sniper today as she left a world government seminar sponsored by the United Nations.

Roman was entering her limousine at the entrance of Ludwell Hall, the recently completed political research center, when a single shot, fired from an adjacent park, struck her in the head.

A spokesman for the Boston police says, "The shot was obviously fired by an expert marksman—a sniper. We have no suspects at this time." Police are scouring the park for clues, and witnesses are being questioned.

One eyewitness told reporters at the scene that "the shot sounded like a board cracking, and then the lady did a backward flip onto the sidewalk."

(Desk Eds: World reactions, backgrounders, and updated obit material are in prep for A Wire distrib. Also in prep is major sidebar on possible link between the Roman assassination and last week's sniper death of Attorney Lou Pizarro. Both were members of the so-called "Ringmasters.")

BULLETIN   BULLETIN   BULLETIN

Seven

A media feeding-frenzy had swirled through St. Augustine from the moment Frank Cooper's name appeared on the local police blotter. The narrow old streets seemed to become instantly choked with vans, satellite dishes, and rental cars, and Restoration District hostelries had throbbed with the joyous reunion chatter of reporters and stringers from the broadcast and cable networks, from the wire services and syndicates, from the Southeast's major dailies, from the news magazines and supermarket tabs. Media people who would never read a novel in their lifetimes—and wouldn't otherwise have given Frank Cooper two sound bites or three lines of agate—had fallen into lockstep behind the *New York Times,* chanting variations on its section-front eulogy of "an internationally acclaimed writer of espionage thrillers" who had expired in a manner "reminiscent of his own ensanguined fiction." And when they weren't pushing microphones, cameras, and notebooks into the faces of city commissioners, bartenders, shopkeepers, and cops—from

Chief Nolan to the off-duty patrolman directing traffic at the
Benefit Sunday Tea Dance—they had been readying philo-
sophical insight pieces or "thumb-sucker segments" that
asked, "Why Are Novelists' Lives So Star-Crossed?" or "Is
the Novel of Entertainment Doomed?" or "Frank Cooper:
Was He a Victim of Our Declining Literacy?"

The commotion had lasted for three days ("which,"
cracked *Time*'s media critic Al Kibbee, "is about three days
longer than it was worth"), and then the pack was off in chase
of Brunhilde Feigenbaumik, movie and recording star, who
had been freed on bond after her arrest in Washington for public drunkenness, disorderly conduct, indecent exposure, and
lewd behavior deriving from an impulsive hard-core love session with voluptuous, equally stoned Melanie Sczmoewzsktz
(pronounced *Smith*), a senatorial aide, in the tourist-packed
Capitol Rotunda at high noon.

For all the heavy duty the murder had placed on her, Tina
Mennen had loved every crummy minute. She had been excited almost to the point of exhilaration, even in the midst of
caving-in weariness, not only by the chase but also by the chas-
ers—the raunchy, blasphemous, booze-swilling, pot-smoking
egomaniacs of tabloid TV and supermarket scandalabras, and
the tweedy, supercilious prigs of the so-called mainline print
media who let it be known that they were on this rhubarb only
because they were between think pieces and were helping out
cretinous editors who were momentarily shorthanded. They
were all industrial-strength pains in the ass, and she wanted
someday, more than anything she could think of, to be one of
their pack. It was part hero worship, part envy, part amour
propre, part love of adventure, part spiritual calling, and
wholly consuming.

Her problem, as she saw it, was provinciality. The stuff of
great news coups rarely lurked in Kiwanis breakfasts, Grange
halls, and Junior League banquets. The lightning of big-time
felony could strike anywhere, as the Cooper slaying had
shown. But here she could spend her whole life waiting for a
similar bolt, and even if it were to happen she'd be lost without
a trace in the subsequent paparazzi storm. And the chewy,
award-winning stuff—huge, internationally significant eco-

nomic, social, and political events that could be searched out and exposed to the world under her exclusive byline—were about as probable in this burg as Dairy Queens on Mars.

Even so, she never stopped dreaming, watching, and waiting. No fender-bender, no club luncheon, no quilting bee, no kitchen fire, no missing-person report was dismissed before she had considered its dramatic potential. (But not without cost. Her boss had snapped only last week, "You have the makings of a great reporter, Tina, but we just can't afford to have you spend three goddamn hours interviewing a woman who lip-syncs canaries, for chrissake.")

So it was not unusual for her to have seen something unusual in a darkened school's being surrounded by vehicles.

She had been to Palatka, where a St. Augustine couple had restored and reopened a fifties drive-in theater. She'd watched the opening reel of a one-star thriller, shot a couple of pictures, made a few notes, then headed on back, taking a shortcut through potato country. As she passed the Gum Tree Private School on County Road 14, it struck her that there was an unseemly number of cars, vans, and pickups in the parking lot and along the adjacent lane, especially in view of the fact that very few lights showed anywhere in the building. Curiosity gathering, she parked at the edge of the lot and made her way on foot to the alley beside the school's gymnasium.

Craning at one of the wire-reinforced windows, she was able to see into the dimly lit gym, where a group of guys of various ages was going through the manual of arms with shotguns and plinking rifles. Since men were generally dorks anyhow—little boys, playing with toys—it wasn't exactly pulse-quickening to see these dudes making like cadets. What caught her fancy was the fact that they were doing it in a virtual twilight. How come?

It was very cold that night, so she was wearing slacks, a lined jacket, and her favorite bubba hat, which obviously caused the man who had stepped out of the shadows to assign her the wrong sex. "You comin' in, buddy?"

She turned to face him in the gloom.

"You're late, and you ain't got a rifle."

She shrugged.

"And the CO ain't gonna like that hair of yours. He's death on guys with cute hair."

"What's going on here, mister?"

"Hey, you ain't a guy. You're a woman."

"I'll be damned. So *that's* why my jock strap keeps slipping."

"You ain't supposed to be here. Let's take you to the CO to see what he says about this."

"Get your hand off me, or I'm not going anywhere."

"C'mon, baby, into the gym."

She uncorked an arm-snap and hip roll, learned in her martial arts course at the university, and, much to her astonishment, the man went tail-over-tincups into the nearby shrubbery. However, he set up such a commotion, thrashing about, shouting dirty words, that several others came running, and then she was being half-carried into the gym, where at least thirty men and teenage boys were going from shoulder arms to present arms in the cadence rasped by a tall man in coveralls and a Ranger beret.

"We found this woman sneakin' around outside, Colonel."

The tall man turned, and Tina found it possible to be amused. It was Claude Abernathy, retired Army big shot and St. Augustine's preeminent realtor.

"Hi, Claude."

"Tina—what in the hell are you doing here?"

"I asked first."

"This is a private gathering. For men only. By invitation only."

"Sorry. I really didn't mean to crash the party. But when I saw all the cars I did my reporter's thing and your pals grabbed me and *made* me crash the party. So I ask again: What's the party all about?"

"This is most awkward. We're simply not ready to talk to the media."

"Hey, Claude, I'm not the media, I'm Tina Mennen, the one who translates all your Board of Realtors PR releases into understandable English. Besides, what's to be so secret about?"

Abernathy thought that one over for a moment, then, with

his features taking on a realtor's let's-deal smile, he said, "Well, you're right, of course. There's nothing here we can't talk about."

"So what is here?"

"Just some men indulging a hobby, Tina. Men who've always wished to make the military their career but, for various reasons, were unable to do so."

"You mean you're guys just playing soldier?"

Abernathy's smile tightened but remained where he'd put it. "It's bit more than that."

"Like what? And why are you doing it in the dark? With guards at the door keeping women out?"

"It lends an air of realism. The feel of martial conditions. A mood kind of thing."

"Who gave you permission to do it in the school here?"

"It's a private school, and I'm chairman of the board."

"What's your group called?"

"We don't have a name yet. We're just friends, indulging a hobby."

"Can I do a story on it?"

Abernathy shook his head solemnly. "We'd rather you didn't. We're not ready. When the time comes, you'll be the first to know."

"What time is that?"

"The time when we're ready."

"To do what?"

"To talk to you."

"Come on, Claude—you're jerking my string."

"No, Tina, I'm most respectful of your status as a reporter. I'm asking that you respect our privacy. At least for the time being."

She saw that much of the problem here was the presence of so many others. Abernathy was being circumspect because the group was watching, listening, to see how he would handle this intrusion.

"Okay, Claude, whatever you say. But I expect you to let me know first when the story's ready."

"You can count on it." To the guards, Abernathy said,

"Please escort this young woman to her car and see that she's not hassled further. She's a friend of mine, and she'll give us all some great publicity, by-and-by."

The two men stayed with her until she had driven out of sight around the bend in the lane. When she reached the black-topped county road, she turned out her car's lights and cut a quick U. After a few yards' backtracking, she parked in the cover of a cluster of moss-draped oaks and, holding close to a hedge, scurried, crouching, to a clump of wax myrtle, from where she had a fine view of the parking lot and the gym entrance.

She took the prone position and checked her camera. Thanks to the drive-in movie assignment, it was loaded with fast, night-conditions film, and the softly illuminated exposure counter showed four shots remaining on the roll.

She waited, trying to ignore the cold and the fact that she had to go to the john.

After half an hour of this, the meeting broke up, and the group filed out of the gym. They spoke softly, engaged in no horseplay, and went directly to their cars and drove off in a muted thunder. Which seemed very odd to Tina, since she had observed the conclusions of enough service club and church meetings to know that men are inclined to be school's-out ebullient in the parking lot.

Something else was odd, too. Claude Abernathy remained behind, pacing beside his dark blue Buick and frequently checking his wristwatch.

At 10:58 by her own watch, headlights flared on the lane and moments later a black Cadillac jounced over the rutted entrance to the parking lot and pulled to a stop under the wan glow of a pole light. Abernathy, shoulders squared, strode briskly to the car and opened the left front door—deferentially, the obsequious doorman.

A short man, somewhat lumpy in an otherwise stylish Chesterfield, slid from behind the wheel and came out of the car's darkness to stand, looking around and blowing on his cupped hands, seemingly unmoved by Abernathy's greeting.

"Well, now," Tina muttered, "just what would District

Judge Abner Hefflefinger be doing out in this nowhere upon a midnight dreary? Somebody please tell me.''

Nobody did, so she busied herself with the problem of how to get close enough to hear without being heard. Fortunately a wind had begun to stir, and the resultant fluttering of winter-dried foliage turned the trick. She was able to slither into the shadow of a wild cedar that placed her within twenty feet of the two men.

But the blessing became a curse: The breeze-restless leaves that had covered her move now made it impossible for her to hear the conversation clearly. A few words—''shipment,'' ''Miami,'' ''speed up''—came through, but there was no context, and no revelation of any significance. But the light and the angle were okay, so she shot her four remaining pictures and held the camera under her jacket to muffle the sound of its automatic rewind.

Abernathy suddenly led the judge across the lot and into the adjacent athletic field, where they stood beside what appeared to be a small equipment shed. The colonel became quite animated, his arms making arcs in the air, his words coming fast. The judge, impassive, nodded, checked his wristwatch, and, saying nothing, headed for his car.

A brief farewell, then he drove off, leaving Abernathy to the night and Tina to her hurried, limping flight for the VW and the search for a bathroom.

Any bathroom.

Eight

Sergeant Nickerson was leaving the house as Cooper pulled into the driveway. The detective waved, then came down the walk and motioned for him to lower the car window.

"What's up, Sergeant?"

"Manfred just gave me the phone log Mrs. Farman prepared for me before she left on vacation."

"Phone log?"

"I want to see who your dad might have talked to the week before he, ah, moved on."

"Need anything else, let me know."

"By the way: the lab confirms that it was your dad who drew that squiggle on the Christmas package. Have you come up with any ideas on what it might mean?"

"Sergeant, you have no idea how much time I've given to that. The more I wonder about it the less it means. I can't imagine what he was trying to tell us with that thing."

"Keep trying. So what are you doing here this evening?"

"Going through files. The lawyers need some papers."

Nickerson peered through the window, his cop's eyes taking inventory of the Ford's scruffy interior. "Do you like this better than a car?"

"Don't knock it. It's paid for. It runs."

The detective sniffed. "How come your daddy didn't spring for something better?"

"Because he was stingy and I have pride."

"Stingy? The old man didn't share his wealth with you?"

"Come on, Nickerson, what are you saying? That as my father's only living relative I got tired of waiting for my inheritance and decided to hurry him along? Is that what you're saying?"

"Hey—what the hell are you so pissed off about? I didn't say any such thing. Did I say any such thing?"

"Up yours."

Cooper threw the Ford into gear and plunged up the drive, around the house, and into the garage in an angry squealing of tires.

Frank Cooper had done virtually all of his writing in later years in what had been the servants' quarters, a suite above the four-car garage and workshop. His desk and office equipment occupied the former parlor, which, as the largest and most pleasant of the rooms, offered an excellent view of the river, the Vilano inlet, and the ocean beyond. There were two bedrooms, a kitchen-dining area, and a bath—a combination which obviously had been intended for occupancy by a man-and-wife butler-housekeeper team. Frank had kept the bedroom next to the bath to its original purpose, while the other was a kind of library, with two walls lined floor-to-ceiling with books and its remaining space given to file cabinets stuffed with computer floppies. Louise Farman's secretarial office was in the first-floor reading room of the main house, where she handled correspondence, answered the phones, and kept in touch with her boss via an intercom. Manfred Kohlmann's digs were in the main house utility ell, from where he supervised those called in to keep house and grounds in order.

Coop had long suspected that the apartment was where his

father had spent most of his later life—writing, eating, sleeping, and doing those arcane things novelists do in what Frank had called "the writer's dreadful isolation." The suspicion was now upgraded to a conviction, since the rooms, for all their museumlike stillness, were rich with the retained feel of him. "A house, like a dog, takes on the essence of the one to whom it belongs," Frank had assured Mom and him in one of his long-ago dinnertime monologues. And here—now, in this quiet place redolent of furniture polish and books—was confirmation.

He sat at the desk and stared out at the distant sea and wheeling gulls, suddenly aware that his earlier depression had been replaced by an indefinable foreboding. It was more, larger somehow, than the irrational rage stirred by Nickerson. Greater than the unsettling puzzlement over his future as a journalist. Almost as dire and prodigious as his father's murder. Something apocalyptic was about to happen. To him. Personally. He simply knew this, as he knew the Matanzas tide would turn.

"There you go again, Mom," he said aloud, sardonic.

He turned, startled, at a soft sound from the doorway behind him.

"Oh. Manfred. I didn't realize you were there."

Manfred—tall, dour, skin like parchment—nodded stiffly, a suggested bow in the German manner. "I'm sorry, sir. I am sorry to intrude."

"It's all right. I'm just sitting here, talking to myself. What's up?"

"I must tell you that the detective fellow, Nickerson, was here and asked me to provide him with the phone log Mrs. Farman keeps. I, ah, tried to resist, but he was most forceful, saying he could get a warrant, and that sort of thing. He—"

"That's okay, Manfred. I saw him in the driveway and he told me. No big deal."

"I think he suspects you of your father's murder."

"Tell me something I don't know."

"You must be very careful of him. Policemen cannot be trusted."

"Hey, old friend, he's just a small-town cop. He isn't the Gestapo. He has to prove I killed Dad, and that's going to be impossible to do, because I didn't."

"The size of the police force has little to do with it. The policeman's job is to keep order. Murder is disorderly. A murderer must be found and punished, first, to show the people that order has been kept, and second, to warn the people who are considering murder not to do it. For a policeman like Nickerson, it matters little who serves as the murderer so long as he has one to bring to punishment."

Cooper sighed, vaguely annoyed by such deep cynicism. "I realize you had a lot of trouble in Germany, Manfred. Dad told me several times that you were brutalized. That was then, a time when rotten people did rotten things for a rotten government. This is now, in the U.S.A. I'll admit that things aren't exactly ecstatic in the country today, and we've got a lot of pushing and shoving and yelling. But cops are still pretty much on a short string."

The old man shook his head. "I cannot agree. The police here are like the police anywhere. The greater the turmoil, the disorder, the shorter their tempers and the more brutal they become. Besides, Nickerson is personally an ambitious man. But there is a larger problem."

"Like what?"

Manfred stood in that motionless way of his, seeming to ponder the question. Then: "Your father kept a revolver in his desk drawer. A thirty-eight-caliber Taurus revolver. I looked for it the day after his, ah, death, and it was not there. I can find it nowhere—in the house, the garage, the apartment, the garden house, the boathouse. Nowhere."

Cooper sat forward in his chair, uneasiness gathering. "So what's your point?"

"I have not reported this to the police."

"Why?"

"I worry that he was murdered with his own weapon. The police may think that you—or I—used it to kill your father and then disposed of it."

Cooper shook his head, dismayed. "Hey, Manfred, for

God's sake. Even if the killer did use Dad's gun—which is only speculation—that doesn't mean it was you or I who used it. Anybody could have found the gun and used it. Hell, even Dad could have used it to defend himself, was overpowered, and shot with his own gun. Right?''

"Quite so, sir. But there were no signs of struggle. I do not trust Nickerson to accept that possibility. It would be much easier for him to suspect those in the house who had knowledge of the gun.''

"Hold on, pal. I didn't even know Dad had a gun, let alone where he kept it.''

"Yes, sir. You know that, and I know that. But I don't trust this policeman to believe that. He needs you, and if he knew about the gun he would arrest you, I'm sure.''

Cooper gave that a moment of thought. His uneasiness deepening, he asked, "So what are we going to do? Tell Nickerson about the gun? Or say nothing and hope it never plays into all this?''

"You already have my answer to that, sir.''

"Yeah. Which means I'm asking me.''

"You would be well advised, sir, to say nothing. I have had much experience with men like Nickerson, and he cannot be expected to be anything but a hungry policeman.'' Manfred paused, then added, "I believe I have said enough already, sir. If there is nothing further, I'll retire now.''

As the old man turned to leave, Cooper held up a hand. "Just a second, Manfred.''

"Sir?''

"I don't know what your plans are, now that my father's gone. But I'd sure be pleased if you'd stay on here, doing for me what you did for him.''

Manfred's expression changed not at all, but a faint glimmer appeared in his ancient eyes. "You will be keeping this house, then?''

"I don't have the heart to sell it to strangers.''

Manfred gave his half-bow. "I am most happy to assure you that I will remain at my post, sir.''

"Good. That's settled, then. By the way, I'm instructing Mrs. Farman to increase your pay by twenty percent.''

"That's most kind of you, sir." A pause, then: "Will that be all, sir?"

"Yep."

Cooper sat, motionless in the twilight, pondering Manfred's disturbing revelation and prognosis. Was this the calamity he had been expecting? It had been bad news, to be sure. But was it *the* bad news?

Suddenly exasperated by all this doom and gloom, he put his mind to the paper chase.

Mrs. Farman had left three fat file folders on the desk, aligned meticulously and carefully labeled. One contained receipts for the past year's purchases of office supplies and miscellaneous payments out of petty cash; the second held copies of letters to and from the agent, Charlotte Davis, and Obelisk, Inc., all dull and routine; the other contained photocopies of all the contracts for subsidiary sales for *The Götterdämmerung Machine*—paperback, foreign publication, book club sales, various serializations, and a three-month option on the motion picture rights from Cosmos Productions. Cooper leafed through these, expecting no surprises and finding none. As he pushed himself away from the desk and rose to go to the bank of file cabinets he noticed a dusty brown briefcase in the corner behind the printer stand. He placed the case on the worktable, and when he opened it, the smell of mold was heavy. Inside were two pencil stubs, some decayed rubber bands, and a file folder labeled simply, "Coop."

It was a trip through time. Yellowed snapshots of him. As a kid on a bike. Cavorting with Skipper, his mutt. At the beach, holding two fingers behind Billy Oswald's head. Arms around Mom, squinting into the sun. In his football uniform, arm cocked for a pass. At the wheel of his hot rod. In his mortarboard on graduation day at Columbia. On the front steps, somber in his Marine Corps greens. A clipping of the press photo of him in Bosnia, all rigid and GI as General What's-His-Face gonged him with the Navy Cross.

And a letter—handwritten, undated, incomplete—to "Coop, my dear son."

It read:

Of all the bitter ironies that have marked my life, the most inexplicable is that which allows me to make a living by writing in a language having words I seem unable to speak.

I can lecture in it, to be sure. I can prate. I can pontificate on inanities, from galactic black holes to black-eyed peas. I can joke and razz. But for all this noisy glibness, and despite my most earnest attempts to do so, I am entirely unable to take your hand and utter three simple words:

I adore you.

Is it because I consider it unmanly? But how can that be, when you came from me, a man? When you came from the woman I—a man—adore and who, in her tormented way, likewise adores you?

Is it because I fear rejection, being so unworthy of adoration in return? Unlikely, because rejection has been my lifelong companion. From my father's denial of me as his son, through decades of the literati's calculated snubs, to my excommunication as a husband by a wife who has been medically diagnosed as alcoholic and manic depressive, I've long since become inured to the pain of rejection.

The fact is, I

Cooper took the unfinished letter to the easy chair beside the big window and, in the fading light, read its nineteen lines a dozen times. Then he folded it carefully and, after returning it to the folder, he sat, unmoving, watching the twilit bay and listening to the call of circling gulls.

The story of his life: watching and not seeing.

Missing the boat.

The phone rang.

"Hello."

"Coop? Stan Tremaine."

"Hi, Stan."

"I hope you're sitting down."

"Why?"

''The Lord giveth, the Lord taketh away.''

''What's that supposed to mean?''

''One day I announce that you're rich. The next day I announce that somebody plans to make you less rich.''

''Come on, Stan. What the hell are you talking about?''

''I've just received a certified letter. Frank's estate—meaning you, of course—is being sued for twenty-two million dollars.''

Nine

While the others foraged at the buffet, rattling coffee cups and poking among the mounds of Danish, Dr. Edmund von Ludwig, managing director of Rettung Internationale, sat at the head of the boardroom table and, pretending to review his notes, steeled himself for the dreary hour ahead. Presumably Takai, seated at the far end of the table, was likewise occupied; motionless, only occasionally blinking, he stared fixedly at the Munich skyline beyond the huge window, seeming to be lost in some private rite of preparation.

One of Ludwig's personal burdens was his propensity for reminiscence, and it plagued him now with vignettes of the first-class boards that had served the foundation in the past. They had been sharp, eager, benevolent, and worldly-wise—a real pleasure to work with in those years of exciting achievement. This current crop—Takai excepted, of course—were clowns, handpicked not for their strengths but for their vulnerability to manipulation.

Rettung Internationale had been established as a charitable

foundation under United States law in 1952 by Frank Cooper, a novelist and ex-GI who had come into money, and Anton Rettung, a successful German businessman who had spent the World War Two years in Japanese-occupied territories. Both had been appalled by the suffering caused by the Nazis— Frank as a soldier-witness, Rettung as a wanderer returning to a homeland that had been dishonored and laid waste. The two had met at a Munich cocktail party, and in the friendship that subsequently developed they recognized their special kinship—the determination to help survivors of the Holocaust and its derivative miseries. Cooper had given a million dollars, proposing that the foundation be named for Rettung, since, by happy coincidence, *Rettung* is the German word for "rescue." Rettung had put up an additional six million—his only proviso being that, whatever Cooper's fortunes in the capricious world of literature, Cooper would serve as permanent president and he, Ludwig, a lawyer and longtime friend, would be appointed managing director.

Rearranging the papers before him once again, Ludwig felt a smile forming at the recollection of the first press reference to Rettung Internationale as "the Ford Foundation of Europe." It was a source of great personal satisfaction that, with the help of several strong boards, he had managed to attract many heavyweight donors and bring a number of lucrative acquisitions and investments under the Rettung umbrella. The foundation had not only helped numerous Holocaust survivors over the years but had also moved into many areas of charitable giving, from gifts to universities for social science research to technical aid programs for the improvement of education, farming, business, industry, and public administration in underdeveloped countries.

Five years ago, after nearly four decades of progress, the foundation had suffered a staggering blow. In a matter of weeks, Anton Rettung had been sucked into the oncologic bog and three of the five-member "good" board had died in a plane crash. The remaining two, made suddenly aware of their own waning mortality, resigned and went off to fulfill unrealized childhood ambitions. And by three years later, when Frank Cooper's participation had dwindled to cameo appearances at annual meetings, Rettung had become essentially a one-man show, with Edmund von Ludwig calling the shots for the current board, which he had personally selected as foils for his own ambitions and slid past the ailing Rettung and the aging, increasingly indifferent Cooper.

But the resulting boredom had become stifling, so last year, when Oko Takai had approached with his bizarre and exciting proposal, their pact followed swiftly. To get the plan under way with minimum delay, Ludwig had created an additional board seat, to which Takai's election had been easily maneuvered.

As always, there was a flip side, and the personal price exacted from Ludwig had been twofold: an inexplicable sense of guilt and an obligatory association with these egotistical yo-yos, whose sole reason for an alliance with Rettung was to present prima facie evidence of their respectability to a doubting world.

He was brought back to the present when Takai coughed gently and said, "We're wasting time, Edmund."

"Sorry. I was daydreaming." Ludwig tapped a tumbler with his pen. "All right, ladies and gentlemen, let's have a meeting, shall we? Please take your seats."

The group, of course, disregarded the request; each was accustomed to absolute authority in his own realm and was therefore as spiky as a porcupine in matters of image and protocols. To sit down at once at anyone's bidding would be to admit to being a lesser god.

Five minutes later, when the point had been made and everyone was seated and the shuffling and clatter had subsided, Ludwig said, "Since this is a special meeting, we'll go directly to new business. I'll begin with a rundown of the situation and how it's to be resolved under the Rettung Foundation's certificate of purpose. Members are, of course, invited to comment or ask questions at any time, but we'll attempt to hold to the nut of things and complete the business with this one meeting. So whatever each of us can do to facilitate—"

Allison-Dutton broke in gumpily. "Brandy. Where's the brandy for my coffee?"

Ludwig shot a glare at the steward, who stood discreetly at the buffet. "See to it."

"And this croissant has an almond undertaste," Madame Doubet whined. "I detest the flavor of almonds. Why is it I can never come to Munich without being served almond-flavored things?"

Enzo Tataglia waved an irritable hand. "For God's sake, Ludwig, let's get on with it. Are we here to nosh or to discuss this succession thing?"

Ignoring the question, the steward's fussings, and the stage whispers of the French grande dame, Ludwig sat, silent and haughty, until he at last had the attention of the six.

Melissa Andrelou, the wifty Piraeus shipping heiress, sighed impatiently. Allison-Dutton, the London oil baron, shoved aside his coffee and tossed off the glass of brandy. Tataglia, the Milano playboy-industrialist, studied a thumbnail. Madame Doubet, monarch of the Paris-based fashion universe after a lifetime of shameless exploitation of talented underlings, rattled her many bracelets, patted her wig, and took up another croissant in her pudgy fingers. Sam Goodman, the beady-eyed, balding New York media overlord and owner of a hundred acres of skyscrapers in various uptown downtowns, drained his coffee cup, then belched. Takai, the diminutive Kyoto electronics king, appeared once again to be lost in thoughts of things elsewhere.

Ludwig cleared his throat delicately and got to business. "We have, unhappily, been struck a double blow within a mere several weeks. With the loss of our founder and elder statesman, Anton Rettung, and our dear friend, cofounder, and president, Frank Cooper, it was necessary to call this special meeting so that we might deal with the matter of succession, which has been rather awkwardly on hold during Herr Rettung's long illness. Now, on the heels of his death and the Cooper tragedy, we are confronted with an additional complication—a further clouding of the question as to how this body will be shaped and how it will function."

Goodman sniffed. "We all know," he said sarcastically, "that you've always got the last word. Why don't we just make things simple and rubber-stamp whatever you've already decided?''

"The foundation," Ludwig said coolly, "is required to observe specific protocols—one of them being that the board function fully as a board. I realize your suggestion is well intended, Mr. Goodman, but if we were to follow it we would be very much out of line."

"If you're telling me to stick it in my ear, Ludwig, why don't you just say so without all the fancy goddamn lingo?''

Tataglia groused, "Oh, come on, Sam. Stop fussing and let us get on with this thing."

"Hear, hear," Allison-Dutton put in.

Madame Doubet's plump cheeks bulged with croissant, but she managed a question. "By the way, has the cause of Herr Rettung's death been officially established?''

Ludwig sighed sorrowfully. "An autopsy after organ-donor procedures confirmed that it was a massive coronary."

Goodman, in an obvious attempt to recoup and show the others that he was no mere grump, said, "I just wish I could have met him. I've been on this board for three years now and not once did I ever lay my eyes on The Main Guy."

Melissa Andrelou seemed to be pleased with the chance to flaunt her seniority. "I met him twice. He was a very imposing gentleman. Dedicated. Very dedicated. I always expected him to outwit his doctors and show up among us."

Goodman countered with a little joke. "And it's my guess that, if Cooper could find a way to outwit God, he'd be here, too. Now there was one dedicated guy."

There was a moment of silent embarrassment in which the others dealt with this gaucherie. Ludwig moved quickly to apply balm. Goodman was an insensitive, insolent man, to be sure, but his millions were important to the foundation and he therefore worth a bit of forbearance. Smiling dimly, he said, "Indeed. Mr. Cooper never missed a board meeting. Not once in forty-five years."

Allison-Dutton pointed to his empty brandy glass and the steward sped to pour a fresh one. "The papers and telly," the Englishman said, "made much of Cooper's being shot to death in his own house. Rum show, what?''

To slow the accelerating rush into gossip, Ludwig said, "Which sad event is the rationale for this meeting. So let us, please, concentrate on the business of the board."

"So okay," Goodman snapped. "So where do we start?"

"The bylaws are quite clear on the matter," Ludwig answered in his prim, pedantic way. "They provide that, precisely three months after Mr. Cooper's death, his son, Matthew, automatically replaces him."

A ripple of wry amusement stirred among those at the table. "Surprise, surprise," Goodman said, snickering. "So why in hell have we all come all this way to attend this frigging meeting? If it's so cut and dried—"

Ludwig held up a silencing hand. "That's our problem. It isn't that cut and dried. I called the meeting because I received a fax from Stanley Tremaine in Jacksonville which informed me that Matthew Cooper, while he admires the work done by the Rettung Foundation and would very much like to join us, cannot take his father's seat on the board at this time."

"Well, how the hell come?"

Ludwig glanced at Goodman. "Frank Cooper's estate, which Matthew inherits, is being sued for libel. The pressures of the pending legal action—the preparation of the defense and all that—will demand almost every minute of Mr. Cooper's time. This promises to be a major case involving a rather complicated, interwoven series of procedures, and Mr. Cooper feels he wouldn't be able to give the foundation the amount of attention it deserves."

Another stir moved about the table.

"Libel?" Andrelou asked, eyebrows raised.

Ludwig nodded. "Mr. Tremaine advises me that the estate has received a demand for retraction or correction under the Florida code. The demand is, of course, being rejected, so now the mechanisms for a formal suit—to be tried in a U.S. district court—are under way. The plaintiff is a German national named Siegfried Ramm, who alleges that Mr. Cooper's novel, *The Götterdämmerung Machine,* issued last fall, contains a vicious libel that has brought pain, suffering, and humiliation to Ramm and his family. Herr Ramm claims that a central character in the novel, while given another name, is an otherwise cruel and barely disguised representation of himself.''

"So what the hell's wrong with that?" Goodman broke in. "Any goddamn piece of fiction, from movies to paperbacks, can remind somebody of somebody. I'm a media guy, and I know for a fact that if somebody gets pissed off by some kind of coincidental similarity, there isn't a frigging thing he can do about it. The similarity has to contain defamation that damages the somebody's reputation or holds him up to public ridicule. Even then he has to prove malice.''

"Which," Ludwig said quietly, "is exactly what Herr Ramm claims Mr. Cooper was—ice-cold malicious—when he has the novel's Ramm-like character openly admit to being a war criminal.''

Takai appeared to take interest for the first time. "I assume you refer to World War Two.''

"My sources say that the novel has to do with an American counterespionage operation in Nazi Germany in 1945. Ramm was a high-ranking Nazi official at that time—he admits it, has even done jail time under the German national Denazification laws of the 1950s.''

"So what's he bitching about?" Goodman sneered.

"Ramm was never charged or convicted of war crimes. Nor has he ever confessed to them to anyone.''

"That's gotta be the dumbest thing since marshmallow screwdrivers. A sick-dick Nazi with a rap sheet from here to there suing somebody because they called him *names?* Loon City, man.''

"Apparently there's a line—a difference. The man was jailed by Germans for his leadership role in a government that brought ruin and injustice to the German people. He was never charged under United Nations statutes for crimes against humanity. It's a matter of specific laws and jurisdictions.''

Takai said, "A case of this, ah, gaudiness will receive rather wide publicity, I should think.''

"I am afraid so. And I think it's to this board's interest that a statement be drafted making it clear we are in no way involved—that, while Frank Cooper was a guiding light of this foundation, his literary affairs were separate and distinct. As soon as the suit becomes a public document it's subject to media inquiries, of course. But for now, attorneys for both sides have agreed to refrain from public discussion of the matter until the depositions are complete and the suit moves to trial.''

Another silence followed.

Madame Doubet, continuing to chew, said, ''So then, dear one, where does that leave us?''

Ludwig cupped his right hand and evaluated its manicure. ''We must act on Herr Rettung's nomination of me as chairman and chief executive officer.''

The group gave this a moment of surprised, silent thought. Then Goodman, leaning forward in his seat, his eyes narrowed, his voice heavy with challenge, said, ''I don't care what the hell you call this. To me it's out-and-out rubber-stamping.''

''Not so, Mr. Goodman. It won't happen if you and the other board members turn it down. Actually, Herr Rettung said he expected you to vote, either to elect me or to choose a CEO from your ranks.''

Goodman snapped, ''Do we have a letter to that effect? A letter of nomination?''

''No. It was simply Herr Rettung's decision, announced during my visit that day. He seemed to be concerned about his deteriorating physical condition and said that he felt the board should put me entirely in charge.''

''That's pretty goddamn unusual, pal. There should be a letter of confirmation.''

Takai chuckled. ''I can set your mind at ease, Mr. Goodman. I was also at that meeting, and I can confirm the nomination. And I can also testify that, in a private conversation only moments before his fatal attack, Herr Rettung told me of his intention to formalize the nomination in a letter to be faxed to each of you that afternoon.''

Another interval of silence followed, broken when Ludwig sighed. ''Let me make a point here, please. I'd like you all to understand that I really don't relish the idea. I am not anxious to take on a promotion that will add thirty-hour days and ten-day weeks to my already heavy work load. At this stage of my life I would much rather decelerate. So if anyone here would like the job, I'll be most happy to nominate you and call for unanimous approval.''

All eyes turned to Goodman, who eventually shrugged and pretended interest in the rococo ceiling.

Ludwig, feigning weary surrender, said, "So, then, let's be about it, shall we? Each of you in favor of my assuming the duties of both the chairman and chief executive officer—as wished by our founder—please raise your hand.''

Takai counted. "It is unanimous. Dr. Ludwig is our chairman and chief executive officer.''

Twilight was settling when Ludwig returned to his office. He went to the cellarette and poured himself a generous cognac, then took the glass to the large window, where he sank into the overstuffed Francini chair and sighed the sigh of a man just released from perdition. Sipping the drink and moodily scanning the violet Tyrolean crags thirty miles to the south, he used his free hand to tap out the numbers for Takai's private Ammersee phone.

"Yes?''

"Edmund here. How do you think it went?''

"Goodman could be difficult, since he's the only board member who shows any signs of thinking. But I suspect he'll calm down if you assign him to an ego-salving subsidiary chairmanship. Our most pressing problem at this point is young Cooper. Simply by existing, he represents a major threat.''

"I agree. Any suggestions?''

"You need do nothing. My specialists are already moving on the matter.''

"Isn't that rather extreme?''

"You must learn not to ask such questions, Edmund.''

"Well, on the heels of the Frank Cooper thing—''

"Good night, Edmund.''

Ten

Cooper had agreed to meet Tremaine at his Ponte Vedra beach house, which turned out to be about an acre of glass and stone and splashing fountains on a mountainous dune with nothing east of it but whitecaps and Morocco.

Arriving two minutes early, he found Tremaine standing in the driveway circle, chatting with a large man at the wheel of a stretch Cadillac that shimmered in the autumn sunlight. After parking his Ford in the shade of a split-stem oak, Cooper crossed to where the lawyer stood, saying, "I'm paying you too much, Counselor. The last time I saw this house it was called Taj-Something."

"Pretty, isn't it. I'll show you around when we've got more time." Opening the Caddy's rearmost door, Tremaine said, "Meanwhile, climb in. We'll work on the way."

"You rented this limo just to take us to St. Augie?"

Tremaine smiled. "A year or so ago I realized I was too old and cantankerous to continue driving in Jacksonville's traffic, where everybody—even little old ladies in sneakers—

dogfights at Mach six for a single car's-length advantage. I never did anything about it. Last week I nearly got killed on the Butler Boulevard by some nut who passed and cut me off. So yesterday I leased this rig and hired Albert to drive it. I can close the curtains, set up a table, and work in sweet ignorance of the combat outside.''

"Makes sense.''

They settled into opposite corners of the backseat and, when Albert had them sizzling south on A1A, Tremaine said, "I'm sorry so much is coming at you at once, Coop. Your father's murder and the press rumpus over that and your inheritance are gross enough. But now this—this Nazi's attempt to plunder the estate—I don't like it one bit.''

"I'm not so crazy about it myself.''

"Cranks. God, I hate them.''

Cooper shook his head. "It's not the cranks who worry me. It's the ambitious dudes. Nickerson, for instance. If there's anything Nickerson isn't, it's a crank. He's something a lot scarier: an ambitious cop, a sergeant bucking for lieutenant. Which means he'd dearly love to nail the killer of Frank Cooper, famous novelist. Which further means that if he's led to see me as a sitting duck, he'll get so busy establishing his case against me he won't have time for suspecting and nailing anybody else.''

Tremaine thought about that for a moment. "Well," he said finally, "I've told you about the perils of wealth. Here's where I show you one of the advantages.''

He picked up the phone and in quick succession tapped the memory and speakerphone buttons. After two rings the phone lifted at the other end.

"Commissioner Santos.''

"Stanley Tremaine here, Bert.''

"Well, hello there, Counselor. This is a pleasant surprise. How the hell are you, anyhow?''

"Excellent, thanks. You?''

"Great, great.'' The slightest of pauses, then: "What's on your mind, Stan? Must be important for you to come in on my private line, eh?'' Santos laughed uneasily.

"A city detective—ah, Nickerson, Sergeant Nickerson—

has been investigating the murder of Frank Cooper.''

"So I understand. Nick's one of our best."

"Does he have any reason to suspect Frank Cooper's boy?"

There was a longer pause, this one accompanied by a tension that could be felt here in the car. "Hell, Stan, you know I don't know anything about police department investigations. And I couldn't discuss them even if I did."

"Come on, Bert. This is Stan Tremaine, not some yuk from Red Dirt Junction. Answer the question."

"Well, in a case like this, a lot of people, their relationships, et cetera, are looked at. And I'm sure Nick is looking at young Cooper. Nothing serious yet. Strictly routine, you understand. And—"

"I'd like Nickerson to be taken off the case."

"Hey, Stan, you can't just—I mean—"

"At once, please."

Tremaine hung up and, smiling faintly, gave the incredulous Cooper a sly wink.

"It'll happen? Just like that?"

The lawyer nodded. "Just like that."

"Either Santos is scared blind by big money, or he owes you something heavy. Maybe both, eh?"

"Another piece of advice, Coop: Never ask questions in such situations. Never say anything. Simply accept the result. You must learn to let me or your designated aides operate and deliver. You don't want to know the details. You must stay out of the trenches—above the battle."

Cooper exploded. "Goddammit, Stan, you know how I hate this kind of crap. I've spent most of my professional life going after the bastards who pull these rotten strings. And now you want me to *join* them?"

"You really don't have a choice. Unless you want the Ramms and the Nickersons of the world to hang you out to dry. The Ramms will try to steal you blind; the Nickersons will try either to use you as a stepladder or to punish you for your good luck."

"Good *luck*? Jesus to Jesus—this is supposed to be good *luck*? Having my world turned inside out, having to give up a career, having to fight corruption with corruption, change my freaking phone numbers, surround myself with a platoon of goons just to get a goddamn hamburger? What's next? Having you tell me when I can go toi-toi?''

Tremaine took off his glasses and rubbed their lenses with a snowy handkerchief. ''Easy, Coop. I'm on your side.''

Even in his anger, Cooper saw that it was a lawyer's cool, deliberate stage business, calculated to interrupt and valve off the surging heat, and he found it possible to be grateful. After a protracted interval, he managed to say, ''I'm sorry, Stan. You didn't invent this crummy world.''

''No offense, Coop. But I do suggest that we've just seen another reason why you should disappear for a week or two of R and R.''

''Yeah.''

''Meanwhile, let's talk some business.'' Tremaine slid into the rear-facing jump seat and lowered the fold-down table. Reaching into his briefcase, he withdrew a fat folder, which he placed on the table before him. ''Have you done any sorting of your father's papers yet? Any at all?''

''I made a start, but all that did was tell me I'll need four years just to go through his stuff, let alone to categorize it.''

''We don't have four years. There'll be a deposition within the month, and the Ramm people will be demanding all documents that pertain to the novel at issue. That's why we're going down there this morning, remember?''

Cooper shifted testily in his seat. ''Hold it, Stan. I'm in no mood for sarcasm.''

''I'm not being sarcastic. I'm being urgent. We don't have a bunch of time.''

''I just can't get it through my head: How come that Nazi bastard has the right to go through Dad's personal papers? And before we even go to court, for hell's sake.''

''It's the way things are done, Matt.'' Tremaine's tidy face assembled an expression that suggested a preacher preparing to explain God to a child. ''Ramm's attorneys have demanded a correction or retraction, as required by Florida Code Seven-Seventy-oh-one. The demand came to me, as administrator of the estate, and a like letter went to Obelisk, as publishers of the work. The demand was rejected by all hands, of course, and

Ramm's next move is to file suit—in all likelihood in U.S.
District Court, because he's a foreign national suing a U.S. citizen's estate for more than fifty thousand dollars. And—"

Cooper broke in. "You mean Obelisk is a codefendant? The
publishers will be in it with me?"

"Not necessarily. I've had a phone conference with Eli
Abrams, the Miami attorney who is signing the pleadings for
Ramm's Munich lawyer, Max Mueller, and he's indicated that
Ramm holds Frank responsible for the libel and that Obelisk is,
in essence, not a participant in the libel but a victim of it. In
other words, the letter to Obelisk was pro forma, but Obelisk
will probably not be named in the suit."

"That doesn't make a hell of a lot of sense. Ramm stands to
make even more money from a big publishing firm."

"Ramm insists that Frank personally, calculating, viciously
libeled him—an act that Obelisk really had no way of knowing was taking place."

"Sheesh. How preciously fair of him."

"Fair? I don't think so. I think he'd just rather not tangle
with the Obelisk crowd. They've got a regiment of lawyers
who eat raw meat and battleship hulls."

"How about publicity? I don't want a drumfire barrage of
supermarket tab stories about how some Teutonic Tamerlane
is about to take my riches away. I've had enough of that kind of
trouble as it is."

"There won't be any publicity at all for a while. At this
point, it's mainly a private matter—an exchange of nasty letters and oily phone calls. Abrams won't call in the press because he wants first to see if we will settle quietly, out of court.
And I'll keep him dangling on that one, as long as I can."

Tremaine riffled through the papers on the table, his lips
pursed, his eyeglasses glinting. Cooper's gaze went to the
passing seascape—the rolling dunes, the sea oats, the sparkling green ocean beyond. A formation of pelicans wheeled
majestically above the beach, and, offshore, a pair of surfers
lay on their boards, paddling along in a futile search for a useful wave. Again the fleeting restlessness which was really a
plea: Why must he be here, when he wanted to be in some
there?

Tremaine broke into his thoughts. "Are the documents assembled by Mrs. Farman complete? I mean, is it possible that Frank stored material elsewhere, as well?"

Cooper sighed and shifted in his seat. "Beats me. We can ask Mrs. Farman."

"I already have. She says the cabinets in Frank's digs and the cartons in the garden house are the only ones she's aware of."

"So why ask me?"

"Because, damn it, you are Frank's son and may know things that she doesn't. You may even know things you don't know you know."

"This is madness."

"Maybe. But it's a madness that can put a heavy dent in your inheritance if we don't deal with it properly."

"So what's next?"

"When the suit is filed, there'll be a summons requiring us to answer within twenty days—if it goes into federal court, as I'm sure it will. The courts—both state and federal—provide, under Rule Thirty-four, for requests for production of documents for copying or inspection. We have thirty days to respond, either, 'Okay, here they are,' or 'Stick it in your ear, pal.' But Abrams indicates that he'll ask for a deposition preceding the formal request for documents. That will let him determine what documents are believed to exist and where they're located."

"Sounds like he's fishing."

Tremaine's glance showed amused respect. "Very perceptive of you, Coop. That's exactly what he's doing. He wants to identify documents that have the best chance of nailing us to the wall. And then, goodies in hand, he'll march us into court and nail us to the wall."

"Which also sounds like he's expecting us to hand him the hammer and nails."

"It's a cruel world, dear boy."

"Will Ramm be sitting in on these depositions?"

Tremaine smiled dimly. "Another good question. Ramm will not be sitting in on anything. He won't even be in court, if it comes to that. As a former SS officer—a Standartenführer, I think it is—and as a German national convicted under Germany's Denazification laws, the Immigration and Nationality Act forbids his entry to the United States. Period. His only way to collect is by way of a judge and jury listening to lawyers and depositions.''

''Ah, yes. The American Way: a dirty rat fink who isn't acceptable to our system can use our system to pick the pockets of those who are acceptable to our system.''

''Cruel World, Chapter Two.''

''Well, what if we want to ask him some questions? I mean, we're not expected just to sit frozen while he does a long-distance number on us, are we?''

''Not at all. I'll question him in Germany, under procedures that allow depositions in foreign countries for cases to be heard in the States. We'll get in our licks, Coop.''

''As the old saying goes: I wonder why that doesn't make me feel better.''

They worked through the morning, had sandwiches and coffee brought to the office by Manfred, then continued until nearly four o'clock. They concentrated on the material taken from the file drawer labeled ''Götterdämmerung,'' but most of it was routine correspondence between Frank and various technical reference sources: requests for World War Two military campaign data from the Pentagon's historical section; requests for CIA documents under the Freedom of Information Act; interchanges with individuals identified as members of War Two's Office of Strategic Services; Air Force weather reports for Bavaria and the Austrian Tyrol for the period January to May, 1945. The drawer also held a sheaf of Wehrmacht correspondence, accompanied by tactical terrain maps for the Rhineland and Oberbayern; mimeographed phone listings for Eisenhower's headquarters at SHAEF, later US-FET, and for Patton's Third Army at Bad Tölz; organization charts for the U.S. Army Counter Intelligence Corps, the British Army of the Rhine, and the U.S. Seventh Army's engineering sections. There was also a worn yellow photograph of a tall, serious young man dressed to the nines as a German officer, Iron Cross on his ribs, Nazi eagles everywhere.

"Hey. Look at this, Stan. A snapshot of Manfred in his salad days."

Tremaine looked half startled, half pleased. Reaching out eagerly, he said, "Let me see that."

"Looks like a character in an old James Mason movie."

"Mm." Tremaine slid the photo into his briefcase.

"Hold on, Stan. Maybe Manfred would like to have it."

"No way. It's part of a legal proceeding now. Sorry."

"A lousy Brownie shot of a dude in a war nobody remembers? Come on, Stan, get real."

"It's not up for discussion," Tremaine said (somewhat snappishly, Cooper thought). "The picture stays in my files." He began gathering papers. "It's all my baby from here on. If it's all right with you, I'll have Albert return tomorrow morning, bundle all these boxes into a van, and haul them to my office."

"Fine with me. But does everything stand still until you guys complete your search of the papers?"

Tremaine shook his patrician head. "Not at all. The staff assistants will do the actual searching. Meanwhile, I'll be taking care of three things: First, the nuts-and-bolts prep work for a preliminary hearing in which we'll try to establish that SS Standartenführer Siegfried Ramm is a notorious public figure and, as such, is open to the same rules of public criticism as an American politician is—namely, that regardless of the truth or falseness of the book's inferences about Ramm, an acknowledged notorious person, there was no libel if there was no actual malice. Second, I'll be reading *The Götterdämmerung Machine* for the umpteenth time to determine just what the hell all the shouting's about. And third, I'll be going to the bathroom, which is something I've had to do for the past hour."

"It's down the hall to the left."

"While I'm doing that, would you please run down and tell Albert I'll be there in a minute or two?"

Albert was leaning against the Cadillac's left front fender, smoking a cigarette and taking in the descending twilight. He was tall and wide, and his blue gabardine suit was put to some important stress tests by the musculature it encased. His eyes, black and noncommittal, turned slowly to regard Cooper's approach.

"You don't look like an Albert," Cooper said.

"I usually answer to Al." The voice was soft, throaty.

"That fits better, I'd say. What's your last name?"

"Milano." He took the cigarette from his mouth and shredded it, coal and all, between his thumb and forefinger. "Something I can do for you, sir?"

"Mr. Tremaine will be with you in a minute. He asked me to tell you that."

"Thank you, sir."

"You've had a long day. Just standing around, waiting. Sorry we took so long."

"I'm used to it. No big deal."

"Well, drive carefully. The road is filled with chopped almonds."

Cooper was heading for the house when Albert's soft voice called after him. "Can I ask you a question, sir?"

Turning, curious, Cooper said, "Sure. What's up?"

"Do you know anybody who drives a cream-colored Mercury?"

Cooper thought for a moment. "Can't say I do. Why?"

"A cream-colored Mercury followed us this morning. From Mr. Tremaine's house to St. Augie."

"Oh? You're sure?"

"I made a few moves—fast drive, slow drive, an untelegraphed turn—and the Merc stuck to me like plaster."

"So that's why you peeled off A-One-A onto Magnolia. I wondered about that." A taut pause, then: "Could the Merc have been following Mr. Tremaine?"

Albert shook his head slowly. "I have no way of knowing. You or Mr. Tremaine, we were being followed."

"What happened to the tail?"

"Parked down the street for a while, then headed off for San Marco. Hasn't shown since."

"I don't suppose you happened to get the Merc's plate number?"

"No. I didn't happen to. I got it deliberately." Milano fished in the breast pocket of his jacket and came up with a slip of paper. "I wrote it down on this."

"You're a right handy kind of dude, Al."

"Handy's my thing."

"Appreciate this a lot."

"Don't get carried away. Having a plate number is one thing. Finding out who it belongs to is something else. The cops won't give you a make unless you tell them why you want to know. And even if you tell them, they might not like your reason and tell you to bug off."

"Not to worry. As a card-carrying newsman, I've got a few good connections." Cooper studied the other man's somber face for a time. Sighing, he said, "I guess the message is clear, eh?"

"Yes, sir. I'd say the message is that you better watch your ass."

"Thanks, Al. I really appreciate the tip."

"You need any help, just say the word. Any friend of Mr. Tremaine is a friend of Al Milano."

"You like Stan, eh?"

"He's helped me prime-grade by giving me a job."

"Where do I find you?"

Milano pulled out a thick wallet, thumbed through it, and produced a card. "Call that number. If a woman answers, be happy for me."

Pete Mitchell, the *Times-Union*'s police reporter, knew a deputy in Alachua County who knew a guy in Tallahassee who, for reasons never fully understood by Pete, would do a make on plate numbers, no questions asked. Cooper had availed himself of this connection several times, and all it had ever cost him was a box of Twinkies, confections which Pete dearly loved. For the promise of another box, Pete agreed to run down the cream-colored Mercury.

Cooper was dozing over a talk show when the phone rang. "Yo."

"Hey, Coop, Pete here. I got an ID on that plate."

"That's great." Cooper groped for a pad and pencil.

''The number is for a '94 Mercury four-door owned by Jansen Auto Rental, Orange Park.''

''Well, that's a start. Now I got to figure a way to find out who's renting it.''

Pete's yawn was loud in the receiver. ''Not to sweat, guy. I did some calling around, and it turns up that Jansen—a pretty straight arrow, by all accounts—is a mystery-story fan. On a whim I called him and told him you, the son of Frank Cooper, needed to know who was tooling around in the Merc, and he just about flipped. Seems your dad was his absolute favoritest author, and what you want, you get.''

''So what do I get?''

''Jansen says the Merc has been rented for the week by Billy Logue, a beach bum who pays for his surfboards by changing tires and pumping gas at a Texaco station on Roosevelt Boulevard.''

''What's a dude like that doing, renting cars?''

''Beats me, dad. To impress a girl, maybe. Jansen says he ordinarily wouldn't rent to somebody like Logue, whose elevator doesn't quite reach the top floor. But in the short time he's been around, Logue's shown himself to be ambitious and a hard worker. Besides, he's got a Harley hog that's worth more than the car and which he left as a kind of collateral, you know?''

''Yeah, well . . .''

''Any of this stuff mean anything to you, Coop?''

''Not yet. But thanks anyway, Pete. Your Twinkles will arrive tomorrow.''

Now that he was fully awake and into the telephone mode, he decided to call Jeff Middleton and settle another question that had been nagging him. Jeff was something rather important in the Jacksonville FBI office—just what had never been clear to him—and one of his jobs was to deal with media inquiries. He was a somber man whose only joke was that he had never knowingly misled a reporter—but he misled all reporters unknowingly all the time.

''Hey, Jeff—Coop. Sorry to bother you at home, but I've run into something here you might give me a hand on—and, at the same time, make sure some glob isn't playing G-man.''

"So what's the problem?"

"I've been asking the Bureau for documents under the FOI Act, and several of the trace slips refer to or are signed by an Agent Albert J. Milano. On an unrelated crime matter I'm working on I've run across a dude, name of Albert Milano, who might be your Albert J. Milano. If he is your guy, he seems to be working something delicate, so I can't just walk up and ask him, 'Hey, you the guy who's been signing trace slips?' But it's important for me to determine, one, should I play dumb and stay out of his way, or, two, can I confide in him and ask his help? Could you tell me whether he's your guy?"

"What's he look like?"

"Six-three, big all around, like a very tall jukebox. Straight black hair, thick, worn in a pompadour. Deep-set, blackish-brown eyes; a nose that's been broken; olive complexion. Husky voice, bass, I'd say. Talks slowly, easily, and is surprisingly agile for a man that big."

"Are you in an emergency situation, Coop?"

"Not yet. But I could be if I don't get some instructions on Milano as soon as."

"Where are you now?"

"In St. Augie, my dad's house. Phone: five-fifty-five, forty-eight, twenty-eight."

"Okay. I'll query and be back to you. Say about an hour, maybe two."

"Great. Really appreciate this, Jeff."

"No sweat. If the guy's a phony, we owe you."

Middleton called back in less than an hour.

"Hi, Coop. The request is that you play dumb and stay out of Milano's way."

"You got it, Jeff. Thanks a bunch."

"We thank you for checking."

NEW YORK (USP) — Steven Bartlett, financial mastermind in some of the nation's most ambitious real estate developments and personal counselor to Third World potentates, died tonight after being struck by a sniper bullet fired into his limousine.

Bartlett was pronounced dead in the emergency room of a Manhattan hospital twenty minutes after the shooting. Police say the financier was being driven from his office to his Park Avenue home and the car was slowing for a stop at the entrance when the shot pierced the car's rear window and struck him in the back.

Ironically, according to Amy Howard, Bartlett's longtime companion, "the car was leased for just the one day because his regular limo — the one with the bullet-proof windows — was in the shop, having a leaking gas tank fixed."

Howard, who was riding beside Bartlett, suffered cuts from flying glass and was released after treatment.

Bartlett was the third prominent American to be slain by snipers in less than two weeks. Police authorities of three states say there is no evidence linking the attacks, but J. William Goodhart, spokesman for New York's mayor, said tonight that "a lot of people are putting a lot of study into that possibility."

Meanwhile, President Fogarty has expressed "deep regret and anger over the loss of three friends and advisers in such a dreadful, wanton way," and has announced that he would have the FBI "evaluate the crimes" with a view toward federal violations.

(Desk eds: More to kum from our Washington bureau. Also complete wrap on an anti-Ringmasters conspiracy theory and an updated obit on Bartlett, plus later statements from Fogarty and other politicals identified as Bartlett's protégés.)

Eleven

A fter lunch, when Nickerson got back to his office—
which was no more than a cluttered desk, two chairs,
and a file cabinet surrounded by a plastic partition—he
found one of the chairs filled by a man about the size and shape
of a soda-dispensing machine.

The visitor stood up and held out a shovel-size hand to display an ID case. "Sergeant Nickerson?"

"Yep."

The man's voice was soft, smooth. "I'm Al Milano, a special assistant to Congressman J. Fenimore Quigg, chairman of
the House Special Subcommittee on International Trusts. The
duty officer gave me permission to wait for you here."

"So what brings you down from Washington, Mr. Milano?"

"The subcommittee needs information about some North
Florida subjects—two of them locals here—and I thought you
might be willing to tell me what you know about them. Background stuff, and like that."

"Sit down. Coffee?"

"No, thanks."

Nickerson took his place behind the desk and watched Milano resettle on the chair, a performance evocative of Kong alighting on a bar stool. "Could I see your credentials again, please?"

"Sure. The one in the left window is my congressional attaché's ID. On the right is my D.C. investigator's ticket. The photos make me look like Shirley Temple, but they're close enough. You want anything else?"

"That'll do for now. So which two locals?"

"Frank Cooper, the writer, and his son, Matthew."

"Hey, those dudes have been all over the tube and the sheets for the past two weeks. Where've you been—Mars?"

Milano smiled. "I mean I need poop that hasn't been on the tube. Local reputation, how they get along with their neighbors, sex and drinking habits, rap sheets if any. You know—the kind of stuff that might queer them for appointments to federal jobs."

Nickerson sniffed. "I can't imagine either of them wanting a federal job. Frank's dead and Matt has turned into the local Croesus."

"It was only a manner of speaking."

"Well, in a manner of speaking, I can't give you anything that could conceivably be valuable to a congressional subcommittee. Law-wise, both—what did you call them? subjects?—are clean whistles. I'm still questioning young Cooper about his father's fall. So far it hasn't turned up much. But I'm on him."

Milano brushed some lint from his jacket sleeve. "What about Stanley Tremaine, that Jacksonville lawyer who's tied in with the Coopers? Know anything about him?"

"Only that he's got a long reach and he gets heap big annoyed when somebody gives him a problem. He's been around a lot of years, has had a bunch to say about how North Florida operates. Holds a lot of markers—even here in St. Augustine."

"What kind?"

"He owns a lot of real estate. Investment stuff. He owns a

lot of pols, too. Contributes the legal maximum to campaigns, does favors. Specifics I can't give you. He and I don't run in the same circles.''

"Is he still ambitious?"

"Sure comes across that way, from what I see and hear. My general impression is that he's still reaching for the brass ring. He's got all a man could ever want, but he keeps reaching.''

Milano took a moment for some thinking. Then: "Back to young Cooper. You think he might have offed the old man?''

"On a homicide, I suspect everybody for ten miles around the body. I'd suspect you, if you'd been sitting in that chair there on the night of the killing.''

"Enthusiastic about your work, eh?"

"Am I ever. I'm a prick on wheels when it comes to people who ice other people.''

Milano smiled again, nodding affably. "Good. You're Congressman Quigg's kinda guy. He's state-of-the-art when it comes to being a prick.''

"That's supposed to make me feel good?"

"Not necessarily. It is supposed to make you more likely to give Quigg a call first if you decide to bust young Cooper. The congressman would consider it a great favor. A favor he'd be real generous in rewarding.''

Nickerson pushed back his chair and stood up. "I've got to run along, Mr. Milano. Hope you have a nice trip back to our capital city.''

Milano, unfazed by the abrupt dismissal, pulled a card from his pocket and placed it on the desk. "Thanks. Meantime, call me at this number if you decide to move on Cooper. The nation will be in your debt.''

"Quigg's the nation?"

Milano heaved himself erect and headed for the stairway. Over his shoulder he said, "In a manner of speaking. Sort of sad, too. Wouldn't you say?''

Chief Reggie Nolan's office in the northwest corner of the new police building on King Street made him appear to be a middle-management honcho with United Rigmarole Corporation. With its contemporary furniture and computer center, there was little to suggest a police station's oppressive atmosphere of sweat, disinfectant, sorrow, and fear. Despite this appearance of princely disdain for the grubby Sturm und Drang of his profession, he was, in reality, a hell of a cop, widely respected for his all-around savvy and what the mayor would always refer to in his annual Police Banquet speech as "unwavering, straight-arrow loyalty to his city and to the people he commands." Nickerson always felt uneasy when the chief was around—the edginess of a sinner in the presence of a priest—and he was now feeling it in spades, standing here as the focus of the man's unblinking gray eyes.

"You wanted to see me, sir?"

"Sit down, Nickerson." The chief nodded at the severe oak chair placed centrally before his massive desk.

Legend had it that Nolan used the chair, a Victorian anachronism in the sleekly modern setting, to discomfort politicians and favor-seekers who took up his office time, a kind of slow-motion ejection seat guaranteed to cause those who sat in it to look for an excuse—any excuse—to get the hell out. There had to be truth to the report, Nickerson decided, because the damned thing would make a cold marble slab feel like a water bed.

"I've read your case file on the Frank Cooper homicide, Nickerson."

There was a momentary silence.

"Cooper was a very important citizen of this town."

"Yes, sir."

"You're a good note-taker. I like that in a cop. Good notes can be the difference between conviction and acquittal. Do you have any ideas—beyond the material in your report—as to who killed the man? Any hunches, wispy leads, outer-space vibes?"

Nickerson was surprised, pleased. The chief himself was inviting him to lay out, not what was restricted to the facts and clues, but what he felt, suspected. "Yes, sir. Any homicide detective worth his salt listens to his hunches."

"What are yours in this case?"

"Something's fishy about Matt Cooper, the writer's son. He doesn't ring a clear tone when you tap his bell. My gut tells me he's been, ah, sort of overly anxious to come into his inheritance.''

"Have you questioned him about this?''

"Yes, sir. Naturally.''

"Was your questioning direct, or cute?''

"If you mean did I make my suspicions evident to him, I don't think so. I've tried pretty hard to give him a fair shake all along, and I haven't tried to entrap him with cutes. But he seems to resent even the slightest hint that he might be, ah, vulnerable, and when I nudge into that area he gets, well, sore—combative.''

"Which makes him even more suspicious, eh?''

"I try to keep objective in my prelims—all my case files. But yes, I admit he looks weirder all the time.''

"Judge Hefflefinger doesn't give him much, I'll tell you. I saw the judge at the Duval League dinner the night before last and he and I and Claude Abernathy were yakking about this and that and somehow Cooper's name came up. Hefflefinger says Cooper's the worst kind of news guy, the kind that gets onto something insignificant and tries to blow it up into a big deal, all out of proportion to what it really is. He says the man's a menace.''

"Abernathy has no reason to love Cooper, either,'' Nickerson said, "after the number Cooper did on that Crescent Beach real estate scandal. Claude got splashed by a lot of mud Cooper dug up on that thing.''

Nolan turned in his swivel chair to examine the day outside his window, and to Nickerson, whose backside was already numbed by the merciless oak, it seemed the interval of silence would never end. Just as he began to wonder if the chief had actually dozed off, the big man turned and nailed him with those gray eyes.

"I got a call from City Commissioner Bert Santos. He wants you off the Cooper case.''

"Santos? What's his beef?''

"He says Tremaine, Cooper's lawyer, claims you've been harassing Cooper. You've been giving the guy a bad time without charging him with anything.''

"That's plain bullshit. Besides, what the hell's Santos got to say about what comes down in the police department?''

''He heads the goddamn Public Safety Committee, is the mayor's brother-in-law, and is president of every freaking civic club between here and Mars. He sings the lead in The Appropriations Follies, and his wife chairs the Florida Auxiliary. Other than that, he's not very important.''

''Come on, Chief—he's a fuggin' politician. Besides, if he has anything to say to the cop shop he's supposed to go through the city goddamn manager.''

''Are you lecturing me on government organization, Nickerson? If you are, knock it off.''

Nickerson shifted on the chair. ''So you're going to take me off the case? Just because a Jacksonville society lawyer has put in an unsubstantiated beef?''

''Of course I am. And I'm putting you on a month's leave of absence, so you won't even be around to clutter up the police station.''

Nickerson pushed himself to a standing position, his face a deep red. ''This is a bum rap, Chief. You're knocking me out of my pay for a month just to stroke a pissant politician. And—''

Nolan held up a hand and broke in, his voice loud and harsh. ''That's enough, Nickerson. You better shut up before you find yourself saying something I can't forgive. Besides, who said anything about no pay?''

''What?''

''I'm taking you off the case, so I can tell that miserable asshole, Santos, that you're officially off the case. I'm putting you on a leave of absence—*with* pay—so that you can, unofficially and on your own time, pursue any unfinished police work that suits your fancy. A working vacation, sort of.''

''The Cooper case is unfinished police work, Chief.''

''I didn't hear that comment. I don't want to hear what cases you'll be working on. And especially I don't want you to get caught working on cases, because it might embarrass me and get Santos on the warpath. This working vacation is between you and me, and I don't want to hear one lousy thing about what you're doing or what results you're getting until you have something very damned definite—something that nails down a suspect. We talk only if you've got something significant. Understand?''

Nickerson, dazed, managed to say, ''Yes, sir.''

''Now get the hell out of my office, finish your day, and get lost.''

Manfred had always been a patient man, accustomed to waiting, to watching others until they made their mistakes. He had learned long ago as an SS Sturmführer and Gestapo agent—even before that, if he considered his five-year wait for Lotte to marry him—that patient waiting eventually resolves questions and dissolves difficulties. Time, he would often remind himself, is always on the side of the tenacious, the forbearing. It was this quality that had enabled him to endure uncounted nights in dank alleys, to watch, unblinking, hour upon hour, simply to catch a glimpse of a fugitive, or a miscreant, or a communist spy. He was admittedly not the most brilliant of enforcers, but there was no denying his ability to wait and endure the petty hardships that belabor the man with a badge.

His old eyes watered, his back ached, his legs were cramping, and his bladder cried for relief, yet he stood fast in the broom closet's dusk, door cracked for a view of the men's room entrance and the wall phone beside it. He had entered the saloon and taken his post here just before five o'clock, when the day-shift policemen, leaving City Hall for whatever warrens they called home, would begin to drift in for drinks.

At precisely five-thirty, he picked up the battery-powered bag phone slung on his shoulder and tapped in the number of the pay phone, the only ornament (beyond the penciled obscenities) on the grimy walls. There were ten rings before a waiter came in from the bar and answered angrily. ''This is the pay phone at Sammy's. Who do you want?''

''Is Sergeant Nickerson there?''

''Just a minute.''

The waiter, letting the phone dangle, ambled off for the clamorous bar. Manfred returned his phone to its bag and removed the knuckle-knife—a souvenir of his duty tour in Paris in 1943—from his pocket and affixed it to his right hand.

As he waited, he felt his pulse quicken and the adrenaline begin to flow.

Nickerson appeared in the doorway, blinking in the transition from dimly lit bar to the glare of the hallway. Then, spotting the dangling phone, he strode across the cracked linoleum. With his back to the broom closet, he picked up the instrument.

"Nickerson."

Manfred eased open the closet door and tightened his grip on the knife.

"Hello. This is Nickerson. Hello?"

At the very instant Manfred prepared to take the three quick steps from the closet, to speed his arm through the classic assassin's swing, and to plunge the knife into the detective's lower back, the barroom door banged open and a graying man came through, unzipping his fly.

"Hi, Nick. What's up?"

"Somebody's playing phone games. How you doing, Lou?"

"Got the senile citizen's disease. I need to take a leak every half hour anymore. Grab a barstool, and I'll buy you a snort when I come out."

"That's something I never thought I'd hear you say."

"Bullshit. I'm the world's most generous guy."

"And the biggest liar."

The two laughed together, then went their separate ways.

Manfred returned the knife to its pocket in the phone bag, sighed the sigh of resignation, and went out the alley door and into the evening.

Twelve

Cooper drove Route 16 to Green Cove Springs, then cut north along the St. Johns river to Sylvan Haunt, one of those shake-shingle country club developments that feature cutesy gate houses, serpentine streets, and usurious mortgages. Roscoe Macabee, it turned out, was not one of the property owners but the ancient, whiskey-nosed father-in-law of a society doctor whose house and outbuildings occupied a site only slightly larger than Rhode Island.

"I appreciate your willingness to see me, Mr. Macabee," Cooper said, settling into a lawn chair with a view of the river and a horizon smudged by distant civilization.

The old man shifted in his chair and pointed with his cane. "See that stretch of shoreline over there?"

"It's right pretty."

"That's because they wanted to build a marina and seaplane base there and I wouldn't let 'em."

"Oh?"

"Bet your ass. I wrote a letter to the editor of the local paper, and by God, it was what finally turned the land rapists to rout. The word processor is more powerful than the bulldozer, eh?''

"No question about it." Cooper drew a notepad from his jacket pocket and placed it on his knee. ''The reason I asked for an appointment—''

"Of course, I don't use a word processor. I just said that to sound state-of-the-art. Typewriter's my weapon. I made a hell of a living with my old upright Royal.''

"Well—''

"Those guys say they're newspaper guys these days make my ass tired. They're not newspaper guys, they're gooey romance novelists, for chrissake. Saw a lead on a hard news story the other day that had five hundred fancy words about dark clouds and bitter wind and rustling trees but nary a mention of what the hell the story was about. Had to read to the goddamn jump to learn that a kidnapped baby had been found unharmed. Guy hand a story like that into the city editor of the Philly *Bulletin* and he'd have had his ass out the door before lunch, I kid you not.''

Cooper gave him an amused, skeptical glance. ''That's unusual these days. Five-hundred-word leads aren't very likely where the news hole gets smaller by the minute.''

"News hole my bunghole. All I hear from you young twerps is complaints about shrinking news holes. Bullshit. You'll dish up a measly three-inch story about eighty people being killed in a plane crash in Rockefeller Center but will run three yards of syndicated text and a four-color spread about the glorious petunia gardens of Bellyacre Castle in Ham-on-Rye, England. What the hell kind of newspapering is that? That ain't newspapering—it's TV bean breeze.''

"I asked for this interview so that—''

"Want a drink?''

"Ah, no thanks.''

"Well, I do.'' Macabee pulled a half-pint from his jacket pocket, unscrewed the cap, and took a noisy swig. Replacing the cap and returning the bottle to its nesting place, he examined Cooper with new interest. ''You say you're with the *New York Times?*''

"No. The *Times-Union* in Jacksonville.''

"Why did you want to see me? You haven't said yet."

"I'm doing a feature on Frank Cooper, the novelist, and in digging around some old files I came across a great profile you did on him for the *Philadelphia Bulletin* in the early fifties. And—"

"Frank was murdered not too long ago."

"Yes. I—"

"Shot to death in his own kitchen, for chrissake."

"I know—"

"Hell, I didn't realize he was living in St. Augie. Knew that, I'd have given him a ring. We were old army buds. No shit."

"About the profile you wrote on him—"

"I remember that sucker. I wrote the sumbish on a Monday, when I had the mother of all hangovers. It took them two weeks to decide to run it because my editor said it was written so goddamn well he was sure I'd copied it from somewhere. I don't know how he'd know; the bastard was illiterate."

"Where did you interview Mr. Cooper?"

"In a saloon down the street from Wanamaker's. He was on tour to sign copies of his new novel, and the store was one of his stops."

"Were you the *Bulletin*'s book page editor?"

The seams in the old man's face took on new seams as he broke into a grin. "The *what?*" The grin became a guffaw. "Excuse me, buddy, but—hah-hah—" he coughed, a barking sound, and, recovering, took another gulp of whiskey. A moment given to wheezing and then he pulled out a handkerchief and dabbed at his eyes. "Back in my day, pal, book page editors were all pipey and tweedy and profound and always looked like they smelled something bad. Look at me: Can you imagine this guy here"—his bony hands swept the length of his torso—"doing the Ivy League thinker scene? No way. I was a *newspaperman*. My beats were cops and City Hall."

"So how come—"

"Did I write a profile on Frank? The city editor heard I'd known Frank from way back and told me to do a piece. We met in Paris after the liberation in '44. I was a staffer on *Stars and Stripes*, and Frank was on R and R after some kind of secret duty tour with the Maquis—the French underground—and we did some drinking together in Pig Alley, the Montmartre, other places. He was always asking me about writing, and how it's done, and how the hell you do this and that to get an idea onto paper. Now there was a thinker, I'll tell you. He was full of ideas, and deep thoughts, and he had a way of articulating some of the most abstract, abstruse concepts, I kid you not. Hell, he could talk even better than he could write. But that was before he'd done any writing, and we'd talk our asses off.''

Cooper made some notes. "Secret duty? You made only a passing reference to that in your profile.''

"Right. I was concentrating on the guy's character and artistry. You get into a guy's war service and that takes over the article, no matter how hard you try to subordinate it. War's gaudy, and it's easier to write about than those things that makes a man what he is. And Frank's war service was plenty gaudy, I'll tell you.''

"What did he do? Did he ever say?''

"Never. But I did some checking around, and I found out that, while he wore the uniform of a U.S. Army sergeant, he was really an agent in the OSS. Three paradrops into Nazi-occupied France. Established a daisy chain of informants from Le Havre to Vienna. Then, after the war and before OSS segued into the CIA, he was agent-in-charge of a huge 1945 intelligence caper in Germany, code-named—what the hell was it?—Oh, yeah: 'Slingshot.' See why I didn't go into his war record in my profile?''

Cooper nodded and made a note. "Slingshot?''

"Yeah. *Stars and Stripes* gave it a hell of a play. I remember. I edited the wire service stuff on it out of Ike's headquarters in Frankfurt.''

"I can see why you left it out of your profile. The tail would have wagged the dog.''

"But there was another, larger reason why I didn't go into it. Frank wouldn't let me. He gave me the interview only on the promise that I wouldn't ask him about the war, what he did in it, and like that.''

"Why do you think that was, Mr. Macabee? Modesty?''

"Hell, no. It was more subtle than modesty, although Frank was basically a modest kind of guy. No, it was something more than that, something deeper. Something had happened to him between our drinking tour of Paris and the day in Philly. When I first knew him, he was a piece of work, I'll tell you. Intelligent, intuitive, aware, but, at the same time, a fun-loving hellraiser who could drink and wench even better than me—which took some doing, believe me, since I made Frank Harris and Henry Miller and all those glamour-puss hotshot expatriates look like choir boys. No, it was a kind of, well, sadness. Yes, that's it: a sadness. Like he'd lifted the lid of hell and peeked in. I know that sounds melodramatic and clichéd and all that crap, but, goddamn it, Frank had changed—still smart as hell, still eloquent, but sad underneath it all. That day in Philly I saw that, for all his success and fame, Frank wasn't enjoying life much.''

They took a moment together, Cooper to make more notes and Macabee to upturn and drain his bottle.

''When you were in Paris together, did Mr. Cooper ever do more than talk about writing? Did he actually do any writing?''

''Twice. And both times he let me read the material.''

''Was it good?''

''Hell, no. It was a triumph of mediocrity. Overwritten. Eight words where two would do. As I say, he was a very articulate gent. But verbose. Know what I mean?''

Cooper smiled. ''Sure do. My editor's always on my case for being verbose.'' After another pause, he asked, ''If he was such a mediocre writer, why do you think he became such a huge success?''

''Beats me. I read his first two novels, then gave up. I could never figure what all the shouting was about, know what I mean?''

Cooper shrugged. ''There's a lot of that going around. Books, movies, tapes, TV shows—they're all being sold like breakfast food and cars now.''

''You got it, buddy,'' Macabee grumped. ''Hype. Hype does it. You hear something's good, over and over, you begin to believe it. But you know something? I've since read all the Cooper novels, and they kept getting better. They began to live up to their hype. The last one—*The Götterdämmerung Machine*—was super. Literary, even.''

"Mm. I happen to be reading that one right now."

"Well, Frank was like his books. He'd grow on you. Keep getting better. First time you met him, seemed like a stand-offish stuffed shirt. Snooty, sort of. Then, time went by, you'd see the humor, the smarts, the kindness. And the lousy self-image. Frank didn't really like himself much. And I think that's the part that grew and made the change in him—brought out that sadness I was talking about."

Out on the river, a motorboat hummed in a wide circle, and an egret, startled, lifted off from the reeds at the foot of the lawn. Somewhere up the rise behind them, beyond the trees, a car horn sounded and two men shared a laugh.

Macabee rose to his feet and, wavering, gave Cooper an amiable, boozy examination. "Going to cut out now, buddy. Got to get another jug."

"Well—"

"Need anything else, give me a hoot on the hooter."

"Ah—"

"I like you. Don't tend to like young squirts these days. Self-centered snots, mostly. But I like you. Don't ask me why. Maybe it's because you remind me of Frank. I really liked that sumbish." He tottered off, muttering.

On the drive back to St. Augustine, Cooper held the Ford to a moderate speed, opening the windows and enjoying the day. The old man's parting words had surprised him, cheered him somehow. People had always made a thing of "the Frank Cooper look." As withdrawn and taciturn as Frank could be in public, this persona seemed rarely to cool the public's warm response to his calm, deep-set eyes, which suggested candor, curiosity, and private amusement, and to what Mom called "that small, mysterious smile." In fact, Mom was the only one ever to show discomfort over Frank's good looks, which was understandable, seeing as how she adored him and could be expected to resent the admiring female glances sent her husband's way.

In any event, it was sort of flattering to have someone—an unsuspecting old geezer, at that—say he looked something like his father.

But the old geezer had done him an even bigger favor. He had unwittingly confirmed that the doodle on the Christmas wrapping was a slingshot.

At the moment of his death, Frank had pointed to his life.

"Look at Operation Slingshot," Frank was saying, "and you'll find who killed me."

Motion astern, and he glanced into the rearview mirror.

A cream-colored car. A Mercury, maybe?

Coming fast, turn signal blinking the intention to pass.

He eased to the right. It was a two-lane highway, and he was approaching the long bridge over the wilderness of Riddle Creek and its bordering marshes and clustered fishing camps, so there was little leeway. As the whitish car pulled alongside, he ventured a glance, aware now that it was a Mercury and that it was sidling in.

What in hell was the man doing?

He had no time to resolve the question, becoming instead instantly consumed by the concussion of the sideswipe, the grinding and tearing of metal, the tortured howl of tires, and the struggle to keep the Ford from satisfying its need to slew and spin and roll.

Then, from the core of terror, he saw the sky and earth twice change places, the uprushing of trees and tangled brush and, below them, yellow-scummed water. The windshield buckled, and a glowing mist seemed, by closing about him, to mute, then silence the frightful clamor.

In time, there was an upside-down settling, the sound of intermittent cracking and breaking, a distant rustling.

In the green half-light, in the gentle swaying, in the numbness, an understanding.

The slingshot sketch was meant for him.

Thirteen

Tina had lunch in her St. George Street apartment whenever possible. It not only saved money—an item in short supply for a beginning reporter on a small-town daily—but it also gave her a quiet time in a pretty place at the midpoint of her workday's clang and boom.

She needed the break especially much this day. After a solar flare of national media attention, the Cooper murder had subsided to several paragraphs on the B-section front and, unless there were sensational developments, such as an arrest or a confession, it would soon drop out of the news hole altogether. The story had tyrannized the local staff—confiscating great chunks of the forty-percent portion of the sixty-forty ad-space-to-news-space ratio, demanding of all hands uncounted hours of overtime and straining budgets, from photo lab to phone bills, to the twanging point. Now it was back to routine, and no one was more grateful than Tina Mennen, who had been pressed into hundred-hour days as police radio monitor, microfilm background researcher, typo-sniper, and all-around gofer. Meanwhile, all the macramé contest winners and champion gardeners and prom committee chairpersons were rattling management's cage with angry queries as to why Mennen hadn't published those press releases they'd sent her weeks ago.

She threw her car keys on the kitchen table, kicked off her shoes, took a Coke from the fridge, and stood, sipping, while sorting the bills that had been pushed through the mail slot by Augie Winkler, the most dour of all postmen.

The sofa was under the front window, and she sank into its cushions, sighing. Lifting her skirt, she swung her body full length into the patch of glowing sunlight. Glancing at her legs, she thought of Bert Santos's furtive evaluations, and she felt the need to shudder. Santos, a recently elected city commissioner whose prominence in the synodical hierarchy of the First Universal Church of Saints, Reformed, guaranteed his respectability, was a leg man. She had discovered this during a ho-hum interview for her ecological feature. As they had made small talk in the anteroom, he kept watching the women at the files, his gaze never rising above their hems. She had subsequently been invited into his office, ostensibly to discuss his proposed tree restoration ordinance, and his pompous oration had been interrupted by a phone call. As he intermittently talked and listened, she'd used the interval to make notes. The glass doors of the bookcase had mirrored his lowered lids, the slackness of his mouth, as his gaze moved up and down her, and she saw that her legs absolutely totaled him.

Hypocritical, adolescent squid.

She was considering lunch (should she finish the tuna salad or open a can of soup?) when the doorbell chimed.

"Who is it?"

The voice beyond the door was muffled. "Nickerson. Could I see you a minute?"

She pulled herself into a semblance of womanhood and opened the door. "Happy New Year. Am I being raided?"

"Nope. I just dropped by to chat."

She nodded at the easy chair. "Sit down. Want a soda?"

"No, thanks."

She returned to the sofa and sat in its sunlight. "How are you making out on the Cooper murder?"

"Can we talk about that?" he asked, taking the designated seat.

"Sure. But, as you know, I'm not one of journalism's big boppers. All I know is what I pick up as a newsroom yard-bird."

Nickerson's blue gaze wandered to the street beyond the window, where the fatties in shorts and funny hats did the tour-ist thing. "Well, I don't expect you to solve the case. I'm just tying up some loose ends."

"Like what?"

"Like did you see Matthew Cooper at any time on the night of the murder?"

"The nouveau riche kid? Had coffee with him."

"Where was that?"

"At the Italian restaurant on St. George Street."

"How long were you there together?"

"Heck, I don't know. How long does it take to have a cup of coffee?"

"You left the restaurant together?"

"No way. I had to leave. I was working on a Watch Night feature."

"You have any idea when Cooper left?"

"Not really. I saw him later, though. On San Marco. He was unlocking a really grungy red Ford, which, I suppose, is his. He said he had a date to see his daddy. A Christmas tradition kind of thing."

"About what time was that?"

"After eleven, I think."

Nickerson made a note on his pad. Without looking up, he asked, "What did you and Cooper talk about?"

"Not much. He seemed to be in a foul mood. He was ticked off at his old man, it seems."

" 'Ticked off'?"

"It was pretty clear that he wasn't happy with the way his father treated him. He called him 'Dracula.' "

"How well do you know Cooper?"

"Only what I read in the papers. And I attended a seminar of his. I admire his articles. But I'd never really talked to him before that cup of coffee." She hesitated. "When it became pretty obvious that he didn't like me much."

"Then you aren't, ah, romantically involved?"

She laughed softly. "You've got to be kidding. He's old enough to be my father."

"He's only thirty-five."

"He's thirty-six if he's a day."

"His driver's license says thirty-five. *Who's Who in the Southern Press* says thirty-five."

"Well, either way, he's still ancient."

"So your only relationship with Cooper is a professional one—is that what you're saying?"

She regarded Nickerson with sudden wariness. "What's going on here, Nick? Why should I be saying anything at all about Matthew Cooper?"

The detective waggled a peacemaker's hand. "No big deal. I'm just doing the working cop scene."

"Well, I admit that he's pretty high voltage, and lots of women wouldn't mind it a bit if he banged on their doors. Smarts, looks, nice manners, a cool job, a famous daddy. And he's single and rich. I mean, he's got it all. But he doesn't light my fuse, and that's a fact."

"Does he light any fuses in particular?"

Her eyes narrowed. "You mean does he have a playmate?"

"Well, yeah."

"How should I know? I'm not sure a guy that old can have sex."

Nickerson smiled. "You just said he has it all."

"Well, that's one thing I have no idea if he has."

"Your face is very red."

"My face always gets red when I'm embarrassed or mad. It's a family curse."

"What are you embarrassed or mad about now?"

"I'm mad about your barging in here, asking a lot of weird questions."

"It's my job to ask weird questions."

"Well, it isn't my job to answer them. So why don't you just toddle on down to the station house and beat up a prisoner or two, eh?"

"In a moment." The detective made another note.

She glanced at her watch. "I've got to be back at the paper by one. And I haven't had my lunch yet."

He finished his scribbling and gave her one of his friendly-cop glances. "What were you doing the night of the murder, Tina?"

"I was at the Night Watch parade, trying to zero in on an article."

"Do you remember what time you got home?"

"Midnight. A little after, maybe. Why?"

"You came home alone?"

"Well, no. I had a guy and five other couples with me, and we gang-banged until dawn." Her face had taken on the color of an eggplant.

"No need to get sarcastic—"

"It's none of your damn business whether I came home alone or not."

"You didn't see Cooper at all after that coffee?"

"I told you I did, damn it. I told you I saw him on San Marco Street."

"But you didn't talk to him?"

"No, I didn't talk to him. In all truth, I don't care if I ever talk to him."

"Why is that?"

"He patronizes. He condescends. I tried to be friendly, but he told me to bug off. He doesn't like me, and I sure as hell don't like him. And, if you want to get right down to cases, I didn't like the way he talked about his father."

"What way was that?"

"It wasn't what he said, it was his manner. He had an attitude. I got the definite impression that he resented and feared his daddy."

"Do you think he was capable of killing his old man?"

"How the hell should I know? What are you trying to do—make him a suspect, or something?"

"As I say: just doing my job."

"Your job stinks."

Nickerson closed the notebook, slid it into a jacket pocket and went to the door. Before leaving, he paused and gave her a look. "You got that right," he said.

BULLETIN   BULLETIN   BULLETIN

VAIL, CO (USP)—Barney Griswold, Chicago banker and legendary "chairman" of presidential "kitchen Cabinets" through three administrations, was killed by a sniper today as he stood talking with friends on a ski slope here.

Griswold's slaying occurred only two days after that of his lifelong friend, New York financier Steven Bartlett, and within a month of the sniper deaths of two other political and business associates, lawyer Lou Pizarro and educator-political savant Eleanor Roman.

President Fogarty has ordered an FBI investigation of the shootings, expressing concern that the similarity in the backgrounds of the victims and the characteristics of the crimes themselves "would seem to show evidence of an interstate conspiracy."

In a statement issued to-night, the president said that "each of these distinguished Americans has played a key role in establishing the shape and tone of at least three administrations and, indeed, at the time of their deaths were advising the leadership of both political parties on socioeconomic trends that will weigh heavily in next year's national elections."

Fogarty said, "There has to be a plot—a conspiracy—to do away with such gifted individuals, and I am asking the Bureau, in collaboration with all police forces nationwide, to examine this possibility. These killings must stop and the perpetrators must be brought to justice."

Skiers in the vicinity of the shooting are being questioned by Colorado police officials, but they have not yet issued statements.

(MORE TO KUM)

(Desk Eds: This story, currently in work, will carry flankers and sidebars based on the furor currently sweeping the nation's political establishments over rumors of a conspiracy to

"cleanse" government of "officials identified with 'the status quo.'"

The story is growing larger and more complex by the hour. We will supply you with A wire updates and backgrounders ASAP.)

BULLETIN   BULLETIN   BULLETIN

Fourteen

The shower was a gray wash that descended like a translucent curtain from the lead-colored twilight sky. Tremaine stood by the window, listening to the storm and watching unhappily as a file of Muscovy ducks waddled across the sodden lawn, down the landscaped slope, and into the rain-pebbled pond. He sighed, then turned to his desk and once again gave gloomy consideration to the search teams' reports.

They would have to do better than this.

The meter was running.

He returned the reports to their folders and, picking up his marked copy of the novel, reread the passage in which Standartenführer Dekkar wiped out the village.

Flimsy. Flimsy as hell.

He set down the book and returned to the window. The ducks had retained their single-file formation and were cruising sedately, unmindful of the lashing downpour. His mind went to the day in his childhood when he'd stood under the trees and expended a whole box of BBs from his Daisy pump rifle in a futile attempt to hit a string of mallards that idled, aloof and disdainful, on Uncle Charlie's cattle pond. The metaphor did not escape him. He thought sourly: *I've spent my whole life pumping away and never even ruffling the world's lousy feathers.*

And now these searches, his latest exercise in seeming futility.

Four ace diggers, coming up with zilch. Tillie and Sam, filtering through the Frank Cooper material for nearly a week— box upon box, folder after folder, even two full trays of floppy disks whose access, directories, subdirectories, documents, subdocuments, and printing codes had to be translated and read—and coming up with no trace of the FBI letter, or of whistle-blowing in any form. Harrison and Mike, fruitlessly fine-toothing the federal galaxy, examining bios and legal histories of no less than eleven political and bureaucratic quasars who would seem to be open to the Takai offer. It was maddening. In Matt's case, either there remained files yet undiscovered or Matt had already discovered and withheld them. The latter possibility was the least likely of all, of course, because Matt had shown little interest in the documents. Matt, it seemed, was so inured to the newspaperman's penury he was treating his inheritance and the threat to it as some kind of off-the-wall fantasy—a skit out of "Saturday Night Live." So the idea of his having spent hours poring over the mountain that had already benumbed a pair of paralegals was simply unacceptable; that he had found the FBI letter and its warning about Slingshot-cum-Yankee Doodle was as feasible as a bicycle tour of Neptune. In the Yankee Doodle matter, the government notables most likely to satisfy the scheme's requirements were proving to lack the two key "abilities"—malleability and vulnerability.

Still—

The intercom warbled politely.

"Yes?"

"Mr. Abrams calling from Miami on line two, sir."

He sat at the desk and put the phone on speaker. "Hello, Eli. Is it raining down there?"

"Like you wouldn't believe. We got the poor man's Venice going here."

A pause followed, and Tremaine sensed a tension at the other end.

"What's up?"

"The Cooper libel. You got a minute to talk about it?"

"I've always got a minute to talk to you about anything, you know that."

"Sure. It seems we've run into a bit of a complication. In Germany, that is. And it could throw us—you and me—into a water-treading situation, sort of."

"Oh? What kind of situation is that, Eli?"

"My client refuses to engage a German lawyer."

"You mean he doesn't want German representation? He wants you to carry the freight exclusively?"

"Well, yeah. He had a guy, Max Mueller, a Munich lawyer with a national reputation, make the initial contact with me and ask me to sign the pleadings with him and appear in court, and like that. But today I got a letter from Mueller informing me that he'd withdrawn from the case at Ramm's request and that it will be up to me and my firm to bring the suit and carry it into court, if things go that far."

Tremaine, an old campaigner, caught the nuance at once. "*If* things go that far? Do I hear out-of-court settlement in your voice, Eli?"

"Hell no. Your client has libeled my client, and we're going to take you to the cleaners. But with a German lawyer out of the picture, I'm going to have to find myself a good legal interpreter to handle depositions—even my own goddamn conversations with Ramm, for that goddamn matter. That's going to take a little time."

Tremaine cleared his throat delicately. "Well, as responding party, I've got only twenty-two days left either to object or to produce documents for copying or inspection under Rule Thirty-four. I'm having hell's own time trying to sift out all the pertinent material from a godawful mountain of files, which means I've got my own problems up here. Sobs of pity for you I can't seem to work up, Eli."

"Hell, man, I don't want your pity. I want to know if you'll accept a hiatus—a delay that will enable me to locate and engage the interpreter."

"The burden falls on you, Eli, not me. I've got an interpreter. But an interpreter wouldn't solve your problems anyhow. You don't have a case. The best way for you to handle things at this point, as I see it, is to back out—kill the suit. Which, by the way, might offer an excellent face-saving device. You can explain to Ramm that if he denies you German representation and expects you to go solo in face of great language and communications difficulties, you will have to withdraw, too. You can pick up your fees to date, then get out before you have to pump a lot of mud in a hopeless cause."

"Hopeless cause, my ass. Have you read *The Goddamn Machine,* or whatever it's called?"

"Certainly."

"Right there, on that page where the Nazi officer tells his machine-gun guy that they're both war criminals, right there is enough to tear your balls off."

Tremaine sniffed. "On that page—and elsewhere in the book—the Nazi officer is called Dekkar, not Ramm. And nowhere in all four hundred twenty-two pages is there any discernible malice toward your client, by whatever name. So you're already pumping mud, old friend."

When Abrams answered, it was in a conciliatory tone. "Hell, Stan, let's not try the case on the frigging phone."

"I don't want to try the case at all. Why don't you just drop it? Tell Ramm he's wasting his time?"

"No way."

"Well, suit yourself. But get this, Eli, old friend: Ramm isn't the only one in the document-demanding business. I'm going to demand that he produce his German military records, where he served and in what capacity. I'm going to demand his *Fragebogen* from 1945. I'm going to demand his military *Soldbuch.* I'm going to demand his SS *Ausweis* number, his police record, his credit rating, his goddamn blood type, for that matter. That Nazi son of a bitch is going to dance to a very long whip, and I suggest you write him to that effect."

"What the hell is a *Fragebogen*?"

"A questionnaire issued to German adults by the American Military Government after the occupation set in in '45. It was a detailed political-economic-military autobiography which, if falsified, put the German who signed it in the slammer for a goodly period."

"What's a—what did you say?—a sold-book?"

"A World War Two German soldier's paybook, which noted the details of his service, including everything from his service serial number, the units he served with, what he got paid and when, what campaigns he was in, what medals he won, his rifle number, his pistol number, his girlfriend's goddamn phone number, just about. If Ramm was a German soldier anytime between World War One and the end of World War Two, he had one. And when he became a member of the SS, his *Ausweis* number is the key to all his records in that organization. I'm going to ask Ramm to produce all those suckers, and we'll see just what kind of wonderful fellow he was back in the goose-stepping days. If that bastard wants a pissing contest, he'll be drowned before he gets his fly open."

Abrams's voice was full of unalloyed curiosity. "How did you learn about those things, Stan?"

"I was there, dear boy. I was analyzing *Fragebogen* and *Soldbücher* before you babies ever let your first booms."

There was silence at the Miami end.

"Are you still there, Eli?"

"Yeah. Yeah. Say, Stan, could I get back to you? I mean, give me a day or two and I'll be back. Okay?"

"One day, Eli. One day."

"I'll call."

The dial tone came on, and Tremaine hung up.

When he returned to the window, he was smiling.

He'd just returned from lunch when the intercom buzzed. "Yes?"

"Mr. Cooper on line one, sir."

Tremaine lifted the phone. "Hello there, young man. How are you feeling today?"

"Stiff and sore and a bit singed. But I'm out of bed and being spoiled silly by Manfred and Mrs. Farman."

"Good. It could have been a lot worse."

"Tell me about it. There I was, upside down in the wild gums and wax myrtles. If those three fishermen hadn't climbed down the bridge and hauled me out of the treetops before the Ford blew I'd have been a French fry."

"I got their names and addresses from the highway patrol, and I've sent them thank-you letters and cash rewards, as you requested."

"Did the fuzz get a lead on the Mercury?"

"Not yet. Nobody got the tag number."

"Well, I did. It's Florida IIJ-fifty-six-I, owned by Jansen Auto Rental of Orange Park and rented for the week by a gas station jockey name of Billy Logue. I don't know why Logue has a hard nose for me, but I intend to find out."

"Easy there, Coop. Logue has proved he's homicidal. You'd better give your information to the cops."

"I will. But I'll check a couple of my sources, too."

"Who gave you the tag number?"

"Your driver, Al Milano, nailed it. I gave it to a reporter friend of mine who gave it to some angle-man in Alachua County who runs tags for a price."

They sat quietly for a time, thinking about this. Then Cooper said, "What gets me is why in hell would a gas station gofer rent a bright-colored car to make a hit in broad daylight in front of witnesses? Logue and I are strangers to each other. So the only reason Logue would want to thump me is because someone hired him to thump me. But a good hit man is smart, secretive, and expensive, and Logue is said to be a beach bum with a dim bulb. If I know that, so must the guy who let out the contract. Which suggests that Logue wasn't hired to kill me—he was hired to make some kind of statement."

Tremaine let doubt sound. "Well, I don't know—"

"Got any better ideas?"

"If I did, I'd tell you."

There was another brief silence.

"I need another car, Stan. Should I write a check on that account you set up for me?"

"Of course not. Capital items are leased through Cooper

Enterprises, Incorporated, whenever advantageous. But in this case you already have a car.''

"I do?"

"Your father's Dodge."

"All respect to the Iaccoca legend, but I'd like something a little less nerdy than a weary, tan 1986 sedan."

"That car, for all its humdrum appearance, is anything but humdrum. Behind its solemn middle-class facade beats a muscular, custom-built heart. There's a special high-performance motor, racing car suspension, and all terrain capability, with tires to match. It's very fast, very nimble, and very tough. And it's bulletproof."

"You are jesting."

"People of substance—and your father was that, in spite of his naturally modest tastes and low visibility—are subject to assault or kidnapping. They learn to drive defensively, drably, and seldom. For them, chauffeur-driven battleships are for the daily grind; nondescript tanks are for those special, covert solos.''

"I'm not about to travel around behind a chauffeur."

"Very well. So the Dodge is your tank."

"But, my God—tan? What kind of color is that?"

"Tan is the color of prudence."

"What a pain in the ass."

"Isn't it, though."

"I'm taking a couple weeks of vacation, as you suggested. But I just can't bear the thought of driving up to an old Marine buddy's house in a grandfatherly sedan."

"Believe me: compared to that disreputable Ford you had, the Dodge looks like a pimpmobile." Tremaine coughed. "Is that what you'll be doing? Visiting an old Marine buddy?"

"Buddies. A couple in L.A., a couple in Seattle."

"Good. When will you be leaving?"

"The day after tomorrow."

"You'll give me your itinerary, of course."

"Can't. I don't know it myself."

"Hold on now. I'll have to know where to reach you."

"I'll call you. Every day. Honest."

''Well, I'm going out of town myself for several days. My godchild, Penny Benedict, is being married in Washington next weekend. She's the daughter of Senator Meredith Benedict, a lifelong friend, and it's an absolute must appearance. If you call, leave the message with Albert at the Ponte Vedra house. He'll be watching the place while I'm gone, and I'll tell him to be on the alert for you.''

''Okay, Stan. I'll be in touch.''

Tremaine listened to the dial tone for a moment, then hung up. He returned to the window to find that the ducks had departed.

This time his smile was even broader.

''Sam?''

''Yes, Mr. Tremaine?''

''What are you doing right now?''

''Tillie and I are in my office, going through some of the boxes from the garden house. It's mainly crap, up to now. Frank's correspondence with some movie people, some IRS worksheets going back to 1960. Lots of junk.''

''I've got news. Matt leaves on a two-week, get-lost vacation the day after tomorrow.''

''Hah.''

''I want you and Tillie to turn his Jax house upside down. Check everything and anything he's ever touched. Tear out walls, if you have to. Look for keys—safety deposit boxes, airport lockers, that kind of thing. Also do a surreptitious shakedown of Mrs. Farman's office and her condo at The Shores, the same for Manfred's apartment at the Water Street house. I mean, do a number. Right?''

''What if we're caught doing all this?''

''Caught doing what? You are legitimate legal reps of a legitimate client who has given your law firm permission to conduct a search of his property for a missing document.''

''I wasn't sure Coop had given us that kind of blanket.''

''He gave it to me. Which means you have it, too.''

''Got you, boss. We'll start tonight.''

Fifteen

Tina had fudged a bit and asked for a day's sick leave, knowing that her boss would never have given her permission to devote so much spec time on a stakeout of somebody so colorless and predictable as Claude Abernathy. She had difficulty herself believing that the realtor was worth such attention, and it took several recitals of the rationale—a kind of saying of the journalistic beads—to keep her in the VW, watching through a hefty ligustrum bush the traffic that came and went at the small but elegant office building from which Abernathy plied his trade:

There is something very peculiar about a real estate broker who meets in a dim gymnasium with a bunch of geeks who have the hots for soldiering. There is something even more peculiar about said broker and geeks being visited by a prominent Jacksonville judge. So why not watch said broker for a day and see what other peculiar things he does?

But as the day wore on, as her butt became increasingly numb, and as the blue Buick remained, solemn and aseptic, in the reserved parking space stenciled MR. ABERNATHY, the question was topped by the larger question.

Was she herself being peculiar?

What was so special about a man indulging a hobby shared by other men—peculiar men maybe, maybe not—including a district judge?

What was she trying to prove here?

No answers came forth. But in the listening for some, the undeniable became the certifiable: Her hunch mechanism, that little energizer which, when triggered by the curious or inexplicable, turned and whirred somewhere in her rib cage, was now in overdrive.

Professor Aaron, the Advanced Reporting guru on State's journalism faculty, had made a thing of hunches. "The world is full of news reporters," he'd said in his wearied pedant's drawl. "Some are insensitive clods, most are bleak little timeservers, and a bloody damned few are excellent practitioners. And then, glory be to St. Inkstain, there is that marvelous handful of great reporters—those men and women who are not only masters of their trade but also are endowed with that sixth sense, that superb hunch mechanism which leads them, tantalizes them, drives them until the orgasmlike release that comes with their full disclosure of the previously unknown or unrecognized. You, here in this class: You must take a merciless personal inventory, and if you find no evidence of this hunch mechanism in your id, or in your heart and bowels, run out of this room, don't walk, to the nearest career guidance counselor's office. I guarantee that you will never be a great news reporter, and I assure you that there's little reward or fun in journalism for those who aren't or can't be great. I know whereof I speak. I ran from the newsroom and into the lecture hall because I am the personification of that wretched little dictum, 'Those who can, do; those who can't, teach.' "

She had remained fast in her seat, because she knew without an inventory that, of the characteristics she owned, her hunch mechanism (she preferred to call it intuition) was the strongest. It had helped her to graduate with honors, and now it was telling her—flat-out—that Abernathy and his group were up to no good.

* * *

An hour after Tina had eaten her peanut-butter-and-jelly
sandwich and sipped a cup of coffee from her Thermos, Abernathy came through the plate glass doors. He paused at the top
of the Mexican tile steps, considered the worsening weather
with obvious disapproval, then stepped briskly to the parking
lot and into his car.

He drove through a drizzle straight north on U.S. 1 to the
I-95 junction, then doglegged back to cross the Buckman
Bridge to Roosevelt Boulevard. There he cut south to Orange
Park, where he finally pulled into the crowded parking lot of a
Burger King restaurant whose interior appeared to be teeming
with midday noshers of all sizes and shapes.

She parked the VW in the lee of a huge motor home with
New Hampshire plates, easing the car forward just enough to
permit a good overall view of the restaurant and its comings
and goings.

Despite the mob, Abernathy's tall figure was easy to follow.
He inched his way through the coffee line, then carried his cup
to a table in the corner, a happy choice, since the corner,
formed of glass, was prominent in her field of observation. He
sat there, sipping.

Exactly seven minutes later a black Caddie pulled into the
lot and disgorged the dumpy figure of Judge Abner T. Hefflefinger, who also acquired a cup of coffee and settled into a
chair at Abernathy's table. The two seemed to have little to talk
about. Four minutes later, a third man came out of the coffee
line to join them.

"I'll be go to hell," Tina said softly, uncasing and cocking
her camera.

She shot a full roll of the three as they talked. The most interesting action came when Stanley Tremaine passed en-
velopes to Abernathy and Hefflefinger.

"Ah, the payoff. Payoff, you say? Payoff for what? That,
Tina, dear, is what you're going to find out."

She watched until the meeting broke up and the men drove
off on their various ways.

She followed Abernathy back to his office and then she went
home for a shower, in which she did a lot of singing.

* * *

Cooper parked in the municipal lot on Hypolita Street and cut through the Spanish Garden to the house on St. George, where, according to the phone book, Tina Mennen had an apartment. It was a hoary building with lots of balconies and a mossy shingle roof, typical of those lining a street which, since 1600-something, had enticed swarms of itinerant go-getters, from Sir Francis Drake, seafaring London hijacker, to Gert Gismo, antiques collector out of Scranton, P-A. But the contemporary swarm was virtually nonexistent this afternoon, thanks to the opaque sky and intermittent drizzle, and the silent streets, further dispirited by the smog settling from chimney pots, suggested the opening credits of an English horror film.

He tapped on her door, then held a white handkerchief aloft. When she opened the door, he said, "Truce?"

She stood there in a bathrobe, fresh-scrubbed and blinking. "What are your terms?"

"Contrition."

"In what form?"

"My apologies for being such a wart in the restaurant that night."

There was an interval given to mutual appraisal.

"So what's with the bandage on your forehead?"

"I totaled my car day before yesterday. Out on the Green Cove road."

"Gross."

"Am I allowed to come in?"

"Sure. Hang your raincoat on that hall rack. While I get some clothes on, you can pour us coffee. It's on the table by the sofa."

He had seen to it and was sitting in the armchair beside the fireplace when she returned, wearing a denim jacket-and-slacks combo. She settled into the sofa cushions and regarded him soberly. "For a dude who's become Florida's answer to Daddy Warbucks, you're not making it, pal. You've got a head of hair and pupils in your eyes."

They exchanged polite smiles.

"I tried to call you this morning. But the newspaper said you were off today. So I came over here."

"Why?"

"To apologize."

"You're lucky to find me here. I just got back from Orange Park."

He rose from the chair and went to the French doors, where he stood, hands in his pockets, rocking on his heels and looking out at the dreary street. "You say you speak German, Tina?"

"Gewiss. Meine Eltern, auch meine Schwester und ich, sind gebürtige Deutschen. Daher spreche ich Deutsch eben so gut wie Englisch." She paused, then made a little joke. *"Leider ist mein Englisch nahezu katastrophal."*

"All r-i-i-ght."

"So what are you getting at?"

"Do you have any vacation time coming?"

"One week. And ten days saved-up comp time."

"How would you like to make some money?"

"Doing what?"

"Translating. Reading some World War Two German military documents from my dad's files and telling me what they say."

She gave him a cool, wry look. "This from the zeke who tells me he never gives a hand to other newsies?"

"Only on news stories. On news stories I work alone, keep my byline intact. No collaborations. But . . ."

She gave him a lingering stare. "Did it ever occur to you that such a sword cuts both ways?"

"What do you mean?"

"I mean, your insistence on exclusivity on a story and its sources could backfire. You'll never know how many stories you've missed because your hard nose has turned off other newspeople who might otherwise have been willing to bring you aboard on something real. Even share a byline with you, maybe." She watched his face closely.

He laughed softly and shook his head. "There ain't no such newsperson. Nobody shares stories willingly."

"Well, I'd share a story with you if I thought I could trust you not to take it over and run off with it and leave me pumping air."

"Take it from me, Tina: Get rid of that kind of naivete right now. If you want to be a hotshot reporter, the only time you drop crumbs to another working writer is after you've eaten all the loaf you can hold."

She shrugged. Her face was pink.

"Besides, I don't want your help on a story. This is personal business—a family history, sort of. An investigation into what my father was working on at the end of the Big War. It's strictly a personal matter."

She placed her cup and saucer carefully on the table. "Well—I don't know. I sort of planned to use my vacation to work on a story. Something rather special."

"What kind of vacation is a vacation you use to do the work you do when you're not on vacation?"

"As I say, this is pretty special. A thing I picked up on when I was out in the boonies the other night. I suspect it's hot—real hot—and I don't want it to cool off. Besides, even though I'd be on my own time, I'm not sure my boss would be so crazy about my working directly with a *Times-Union* sharpster. Personal or not."

"No problem. I've quit my job at the *T-U*."

She gave him a look, surprise in her large eyes. "You did? When?"

"Officially, yesterday."

"My God. That was a great job—"

"Sure was."

She nodded, thoughtful. "Well, why work, eh? Now that you're loaded—"

"Money had nothing to do with it. I've got something that's more important. Something I've got to do."

"Tracking down your father's killer? Revenge?"

"Something like that."

"I thought you didn't like your father."

"I don't know where the hell you got that idea."

"The things you said, the way you acted."

"Two things my dad and I had in common. One was that we looked a lot alike. The other was our ability to say and do dumb things that give people the wrong idea about us."

She sat quietly for a time, thinking. Then: "Say I give you

the vacation week and save the comp time for my own project. What's in all this for me?''

''A hundred bucks a day for a guaranteed ten days. Plus any expenses you might incur. I don't foresee many of those, since you'll be working in my father's office in the Water Street house, but they include meals, mileage, that kind of thing. And Mrs. Farman and Manfred, the houseman, will be there to give you a hand if you need anything special.''

''Where will you be?''

''In Washington, mostly. Only you three will know that, by the way. Everybody else—everybody—will be told I'm visiting friends out West. And I'll check with you daily to let you know what I'm up to.''

She thought some more.

''A guaranteed ten days, meaning you'll get a thousand dollars even if you finish in five days. What say?''

She sighed. ''That's very generous. And I could sure use the money. My VW is fresh out of *Fahrvergnügen,* seeing as how it needs new umlauts.''

''Get it fixed and send me the bill. Meantime, you can use Dad's Jeep.''

His attitude—his straight-up, no-excuses apology—had made some kind of difference.

Moreover, for an old guy, he looked especially nice today. Standing there in the light of the misty noon, neat and clean in his Oxford cloth shirt and tweed jacket, his preppy tie centered, his trousers creased, his loafers glistening, he could be an ad in *Gentlemen's Quarterly.* And in this new perception of him was the core understanding that he was seeing her in a new light, too. That night in the restaurant, she'd played the smart-ass ingenue, the sort of female that gives females a bad name, and she sensed that today he had duded up to show he had seen through her act and respected her anyhow. It was all very heady and indescribably subtle. In any event, the two horses' asses of Luigi's pasta palace were gone, their glib antipathy replaced by—what was the word? ''Friendliness'' was too strong; ''civility'' was too weak. He still communicated aloofness and a tendency toward sarcasm, and she knew she was, as usual, a bit too mouthy; but for all that, their initial abrasiveness had been smoothed, in these few electric minutes, by a tacit, reciprocal absolution. *Forgive us our phoniness, as we forgive those who phony against us.*

Giving him a sidelong glance, she decided that centerfold material he was not; a brilliant conversationalist he would never be. But there was a sweetness, a gentle amiability and roguish humor lurking in the mix. And he *was* rather great-looking in a middle-agey way, and—she couldn't deny it—sort of sexy.

What he was proposing was, of course, preposterous, since she was totally committed to her job. But in this suspended moment, when they each were presumably counting the potential costs of their working together, she could anticipate relief from the fear—an anxiety so intense it had become physical pain—that had ground at her in recent weeks. It was rooted in her gathering sense of an ever more crowded world, a profession overpopulated with rivals who would kill for a single rung on the ladder, a melancholy belief that her talent and skill and hunch mechanism would never be enough and that political correctness and luck—blind, sweepstakes-winning luck—were the reigning criteria for success, not only in journalism but in life itself. It was expressed in a creeping hysteria that told her, those nights she lay awake in her dark and lonely bedroom, that no matter how hard she tried, no matter how much skill and purpose she could bring to the journalistic workplace over her life span, no one would take note, nothing would ever happen. She would sink without a trace into newspaper history, just another solitary woman who had failed to scratch the armor of a masculine world. The feeling had grown in intensity over recent weeks, and she had longed for a break, any kind of break, that could save her from running aimlessly, screaming, as she'd seemed ready to do when awakening from her fitful sleep this morning. It had been this near-panic situation that had caused her to call in sick and begin her stalking of Abernathy.

But here was the clearest-cut break of all, a fall into an entirely different world, to be legitimized by honestly earned pay from a presentable employer on what appeared to be a heartfelt, albeit quixotic, quest.

"Are you hungry yet?"

"Starved. Let me take you out for an early supper."

She shook her head. "Stay right where you are. I'm famous for my omelettes, which are so light they levitate."

"Does this mean you'll take the job?"

"Tell me about it while I go into cuisine mode."

The drizzle had lifted, hurried along by a fresh breeze off the Matanzas. Cooper left Tina's place at about seven-thirty and drove over the Bridge of Lions to Anastasia Island, where he parked in front of Nickerson's Comares Avenue condo. Nothing happened when he rang the doorbell, so he returned to the Dodge and waited until eight-fifteen, when Nickerson's Chevrolet finally came around the corner and squeaked to a halt in the driveway. The detective was heading for the house when Cooper called, "Yo, Nick. Got a minute?"

Nickerson turned, blinking and wary. "Cooper?"

"Come on. Get in my car. I have a question."

The detective's face reddened. "Bug off, rich boy. I don't answer questions, I ask them."

"Please."

Nickerson snapped, "You're wasting your time. I'm not on the case anymore."

"That's what I want to talk about. I've been sitting here a long time, waiting to talk to you about that."

"Poor baby."

"You were jerked around. And I don't like it any more than you do."

Cooper could see the indignation, for all its intensity, make way almost at once for curiosity. He leaned across the seat and opened the passenger-side door. "Come on, hop in."

The squat man, pale under the wan streetlight, climbed into the Dodge, smelling of tobacco and whiskey. Settling into the seat, he gave Cooper a truculent stare. "So what's on your mind, rich boy?"

"First, my assurance that I had nothing to do with your

being taken off the investigation of my father's murder.''

Nickerson sniffed. ''Come on, get real. There's only one arm that can reach down into our department that far, and that's Stan Tremaine's. Stan Tremaine is your lawyer. You think I can't string that together?''

''I had no idea Tremaine has that kind of clout. He unpacked it right in front of my eyes, without once asking me did I think it was a good idea. Well, I thought it was a rotten idea, and you have my apologies.''

Nickerson sniffed. ''Big deal. So what are you going to do—have me reinstated and promoted to inspector?''

''Cooper does not equal Tremaine. I can't do anything for or against you, and I think you know it. And I think you know that I wouldn't play dirty even if I could.''

Nickerson's glare broke, and he peered through the window at the blustery night. ''You said you had a question.''

''Do you take off-duty jobs?''

The glance was incredulous. ''You've got to be kidding.''

''No. Does the department allow you to moonlight?''

''I don't direct parking at house parties.''

''I need advice. Could I hire you to educate me on police procedures and techniques?''

''What the hell does that mean?''

''I mean, I'm trying to find out who killed my father and why. I'm a damned good investigative reporter. I know how to follow paper trails. But I need backup. Some heavy-duty violence has already come in on me, as you damn well know, and I need a guy like you to advise me on how best to cover my butt while I'm chasing paper. What say?''

Nickerson looked pained. ''What do you mean, a guy like me?''

''I did some deep-dish browsing through the St. Augie newspaper's back files yesterday. They had a wad of clips on you—how you've been a homicide specialist for nine years and all that—and the best one was a profile they ran after you won your third Cop of the Year award, in which it told how out of some forty or fifty homicides you investigated, only two— both of them involving German tourists—remain unsolved.

That makes you a real hotrock in my book, and that's what I mean by a guy like you."

"Those Germans were hit," Nickerson said, his tone a touch defensive. "It's hard to solve a homicide when it's a Mob hit."

Cooper let his curiosity show. "German tourists hit by the Mob? That's sort of unusual, isn't it?"

"There is nothing usual about the Mob. But they had to be Mob hits. They were so neat, so advertised."

"Meaning the Mob wanted the bodies to be found, right?"

"Yeah. The Mob never kills just for the hell of it. They kill to advertise—send messages. The German dudes weren't tourists; they were ID'ed as members of a neo-Nazi gang in Munich. They were executed, shot behind the ears, and left in their rented cars in downtown parking lots. It looked to me like the message was, 'Krauts, This Space Is Reserved. Signed, The North Florida Mafia.'" Nickerson smiled faintly at his own joke.

"They were killed several years apart, right?"

"Yeah. Which makes it even harder to come up with a linkage."

Cooper shrugged. "The fact remains: You have a helluva record, and I'd like you to do a job for me."

"If you're all that anxious to spend your millions, hire a Pinkerton. Why me?"

"Three reasons. First, I owe you one. Second, I like your persistence—your attitude leaves a lot to be desired, but I like your persistence. And third, I hope that while you're advising me you'll pretty soon see that I had no involvement in my dad's murder."

"I never said you did."

"Hey, man, cut the crap. I'm your only suspect. You know it, I know it, and Stan Tremaine knows it. This way, you'd be sort of unofficially back on the case."

"How would that go down with Tremaine?"

"I'm more than a little ticked off over the way he put the nail into you. I think he was showing off, and I don't need that. But more important, I want to keep you in the background—

an ace in my sleeve. The fewer people who know about our arrangement the better. Stan included.''

''What's the job pay, and how long would you be paying?''

''Ah, the good part. I just want you to be available to answer questions for me—nothing that would compromise your work at the department, nothing that would ask you to violate your confidentiality rules or to enter a conflict-of-interest situation—but generic, procedural stuff. Techniques. For this, I'll pay you a hundred dollars an hour, plus expenses, if any. And you'll get the hundred for any portion of an hour. You send me a bill every week, my secretary will check your bill against her time sheet, and you'll get a check in the mail the next day.''

''You're saying that if I spend an hour and a half answering your questions I'll get a full two hundred?''

''You get a hundred for a minute, two hundred for an hour and one minute. If our clocks disagree, my clock decides.''

Nickerson gave him a wry, sidelong glance. ''You must want to prove yourself to me real bad.''

''You got that right. And I'll give you a hundred bucks right now for answering my first question: Who, in your estimation, would provide me with a first-class security service? I don't mean burglar alarms. I mean, like, riding shotgun. Covering my ass when I run down to the local hamburger joint some midnight. Hiring the right people to cover me when I pop off to L.A., or Chi.''

Nickerson laughed softly. ''That's easy. Me.''

''You? How could you do that? You've got a job.''

''The hell I do. I'm on a one-month terminal leave of absence without pay.''

''What?''

''I told Nolan that I didn't like working for a chief who jumps through hoops for local hotshots. I told him sort of, ah, impolitely. He wants my badge.''

''I sort of hit you at the right time in your life, eh?''

''Couldn't have been righter.''

''I'll need to revise those dollar figures. I'll work up a salary scale when I get back to the house. I'll call you. What's your home phone number?''

Nickerson took a pad from his coat pocket, wrote the number, and handed over the sheet. ''When do I start?''

''Tonight, if my offer's acceptable.''

''Hey, it'll be acceptable. Anything over nothing is acceptable to a guy who's got nothing.''

''Come by the Water Street house at ten.''

''So now that I'm an employee, what do I call you?''

'' 'Sire' will do.''

Nickerson sniffed.

Sixteen

Beauvin, France
November 17, 1944

Standartenführer Otto Dekkar stood, alone and appearing to be lost in thought, beside the weed-choked fountain in the miserable village square. His leather greatcoat, draped neatly over his shoulders, and his service cap, with its polished black visor and gleaming silver Hoheitsabzeichen, made him seem even taller and, oddly, more lonely. The wind had become restless and cold, carrying the smell of oncoming winter, so he pulled the coat closer about him and raised its collar. His expressionless yellow eyes turned slowly to regard Obersturmführer Bechtel, who waited politely and attentively, the model German officer, to the flank of his machine-gun section.

"Are they all here, Bechtel?"

"Yes, Standartenführer. The roundup produced those nine males against the wall there."

"What about the women and children?"

"A dozen females of various ages and sixteen children, from infants to ten-year-olds, are being held in the church cellar."

"Have any of the men shown a willingness to cooperate?"

"No, Standartenführer."

"Not a word, a hint?"

"No, sir. Nothing."

Dekkar's strange pale eyes narrowed, and a muscle moved in his meticulously barbered jaw. After a time he said quietly, "Very well. Set fire to the church. Then give each of the men a last chance to answer the question. If they still refuse to talk, the fire will continue, the women and children will die in the cellar, and the men will be shot, each in his turn."

"Most respectfully, Standartenführer, but that could be construed to be an atrocity—"

"Don't be so fastidious, Bechtel. The world has already condemned the SS. The world already denounces you and me as war criminals. So let us show the world how skillful we are, eh?"

There it was.

The only place within the bounds of more than a hundred thousand words to mention directly—even indirectly, for that matter—war crimes or atrocities. Two complete readings of the novel had failed to produce anything else that might feasibly trigger a libel suit.

In the complex algebra of law, could Dekkar equal Ramm?

Cooper placed a marker on the page and closed the book.

He was very tired, having spent most of the day clearing out his cubicle at the newspaper and completing a particularly stressful employee exit interview with Gert Shaw, and he was now at the point where his eyes seemed unwilling to deal a moment longer with language in any form. He shut them and, resting his head against the high leather back of the swivel chair his father had called "Mount Nates," he listened to the gentle hiss of the rain against the windows and replayed in his mind the gray November day, the bleakness of the French village, the cluster of old men and boys melting into a bloody heap as the machine guns chattered. He was deeply sad and unaccountably tense.

He had been reading since late afternoon, so engrossed by the labyrinthine zigs and zags of *The Götterdämmerung Machine* he hadn't left the chair—even for the supper of soup and chicken salad brought in by Manfred in the middle of chapter nine. Perhaps it was his changing perception of Frank Cooper, the man, or maybe it was his awareness that the book—for all its entertainment value—had become a legal document, but he had never before appreciated the reach of his father's mind and the vigor of his prose. The difference between the first novel, *A Job for Despair,* and *Machine,* the last, was extraordinary. The first had been formula treacle; the last, an elevation of the thriller configuration into genuine literature. Yet the writing itself was virtually overshadowed by *Machine*'s stunning exhibition of technical savvy; the story dealt with wartime espionage and its ancillaries, and the detail he brought to it left no doubt as to Frank Cooper's intimate knowledge of intrigue and its practitioners.

The novel's central theme involved a war's-end plot of Martin Bormann, Hitler's brutish "secretary," to desert the doomed Führer and flee to Brazil via submarine, taking with him a prototype atomic trigger mechanism developed in Nazi laboratories. Code-named *Götterdämmerung,* or "Twilight of the Gods," the device converted standard aerial bombs and long-range artillery shells into rudimentary, low-yield nuclear weapons—a piece of machinery whose clandestine auction among the oligarchs of the world's emergent nations would most certainly make Bormann a billionaire. Charged with delivering the device from the lab near Munich to a rendezvous with the sub off Lisbon was Otto Dekkar, an SS Standartenführer whose zealotry was a legend among even the most fanatical Nazis.

Since the Allies controlled the air over Western Europe, Dekkar knew it would be unacceptably risky to fly the machine across southern France to a secret landing strip on the Portuguese coast. So he handpicked a small SS crew to truck him and the device from Munich to Mulhouse and then across the underbelly of Vichy France to Portugal's northern border. He and the crew would be disguised as French civil engineers, en route to the site of a proposed bridge across the Salmson gorge.

The story evolved in parallel story lines, one covering Dekkar and the Nazi preparations, the other following Allen Ross, an American undercover agent in Germany, who learned of the scheme and set up an elaborate counterploy to intercept the delivery and divert the machine to Eisenhower's G-2 at Supreme Headquarters, United States Forces, Europe.

The novel's two story lines converged during a hellish blizzard that swept Bavaria and the Black Forest area in March of 1945. Ross and his team attempted the intercept on a lonely stretch of road beside the Ammersee, a large lake southwest of Munich, but in a vicious firefight, Dekkar lost control of his truck and he and the Götterdämmerung machine skidded onto the frozen lake, crashed through the ice, and sank in a hundred feet of black water. Dekkar and Ross survived the incident, and the rest of the novel was given to their fruitless and mutually destructive struggle to salvage the priceless machine.

The whole thing, Cooper decided now, was a metaphor for the world's guaranteed failure to control the atomic genie.

"Sneaky, Dad," he said aloud. "But hardly libelous."

He was in a strange city, alone on a rainy night, and his pockets were crammed with thousand-dollar bills which nobody—cab drivers, short-order waitresses, hotel clerks—would accept. And so he wandered the empty streets, cold and hungry and lost, alternately oppressed, first by panic, then by a terrible sorrow. He was banging on yet another darkened door when a hand touched his shoulder, and he spun around, surprised and frightened, to confront the marblelike features of Manfred.

"Mr. Matt. Wake up, please."

"What? Who—"

"It's Sergeant Nickerson, sir. He's in the main foyer."

"Why didn't you just buzz me on the intercom?"

Manfred seemed to have expected the question. "If I'd done that, Mr. Matt, he would have known you are here. I wasn't sure you wanted to see him. This way I could tell him you'd

been in the garden house and I'd have to go out there to see if
you had left.''

Cooper felt a smile. ''Good thinking, Manfred. Thanks. But
I'll see him. Bring him on over, will you, please?''

''Sir—''

Cooper's eyes, focused now, saw something different in the
old man's face—something he had never before seen there. It
was subtle, partly buried in the seams and crags and barely discernible in the watery blue eyes. But having seen it in its many
forms and shades of intensity while in the Balkans, Cooper
was unable to miss it now.

Fear.

Manfred was frightened.

''Something bothering you?''

''All policemen bother me, sir. When they come calling at
night—''

''He's just a busted cop I've hired, Manfred. He isn't the
Gestapo.''

''Sir, I must—'' The old man's voice fell off.

''Must what?''

Manfred shook his head and blinked, as if trying to shake off
a burden. ''I'm sorry, Mr. Matt. It's none of my business. Forgive me.''

''No problem.''

As Manfred ghosted off, Cooper went into the bathroom,
where he washed up and combed his hair and, squinting into
the mirror, eventually detected signs of human life.

He was back at the desk when Manfred returned to usher in
the detective.

''Hi, Nick. Have a seat.''

Nickerson sat in the wing chair, his gaze wandering about
the room. ''I've been all over this property in the past couple
weeks, and this is the nicest part, hands down.''

''My pappy practically lived here.''

''Don't blame him.''

''I'm going to drive up to Bayard this evening. I want you to
ride shotgun. I don't want another experience like the one on
the Riddle Creek bridge.''

''Are you still unwinding from that?''

"I wake up nights singing 'Rockabye Baby.' "

"It never really goes away. I still dream about my first shootout."

"Tell me about it. Bosnia's my constant companion."

There was a pause. Then: "What's in Bayard?"

"A guy named Billy Logue. He works for a Texaco station in Orange Park. I called the station this afternoon and the manager told me Logue lives in a mobile-home park near the Bayard dog-racing track."

"So?"

"I want to ask Logue some questions about the rental Mercury that ran me off the bridge. He picked it up at Jansen's. I want to know who he delivered it to."

"Why don't you just call him?"

"I want to eyeball him. And wave a couple of dollars under his nose. People respond to the smell of dollars."

"Like me, eh?"

Cooper gave Nickerson a moment of sober inspection. "Do you have second thoughts about this, Nick? Does working with me demean you somehow?"

The detective waved a dismissing hand. "Hell, I was just kidding. I'm real easy about our deal. To tell the truth, I almost fell off my couch when you called this afternoon. I mean, a thousand a week is a helluva baby-sitting fee."

"Well, I didn't mean to poing your pride, or anything."

"With money I don't have any pride because I've never had any money to speak of. Starved my ass off as an orphan kid, worked for three cents a year in fast-food joints, boatyards, saloons, whorehouses, paper mills, car washes—you name it— to get enough education to be a cop. Which, as you know, pays about four cents a year. Upset about your deal? For a guy like me, who needs money more than anybody and would do anything to get some, the idea of being upset is to laugh."

"You have any problems moving into those rooms next to Manfred's in the service ell?"

"Nope. I'll just sublet my apartment."

"No women on the premises. For one thing, Mrs. Farman would have a hemorrhage. For another, it gets too busy, too complicated."

"I've had my Significant Other for nine years now. And I always go to her place."

"Good. Be sure to give her number to Mrs. Farman."

"I'm not there all that much."

"Okay. Bayard, anyone?"

The January chill had settled hard over the land this black, rain-spittled night, and Route 1 was virtually devoid of traffic. They said nothing for almost all of the eighteen-mile drive, subdued as they were by the sounds of the buffeting wind, the sizzling tires, and the metronomic clacking of the windshield wipers.

Cooper gave much thought to the paradox represented by his father—the earthy man of moods and movement and laughter and deep, protracted silences, as compared with the spiritual man revealed in the shard of a letter proclaiming his love for his son. The letter, in the metaphor of the moment, had shown Frank to be the chalky beams of the headlights; Mom was now the surrounding darkness. For all the marital gloom that had obscured his world, and despite the limited light he could generate, Frank had kept everything on some kind of road. Now, even as Cooper savored those wrenching, incomplete, yet wonderfully illuminating sentences, his pathetic, tormented mother obtruded. Now, behind the wheel on this rain-swept highway, he felt a gathering of the prescient uneasiness that linked him to her and her lonely and lethal afflictions.

Nickerson broke their silence briefly. "This car rides hard for a Dodge."

"It's the suspension. My old man had the whole car beefed up."

"Oh."

Cooper's uneasiness grew after they had passed Race Track Road and were approaching Bayard. The misty sprinkling had become an insistent, driving rain, making the driving wretched and the visibility almost zero. But the tension was larger than mere concern about the weather. It was, well, Mother again.

"Turn right here," Nickerson said.

Cooper nosed the Dodge slowly onto a narrow lane whose

ancient blacktop was rutted and holed and awash with angry runoffs from the surrounding pine woods. A quarter mile of this, then a further narrowing at a gate where a hand-painted sign announced EVERGREEN ACRES MOBILE HOME PARK, NO THRU TRAFFICK.

Nickerson peered through the side window. "See that mailbox? Those lights? Number three. Two more to go."

"He won't be there," Cooper said suddenly.

Nickerson gave him a sidelong glance. "What the hell are you talking about?"

"Logue. He won't be there."

"How do you know that?"

"I just know."

They pulled to a stop at number five, a box of grimy aluminum whose windows were dark, except for one. Huddling in their raincoats and following Nickerson's flashlight beam, they left the car and made their way along a gravel path to the side door. There was no bell, so Nickerson pounded on the streaming metal siding of the house. A miserable wait, three more vigorous poundings with no result, and Cooper said, "Come on. Let's go. He's not home—just like I said."

"Wait. There. In the woods over there. A car."

It was a Mercury, its cream finish smeared by mud, its right flank torn and scraped, its doors locked.

The flashlight glare showed a young man sitting upright in the back seat. His mouth was open, and his glassy blue eyes stared—vacant, unblinking—at the car's ceiling and the universe beyond. Blood was everywhere.

"You were wrong," Nickerson said. "Logue *is* here."

"We don't know for sure that it's Logue."

"Want to lay some bets on that?"

"Well, whoever it is, we've got to call the sheriff." Cooper turned and made for the Dodge.

Nickerson, striding along with him, said, "Give that a thought or two."

"Why? There's a dead body back there."

"Use that car phone, and you'll be here the rest of the night, making statements, explaining yourself."

Cooper slowed his pace, came to a halt, and stood in the rain, regarding Nickerson thoughtfully. "I've got to go to Washington tomorrow," he said.

"When you called Logue's boss for this address, did you give him your name?"

"No. I said I was a pal of Logue's from Atlanta."

Nickerson nodded. "All right, then. We go back to St. Augie, dry off, take a stiff drink, and go to bed."

"What about the dead guy?"

"I don't suppose he'd mind."

The house had been fitted with three phone lines: the main number, for general use and with extensions throughout, including the garden and boathouses; a second connected solely to Frank's office above the garage; and a third for use by Mrs. Farman when the main line was otherwise tied up. Manfred's apartment, because he seldom made personal use of a phone, had both an extension jack linking it with the main line and a two-way intercom for talk with Mrs. Farman or Frank.

Manfred had considered the installation of a private, unlisted line for himself but had ruled it out when, first, he discovered how much it would cost and, second, when he conceded that Lotte was the only person he called with any frequency and that when he did call her it was always at night after Mrs. Farman had gone home and after Lotte had arrived home from her Daytona art supply shop, The Smock and Beret.

Another complication was the fact that all mail, including phone bills, was delivered to Mrs. Farman. Bills for the main line would report any toll calls he made from the phone in his room, so for privacy's sake he had an arrangement with Lotte in which he'd reimburse her for those collect calls he made to her and for whatever other long distance calls he billed to her phone in emergencies.

This night he'd tried to set up a call to Wolfgang the moment Mr. Matt and Nickerson had left the driveway. But the overseas operator unaccountably had trouble dealing with the billing arrangement and he wasn't put through until Lotte got home from a movie and personally accepted the charges. By then it was after ten o'clock, and he kept a worried eye out for Mr. Matt's returning car.

"Hello."

"This is Putzi, Wolfgang."

"Well, well. How's everything in Florida?"

"Not so good. The fox is in the henhouse."

"You mean Nickerson——"

"He's befriended Matthew and is preparing to move into the apartment next to mine."

"Oh, my God."

"What are your instructions?"

"We must assume Nickerson has wind of the Six-Twenty. Otherwise he would have remained content with the watching game. So you'll have to adjust your program as well. You must be prepared for some direct moves against you."

"I agree. So what I'm asking for is permission to go into heavy preemption. I'll have to make the first move."

"Well, it's obvious that we must protect the Six-Twenty at all costs. Which means some heavy-gauge athletics are indicated. Do you think you're up to it?"

"I have a confession to make, Wolfgang. I've already made a trial run along those lines. And all it proved was that I'm no longer a Nazi superman."

"You mean——"

"I made a move against him. I failed."

"Is he aware of that fact?"

"Oh, no. But the failure told me that if it comes to physical confrontations, I must engage on my terms and my terms only. So I want your permission to move as I see fit."

"Of course you have my permission. We should have eliminated Nickerson at the beginning—when he first began sniffing around."

"I couldn't agree more. But you know how Frank was, how strongly he insisted that we abstain from the old methods."

"Should I try to send you some help? It's very much more difficult to set up in these times, but I can try——"

"No. It's impractical. Besides, they'd probably end up dead

in municipal parking lots, like those other two.''

"All right, then. Whatever you decide will be all right with me. We can't play any more waiting games. He's a minor pest—an ambitious local cop—who's turning dangerous. One way or another, cop or not, you must take him out.''

"It will be a pleasure.''

"Very well, then. Good-bye, Putzi.''

"Good-bye, Wolfgang.''

Seventeen

Congressman Quigg loved parties—especially this kind, where a few of the world's top one hundred egotists, having descended from their senatorial Olympus for an evening, gathered in the name of matrimony to be fawned over by a regiment of subordinate yet equally swollen egos. The rationale here, of course, was the marriage of Penelope Benedict, the sleek and notoriously randy daughter of Senator Meredith Altman Benedict, to James M. Dillingsworth III, intellectual scion of aerospace and cattle-ranching millions, who regularly awed his friends in Palm Beach and L.A. with his ability to complete much of each *New York Times* Sunday crossword.

As one of the unattached lesser mortals in attendance, Quigg was free to roam the site, in this case the south wing of the Windy Acres Hunt Club and Hostelry, the magnetic pole for public-trough snobs and Cabinet-level trysters, located on a Chesapeake Bay prominence in Prince George County. The postnuptial party was very social, to be sure, but, like all things involving senators, also very sotto-voce political. The security was intense, the buffet was extravagant, the music was mellow, the dancing was trendy, the shirts were starched, and the ties were black, but throughout the swirling and clinking and chattering, deals were being cut, loyalties were being forged or forgotten, conspiracies were being launched, and the world's dubious fate was being brought yet another day, another lie, closer.

"God, this is great," Quigg exulted aloud.

A waiter at his elbow asked, "You wish something, sir?"

Quigg, relishing the sudden vision of how far he had come since his salesman days, beamed. "No, son, I'm looking for Stanley Tremaine, the bride's godfather."

"Most of the wedding party are in the card room, sir." The waiter pointed. "Over there, next to the solarium."

"Thank you."

Quigg eased his way through the fragrant, clamorous eddies to the card room entrance, where, for the benefit of those who might recognize him, he stood in an attitude that suggested regal fearlessness in face of the burdens society had laid upon him.

A young woman in an abbreviated skirt and a see-through blouse came from behind to peer into his face and punch a finger into his cummerbund. "Whatsamatta, Pop? Gotta gas pain? Or are you one of the eight million house dicks?"

Quigg managed to control his irritation and project weary amiability. "No to both questions, my dear. It's simply that I can't seem to leave my office in my office."

"You some kinda big shot? Your face is sort of familiar."

He gave her the coup de grace. "I am a member of Congress," he said softly, loftily.

"We all got problems." She laughed, tossing her glistening black hair and displaying brilliant, flawless teeth.

"I wouldn't expect you to understand."

"Understand, hell. My old man's a senator. I was born in a ballot box. Don't give me that 'understand' crap."

Quigg blinked and licked his lips. "Oh?" he said carefully. "Your father is—?"

"Meredith Altman Benedict, current patriarch and the glibbest of ten generations of professional bullshitters. He also has a talent for throwing lousy parties.''

Working to cover his astonishment, Quigg said smoothly, "Then you are the bride?''

"Nope. She and her new old man have already left on their so-called honeymoon. I'm her sister, Annie.'' She sipped her drink and gave him a closer look over the rim of the glass. "You here by yourself?''

"Yes.''

"You mean you came voluntarily—without some Mumsy pushing you into it?''

He laughed, truly amused. "I don't have a Mumsy, happy to say. Actually I came here to meet somebody I've long admired from afar. A member of the wedding party.''

"Who she?''

"Not a she. A he. Stanley Tremaine. Your godfather.''

"Oh. You're gay?''

"No, I meant I admire Mr. Tremaine as a professional manager of large foundations. I'm chairman of the House Subcommittee on International Trusts, you see.''

She took his arm. "Well, hell, no prob. Come on. I'll introduce you. By the way, who put you on the guest list? The only congressman I remember there is John Horner.''

He saw that the girl was not the kind to be conned. He chuckled. "I confess. Call Security. I crashed the party with my congressional ID. But I could think of no other way to get in social touch with Tremaine before he left town.''

Annie laughed, a genuine guffaw. "Security, hell. I should call Walter Reed Psychiatric. Anybody who'd want to crash this crappy do has got to be around the bend.'' She laughed again. "What's your name?''

"Fen Quigg.''

"Oh, yeah. Now it comes to me. You're the guy always blabbing when I flip past CNN. You're a real art form, Fen baby.''

The card room was Elizabethan, with richly glowing walnut paneling, diamond-paned casement windows, massive beams defining the low-slung ceiling, and a lazy blaze flickering in the enormous stone fireplace. Central to this was a long trestle table, which literally seemed to groan under the eroded yet still-mountainous wedding cake and its phalanx of sandwiches, relishes, and glittering bottles. Standing in a cluster between the table and the fire were the party's cadre—Senator Benedict; a reedy, tired-looking woman in a magenta gown who had to be the senator's wife; Senators Allen, Ditmar, O'Toole, Feinberg, and Rossini; Reginald Oldham, secretary of defense; Sherman Dillingsworth, cow-punching astro-nut; Pat Tinker, publisher of *Chronos* magazine; Benjamin Rubin, chairman of the United Broadcasting Corporation; Oko Takai, the Tokyo electronics tycoon; and "Little Jack" Horner, Speaker of the House. And, of course, Stanley Tremaine—tall, cool, immaculate, and polite. Intermixed with these softly gabbling titans were women of assorted ages, sizes, and auras, all of them wearing expressions that spoke of having been in twenty thousand Heres, enduring twenty thousand Same Old Conversations.

The group stirred, coming together somewhat like a rifle squad falling in, and faked both delight at the approach of Annie and a how-wonderful-to-see-you-again ebullience for the Johnny-come-lately headline grabber they admired, envied, or detested, depending on which ax each held to which grinding stone.

The Speaker said, "Well, I'll be. Fen, old boy, how wonderful it is to see you here."

Quigg took the outstretched hand, showing his best side to the women and his most captivating smile to them all. "Good evening, Little Jack—ladies and gentlemen."

Annie, perceiving her mother's puzzlement, crooned, "I can't thank you enough, Mom, for dragging this old darling away from his labors on The Hill. The party wouldn't have worked for me without him."

"Well, dear," Mom crooned back uncertainly, "I knew what it would mean to you."

Annie swept the group with a rebel's smile and said in mock confidentiality, "Fen and I have been lovers for years."

Senator Benedict said, "Arr-r-um."

Mrs. Benedict said, "Sheee."

Quigg laughed. "That's the nicest fib I've heard all day."

Stanley Tremaine said, "Congressman Quigg. You're chairman of the House Subcommittee on International Trusts, aren't you?"

Quigg nodded. "That I am. And I've long admired the reputation you've built at the Rettung Foundation, Mr. Tremaine. A fine, clean operation. I've had some questions about how you do it for some time now, but I've been so unbelievably busy I haven't followed through with a letter."

Tremaine smiled with discernible relief at this promise of escape. "Why not now?" To the Benedicts, he said, "I'm up to here with wine and cheese. You won't mind if the congressman and I toddle into the men's locker for some he-man booze, will you?"

Waving a hand at the frozen smiles around her, Annie said, "I'm off, too. Charlie Dinsmore's waiting for me at the handball court. Plays a helluva game, but I take him every time. Ta-ta."

"Thank you, Annie," Quigg called after her.

She looked back and gave him a wink.

Tremaine took Quigg's elbow and steered him away.

They took off their jackets and sat on a bench, sipping and talking, until two-thirty in the morning. They were virtually alone, the presence of others marked only by the occasional rattling of a janitorial mop pail or the far-off sound of vacuum cleaners.

Quigg told of his bizarre entry into politics, of his discovery that he had talent for "the game," of his rapid progress in committee assignments, and of his personal network of informants and collaborators, both in his district and on The Hill. Tremaine told of his rocky beginnings, of the lessons of The Big War, of his climb into the legal elite, and of his humiliating defeats in his own quests for elective office.

After mutual confidence had been tentatively established by the sharing of these sanitized, glamorized recollections, the conversation drifted into shop talk. The bottle of Scotch had been half emptied when Quigg said, "Just how—specifically—did Rettung get so goddamn big, Stan? I mean, hell, you guys must have started out with one stupendous pile to have been able to shove Rettung into the stratospheric billions, eh?''

''Well, I'm not at liberty to talk specifics about Rettung, but you need only look at the Tremaine Fund, conceived and headquartered in my own office in Jacksonville. I saw early on how U.S. tax laws were stacked in favor of foundations—big or small. And being a small-town lawyer with damned few assets, I started out small, I'll tell you.''

Quigg nodded solemnly. ''Five hundred bucks out of your personal savings account, wasn't it?''

Tremaine gave him a quick look. ''You know that?''

''Mm. I know how you built the Tremaine Fund. At least I know what the paper trail shows, and, adding a bit of my own interpolation, I'll wager I could give you the basic scenario right now. Want to hear it?''

Tremaine smiled, his eyes showing faint annoyance. ''Do I have a choice?''

''Back then,'' Quigg said, reaching for the bottle again, ''foundations could become nearly impregnable tax-free holding stations for capital gains. That's the bedrock on which your foundation and all large foundations have prospered.

''So then, the way I see it, soon after your widowed mother began her long decline into death, you recognized that you had to do something about her estate, which amounted to a large house in Tallahassee and a rather decent portfolio. As her ward, you could either liquidate the estate or keep it until your inheritance as the only child. Either way, you'd pay a hell of a tax—capital gains and/or inheritance. So, with five hundred dollars you established the Tremaine Fund, ostensibly a charitable foundation designed to provide study grants and financial aid to struggling attorneys.

''Your mother dies, and you turn over her house and investments, which amount to some two hundred grand—and which stand to incur a huge capital gain on long-term appreciation—to the Tremaine Fund. By doing that you avoid paying a gift tax, because the investment has gone to a tax-free foundation. Then you have the foundation sell the investment, which enables you to escape paying a capital gains tax. That done, the foundation lends you, the original donor, the entire liquid sum at one percent interest. How come you get such a good rate? Because foundations aren't required to charge the going rate when they make loans. They can charge any rate they want, and it's usually nominal because they're usually lending to their originating angels.

"So you help a few lawyers get on their feet to further legitimize your foundation, then you invest the remaining part of the tax-free, one-percent loan in tax-free municipals which, in turn, pay you three percent, tax-free.

"Then you get down to some really serious operating. Using the same process—borrowing tax-free money at ridiculously low rates—you buy into small companies, gain control of both management and cash funds, and find even more low-interest loans. It doesn't take too many years to parlay your original five hundred bucks into millions. Believe me, Stan, I've found that, at the time you were doing all this, if anything was financially possible, a foundation could do it—completely free of public supervision or regulation. You name it, and it could be done—tax-free and absolutely legal all the way. It's hampered, but not too severely, today, and that's what my subcommittee is looking into. Where do U.S. laws stand, and can they be amended to provide badly needed federal revenue?"

Tremaine said, "Hand me the bottle."

Quigg passed the Scotch, then loosened his tie. "God, if you could do that with five hundred, just imagine what Rettung must have started out with."

"Imagine, hell," Tremaine said, sounding slightly defensive, "they opened in 1950-something with seven million. And that was when a buck was a buck. Rettung soon became one of the largest and most muscular operations in the world, with some twenty-seven subsidiary foundations acquiring and lending to each other, over and over, without paying any kind of serious stateside taxes."

"Well," the congressman said, "as Rettung's North American legal rep, you must be making a nice piece of change on top of your own wheeling and dealing. How come Rettung has never invited you to join its board?"

"We both like things this way. I've made my own pile and I

don't need the hassle. But I do like the association because it
lends a certain cachet to my personal reputation. Rettung likes
it because I'm a savvy, rich-enough U.S. lawyer who isn't always putting the arm on them. Besides, an old army buddy of
mine, the novelist Frank Cooper, was on the board until he got
murdered recently, and between the two of us we were making
out very well. Very well indeed.''

Quigg splashed more Scotch into Tremaine's glass. "Yeah.
Too bad about Cooper. He was one of my favorite authors.
Great stories. Great.''

"Damn straight. Weren't any better.''

Quigg cleared his throat. "You know, Stan, you guys at Rettung ought to start worrying a bit about how you stand to be
treated here in the States. There's a lot of agitation on my subcommittee, for instance, for laying some new hard-nose regs
on the way international foundations do things.''

"Oh?''

"Yep.''

"Tell me about it.''

"Can't. Wouldn't be ethical at this stage. I've already told
you too much, just bringing up the possibility. But you really
ought to start watching your flanks.''

There was a moment of silence.

Tremaine said, "You don't mind if I mention this to our
lobby group, do you?''

Quigg shrugged. "Just don't name your source.''

Another silence.

"Is there anything else we could be doing, Fen?''

"Well, you—Rettung—could eyeball each member of the
sub. Ask them personally if there's anything you can do to reduce government interference in your U.S. operations. But,
come to think of it, that smacks of prior knowledge and could
get a little hairy.''

"So what do we do, then?''

"You could talk to me. The subcommittee goes along pretty
much with what I want, I've discovered.''

"Could we contribute to your campaign kitty?''

"There are formal limits to such contributions. Set by law.''

"But that law doesn't reach offshore banks," Tremaine said

slowly. "Or forbid contributions to any number of political action committees that might operate in your interest. Or restrict the amounts you might receive via escrow investment funds a specified number of years after your retirement from public service. The possibilities are legion, as the saying goes."

"That's true."

"What say I work up something?"

Quigg shrugged again, then slowly drained his glass. "It's a free country."

Tremaine tossed off his drink, sat for a moment, blinking, then yawned noisily and consulted his watch. "Good God. Time for bed."

"Yeah. Big day tomorrow. The subcommittee's examining philanthropic networking, worldwide. Would you like to attend? The session starts at eleven."

"Thanks, no. I've got blue hell waiting for me in Jacksonville, what with the Cooper estate settlement and all."

"I've been reading about that in the *Post*. Young Cooper has come into a real pile, it appears."

"Yes, he's pretty well off now." Tremaine paused. "Coming?"

"No, you run along. I'm going to have a nightcap and do some thinking. Sure glad I finally met you."

On the locker room bench behind the partition, Cooper closed his notebook and turned off the tape recorder, both of which he slid into his jacket pockets. Stifling a yawn of his own, he eased quietly into the corridor and made for the club's deserted main lobby. At the door marked HOUSE SECURITY, he went in and gave bite to his thanks by handing the security chief another two hundred dollars for honoring his outdated *Times-Union* press card and giving him the run of the place. At the desk he slipped the clerk another hundred dollars for closing the locker room and holding off the janitorial people. He also tipped the doorman and car jockey twenty each to assure a happy welcome if he had to come back sometime. Then he drove his rental car to the Holiday Inn four miles down the road, where he took a shower, slid between the sheets, and fell into deep, black unconsciousness.

MIAMI (USP) — Pat Tinker, chief of the Chronos media empire and close friend of four other prominent U.S. business and political personalities murdered by sniper fire in the past month, was himself shot to death aboard his yacht today as he set sail for "sanctuary in the Caribbean."

Tinker had joked at a Chronos board meeting yesterday that "it's getting to be downright chic to be sniped at these days—literally—and, since I've always dreaded being one of the crowd, I'm going to take some accumulated vacation and head for open water."

The media giant's quips about his need for "sanctuary" and "taking it on the lam" proved to be grimly portentous. As his luxurious craft slipped away from its berth at an exclusive East River yacht club, a shot fired from a riverside building blew him out of his deck chair, according to police reports.

(MORE TO KUM)

(Desk Eds: This, the latest in the rash of sniper killings of prominent Americans, has sparked unprecedented consternation among the so-called Elite. Law enforcement agencies, from the FBI to the smallest of police forces, are throwing maximum effort into investigations of the conspiracy theory. Even the recent gunshot death of famous author and charitable fund executive Frank Cooper is being reconsidered. Cooper was slain in the kitchen of his Florida home, and authorities have pronounced it a murder committed during an interrupted burglary. But unofficial reports say local, state, and federal agencies are reexamining the case to see if it fits the pattern established by the sniper deaths of the so-called "Ringmasters," Pizarro, Roman, Griswold, and Bartlett.

A comprehensive on all this is in prep and will be on the A wire for use by a.m.'s of tomorrow.)

Eighteen

The Freedom of Information Act was to investigative journalism what the water bed was to sex: the game itself remained unchanged, but playing it was now more fun than ever.

Congress, in one of its rare spasms of integrity, had enacted the law in 1966 after deciding that the government did indeed owe an accounting to the American public and should make all its records available upon request—not just to lawyers and professional snoops but to anybody. Much to its dismay, the government was reminded the hard way that "anybody" included gung-ho members of the working press; the subsequent decades saw a cavalcade of media exposés, ranging from the U.S. massacre of Vietnamese women and kids at My Lai to President Thomas Wilson Fogarty's high-stakes gambling parties and attendant debaucheries at Camp David.

Cooper, for one, had scored some heavy news beats via the act when his local trail led through federal turf. The process was simple: Write a letter to the agency involved, spell out precisely what was being sought, and then wait ten days while the agency's people dug the stuff from the files. If the agency refused or failed to produce the requested documents within twenty days, you could get a court order. And if the base ten days were too much of a drag, direct examination of the pertinent documents could be had by personally visiting the agency.

The FOI liaison officer at the newly established Military Archives Repository in Falls Church was a trim, cheery woman of about thirty whose name, according to the plastic sign on her desk, was Smathers. Cooper introduced himself as a freelance writer researching U.S. military intelligence activities in World War Two, and Smathers assured him she was anxious to be helpful.

"I need to look at documents," Cooper told her, "that cover a 1945 army counterintelligence operation code-named 'Slingshot.' Not just the operational reports but also the dossiers of the participating German principals, if they're still available."

"Well, then," Smathers said, punching cheerily at the keyboard of a computer on her desk, "that shouldn't be too big a prob. You've got a date and a code name, and that should speed things up a good bit. You have no idea how many people want us to provide historical documents on incidents they don't know when they happened or what they were called or who was in them and all that kind of basic stuff. They just write in or stop by, asking for all sorts of weird material and expecting us to produce it in two minutes."

"I hope I don't cause you too much trouble."

The woman's eyes flitted back and forth as she scanned her scrolling computer screen. "No way. Not with the lead you gave me. Army counterintelligence isn't too big a category here, and most of those activities with code names were handled by CIC. Our CIC files are pretty complete."

"CIC—the Counter Intelligence Corps, right?"

"You got it. Of course, Eisenhower's G-Two had its own CI Branch, but that was a staff section and so most of its work is integrated in our files on United States Forces European Theater, and like that. In War Two, CIC had a peculiar kind of autonomy. It was small in numbers, and its teams were attached to various units for pay and quarters and general adminitration, while getting their operational orders out of its headquarters at Theater level. The teams specialized in security procedures and the investigation of enemy political personalities and civilian resistance movements and sedition and things like that. Hey—here we are. Just as I thought. Slingshot. Classified Top Secret in December, 1944, reduced to Confidential in 1952, then entirely declassified four years later. It's in the CIC file and it's on microfiche. You can read it in one of our cubicles down the hall, okay?''

''Sounds great. How about the dossiers?''

''You read the poop, then say what you want. Okay?''

While waiting for the micros in the viewing cubicle, Cooper went over his notes from last night's eccentric but informative wedding party.

His original intention in visiting Washington had been simply to do some document searches. But with Al Milano pretending to be both a driver for Stan Tremaine and an eye for Congressman Quigg, it seemed fairly certain that Stan would soon be contacted by the congressman—probably (make that most logically) during Stan's tour at the Penny-Benedict-What's-His-Face wedding. For what reason was a question that no good reporter could allow to go unanswered, especially if he was going to be in the neighborhood anyway. So a simple tail job from Stan's digs at the new Shoreham to the hunt club, plus a few hundred bucks pressed into assorted hot little palms there, had given him a ringside seat at the very genesis of a king-size exercise in graft.

Ah, Democracy and the American Way of Strife . . .

Sitting there, mulling all this, he felt the old Spooky Feeling begin to move in. Something had been said during the locker room conversation that resounded faintly, elusively. He had played the tape several times at the motel this morning, but for all his hard listening, whatever it was eluded him. But the impression persisted, and it was especially intense now.

The screen glowed, and he forced himself to business.

In one way, Ramm was right. There was an eerie similarity between the plot of *The Götterdämmerung Machine* and the general operational context of Slingshot. In the novel, American agents struggled to outwit and ensnare an SS officer charged with smuggling an atomic triggering device to a rendezvous with a submarine. In Slingshot, American agents sought to interdict Martin Bormann's master plan for the penetration, sabotage, and eventual usurpation of postwar German government by carefully masked and choreographed Nazi zealots. Both plots unreeled in the same geographical areas— the Rhineland, Heidelberg and the Neckartal, Oberbayern and the Austrian Tyrol. Both plots resolved with a vicious firefight and the loss of the prize in a riddled truck, sunk beyond retrieval in an icy Bavarian lake. Both plots featured a coterie of Nazi bigwigs and German underworld figures who were outwitted by a team of American agents.

At this juncture, Cooper was briefly immobilized by the compound shock of recognition, personal involvement, and a bizarre afterburn of the mourning process. All memoranda addressed to CIC headquarters at USFET carried the signature of the team commander, Frank J. Cooper. Here was the same scrawl that had certified his birth, his school applications and report cards, his motor vehicle learner's permit, and God knew how many other documents which, all those years ago, guaranteed that his progress through the pimpled miseries of the minor were being observed, managed, and usually approved by a reasonably responsible major.

But a truly vexing question—who were agents "Ham," "Eggs," and "Pancake?"—went unanswered. Were they, like Frank Cooper, American CIC people? Or were they German military turncoats? Anti-Nazi German civilians?

Cooper leaned forward, staring raptly at the screen, which displayed merely one of the dozens of memoranda:

TOP SECRET

Memorandum to the Officer in Charge
Operation Slingshot
10 Feb 45

Undersigned, along with "Ham" and "Eggs," traveled this date to Munich for a meeting with Benz, Steiner, Holzmann, and Hugelmeier. Session was in the Zum Goldenen Affe, an inn on the Linzer Allee owned by Lori Altmann, the Bund Deutscher Maedel adjutant and mistress of SS Oberführer Max Dietz. Discussion centered on possible hiding places of Siegfried Ramm and his deputy, Adalbert Klug. Several promising leads will be followed by the group. Will keep you advised.

> Frank J. Cooper
> Team
> Commander

A half century ago. Four young men against the savages. And now, more than five decades later, one was dead and the others—whoever they were, and if they were still living—had to be old and jaded and, once again, confronting the wiles of an old and jaded Siegfried Ramm.

What goes around comes around, eh?

Cooper sank back in the chair, shaking his head in cynical wonder.

Then he opened his pad and spent fifteen minutes writing a list of Slingshot names, ranks, and titles.

He shut off the viewing machine and walked down the hall to the office where Smathers sat, rattling the keys of her computer. She looked up and smiled. It was a nice smile.

"All done, Mr. Cooper?"

"For now. But I'd like to have photocopies of the Slingshot field memos and the military service records of Agent Cooper and, if possible, the IDs and/or records of 'Ham,' 'Eggs,' and 'Pancake.' Also I'd like the dossiers for Siegfried Ramm and the principals, Lori Altmann, Max Dietz, and Adalbert Klug—if they still exist, that is. And—"

"Hey," Smathers broke in, "you're talking a major effort here. It'll take some time. Photocopies I can give you in a few minutes. Dossiers are stored in the mainframe computer complex in Kansas City and require a bunch of bureaucratic paperwork to uncork. And forget the service records. They're not available to the public under the veterans' right of privacy and all that.''

''But I'm the sole survivor of one of the agents, Frank Cooper. He's dead now and I, as a family member, should have the right to see his record.''

Recognition shone in the woman's green eyes.

''Ho. Now I know who you are. You're *that* Cooper. It was bugging me silly, ever since you came in the door. I knew your face, but I didn't connect the Coopers.''

He sighed. ''And now you do.''

''You're the guy on the tube and in the papers. Your father was shot in Florida. The rich author.''

''Guilty as charged.''

A blush of embarrassment moved across Smathers's round face. ''Oh, I'm sorry—I didn't mean to be so—dumb, so insensitive. But I don't meet zillionaires every day and I guess I just—well, please excuse me.''

''I'm as uncomfortable with it as you are, Ms.— Do you have a first name?''

''Helen.''

''Are you sure you can't dig out the service records for my dad and his team members? I'm in a real bind, and it's very important that I see those records if I'm to complete my inheritance. I'll be glad to pay for any expenses your agency incurs.''

Helen Smathers made a sympathetic face. ''Well,'' she said slowly, ''I suppose I could request copies of the docs from K.C. for filing with the Slingshot folio. You know—a routine sort of request to round out existing data.''

''Now you're talking.''

''It'll take a while, as I say.''

''Sure. But you'll hurry it, won't you, Helen?''

''I'll fax the request. That's the best I can do.''

''And meantime, how about the photocopies?''

She pummeled her keyboard. Her face was still a bright pink. ''They're in work, as of now.''

''I sure appreciate this, Helen.''

''I can't imagine why I didn't place you right away. You've

got a face nobody—no woman, anyhow—would be likely to forget.''

"That bad, eh?''

"No-no," she sputtered. "It's a very nice face. I mean to say—''

He gave her a friendly wink. "Careful, Helen, anything more and you'll be into sexual harassment.''

They both laughed.

He returned to the District and the Library of Congress, where he requested a copy of the *Foundation Directory,* a history of the Rettung Foundation, a list of Rettung's current board members and the biography of each, and Rettung's official prospectus and the subsidiary foundations it covered. The material on Rettung itself was bone lean, of course, because (as he had learned from previous investigations) foundations had always—since the dawn of organized, tax-free beneficence—been loath to release anything but the most basic information about their funding and purposes. Even the biographies had been sanitized, simply listing each board member's business address, genealogy, schooling, career resume, and do-gooder associations and suitably snooty clubs.

After three hours of reading, note-taking, and volume-and-page-listing, he arranged and paid for photocopies of the most useful stuff.

Then, briefcase packed and eyes hurting, he left the library and drove into the first McDonald's he could find, where he ordered a burger and fries.

Finishing up, he considered calling Stan and telling him that not one muncher in the place had recognized him. Instead, he went to a pay phone, let his fingers walk through the Yellow Pages, and called the Green Thumb Florist Shop.

"Send a dozen long-stem red roses to Helen Smathers, Freedom of Information officer at the U.S. Military Archives Repository. And enclose a card saying, 'Helen—Many thanks from the zillionaire who, among all the zillionaires you know, admires you the most.' And sign it, 'The Face.' ''

Nineteen

They had tea in the solarium of Takai's villa beside the Ammersee. The house and its appendages were a lavish spread of timber and masonry that had been stained, whitewashed, and shingled so as to provide a contemporary interpretation of the traditional Bavarian *Bauernhaus*. Fresh snow had fallen during the night, so now the frozen lake and adjacent parklands, glittering under the morning sun, suggested a huge confection, heavily iced and laden with whipped cream. Despite the great sums that must have gone into its conception and development, the place struck Ludwig as overdone—kitsch, actually—and a surprising discord in the studied conservatism that marked the lifestyle of Takai, who, it was generally conceded, served as the definitive Japanese billionaire.

As a German, Ludwig was not overly fond of tea, but thanks to his basic unfamiliarity with Asian folkways, and fearing that he might somehow offend his host by refusing it, he sipped at his cup with pretended pleasure. Takai reciprocated by wearing a Tyrolean jacket and by puffing contentedly at an elderly, aromatic Meerschaum. How ironic, Ludwig thought now, that he and Takai—not withstanding cultures, personal ambitions, and angers rooted a world apart—could enter into an epochal allegiance, prodigious in scope and implications, and still need the reassurances that lay in workaday trivialities.

Takai, for all his wealth, was not above his own need for reassurance, apparently. "Do you think Tremaine has enough clout to pull Yankee Doodle together? Or should we replace him?"

Ludwig shrugged. "I don't think there's enough time to replace anybody in this mix. The American election campaigns will begin in earnest in a few months and it takes a lot of time to find the right people. Besides, Tremaine's all right. Even if he isn't all that we'd like him to be, he's sitting atop the very formidable army of influence vendors marshaled for the effort."

Ludwig drew a notebook from his jacket pocket and consulted the first page. "As of this morning, I'm told, our assets include three public relations firms, two in New York and one in Washington, which are sifting data—much of it already computerized for use by members of the U.S. Commercial Reference League—that by Friday will give us a precise confirmation of the people we've enlisted. Moreover, a dozen former high-ranking Washington officials and political campaign directors are confidentially canvassing members of Congress and the Administration and have already purchased the support of twenty-one new allies. The matrix for a national campaign committee has been established and we've bought the aid of Roland Ankoff, the former television baron, who will coordinate the dangling of cash carrots before the key media decision-makers and opinion leaders. In the Midwest, Harry Allen has made great strides in pulling together a cadre for a citizen-supported militia, and the assassination squad mandated by your Tokyo people is already doing a lot of good work under Allen's aegis. All of these parts, oblivious to the whole they compose, are in momentum, and so, even if Tremaine were to bobble, the mass would continue to move, our human resource analysts at the foundation would provide the list, and you would make the ultimate judgment. But Tremaine is not really likely to bobble. He's highly intelligent, and he's personally very well connected, not only in the South but also in the Rust Belt and the fulcrum areas of the West Coast. Though his earlier personal aspirations for public office met with failure, his wealth and social connections assure him a respectful reception wherever he goes. For instance, he was recently invited to speak at a meeting of the notorious Ringmasters, who, with various memberships, have placed their imprimatur on all presidents since World War Two. To appear before the Ringmasters is to be certified as a very important American opinion leader.''

Takai shrugged. ''That's an encouraging sign, of course. I'd be much happier if Tremaine had appeared before the Ringmasters after we were in business than before. That's not possible now, of course, what with the assassinations of five of the six Ringmasters, but still——''

''Tremaine says such appearances provide us with excellent contacts and observation posts, so to speak.''

''In any event, I want you to tell Tremaine to stop meeting and talking and get cracking.''

Ludwig hid his resentment of Takai's imperious tone. ''Tremaine is sold on Congressman Quigg. But Quigg is such a lump in some ways. He's often so simplistic he seems naive. To him, everything is black or white. Moral or immoral.''

''He does seem to sermonize a bit,'' the Japanese agreed.

Ludwig looked for the bright side. ''Well, we all get a tad supercilious when we've had our own way for so long.''

Takai made a little joke. ''You should know, eh?''

''Ha,'' Ludwig said loftily, playing the game. ''I act superior because I am superior.''

Takai chuckled. ''Seriously, though, Edmund, you should be rejoicing. The turning point has come. In Quigg we now have the axle on which the Yankee Doodle plan can ride.''

''I certainly hope so.''

''Faith, Edmund. You must have faith. I am delighted, of course, that the computer is already so sanguine about Quigg, and I'm certain that Friday's precision profile will confirm his correctness. But my own hunches, which I trust far more than any computer profile, tell me that Quigg is made to order. As a commodity, he's smart, attractive, and, when the occasion demands, enormously personable. In my Congress-watching, I've had the opportunity to study him in action, and the total impression was that Quigg, for all his bombast and middle-class gaucheries, was a straight and attractive arrow. But my hunch mechanism said something else lurked there, and with Stanley Tremaine's electrifying report that Quigg is really a rascal—purely corrupt, single-mindedly ruthless in his pursuit of graft—well, I couldn't be more pleased. He has put us on the march."

"Well, I'd feel a lot easier if Matthew Cooper had been tucked away. I can't imagine why it's taken so long for your people to do something about him."

This smacked of criticism, and Ludwig's heart sank. With Takai, there were certain lines one never crossed. He liked jokes, yes, and made them frequently. But it was quite obvious that he did not appreciate jokes when they were on him. He was even less tolerant of gratuitious criticism—criticism of any blend, actually—and Ludwig feared that he'd unwittingly entered taboo territory.

Once again, though, Takai surprised him by agreeing. "You are not alone in your puzzlement, my friend. I have sent some of my best technicians against him, only to have the technicians outwitted and victimized. But I am moving to correct all that."

"Sorry. I get quite discouraged sometimes. I—"

"Faith, Edmund. Faith."

With nothing left to say, they fell silent.

Ludwig's uneasiness compounded, melding with guilt. The mere mention of faith could do that, overcoming in an instant his years of suppressing his God—and—church heritage. As the son of a dairy farmer, he was steeped in Bavarian Catholicism and its ethos, but the subsequent decades of striving, of making it up the socioeconomic mountain, had served ultimately as a spiritual novocaine, numbing him to the jabs of conscience and his inherited passion for justice and righteousness. Rettung Internationale, the quintessential do-gooder agency, was in fact an apt metaphor for his own persona. On the obverse were altruism and generosity; on the underside lurked a ruthless, insatiable lusting for material wealth and its concomitant power. By directing Rettung's worthy affairs he had gained, through a kind of osmosis, a sense of being good himself—or at least better than he occasionally perceived himself to be. Yet on the reverse side of his general Gemütlich-keit lurked this dark hunger and its attending—what? Uneasi-ness-cum-guilt?

The echo of childhood confessionals?

Takai broke the silence. Examining the coals in his pipe, he said, "I want you to concentrate on Tremaine. Put real pres-sure on him. He must nail down Quigg and put him to work at once. He must accelerate the overall process even more. The preparatory publicity has been going extremely well, I think, with maximum coverage of the assassination schedule in par-ticular. Tell him to step up the key disbursements, the conclu-sive winnowing. And remind him that, although he's expected to maintain the strictest confidentiality, he must be sure that his maneuverings have at least the superficial appearance of legal-ity. This in case they come to the attention of the nonparticipat-ing media, or are otherwise exposed. However things go in the States, though—win or lose—Rettung people simply must not in any way be linked to the exercise."

"Tremaine is quite experienced at this kind of thing," Lud-wig said.

"I expect him to prove that to me."

"I still say that Matt Cooper poses the major immediate threat. He's the only unaligned American individual with a, ah, an understanding of things."

Takai said nothing, which said much more than if he had made a speech. He left the window and crossed to his huge desk, where he stood, fingering the telephone, and Ludwig un-derstood that the meeting was over.

"Well, then, I'd better get back to Munich. There are many things to do. Thanks for the tea."

As Ludwig made for the door, Takai added softly, "Cooper will, one way or another, be persuaded."

"I have no doubt of that, my friend. Your powers of persua-sion are legendary."

Twenty

Nickerson liked his new digs in the Water Street house. The living-dining room, kitchenette, bedroom, and full bath constituted luxury he'd never known, not so much because of the number of rooms—he'd had the same in his Anastasia Island apartment—but because of their size and feeling. With high ceilings, French doors opening onto a wide deck shaded by oaks, windows that actually raised and lowered, carpeting that went from here to there, plus furnishings that might have come from a museum, it was a suite that would make a nice spread in one of those dentist's office magazines. It even had its own walk-around phone, which was ringing insistently when he stepped out of the shower.

"Hello."

"Nick? Duke Russell. How you doing?"

"I'm standing buck naked in a pool of water, that's how I'm doing."

"Sorry to bother you at home. You are home, aren't you?"

"Yeah, sort of. Why?"

"The phone number's different. The number you gave me is different from the one in the book."

"I'm shacking up for a couple weeks. It's good for the old prostate, they say."

"Oh? Well, anyhow, I got the poop you wanted."

"Hold a second." Nickerson toweled himself quickly, pulled on his robe, and went to the desk. Pencil poised over a notepad, he said, "Okay. Shoot."

"I called in some markers in the Duval sheriff's office, which was the only way I could tap into the police info network without my boss knowing about my doing favors for a guy no longer on the case."

"All right, Duke, I get the message. So I now owe you one. So what did you find out?"

"Well, the FDLE lab has reported on the mutilated bullet taken from Frank Cooper's body. It matches with the one taken out of Billy Logue."

"How could they tell that? The Cooper slug looked like a wad of parked chewing gum."

"There was enough of the slug left intact—weight, composition, number of cannelures, and that kind of crap—to determine that it had been fired from the thirty-eight revolver that killed Logue."

"Was enough left for comparison firing?"

"That's what the report suggests. 'If you locate the weapon, send it to us for a comparison,' et cetera."

"Yeah. Hey, I really appreciate your assist on this."

"Sure. Anything else you need out of me?"

"Not right now. Just let me know if they find a suspect thirty-eight and run a comparison. Meantime, thanks for this. It helps, big-time."

"Okay, pal." Russell hung up.

Nickerson got dressed, then put in a call to Betty Sims. "Anything going down?"

"Nope. Milano's still at the Tremaine house."

"You're sure he couldn't have left without your people seeing him?"

"No way. The house is in full view of the beach club, and I've had my girls on shifts, watching. He spends hours sitting on the patio, looking at the ocean. His car hasn't moved an inch, either. I think he's waiting for someone.''

''Tell the girls I appreciate their help. And you know how I feel about you, eh?''

''Do you have any idea how tricky it's been, posting girls at the club without clients? The bartender's getting damned curious, according to Lola.''

''Well, Betty, everything in life is a hassle, eh?''

''Up yours, Nick. You're supposed to be my Main Man. So how come you're blackmailing me?''

Nickerson laughed softly. ''I'm not blackmailing you, dear heart. I'm just not blowing the whistle on you for running girls out of a house in a resort area.''

''It's still blackmail in my book.''

''Don't be tiresome, Betty. The only thing in your book is a list of johns.'' He laughed and clicked off the phone.

He sat for a time by the large window, staring off at the sun-dappled Vilano inlet and the sea beyond. A lot of things were coming together, and it was time to sort them out, chronologically and logistically. It was tricky, complicated, but he'd begin to see the requisite pattern. Decision made, he picked up the phone again and called the chief's personal line.

''Chief Nolan.''

''Nickerson, sir. I know you told me not to bother you while I'm on this, ah, leave of absence, but I need a favor, and I'm calling you because the cop shop doesn't know I'm working and it would look peculiar if I asked them to—''

''For God's sake, Nickerson,'' the chief broke in, ''get to the point. What do you need?''

''A search warrant. I want to rummage Cooper's house in Jax. Personally, that is.''

''What are you looking for?''

''A weapon. Cooper says he has none, but I want to check his story. It's routine as hell, but I think it ought to be covered, and I'd appreciate it if you could set up whatever paperwork I need to authorize a rummage in Duval County and a certification of any legally obtained evidence I might find there. If I find a weapon I want to be able to take it into court.''

''You know this is a hell of an imposition, don't you? On

me, the courthouse paper factory and the Duval crowd.''

"Yes, sir, I know. But I want to be legal.''

"Shee.'' Nolan hung up.

Tina had never given much thought to war. As a female child of the seventies, when the Nam experience was winding down and the Cold War was proving to be history's most prolonged, expensive, and preposterous game of chicken, her consideration of the subject had been no deeper than an occasional late-night TV action movie starring Richard Foster, who had cute hair and great buns. These, and a few bluebooks and final exams en route to her degree, composed the sum total of her familiarity with the whos, whats, and whys of armed conflict between nations.

So it had been with some curiosity that she tackled the mountain of Wehrmacht documents Coop had piled on the worktable in his carriage-house office. There were message flimsies, crinkled tactical maps, formal correspondence stamped with the red-ink admonition *Nur für den Empfänger;* there were weapons manuals, strategic charts, patrol leader reports, ration cards, mess hall menus, propaganda leaflets, motor vehicle trip tickets, *Fragebogen, Soldbücher,* and *Zuzugsgenehmigungscheine.* Nazi eagles and swastikas were everywhere. *Heil Hitler!* was the standard replacement for *Yours truly. Geheime Kommandosache* was the forbidding designation for everything from attack orders to quartermaster supply slips. The World War Two German military, she decided, had been absolutely label-crazy. Given a roll of toilet paper, the Wehrmacht would surely have stenciled it: *Achtung! Achtung! Dieses Papier darf nur in dringenden Poopenindenpantsengefahr benutzt werden! Heil Hitler!*

She laughed softly.

"What's so funny?''

Startled, she glanced at the doorway, where Coop stood, regarding her with faint amusement.

"I didn't hear you come in. When did you get back?''

"Daytona noonish, here nowish.''

"How was the wedding?''

"It convinced me that I should never get married.''

"It's just as well. Bearing children is difficult for somebody your age."

He crossed the room and, sighing, sank into the easy chair by the window, a soldier home from the wars. "So what have you been doing to earn your keep?"

"You know, it's no wonder the Germans lost that war. If they'd spent nearly as much time fighting as they did writing memos and putting signs on things, they'd have taken London and New York in six weeks."

"Correction, dear child. My dad, who knew a lot about that war because he had been invited to attend, often said that the Germans did win that war. They lost out on the shooting part, but they modernized their industries, commerce, finance, agriculture, schools, and flush toilets on money given them by American taxpayers and then went on to dominate Europe—which was precisely the goal they had set when they went to war in the first place. They won everything they wanted by losing everything they'd fought for."

Unimpressed, she tapped a forefinger on the stack of papers on the desk before her. "I've spent the last three days on this wad, trying to bring the American and German documents on Slingshot into some kind of agreement. I've racked up the essential points of both official versions—one signed by a Colonel Travis, assistant to the Chief, CIC, USFET, the other by an Oberst Schliem, aide to the chief of the Abwehr—side-by-side on the computer. What do I get? A Tale of Two Shitties, that's what I get."

"Isn't there any agreement at all?"

"Sure, on some things. Dates, places, times, people. But when they get into what happened, both reports sound off-the-wall—as if they were written by a pair of bullshitters trying to soft-soap testy bosses."

"I wish you wouldn't use language like that."

"Like what?"

" 'Testy.' Refined women never say 'testy.' "

"What do you know about refined women?"

"Plenty. Fifty percent of my own parents were refined women."

"Do you want to see this rundown or not?"

* * *

She fussed at the computer, pretending to work, but really watching him while he read. He sat deep in the chair, his feet on the hassock, his gaze moving across and down the printout, slowly, absorbed. With a guarded, sidelong stare, she examined his face for evidence of approval. It was important that he be impressed by how well she had evaluated and organized the data. Good organization of material was the bedrock of good journalism, according to Professor Folger, who, although he smelled bad and wore glasses that didn't fit, had otherwise seemed to be on the dime. And, no two ways about it, Matt Cooper was one cool journalist, and, to her mind, impressing him would be like getting a medal, or something.

He seemed to be changing by the day.

It was becoming evident that he'd cared a lot more for his father than she'd originally thought. Things he said, the way his gaze lingered on the gallery of photos on the office wall—Frank, impossibly young, at his typewriter; Frank on horseback; Frank on a movie set; Frank in a GI helmet, mugging with Bob Hope; Frank touching whiskey glasses with Papa Hemingway and having lunch with Darryl Zanuck and squinting up from a sun-dappled swimming pool and snoozing in a hammock—revealed a tenderness that had been completely disguised during their initial encounter.

Which was nothing new, since it seemed to be her sad destiny to misjudge men, to see their strengths and faults only when it was too late, well after her having made a fool of herself. From her first crush to last year's disastrous affair with Tommy Briscoe, her relations with guys had always soured due to her readiness to see something wrong or inadequate in them. No matter how much or how little they attracted her, repelled her, bored her, or inflamed her, she would end up pulling the ejection handle, catapulting them out of her life for what would eventually prove to be all the wrong reasons. Bob Sanders, the football jock, resisted, then summarily rejected because he was so insensitive, and what happened? He graduated with honors in the arts and became the youngest poet laureate in the state's history. Disdaining the overtures of Lou Cassini on the grounds that he had the personality of a fire hydrant, when, within two years, he'd been cast as the romantic lead in a TV soaper. Even Georgie Peterson, her passion for the first three weeks in fifth grade, for cripes sake—eventually sent packing because he lacked a front tooth and was two inches shorter than she was. Georgie was now making six figures a year as a New York fashion model. There were others, but none she could clearly remember, or could manage to remember without reddening with embarrassment.

In any event, the improved Matt Cooper who had come to hire her had continued to soften and brighten in some unspecific way. He now seemed less diffident, more cheery, as if he had completed his passage through the state of mourning and was getting on with life. And what she had originally taken for self-centeredness was emerging as prudence—a wary appreciation of the world's rascality. What she had seen as sulky resentment of his father was obviously no more than a fear of not measuring up to his father's standards. What she had first read as lofty sarcasm was showing itself to be sardonic humor that doted on esoteric puns and witty hyperbole. And—

But hold on: Had he truly changed? Was she at last really beginning to see a man's merits before she threw him out of her life? Or was Coop's new great wealth serving as a prism— catching the average lumen of his personality and intensifying it to a multicolored brilliance that was once again warping her perceptions of reality?

Big money changed people, sure as hell. Worse, big money changed the way people saw people who had it.

Where was she in all of this?

Cooper sat forward in his chair, smiling. "Hah."

"What means 'hah'?"

"Our old friend appears. Siegfried Ramm." He tapped the paper. "Here he is, SS rank and all, as CO of the German's 'Operation Sunrise,' or 'Martin's Six-Twenty.' "

"The man who's suing you. You aren't surprised to find him there, are you?"

"Not really. I've already found him in some of the poop I dug up in Washington. I'm not sure just what this will do for us, but, for better or worse, here he is."

He placed the paper on the table beside him and gave her a wink. "Veddy goot, madame."

"A glob, ain't it."

"The material is a glob, but you laid it out in a hell of a useful way. You're not as dumb as you look."

"Gosh, I hope not."

"Two teams—one American, the other German—reporting two curiously different versions of the same incident. The Americans, with Dad as leader of three agents code-named Ham, Eggs, and Pancake in a caper they called Slingshot, were breaking their butts to intercept Martin Bormann's plans for a postwar, clandestine Nazi Germany. Ramm and his bunch—Max Dietz, Adalbert Klug, and Lori Altmann—were likewise hard at work on what they called 'Operation Sunrise,' apparently trying to smuggle from an indeterminate Point A to an inexact Point B an unidentified something the team often referred to as 'Martin's Six-Twenty,' or, even more often, as simply 'The Six-Two-O.' And what links the two are an identical theater of operations, the same general cast of characters on both sides, the same time span, and the same end result: a big splash in a Bavarian lake. What separates the two is the nature of the conflicting preoccupations. The Yank concern is a clearly defined enemy plan of action; the German concern is what seems to be a thing, a device. And you've boiled down the fifty pounds of paper that says all this to three pages. Nice work, Sergeant."

"Thanks."

A pause followed, in which he stared out at the bay, lips pursed, eyes thoughtful.

"Something wrong?"

"Have you read *The Götterdämmerung Machine*?"

"Eight or nine times. Why?"

"Could there really have been an atomic triggering device? Could the American team—Dad, Ham, Eggs, and Pancake—have *thought* they were after a plan for political action when all the time it was an atomic device the Germans were smuggling?"

She thought about that.

"Well?"

She said, "You sound like a dust jacket blurb."

"You like that, you'll be crazy about this: Even if my father's novel is more truth than fiction, whatever device is involved is lost forever among the glacial rocks under a hundred-some feet of icy water. Today it's a long-forgotten irrelevance—like the war it was part of. So, then, why would Dad, when facing the reality and moment of his own death, scrawl the code signal for the damned thing?"

She shrugged. "Maybe the device isn't so lost after all. Maybe it's still around, or something like that, and your father knew it and was warning somebody."

He gave her a long, unblinking stare.

After a time she waggled a hand. "Are you still here amongst us?"

"You are indeed not so dumb as you look, Mennen."

"You mean I said something good?"

The intercom warbled and Tina pressed the answer button. Cooper said, "Yes, Mrs. Farman?"

"Mr. Tremaine is on line one. He wants to know if any of us have heard from you yet today, because he hasn't. I told him you haven't phoned me—that's no lie, certainly—but I'll check Miss Mennen. What should I say now?"

"Tell him that I've talked to Tina and plan to call him tomorrow—ship-to-shore—at around seven A.M. Jax time."

"Ship-to-shore?"

"Mm."

"What if he wants to talk to Miss Mennen?"

"Tell him she just left. She's starting a two-week vacation—a visit with her folks in Philadelphia."

Mrs. Farman's embarrassment and impatience were evident in the brief pause. She said then, "I simply don't understand why we have to play these children's games with Mr. Tremaine, of all people. He's trying to help us, after all, and I'm very uncomfortable misleading him this way."

"Steady on, dear lady. I'm not singling him out. There are very important business reasons to keep everybody thinking that I'm out of town. Literally everybody but you, Tina, Manfred and Nick. Anybody else wants to talk to me, tell them I'll be back to them."

Mrs. Farman sighed audibly and clicked off the intercom.

Tina said, "Tremaine will be coming here tomorrow. He's going to have lunch with a client, he said, then he'll stop by here to pick up a file. If I'm supposed to be in Philly, I'd better not come to work."

"But you *will* be in Philly. I want you to go there, see your folks, then wait until I call with instructions on when and where to meet me in Frankfurt."

"*Frankfurt?* Germany?"

"The same."

She sputtered. "I can't go to Germany, damn it. I've got a job I have to go back to, and within the framework of that job, I'm picking up steam on a humongous story I don't want to cool."

"We'll only be a few days. A week at the most. The way I count your vacation time, you'll be back with a couple of days to spare. You have a passport?"

"All Mennens have passports. My daddy has made it one of the requirements for membership in our family. So what the hell are we going to do in Germany?"

"Interviews. Paper trail searches. I'll need your German. You'll be doing there what you're doing here."

"What I'm doing here mainly is working on a story. You're part-time, remember?"

"What story is so important it takes precedence over an all-expense trip to Sound-of-Musics-ville?"

"A damned good story, it looks like. Fast-lane stuff."

"Ah, a scandal in the Rose Petal Crochet Club?"

"Come on, Coop, enough with the condescension. You aren't the only reporter who gets good stuff. Give me a break."

"Well, tell me what the story's about."

"The hell I will."

"Why?"

"I don't want you to steal it."

"Hey, I'm an unemployed journalist. Why should I steal something when I don't have anyplace to get it published?"

"You can freelance anything you want, anywhere, anytime. Don't give me that unemployed crap."

"Tell you what: When you're not working on my stuff, you

can cover your story by phone from Germany. Put it on my bill. You can cover some of it by phone, can't you?''

"Some of it, yes."

"Well, then."

"I'll have to clear some of the angles with my boss. You don't mind if I use your phone on my paper's business?''

"You got it."

"And I have some relatives over there. In a Bavarian village called Himmelsdorf. Would it be okay if I made a side trip to say hello?''

"Better yet, make their place your base. I'll know where to get you when I need you.''

"I'll not be traveling with you all the time, then?"

"Not unless you want to make it look like we're living in sin."

"Sheesh."

He punched the intercom button. "Mrs. Farman, please give Tina my telephone charge number, will you? And arrange some air tickets to Philly in Tina's name." He glanced at Tina. "How much time do you need to buy new underwear and socks and get them into a duffel?''

"Give me two days. Tomorrow and Friday."

"Make them first class for Saturday, Mrs. Farman. And then get her some open tickets, first class, dates to come, from Philly to Frankfurt and back to Jax.''

Mrs. Farman's amplified voice was enthusiastic. "Oh, Tina, this is exciting. Aren't you thrilled?''

"My bosom is heaving and my face is radiant."

Twenty-one

Morning, Stan.''

"Coop, for God's sake, where have you been? I've been waiting to hear from you for two days."

"What's up? Why all the urgency?"

"There will be a memorial service for Anton Rettung a week from today. In Munich."

"That's nice. He should have a memorial service, all right. Good man. Do you think his death was one of all these assassinations we've been having these days? Pizarro, Roman, Bartlett, Griswold—God knows who else tomorrow, maybe. And now the fever is spreading, say, with the usual copycat killers popping up in Europe?"

"No, nothing that dramatic. He simply had a fatal stroke in his Bavarian home. Two board members—Ludwig and Takai—were with him when it happened."

"Well, ah, is there something I should be doing about this? Send flowers, maybe?"

"You should attend the service. That's why I called. To get you to the service."

"No way. I can't make it. I'm far out to sea. The only clothes I have are sneakers."

"He was a lifelong friend of your father's. It's your duty to represent your family."

"Why? My family's dead, too."

"Protocol. Courtesy. Respect."

"Theatrics. Posturing. Hypocrisy."

"Well, now—"

"Come on, Stan, get real. I didn't even know the man."

"That's true, but certain things pending can be helped by such a gesture."

"I haven't the foggiest notion of what you're talking about. What pending things?"

"I have been quietly approached by several members of the Rettung board. They aren't—comfortable—with the current arrangement, in which Edmund von Ludwig, the managing director, has assumed the chair. He was elected after you declined to succeed your father on the board. There are signs, according to the members who have contacted me, that Ludwig is getting dictatorial now that Herr Rettung is gone. I've been asked to do some things for the three, and—"

"Hold on. I don't recall declining a seat on the board."

"I declined for you. I thought you weren't interested."

"But I am interested."

"Since when?"

"Since you declined for me."

"Coop, you just aren't making any sense—"

"There's something you apparently don't understand yet, Counselor. You can set up my bank accounts. You can tell me how to buy a refrigerator. You can hire or fire handymen and gardeners in my name. You can buy a thousand shares of Amalgamated Shoelaces in my name, and you can even vote the shares in my name. You can manage my money and my estate. But, by God, you can't manage me. You can't tell me what to do and when to do it, what I think or what I don't think. That's for me to do. And if I'm invited to join Brownie Troop

Number Five, I'll goddamn well make up my own mind as to whether I'll accept or not."

"Let me get this straight, Coop. Are you telling me you actually *want* to be on the Rettung board?"

"That's what I'm telling you. It's a good cause, and I'm not doing too much for the next hundred years, so why shouldn't I give a little time to a good cause?"

"But you can't—I mean, you're going to make things very awkward. The board has already acted in response to your refusal to serve—"

"Correction: *your* refusal, Stan. You refused for me."

"Well, still—I mean—this is most awkward—I—"

"Why the hell are you sputtering?"

"I'm not sputtering. It's just that this is a surprise development which will stir a lot of waves."

"Are you scared of waves?"

"Of course not."

"Well, then. Prepare me a briefing. Give me all the background, the history, the major actions taken and the major acquisitions made since the foundation's foundation. Show me the composition of the board over the past twenty-five years, and give me detailed resumes for each board member. Provide me with everything an active board member needs in order to function effectively. Because that's what I'm going to do: function effectively."

"You'd better think this over carefully, Coop. You are going to be very heavily tied up for at least the next year, perhaps longer, fighting the Ramm thing—"

"What's to be tied up about? You're my lawyer. You're the one who's going to be tied up. All I have to do is show up when the court wants me to recite. Right?"

"It's more complicated than that—"

"Send all the Rettung poop to Mrs. Farman, Stan, marked to my personal attention. I'm going to be the best board member that outfit ever had."

"Good morning, Helen. This is The Face."

"Well, hi, there. You're up early. Let me put you on speakerphone. I still got my coat and boots on. Snowing like everything again.''

"Sorry. I thought early would be a good time to call for a little advice."

"Not to worry. It's quite fashionable for government workers to get to work on time these days, what with all the hotshot government types getting blown away. Did you hear? Lawrence Whittle just got his on the Mount Vernon Parkway."

"The Ag Secretary? That Whittle?"

"Yep. Only an hour ago. Right in the middle of rush-hour traffic. Two vans boxed in his limo and machine-gunned it to confetti. *God*. The District's a madhouse. The honchos are starting to take all this talk of revolution very seriously."

"I don't know why they should be surprised. They've been asking for it for years."

"Feeling sort of cynical this morning, dear?"

"I'm cynical all the time."

"Well, you'd better be careful. With all your money, the revolutionaries are going to think of you automatically as one of the bad guys."

"They already do. You should see some of my mail."

"I'm decoated and debooted and sitting down now. What do I know you need to know?"

"Who, of all the experts on Germany's Nazi period and its political aftermath, is the most expert? I mean, it's got to be somebody who knew what kind of razor Hitler used when he shaved. You know: a detail person."

"Well, that depends on who you're talking to."

"I'm talking to you. You're my favorite archives expert. Who's your favorite Nazi detail expert?"

"If it were me, and I was looking for what kind of razor Hitler used, there's only one guy I'd go to. Hermann Feldstein, who lives in Eheburg, a crossroads between Frankfurt am Main and Oberursel. He has spent his entire lifetime chasing, cataloging, and bringing the main gears of the Hitler period to justice. He's a perishing legend, I'll tell you."

"Does he talk to ordinary dudes like me?"

"Sure. Want his phone number?"

"Well, actually I was thinking about talking to him in person, if I could set it up."

"When do you want to go?"

"Sometime in the next week or so."

"How about if I call him and tell him you're coming?"

"Do you know him that well?"

"He's madly in love with me."

"Oh?"

"With my archives, I should say. We've been pen pals and document traders for years."

"Well, anything you can do—"

"Consider it done. The old geezer will be turning seventy-six next month and it'll give me another reason to call and wish him."

"Cool."

"How are you making out on The Hunt for Red Herrings?"

"Not too great. I'm hoping Feldstein can help."

"Hey, he can help. If the Nazis did it, he knows about it. If they didn't do it, he knows why."

"Helen, I love you madly, too."

"Well, just don't send any more roses. My boss has the hots for me, and I don't want to get demoted."

"You're a victim of sexual harassment in the office?"

"Sure am. And I harass him right back. God, what a doll. We're getting married in April."

Twenty-two

"Hi, Claude. Appreciate your seeing me on such short notice. I'm due to go out of town the day after tomorrow and I'm trying to clear the decks."

"I only have a few minutes, Tina. A client's expecting me down in Crescent Beach."

"May I sit down? It's hard to handle this notepad while I'm standing."

"Okay. What can I do for you?"

"Just answer a few questions, if you will. About the thing in the gym the other night."

"No, Tina. No. I told you then that we have nothing to say yet. We're simply not ready to talk to the press."

"By 'we,' you mean you and Judge Hefflefinger and Stanley Tremaine?"

"Wh—what do you mean?"

"The judge and Tremaine. Are they playing soldier, too?"

"Whatever gave you that idea?"

"Well, I've been looking into the matter since I saw you,

and several interesting things have come to light—among them the involvement of Hefflefinger and Tremaine. And they—''

"You've been talking to Stan and the judge?"

"I've been talking to a lot of people. Here. Miami."

"My God, you know about Miami?"

"Not enough, of course. That's one of the reasons I'm here. To see if you can fill me in on some of these things."

"This is incredible. How did you find out about the judge and Tremaine? And Miami?"

"Hey, Claude, it's my business to find out things."

"Well, I must say I'm absolutely flabbergasted to learn that you've been talking with those two men. That they told you about Miami, and all that. They're the last ones I'd expect to be talking to the media. Especially after all the cautions they gave me on the subject."

"The old 'Don't do as I do, do as I say,' eh?"

"I mean *really*."

"If this is just a simple matter of men indulging a hobby, Claude, why the heck are you so reluctant to talk about it?"

"Well, if you've been talking to the judge—Stan, too— then you know that it's a lot more than just a hobby."

"That's what I'm saying. It's more than a hobby, of course, but what are its dimensions? How big a deal is it? It's got to be pretty big, what with Miami and all."

"Oh, come on, Tina. Miami's only one of the places. It's very important on the supply chain, certainly, but the judge, being the way he is, self-important and politically ambitious and like that, has probably made it sound as if it's the only port of delivery for us. Well, it's not, I assure you."

"I'll admit I was under the impression that Miami was the only place, all right."

"There, see? The man—for all his brilliance, for all his critical importance to this thing—makes my ass tired."

"You and me both, Claude. So what's his true role? I mean, if I got the wrong idea about Hefflefinger, what's the right idea? And, even more important, what else do I have wrong, for cripes sake? Like you: Are you really just small potatoes? It seems to me you're more than that—''

"Is that what he said about me? Did he call me small potatoes? Why, that pompous, insufferable—I was in this thing from the very beginning. Not like him, a Johnny-come-lately who signed on only after he thought it was socially acceptable and politically smart."

"That's another impression I have: You and he don't see eye-to-eye on some things. Right?"

"On a lot of things, believe you me. If Yankee Doodle weren't so important, I'd have told him off long ago."

"Just how important is Yankee Doodle? As you see it, that is."

"Well, now that they've told you about Yankee Doodle and what a big deal it makes them, I don't mind saying that—the Hefflefingers and Tremaines aside—it's the very damned equivalent of Lexington and Concord. There were plenty of egotistical horse's asses in those days, too, but the events and their significance overshadowed them. And that's what'll happen here, by God—What is it, Doris?"

"Sorry to interrupt, sir, but you have a date with Mr. McHenry in Crescent Beach."

"I'm leaving right now. Call him and tell him I'll be a few minutes late. Did you put the contract in my briefcase?"

"Yes, sir. Along with the survey."

"Hey, Claude—"

"Some other time, Tina. I'm out of here. There's a living to be made."

"Okay. I'll call you tonight."

"Excuse me, Judge. You have a minute?"

"What are you doing in this garage, young woman? It's restricted to courthouse employees."

"I'm Tina Mennen, a reporter for the *St. Augustine Record*. The guards let me in on my press pass."

"Well, they shouldn't have. Besides, if you want to see me, make an appointment with my secretary."

"I tried that. She said you don't give interviews. Which seems like she must be wrong. I've never known an elected official who won't give interviews. I take that back. I knew one—and he didn't get reelected."

"Well, what is it you want? And make it fast, please. It's cold and damp in this rotten place, and I have a luncheon engagement I'm already late for."

"I have a few questions about Yankee Doodle."

"Wh—you—Yankee Doodle? What in the world are you talking about?"

"You know. The Miami thing. The thing you and Tremaine are into. I need some backgrounding on all of it."

"I haven't the foggiest notion of what you're talking about."

"Sure you do. The gymnasium drills. The athletic field storage house. The meetings at McDonald's in Orange Park. The payoffs. *That* Yankee Doodle. Judge? Yo, Judge. Are you all right?"

"Wh—where did you learn of these things, Miss—"

"Mennen. Tina Mennen."

"Well, where?"

"Sorry, Judge. You understand confidentiality. The protection of sources, and all that."

"I've got it. Claude Abernathy. You've been talking to Abernathy, haven't you?"

"Sorry."

"That idiotic windbag. How much has he told you?"

"Whoa. If I told you that, I'd be acknowledging Abernathy as a source, and, as I say, you know I can't do that."

"Correction: You just have."

"You're saying that. I'm not."

"Well, then, let me say something else: Whatever that ass has told you, I categorically deny it."

"Even the claim that you are brilliant and absolutely, critically important to Yankee Doodle's success?"

"He said that?"

"Which he? I've talked to a lot of 'he's.' "

"You are playing games with me. That annoys me. And I assure you that I am a very dangerous man to annoy."

"That's the last thing I want to do, Your Honor. I, too, see you as the brilliant prime mover in all this. It would be silly and wasteful for me to annoy you, knowingly or otherwise. And, if I have, I sincerely apologize. But you are also a very sophisticated gentleman, and, as such, you recognize my need to protect the identity of my sources. As I will protect my knowledge of your involvement in Yankee Doodle.''

"I am also sophisticated enough to know that you are putting me on, Miss Mennen. And it will get you nowhere. Now, please, step aside and let me get into my car.''

"Certainly. Thanks for your time. I'm sorry you won't background me. I'll just have to go with what the others have said.''

"Go?''

"Yeah. You know. Do the story.''

"You are planning to do a story on Yankee Doodle?''

"That's what I'm all about. Stories.''

"Then I must warn you again: Even to contemplate such a story puts you in the greatest of peril.''

"Are you threatening me, Judge?''

"Of course not. I'm simply advising you that there are dark and terrible forces at work here—forces that brook no interference or publicity. If I fear them, most certainly you should. Right?''

"Who are they, and why do you, an insider, fear them?''

"I've said all I'm going to say. Good evening.''

"See you around, Your Honor.''

"Tremaine speaking.''

"Abner here. There has been a development I think you should know about.''

"What's up?''

"I was approached this morning by a reporter for the St. Augustine newspaper. She seems to be conversant with Yankee Doodle and wanted me to comment. She plans a story.''

"Oh, my God. Who's she been talking to?''

"She wouldn't say directly. But I think it was Claude.''

"Damn. I've said all along it was a mistake to bring that idiot in.''

"I couldn't agree more. But we need idiots to make this thing succeed, and, unhappily, he's one of the more useful ones. He has a military skill.''

"Well, he's outstayed his welcome, obviously. I'll have to report this to the people abroad."

"What about the newswoman?"

"What's her name?"

"Mennen. Tina, or Trina—I think it's Tina—Mennen."

"Is it possible she's bluffing, blackmailing you? Or maybe even trying to enlist? Looking to get on our media payroll?"

"My impression is that she's a serious journalist."

"All right. I'll have the people abroad look into it. If she can't be bought like the others, the European crowd will have to decide what to do about her. Anything else?"

"No. That's it for now."

"Thanks for calling, Abner."

Twenty-three

Nickerson had a new Ford—a car he had shopped for carefully and paid for out of the transportation budget allowed him by Cooper. It was black and sporty and full of pee and vinegar, but its lines were conventional enough to allow a comfortable anonymity in traffic or on stakeouts. There was a two-way police-type radio that tied him to the little network of security guys he had set up to patrol the St. Augustine property, and a standard cellular phone tuned him in to the world at large. The trunk carried a pair of sawed-off shotguns, a Remington .30-.30 hunting rifle with scope, a box of stun grenades, and boxes of ammo for everything, including the Uzi racked under the dash panel, the .357 Magnum in his body holster, and the .38 Special—which he liked to call his ''special-Special''—in the sleeve under the driver's seat.

Working for a rich guy had its advantages.

This had been an unusual Friday morning, and the car's versatile communications equipment had come in handy. The first call had been from Betty, who called in on the cellular to tell

him that soon after Milano had driven Tremaine to work, a
young woman in a VW pulled into the driveway, rang the bell,
got nowhere with the houseboy, then went down the road a
piece before parking and returning on foot. She sneaked
around the house, peeking in windows like a bush-league Tom,
before giving up and driving south on A1A. She had just left
and was probably halfway to St. Augie. Nickerson, who had
been driving north on San Marco en route to his gunsmith,
figured that, since A1A was the only seashore highway and
there were no arterial cutoffs on it between Tremaine's house
and St. Augustine, Tina simply had to show up at the intersection of A1A and San Marco. Which, of course, she did.

A good thing, too, because if Nickerson knew anything, he
knew a tail when he saw one. She was being followed by a
green Chevrolet, so devoid of ornamentation it had to be a
rental, which cruised behind the VW at a discreet distance and
matched her move for move.

Why would somebody be tailing an entry-level reporter on a
small-town daily?

"Let's find out, shall we, Nick?"

He eased the Ford from his observation point in the county
library parking lot and settled in behind the tail.

Tina took the A1A dogleg to U.S. 1, then fell in with the
southbound traffic. He thought she might be heading back to
her office via the indirect but more easily driven route, but she
fooled him by continuing south to the junction of 207, where
she turned southwest toward Hastings. He tried several times
to sneak a look at the driver of the Chevrolet, but the speeds
and angles worked against it.

Nickerson took up the cellular and dialed his chief day man,
Bucky Lewis.

"I'm on Two-oh-seven, tailing a tail on the Mennen
woman. Anything going on there?"

"All's quiet here, Nick. Cooper's still in the office, apparently getting ready for his trip. Mrs. Farman is doing her thing
and Manfred is bossing around the yard man, who is watering
the plants."

"Nothing unusual, then?"

"Not really. Except Cooper did something a little off his usual routine."

"Oh? Like what?"

"I got this good view of the carriage house and the back side of the main house, where the gallery is, and I saw Cooper come out, make sure Manfred was in the yard, and then go to the main house and down the gallery to Manfred's rooms, where he let himself in and stayed for about ten minutes."

"Why would he do that?"

"Beats me. But I have a hunch that he was doing a shake-down in there. Think maybe Manfred's been stealing silver-ware or something?"

"Not likely."

"So, then, when will you be coming back?"

"Who knows?"

"Any instructions?"

"Yeah. Do a shakedown of Manfred's rooms yourself. See if there's anything out of whack there."

"Okay."

Nickerson hung up and, settling back in the seat, ate a candy bar. He was trying to kick cigarettes, and at this moment, chewing bleakly, he decided that if cancer didn't get him, toothlessness and obesity sure as hell would.

Tina passed straight through Hastings and continued toward Palatka, but a few miles short of the St. Johns River she slowed, then made a turn onto a nameless twig of blacktop winding southwest into a spread of pine and palmetto. The green Chevy fell further to the rear before it made the turn, its driver apparently aware that unless he did he might be spotted by the girl—who, it was now obvious, was up to something very weird indeed.

Making a feint in case anybody in the cars ahead had begun to wonder about his prudently distant presence, he drove past the turn. About a quarter of a mile beyond, he put the Ford through a squealing U and returned to the blacktop to see what the gang was up to. Struggling to liberate his teeth from a seemingly invincible clump of caramel, he dialed Lewis again.

"I'm still on the tail, between Hastings and the river on the road to that private school whose name I can never remember. I don't know where we're going, but I'll report when possible.''

''Roger, boss.''

Going slowly so as to avoid surprises, Nickerson followed the macadam to its junction with the unpaved lane that led to the school. The VW was parked in the lot next to the fence around the athletic field, and he could see Tina talking with a school guard at the gate. The green Chevy was parked behind a stand of wild magnolia in a location that gave him no option but to continue into the parking lot and take cover beside a school bus. Which was all right, because it gave him an even better view of Tina and the guard, who, after some arm-waving and head-scratching, let her through the gate and walked with her to a small storage building at the side of the athletic field.

She walked around the thing. She took pictures. She made notes. She asked questions of the guard, who did some more arm-waving. Then she stooped and appeared to be studying the ground, like those scouts in western flicks looking for tracks telling which-away the bad dudes went.

''You are one weird female, Tina Mennen.''

She shook the guard's hand and headed back for the parking lot, but instead of climbing into the VW she cut across an open meadow and picked up what appeared to be a footpath. Alternately marching, camera gear bouncing on her hip, then pausing to study the ground, she made her way slowly toward a wooded ravine.

Craning, Nickerson saw the Chevrolet's door open and shut and its driver hurrying off for a line of trees that roughly paralleled the path.

He sighed. ''Where's everybody going, for chrissake?''

Leaving the Ford and moving carefully through the trees bordering the lane, he came to the rim of the ravine. There below he saw Tina, kneeling and sifting dirt beside a large, water-filled borrow pit—a kind of man-made lake derived from years of digging for fill dirt by construction contractors. And between him and the girl, crouching in the underbrush, was a man in a red storm jacket and jeans who simply had to be the driver of the Chevy. He was Japanese, and he was powerfully built, with shoulders that went from here to there and hands that were the size of Ping-Pong paddles. He was aiming a scope-mounted hunting rifle at Tina.

Nickerson, taking advantage of the man's preoccupation, stepped up behind him. He thumbed off the safety of his tube-silenced .38 and said softly, politely, "I suggest you drop that piece before I give you three new assholes."

The Japanese placed the rifle on the ground, then, standing, turned slowly, hands out to the side.

"Just who the hell are you, and why were you going to shoot that nice girl there? I'd really like to know," Nickerson whispered.

The man suddenly went into a Chuck Norris mode, glowering, shifting his weight gracefully from foot to foot and making odd little swimming motions with his big hands.

"Okay," Nickerson said, sighing again, "so you're a rotten conversationalist."

The .38 sneezed, and the crouching muscle man, lifted off his feet by the dumdum, spun in the air and dropped heavily into a clump of palmettos.

Tina's voice came up the hill, alarm in it. "Who's there? Is somebody there?"

Nickerson stood in the shadows, silent, unmoving.

He heard Tina say nervously, "I'm outa here."

He watched her scurry up the hill and disappear toward the school. Then he went to the Chevrolet, threw the rifle into the backseat, put the gears in neutral, and rolled the car down the incline to the ravine's edge. It was a real challenge to place the dead man—huge, limp, sacklike—behind the steering wheel.

An easy push, and the green sedan jounced down the slope and rolled into the pond, where it floated for a moment, then quietly disappeared in a soughing, bubbling eddy.

After sweeping away his own footprints with a cedar branch, Nickerson stepped into the trail-obliterating underbrush and made his way back to the Ford.

Sliding behind the wheel and starting the motor, he said aloud, testy, "Threaten me, and you're dead. D-E-D, dead."

Twenty-four

Congressman Quigg had never been to Jacksonville. He was vastly pleased with the towers that glittered in the impossibly bright winter sunlight, with the winding, blue-green river and its multicolored bridges, with the rustling palm trees and the whirling clouds of birds, and with the spread of highways, glitzy suburbs, humming retail malls, and forested industrial parks. It was one hell of a big, busy city, and it appeared, in his midwesterner's eye, to have much of the good and only a little of the bad he had found in Los Angeles.

He stood now at a huge window in the vaulted lobby of the penthouse Jackson Club, admiring the teeming spectacle that ranged outward to the horizon and beyond.

Tons and tons of money at work down there.

Most of it undoubtedly controlled by the expensively dressed, arrantly vain men and women who gathered at the dining room threshold, which was guarded by an unctuous maître d' they called Rudy.

He peered among them for a familiar face, until the voice at his elbow: "Ah, there you are."

He turned. "Well, now. Stanley Tremaine. How very good to see you again."

They shook hands, and Tremaine said, "My most sincere apologies for keeping you waiting, Congressman. But Fridays are difficult, and there was a phone conference with a client I can't afford to ignore, and so—"

"No problem, Stan. I was enjoying your view here."

"Wonderful, isn't it."

"I should say. I have a hunch I could take a lot of this city."

Tremaine made a joke. "I don't think so, Congressman. Most of it's been taken already."

Quigg laughed appreciatively. "By the members of this club, eh?"

Tremaine smiled and winked.

They were personally escorted to table ten by Rudy himself, who, if he'd had a basketful immediately at hand, would have strewn the way with rose petals. Lacking these, he merely flourished his menus as if they were palm fronds hailing the entry into Jerusalem.

After they were seated and Rudy had returned to his post, Quigg said, "Now there is a fellow who takes his work seriously."

Tremaine nodded. "Rudy has done more than anybody on this planet to establish bootlicking as one of the major performing arts."

A study of the menu served to cover their separate gropings for ways to rekindle their erstwhile locker room camaraderie. Charlie Lang unwittingly helped when his tinkling piano segued into a soft rock rendition of the official song of Quigg's home state.

"CNN and your iconoclastic speeches have made you hopelessly famous, Fen," Tremaine said. "Even the piano player recognizes and salutes you."

Quigg beamed and waved thanks to the lanky musician. To Tremaine he said, "I love it. Absolutely love it."

"I really should have met your plane—made more of your

arrival. But your note was quite specific.''

''My staff was adamant: With all these sniper attacks going on, they feel I might make a nice target.''

Tremaine made a wry joke. ''The victims have all been Leets. As a Middle, you're ineligible for assassination.''

Quigg laughed. ''Even so, I virtually sneaked out of Washington.''

''But your fans recognize you anyhow, eh?''

''That's the fun part of my job. Headaches fade when strangers smile and wave. When a piano man I've never met plays my favorite tune. It's great. Really great.''

The waiter came and they ordered chicken au porto, the house specialty, then, after the wine was poured, pretended to listen to the music and enjoy the view.

Quigg, never at ease in any lull, decided to get down to business. ''Your invitation said I could be of help, Stan. So what can I do for you?''

Tremaine seemed to welcome this straightforward shift from playacting to substance. He caressed his lapel in that way of his and asked a question: ''What are your plans for the future, Fen? Will you make a long career of Congress, or are there other things you plan to do after your eventual withdrawal—''

''Or eventual defeat, eh?'' Quigg asked, amused.

''Or defeat,'' Tremaine conceded. ''Nothing is forever.''

Quigg assembled the practiced, level stare that so many mistook for candor. ''Naturally I'd like to stay in Congress long enough to complete the tasks I've set for myself, to achieve certain long-range legislative goals. But living in raw insecurity as I do, never knowing for sure whether I'll have my job two years from any today, it's only prudent to give thought to alternatives.''

''And what conclusions have you reached?''

Quigg took a thoughtful sip of Riesling. ''Nothing specific yet. I rather imagine that I'll hang around government in some capacity, but just how or where is still up in the air.''

''Have you considered lobbying?''

Ah, Quigg thought, *here it is. He's winding up for the pitch.* He cleared his throat and dabbed at his lips with his napkin.

"Of course. But as a legislator from a predominantly rural area, I know few corporations or heavy-duty enterprises, no blocs of employees and stockholders and suppliers and distributors to represent."

"But your congressional experience, the clout you are gathering as a result of your committee assignments, the impressive persona you are building via TV exposure, and above all that marvelous in-your-face brashness that's so appealing to the Middies are already enough to put you in the lobbying industry's fast lane. You've amassed highly salable savvy and sauce, and God knows what some truly muscular financial backing would make of you."

Quigg narrowed his eyes, a business which, he'd learned long ago, intensified the illusion of polite sincerity. "What are you getting at, Stan?"

"Your chairmanship of the House Subcommittee on International Trusts, for instance: What you have learned there, the intimate knowledge of regulatory legislation you've acquired, would be worth a lot of money to my client, Rettung Internationale. Representing Rettung alone, a man with your credentials could quickly become wealthy."

"Careful, Stan," Quigg chuckled. "This is a congressman you're talking to. You must be wary of such claims in the presence of an impecunious man of the people."

"There's no such thing as an impecunious politician."

They laughed together.

"Come on, Stan. What's on your mind?"

The waiter arrived, and they waited in stilted silence while he served. When he'd left, Tremaine answered softly, directly. "As soon as the law permits after your departure from Congress, Rettung Internationale is prepared to engage your counsel on a retainer fee amounting to two hundred and fifty thousand dollars a year."

Quigg sliced away some chicken, picked it up with his glistening fork, and placed it with slow deliberation in his mouth. He realized instantly, of course, that Tremaine had, with a single shot, destroyed whatever objectivity he might otherwise have marshaled when considering legislation that could affect Rettung; no man, no matter how righteous and self-sufficient,

could ever again speak a dispassionate word or cast a vote—
pro or con—without remembering the fortune that lay within
easy reach. So the question was not whether to weigh the proposal; it was to decide how much he would settle for. Chewing
pensively for a time as a means to disguise his shock and delight, he dipped into his bag of marketing lies. "A generous
offer, to be sure. But I've already turned down an offer of two
seventy-five."

It was Tremaine's turn to be thoughtful. "I'm sorry to hear
that," he said eventually. "My client has budgeted the two-
fifty, tops. So it appears that we're out of the running before we
even start."

"If Rettung can come up with three hundred even, I'll be
inclined favorably. Provided, of course, that the fee itself is
augmented by reimbursement of those expenses—travel, accommodations, rental fees, and the like—incurred in the pursuit of Rettung's interests."

"I'll have to consult with my client, of course."

"Of course."

They listened to the piano again.

The main course was virtually finished when their conversation, in the interim given to comments on the food, the
weather, baseball, and the stock market, returned to the luncheon's rationale.

"You still have something on your mind, don't you?"

"Well . . ."

"Come on, Stan. Out with it."

Tremaine, obviously seeing no reason to continue their sparring, came directly to the point. "If certain conditions are met,
a trust called the Lucy T. Quigg Foundation will be established
in memory of your mother, a native of South Carolina, and its
aims will be to provide financial support to those individuals
and groups involved in the restoration of antebellum houses
and other structures in those areas of the United States that
once made up the Confederacy. The fund will be launched
with an initial five million dollars donated by admirers of your
mother's work in restoration. The board will be composed of
three South Carolinians of substance, and they will make you

immediately eligible for a no-interest loan of up to four million dollars.''

"My mother's work in restoration? All she did was update the bathroom in the old family home in Columbia.''

"Ah, but it was an authentic period bathroom.''

Quigg shook his head in disbelief and laughed softly. "My aching ass. You guys really do your homework.''

Tremaine smiled. "In this case, literally, eh?''

Quigg, struggling to absorb all this, sought confirmation. "You would make four *mill* available to me?''

"At once. More, after your, ah, momentum has been achieved. With your knowledge of trust operations, you should be able to do quite well, all in all.''

"You'd be making me instantly rich, as I see it.''

"In a manner of speaking, yes.''

"Tell me, Stan: What am I supposed to do to be worthy of this great blessing?''

Tremaine paused, as Quigg knew he would. There were so many ways to get into bribery, so many words available to convey so many nuances in the arts of face-saving and self-justification. His guess was that this foppish lawyer would opt for mild circumspection.

He was right. Tremaine, leaning forward slightly, lowered his voice. "It's rather important at this stage for you to demonstrate good faith. This can best be accomplished by your subcommittee's recommendation against House Bill Three-seventeen. Better yet, if this proposal sinks quietly and without a trace while under your chairmanship, your good faith will have been demonstrated beyond question.''

"That won't be so easy to pull off. Three-seventeen proposes significant alterations to the tax advantages enjoyed by foundations. It's pretty high-profile and has a lot of popular support.''

Tremaine sniffed. '' 'Popular support' is a fiction. The populace is no more than a large number of individuals, and individuals support only those things they believe to be in their own self-interest. 'Popular support' is merely the coagulation of many individual sets of ambition, greed, envy, and resent-

ment into a momentary, perceived commonality. To overcome
or work around such a clot, politicians need only to break up
the perception or warp it into a new, more easily managed perception. There's much 'popular support' for the idea of social
security, for instance; there's a common perception that everybody should contribute to a fund that guarantees the individual's freedom from fear of old age and incapacity. But if the
politicians decide—for self-serving reasons of their own—
that this 'popular support' should be broken up or negated, all
they need to do is create a new perception in which younger,
hardworking individuals 'discover' that they're being taxed to
death to support all those freeloading old fuds on retirement.
The fact that those old fuds have themselves been screwed—
paying the same tax for decades, contributing to a fund they
could supposedly draw on in their old age, only to find that
their government has used the money to buy tanks and nuclear
subs and that they must continue to pay the tax out of their nest
eggs to make up the difference—is lost in the new, more ex-
ploitable commonality, which is the young's resentment of the
old.''

No wonder this jerk never succeeded in politics, Quigg
thought disdainfully. ''Well, it's a lot easier to talk about creating a new perception than it is to do it.''

''Not if doses of money are applied in the right places at the
right time. There was a time, years ago, when I aspired to public office. I failed every time I tried. Not because I was stupid
or incompetent or unqualified, but because I hadn't yet learned
how to apply the right doses of money in the right places at the
right time. Today, knowing what I do about money, and given
some time, I could eventually persuade the world that *Tyran-
nosaurus rex* was really a chihuahua with a bad case of hives.''

Quigg couldn't help the sarcasm. ''So why don't you run for
something, then? President, maybe.''

Tremaine shrugged. ''Because I prefer to hold the leash, not
to wear it.''

''Ouch.''

''No offense. Most elected politicians—from town councilmen to the president of the United States—wear leashes held
by somebody with money. I'm simply offering you a chance to

take off your little leash and put on one that is much more worth your while."

"So who do you think holds my leash?"

"The farmers and hardware salesmen and little ladies with lace doilies who contribute nickels and dimes to your campaigns. The bush-league millionaires in your district, like Sam Sorgel, Al Binelli, and Orson Raleigh, who have set up that little slush fund for you in Liechtenstein. It's all very small-time and grubby, actually, but small-time or not, you always jump when one of those bumpkins jerks on your line."

Quigg's stare was half angry, half amused. "How did you find out about those guys and Liechtenstein?"

"Money. With enough money, one can find out or do anything. Although in this case it also helped to have a client who owns the bank in Liechtenstein."

"Why, if I'm such a crook, are you being so good to me?"

"Because my clients believe you show great promise as a frontline fighter against their natural enemies. American society today is being subverted by an underground network of cosmopolitan, well-educated, and altogether amoral individuals who hold positions of power in government, commerce, and academia. If you can show my clients ways by which they may protect and expand their interests in such an environment—as they believe you can—your own future is assured."

"Like what kind of future?"

"We believe you have shown—from the days of your hell-raising, incomprehensibly successful campaign as a Mr. Middle-class Nobody against a solidly entrenched political machine to your star-quality prominence of today—that you are presidential. We think that, with carefully prepared fire-and-brimstone speeches and carefully selected talk-show appearances and carefully engineered massaging of the print media, all backed up by mountains of money right down to precinct level, we could get you elected to the presidency."

Quigg's astonishment, as great as it was, could not quite equal the instant, giddy delight that rushed through him on the wings of ego. He had dared to dream the impossible dream, and now here it was, a yearning taking shape, like a three-dimensional figure evolving in a cloud of ectoplasm, given reality in an old man's crooning of manipulation, money, and power. But for all the roaring in his head, despite the pounding of his heart, he struggled to remain impassive. "It seems to me that instead of throwing off my leash, as you put it, I'll simply be acquiring another."

Tremaine took a lingering sip of coffee, then stared into the cup, as if looking for patience there. "Put the fix on H.B. Three-seventeen, Fen. You do that, and I'll show you how to move up—to acquire, and to wear with distinction, the greatest, most powerful, and most lucrative leash known to humankind."

Twenty-five

It's certainly kind of you to receive me on such short notice, Congressman. When a friend called me and told me you were in Jacksonville, I thought it was a great opportunity to meet you—the rising-est star of all the rising stars in Washington."

"Ha ha. I'm delighted, Mr. Cooper. I've long wanted to meet you, too. I've always been a fan of your late father's work. He was a super writer, and I understand you are already close on his heels in professional accomplishment."

"One does what one can."

"Ah, yes. Sit down—there, in that big chair. Hotel chairs are usually awful, but that one's endurable."

"Thank you."

"I regret that I can give you no more than a half hour. I have an appointment at three-thirty then it's back to D.C. Since it's Friday, I want to allow plenty of time to get to the airport."

"I'll take only a few minutes, Congressman."

"How can I help you?"

"I wonder if I might schedule a chunk of time with you. I contemplate a piece for *Chronos* magazine, an in-depth profile of you and your increasingly muscular role as spokesman for the Middies, and it would be necessary for me to, well—I hate the term—pick your brain. To let the reader see inside that maverick's head of yours and gain an understanding of the source and force of your iconoclasm—your rather remarkable courage in standing up to the Leets and the other members of The Establishment. After all, you are virtually alone in your attacks on the status quo, on the Congress and its apparent indifference to the nation's true needs. You're rapidly becoming a folk hero, and I want to let the folks see how their hero ticks, so to speak."

"Well, I must say I'm very flattered, Mr. Cooper—"

"Coop."

"—Coop—and I'll do what I can, of course. *Chronos* is unquestionably one of the nation's most important and widely read publications. They've asked you to do this kind of story?"

"Not exactly. But I have not only a considerable track record but also—again, I despise the term—a big bunch of clout. The editors will listen to me because they can't afford not to, if you know what I mean."

"You've come into a sizable fortune, I understand."

"Money talks with most publications these days, and *Chronos* is no different."

"You would pay them to publish your article?"

"Of course not. They still have the little charades they play in the name of ethics, and so on. The game is more subtle and complex than straight deal-making, but it works the same effect."

"Bribery, the purchase of influence and acceptance, mystifies me. I must confess I'm surprised that it reaches even into the media. I've tended to hold on to the traditional image of the stalwart, objective, fair-minded journalist whose search for the truth is beyond purchase or favor."

"You mean you have never been treated unfairly by the media? I find that hard to believe."

"Of course I've been badly treated. Most newsmen hold me

in contempt because I champion the nation's unwashed; I am simply not one of them or their kind. I don't speak their language, observe their protocols, or genuflect before their deities. Since World War Two, the American media have gone through an evolutionary process in which their members— once rambunctiously middle class—have coagulated in an aristocracy, a kind of snooty ethnicity that places them apart from and superior to the general population. They see themselves as priests in a holy calling—even as gods of reform and righteousness who ferret out and sit in judgment of the transgressions of lesser mortals.''

"That's pretty harsh, Congressman. I have no sense of superiority—''

"Let me finish. There is a minority among your colleagues—both writers and editors—who have retained a sense of balance, have refused to believe or accept the self-serving professional cant, and still perform in what I deem to be the honest, traditional way. From what I've seen of your work, I suspect you are in that minority.''

"You mean you read Florida newspapers?''

"My staff prepares digests of the more interesting and informative articles originating in each state. You are almost always represented in the Florida digest.''

"Well, that's something, I guess.''

"So what would be the focus of this piece you envision?''

"Your work with the subcommittee on trusts and foundations. As chairman, you are among the most watched, most feared of legislators, because you are the wellspring of trouble—or delight—among some of the world's most rich and powerful. You offer a remarkable portrait of ironic contradiction—the plebe who makes emperors tremble. How did you get that way? What in your origins prepared you for such a titanic role? How did you, a mouthy traveling salesman, hack your way from obscure near-poverty to the chair of a group that regulates the distribution of most of the world's discretionary wealth?''

"Well, now, I can hardly wait to find out, eh? Ha ha.''

"Take me, for instance. I am soon to become a member of the board of the Rettung Foundation. That means I will be directly involved in setting the policy and the general operational course of one of the world's mightiest conglomerates of money and raw power. But both as a Rettung functionary and as a working newsman I am, in a way, at your mercy. I can't proceed in either activity without your cooperation.''

''Cooperation? That's a strange word to use in this context.''

''Not so strange, Congressman. I sense that if I say the right words, make the right moves, you will become not my problem but my facilitator.''

''I don't follow you—''

''Let me be blunt. As a Rettung board member, it's fundamentally important to my interests and survival to have as much current information on the other board members as I can get. As is available. For instance, take Oko Takai, the Japanese electronics baron and reputed terrorist. Not only will I be hard-put, on principle, to work with such a duplicitous man, I must also be forever alert to his dark side—his ability to harm me and my personal interests. So it's worth a good deal of money to me to have an inside track on his machinations, especially the moves he makes in America. But I'll need the same kind of data on the other board members. Since this kind of information is regularly harvested and evaluated by your subcommittee's watchdog unit, I am willing to contribute two hundred and fifty thousand dollars to your personal account—in whatever form—for a look at your dossier on the Rettung board.''

''You are attempting to bribe me?''

''Not at all. I am offering you a campaign contribution. I want very much to see you in the U.S. Senate. I think it's only fair that if I help you get there you should help to protect me against the wiles of a ruthless board.''

''There's a problem with that. I have been asked by a group of very influential people to run for president.''

''*Really?*''

''Yes.''

''Now that's wonderful news. Will you accept?''

''This is still confidential, of course. But I think I might just take them up on the offer.''

''Then count me in for five hundred thousand.''

"Well, I must say that's a tidy sum."

"You better believe it is, Congressman."

"The dossier is quite fat."

"Will this check I'm writing permit me to read it? And get whatever updates follow?"

"Of course. At once, by fax. But no checks to me, please. Checks are usually made out to the Lucy T. Quigg Foundation."

"Lucy T.?"

"That's right."

"There you are, Congressman. And here's my card and my fax number."

"I'll call my Washington office and you'll have the dossier within the hour."

"Great to meet you, sir."

"Likewise, Mr. Cooper—ah, Coop. Let's hope that this is the first day of many years of friendship."

As agreed, Quigg was in the hotel's parking basement at precisely three-thirty. Almost at once a motor started somewhere in the gloom and a dark blue Oldsmobile drifted around a corner and pulled to a stop where he stood. The driver's window lowered with a soft whirring.

"Hop in, Congressman."

"Mr. Milano?"

"You got it."

Quigg went around the car, slid into the front passenger's seat, and buckled himself in. He shook Milano's outstretched hand and said, "Take me out of here and into that fantastic sunlight."

"Anywhere special you want to go, Congressman?"

"The airport by five o'clock. For now, let's just drive around."

"Sounds good."

They went over one of the high, colorful bridges and into an area of shaded streets and expensive homes. Quigg experienced a touch of nostalgia, seeing the wide lawns and flowering bushes and steep slants of sun-washed roofs; the best year of his childhood had been spent in his aunt's home in a neighborhood like this outside Cincinnati. The other years were for the birds, what with Pa being sick and out of work so much of the time and Ma doing laundry for the traveling salesmen who hung out in the Ralston Hotel down the street.

"It's pretty here," he said.

"Florida's okay. But it's boring. Give me Washington anytime."

Quigg had nothing to say to that. Instead he got on with the purpose of the meeting. "What has your Towson office told you about my visit here, Mr. Milano?"

"You've hired the company to do a deep-dish study on two subjects: Stanley Tremaine, a big-bucks lawyer and political operator, and one of his clients, Matthew Cooper, sole heir to a fortune left by Frank Cooper, the writer. The office, which has assigned other operatives to provide you with biographical and financial backgrounders, has me on an on-site investigation of the subjects' current activities. My boss called me yesterday to tell me that you'd be visiting Jax on business and that I should pick you up in the hotel garage at three-thirty today. He said you want an interim report on what I'm running into. And that's it."

"So what are you running into?"

"Something strange. It should be pretty cut-and-dried, but some very peculiar vines are creeping into the mix. I entered the case soon after Frank Cooper was murdered in his St. Augustine home. His son, Matt, had found the body and almost right off became the chief suspect, according to Ed Nickerson, the detective assigned to the case, because he—young Cooper—didn't particularly like his old man and stood to inherit a couple hundred mill, which together make a motive for hurrying the old man along. It's all been very heavy-duty on the tube, so I suppose you're up on that.

"Anyhow, Matt Cooper hired his dad's lawyer and pal, Tremaine himself, to continue managing things, and while this was going on, the Cooper estate was sued by a German national name of Ramm for twenty-two mil, the claim being that the writer libeled Ramm by calling him a war criminal in one of his books.

"Meantime, I'd been asking around about the two principals and I heard from Lou Adams, owner of the garage that services Tremaine's cars, that Tremaine hates to drive in traffic. So first I tailed Tremaine and managed to scare the day-lights out of him with a lane-change fender-graze on I-Ninety-five. When Tremaine brought his car to Adams's garage for repair, Adams suggested that Tremaine needed a chauffeur. I 'happened' to be there, naturally, and 'overhearing' the con-versation, said I was an expert driver looking for a job. The following day I was hired by Tremaine. That put me in the game.

"From what I pick up in conversations between Tremaine and Cooper, and from what I learn by some tailing and bug work, Cooper is having some kind of trouble adjusting to his new money. He quit his job as a reporter for the Jax paper and is keeping a very low profile, spending most of his time trying to prepare a defense for the Ramm libel suit. He and Tremaine are going over documents Frank Cooper used to research the book in question, and Cooper has even hired the part-time help of a woman reporter from the St. Augustine paper to translate some of the World War Two German stuff. And—get this—Tremaine, hearing that young Cooper was being given a bad time by Ed Nickerson, who was hot to nail him for his dad's murder, put some heat on City Hall and had Nickerson taken off the case. Nickerson turned in his badge in disgust, and young Cooper, finding out about it, has hired him as a combi-nation bodyguard and security guy."

Quigg waved an interrupting hand. "Why? Why would young Cooper hire the detective who was trying to nail him?"

"You tell me. I haven't heard any discussions about that and my bugs don't carry anything, either. Young Cooper is sort of weird, you ask me. But I have a relationship working up with Nickerson, and I'll try to get a better line on that aspect. Right now, you ask me to guess, I'd say Cooper is sort of buying off the opposition, if you know what I mean. You hire a cop who's out of a job, he isn't likely to give you a bad time. That sort of thing."

Quigg gave him a quick glance. "Do you think Matt Cooper did kill his father?"

Milano shrugged. "Could be. As I say, he's weird."

"In just what way is he weird?"

"Well, for one thing, he doesn't act like a guy who's just inherited a couple hundred mill. He wears the same clothes, lives in the same crappy little termite heaven in Jax—except when he's working in his father's St. Augie office, that is—and has Nickerson drive him around in a middle-aged Dodge that belonged to his old man. Tremaine had to talk him into taking a vacation, and what does he do, for God's sake? He goes to California to visit some old navy buddies, of all things. Most young men in his position would begin a perpetual vacation, complete with yachts and women. That sort of thing."

"Anything else?"

"Ah, yes. The most peculiar of all. He's very casual about dead bodies. He had been tailed by someone in a cream-colored Mercury. I know, I spotted it first and told him about it. One rainy night, I tailed him and Nickerson to a little town named Bayard near Jax here. They went to a double-wide in the wood, where they found the Mercury with a dead guy in it, a guy who'd been shot. What did he and Nickerson do? Go straight home. Never said peep to the police, anyone. Now that's peculiar."

"Did you report the matter to the police?"

Milano nodded. "The body only. Anonymously."

"Why anonymously?"

The big man looked pained. "How was I supposed to explain my knowledge of the subject, Congressman?"

"Was the body identified?"

"Yep. William Olsen, a gofer for Jansen Car Rental in Orange Park. A nobody."

Quigg sighed. "So what are your plans now, Mr. Milano?"

"That depends on you, Congressman. What do *you* want me to do?"

"I'll have to think about that."

"Do you want me to continue driving for Tremaine? Listening in on him and Cooper?"

"I'm not sure. I've already learned a great deal about both through my own contacts with them."

"It never hurts to check your personal observations from another vantage point."

"That's true."

"It would help a lot if I knew something about just what it is you're angling on these guys for. I get the impression you're looking for something, or expect something from them. If I could know a little about that, I could be a lot more helpful, sure enough."

"No, Mr. Milano, I can't share any of that with you. At this point I'm not sure what I expect of them myself."

"Then you need me all the more. I'll just keep driving and listening and reporting. Okay?"

"How do I get in touch with you? Through your main office in Towson?"

Milano shook his head. "That would be a bad idea. Someone might put a link to us that way. Let me call you, say, once a week in your Washington office. Any time better than others?"

"Mornings are best. Say ten o'clock on Tuesdays."

"You got it."

"Now take me to the airport, please."

They made the trip in silence, and for Quigg the day, so brilliant, so beautiful and full of promise after the remarkable, incredibly enriching luncheon with Tremaine and the meeting with Cooper, had become suddenly melancholy, oppressive. Life was so very goddammed complicated. You take a step forward, gain a little edge, then in the next minute the world hits you in the balls and you're back two steps. Living on the rim, teasing the limits of law and ethics, chancing big and fast, that was one thing—the sport of doers and emperors; but consorting with suspected murderers, being on even the foggiest perimeter of their murders, was no sport; it was plain damned awkward. Depressing.

And, yes, frightening.

Twenty-six

Coop gave Saturday to shopping and chores, then, after an early supper served by Manfred in the carriage-house office, resumed work on his flow chart. It was a device he'd often used to sort out the elements of his more complicated investigatory stories for the *Times-Union*—who was really who, doing really what to whom, really when and where, and, if determinable, really why. On a sheet of construction paper he would draw little boxes representing the personalities involved, and he'd connect these with solid lines when their relationship was overt, direct, or public, and with dotted lines when the relationship was either tangential or conjectural. And then he would draw a time-and-place line, on which he would mark the apparent continuity of action evolving from the relationships or from the chemistry generated by the interaction of the personalities themselves.

This particular chart wasn't anything to rave about, seeming to produce not simplification and clarification but complexity and conundrum.

Solid lines connecting:

Box no. 1: Frank Cooper, famous American novelist and a cofounder of Rettung Internationale, a hugely wealthy, worldwide charitable foundation.

Box no. 2: Matt Cooper, Frank's son and newspaperman, and heir to his father's estate, valued at more than 220 million dollars.

Box no. 3: Stan Tremaine, Jacksonville lawyer, wealthy investor, sometime politician, Frank Cooper's confidant and Matt Cooper's estate manager.

Box no. 4: Ed Nickerson, former city detective, now hired as bodyguard and security chief by Matt Cooper.

Box no. 5: Tina Mennen, local news reporter and daughter of a successful Philadelphia travel agent, hired by Matt Cooper as translator and interpreter of German documents found in Frank Cooper's files.

Box no. 6: Siegfried Ramm, former German Nazi residing in Munich area and originator of a suit charging Frank Cooper with libel.

Box no. 7: Eli Abrams, Miami lawyer representing Ramm.

Box no. 8: Roscoe Macabee, retired journalist and wartime buddy of Frank Cooper, who provides key clue to the meaning of "Slingshot," a War Two intelligence operation.

Dotted lines connecting to above and to each other:

Box no. 9: Al Milano, an FBI agent out of Washington, presenting himself in Jacksonville as a private detective ostensibly working for a congressional subcommittee but really (this a good guess) looking into Quigg's possible connections with gunrunning Middies, and who is hired as chauffeur by Stan Tremaine.

Box no. 10: William Olsen, aka Billy Logue, who runs

Matt Cooper off the road and is later found shot to death.

    Box no. 11: Congressman J. Fenimore Quigg, chairman of the House Subcommittee on International Foundations and Trusts and champion of the Middies. He hits on Tremaine for money in return for political favors, is then tapped by Tremaine as candidate for president, and subsequently accepts bribe from Matt Cooper.

    Box no. 12: Edmund von Ludwig, managing honcho of Rettung Internationale, described by Stan Tremaine as being the cause of some kind of trouble among members of the Rettung board, to which Matt Cooper expects appointment.

    Box no. 13: Max Mueller, Munich attorney, originally representing Ramm and overseer of the German depositions for the pending libel trial, now off case, having been fired by Ramm. (Why?)

Questions and possible entries for time-and-place line:

    1. Why did Frank Cooper draw the code symbol for Operation Slingshot at the time of his death?

    2. Who were Frank Cooper's enemies, and how did he get along with Rettung board members?

    3. Who are Rettung board members, really? (Answers being sought via Congressman Quigg bribe.)

    4. Who instructed Billy Logue to run Matt Cooper off the road?

    5. Ed Nickerson says Frank Cooper's death was caused by a single shot from an unrecovered pistol and that the soft-nosed bullet was so deformed lab work could do nothing to identify the weapon or the killer. What kind of bullet killed Billy Logue? Could the same pistol be involved?

    6. When did

The phone rang, a jarring sound in the office stillness.

    "Hello."

The woman's voice was thick and full of native Florida cadences and inflections. "I'm tryin' to call Mr. Matt Cooper. Is this the right number?"

Cooper laughed softly. "Well, now—Mrs. Beatty. How are you tonight, my dear?"

"That you, Mr. Matt?"

"Sure is."

"How'd you know it was me?"

"I'd know your voice anywhere."

"I been tryin' to call you, but you ain't got a listed number, 'cordin' to the phone lady. So I call the Jax newspaper and asked for that lady you said was your boss, a Ms.—" She hesitated.

"Gert Shaw."

"That's the one. Told her I had sumpin' important to tell you but I couldn't find you, and she said sure, you'd let her have your number. And so here I am."

"It's great to hear from you. How's Nellie?"

"Still the smartest cat this side of Perdition. My best friend. Next to you, 'course."

"So what can I do for you, Mrs. Beatty?"

"Not nothin' for me. I want to tell you sumpin'."

"Shoot."

"Well, you know how I keep my wheelchair next to the parlor window so I can see the street and what goes on there. It keeps me ahead of the lonelies."

"Gives you some sun daytimes, too."

"Yeah. And it gives me a good view of your house up here, seein' as how it's right across the street from me, and all. Now, I ain't a nosy-bender, believe you me, so I hope you don't think I'm outa line, callin' you about what I seed there past couple days."

"No way would I think that. That old house isn't worth much, but it means something to me, and I feel good, knowing you're keeping an eye on it."

"Well, that's why I called. I think you ought to come up to Jax soon and check your house to see what coulda been stolen and like that."

"Stolen?"

"You've had four burglars in the past two days. Right in broad daylight, for Pete's sake."

"Oh?"

"Yep."

"You mean people actually broke into my house?"

"Yep. Three guys and a woman."

"Did you call the police?"

"Heck, no. Thought I oughta call you first."

"What did these people look like, Mrs. Beatty?"

"First came a young dude and a girl, in their twenties, early thirties, maybe. Showed up in a limo, rang your doorbell. Then, after a long look around, he put a credit card into the lock and they walked in. Were in there for most of an hour. Came out, got into the limo, and off they went."

"And—?"

"Next was the limo driver. He came back by hisself just before dark Tuesday evenin' and went into the house with some lock jimmies. I seed 'em. He was a big guy, big as a ape. Big jaw. Smoked cigarettes. Stayed only a few minutes."

"How about the fourth?"

"He was a Asian type, or somethin'. Short, tough-lookin', with heavy shoulders and big hands. Mean-lookin' cuss, like one a them guys in the kung fu flicks."

"You're kidding."

"Nope."

"I don't know any Asians."

"Wouldn't wanta know this'n."

"Did they carry out anything when they left?"

"Not as I could see. If they took suthin', it was small. Like they could put in their pockets. That's why I thought you oughta come here and check."

"I can't come right away. I'm getting ready for a trip. And I'm having the house tented for termites. After I get the place debugged I'll check out the contents. Meantime, I really do appreciate your calling, Mrs. Beatty. A real neighborly thing."

"It's you is the good neighbor, Mr. Matt. The way you checked on me by phone every day, got me my groceries now and then, ran down to the drugstore for my pills—all them things."

"Well, you'd do it for me, if you could."

"Ain't many people care about a old widda in a wheelchair. And I'll always think bigly of you."

"When I check the termite thing I'll bring a bucket of chicken, and we'll pig out on your porch."

"Sounds good. Bye now."

The dial tone sounded, and Cooper hung up. He sat for a time, deep in thought.

He picked up a pencil and pulled the flow chart to him.

Add to time-and-place line: Two of Stan's people and Milano sneak into the Jax house. What are they looking for, and why do they think I have it? And who was the Asian?

Very curious.

He punched in Mrs. Farman's recorder: "Mrs. Farman, please set up a daily check on Mrs. Frances Beatty, thirty-seven Palmetto Court South, Jax. She's confined to a chair and is very vulnerable. Call the Mayo people over on San Pablo Road, or somebody equally reliable, and see that she's visited regularly by savvy clinicians and therapists. Also see that all her bills are paid, and that her refrigerator and pantry are stocked. She's a very proud woman and would resent any implication of charity. So if she kicks up a fuss, tell her that I'm hiring her to keep an eye on my Palmetto Court house and that these benefits are in lieu of salary. And tell Stan to have our CPAs make sure the benefits don't interfere with any Social Security or Medicaid payments she might be getting. In other words, get as cute as the law allows. Mrs. Beatty is a personal friend of mine, and I don't want the state or the feds giving her the shaft just because I'm hiring her—or because we've overlooked some wrinkle in the regulations. And also: Ask Manfred to run up there once or twice a month and check on the old gal, just to see how she's doing. She knows him and likes him, so she won't see him as a nosy intruder, or whatever. Thank you."

He sat back in the chair and closed his eyes, aware that a dull aching had formed behind them. Hunger, perhaps. He hadn't eaten anything since noon, and there were times his head would ache when he became overly hungry.

Loneliness, too.

He realized suddenly that he felt very lonely.

Stan Tremaine had spoken of this, the apartness created by money. In the old days—God, they'd been only a few weeks ago!—he would counter moments like this with a quick run down to the Dilly Deli, where he'd smother the whim-whams with a mountainous slab of New York cheesecake, followed by a bit of playful flirting with Dorothy, the waitress with the hots. Or maybe he would just take a walk along by the river, listening to the water and the rustlings of the giant oaks and the far-off sounds of the city. None of that now. Now, Dorothy, never one for halfway measures, would either repel him with saccharine politeness or rape him against the cold cuts counter, just so she could brag that she'd had a jillion-dollar lay. And a river walk was out because the shadows of those same giant oaks provided super cover for skulking ransom artists.

Or today's Billy Logue.

When the desk clock said it was time, he picked up the phone again and tapped in the Bryn Mawr number.

She answered on the second ring. "Coop?"

"Ah. There you are. How was the trip?"

"Great, My dad met the plane, took me to lunch, then brought me home. After a whole afternoon of gab and a dinner this big, Dad's back at the agency, Mom's watching some godawful game show, and I'm being glad to hear from you."

"I told you I'd call at nine."

"True. But one never knows, do one."

"Are you ready for tomorrow's hop?"

"All set. Passport and transport warming up on the line. Bags over laden. Excitement and disbelief at full rich mixture."

"Disbelief?"

"I can't believe I'm really going to Germany. Nor can my parents, who think of me as being eleven years old."

"You've told nobody else?"

"Nobody this side of the Atlantic."

"Good. How about your aunt and uncle?"

"They're as excited as I am. They said the whole village of Himmelsdorf is excited as I am. But I don't see how anybody can be as excited as I am."

"Nothing wrong with that."

"You'll be arriving in Frankfurt as planned?"

"Thursday morning. Meet me at the airport baggage claim at noon and have a rental car waiting. We have a date with Chuck Coleman at the Alpenhorn at one-thirty. He'll tell us where to go from there."

"Okay."

"Well, I guess that's it. I really appreciate your using some of your vacation to help me this way."

"My God, Coop, it's a big hoot for me. I'd never be able to afford—"

"So, then, take care, and have a good flight, hear?"

"Coop?"

"What?"

"Are you all right?"

"Yeah. Why?"

"You sound sort of—down, like."

"Menopause, I guess."

"Oh, sure."

"Well, good night, Tina. See you Thursday noon."

"Right."

They rang off and he sat again for a time, listening to the silence. He was about to climb free of the chair and make a trip to the loo when a light glowed on the main phone panel. Curious, he leaned forward, squinting at the label.

Manfred's line.

Odd. Manfred was usually buttoned down for the night by this time.

The old hunch machine clanked into action, and, lifting the phone, he tapped into Manfred's conversation, recognizing as he did that he could no more have not tapped in than he could have willed a stop to his blinking.

A phone was ringing on the other end. It lifted, and a man's voice said, *"Ja?"*

Manfred's creaky voice: " *'Abend, Wolfgang. Hier Putzi.*"

Again unable to deny his hunch, Cooper tapped the button marked "Record."

WOLFGANG (SLEEPILY): " 'Morgen' meinst du."

MANFRED: "Pass auf! Matthew Cooper fährt dahin."

WOLFGANG: "Wirklich? Wann?"

MANFRED: "Ankunft Donnerstag, um Mittag."

WOLFGANG: "Ferien?"

MANFRED: "Nein. Geschäftsreise. Vielleicht gefährliches Geschäft."

WOLFGANG: "Wie so?"

MANFRED: "Es tut sich etwas. Ich habe die Ahnung, dass er Slingshot wieder ausgraben will."

WOLFGANG: "Scheisshausmaus! Ich dachte die erbärmliche Sache war gänzlich abgestorben—"

MANFRED: "Leider nicht. Ramm hat es aufgeruhrt."

WOLFGANG: "Ramm ist verrückt. Er war immer verrückt. So womit kann ich dienen?"

MANFRED: "Du verstehst das Problem. Tue was möglich ist. Aber sei wachsam. Haifische schwimmen in der Nähe."

WOLFGANG: "Abgemacht. Ich erkenne Matthew nicht, so bedürfe ein Photo."

MANFRED: "Ein Fax ist unterwegs."

WOLFGANG: "Was sonst?"

MANFRED: "Halte mich auf dem laufenden."

There was a click, then the dial tone.

Cooper retrieved the tape from the recorder, sealed it in an envelope, and placed it in his briefcase.

He drew another rectangle on the flow chart:

Box No. 14: Manfred. Loyal servant? Not?

Then he made one more entry on the time-and-place line:

Who is Wolfgang and where is he located?

Twenty-seven

Tomas Niedrig, the mouthy environmentalist who had recently been officially apotheosized as A Very In-Guy by the politically correct arbiters of all things cute and wise, had metaphored in his gaudy best-seller, *My Earth Hates You,* that the chain of tiny Bavarian lakes called The Necklace was "an angry deity's graffito, a middle-finger 'Up yours!' scrawled in blue slashes across primordial plutonic rock." If so, Tina now decided wryly, Himmelsdorf could very well serve as the dot at the bottom of the ticked-off deity's exclamation point. The town sat, Disney-darling and unchanged since Hannibal, at the lower tip of the easternmost lake, where its buildings of whitewashed stone and weathered timber sent out much of the world's supply of pickled pigs' feet and ersatz brush plumes for souvenir-store Tyrolean hats.

Taking in the view from the bedroom balcony of her ancestral home, Tina conceded that early-morning Himmelsdorf made Burp Junction, Montana, look like the Chicago Loop. For Matt Cooper, who considered privacy next to godliness, it would have been the absolute, super-marvelous cat's ass. No-where could possibly be more nowhere than this Nowhere.

Coop.

The anxiety stirred again, and she tried once again to pretend that she wasn't really worried about him. And for the thousandth time since their crazy encounter at the Frankfurt airport yesterday, she pretended to believe that there had been a perfectly valid reason for him to walk right past her and disappear into the crowd.

It was very hard for her to pretend. All her life she'd hated it when, for reasons that always seemed more important than honesty and peace of mind, she would be expected to say yes when her mind said no, when society said smile and her heart said cry. *I want to zig,* her mind might insist. But Status, or Prestige, or Image, or Pride, or Propriety, or Tradition, or any one of the other thousands of social tyrannies would overrule: *Like hell you will—you will damn well zag, hear?* And she would obey, because she was weak and wanted to please—aware as she did so that she would subsequently pay a heavy price in self-contempt.

Coop seemed guaranteed to bring on this kind of thing. It had happened the night they met, when she'd played the wise-ass female Hildy Johnson out of some weird need to impress him; it had happened again last night when, truly puzzled and anxious over the events at the airport that morning, she had pretended delight at the party thrown by Uncle Otto and Auntie Lolo.

The neighbors (meaning just about everybody in town) had come to welcome the Wonder Niece from America, and they'd worn traditional peasant garb: the women in long, wide skirts, long-sleeved white blouses and black-and-gold velvet vests, shiny silk aprons and silver-buckle shoes; the men in leather shorts, open-neck shirts, bright-colored braces, knee-high socks, and velour hats with brush plumes. And when the dancing began, a wild, whirling, hand-clapping, foot-stomping *Schuhplattler* accompanied by Teutonic rebel yells of *"Ju-chuh!"*, she went along, playing the giddy ingenue from America, oohing and ahing about all the darling folkway stuff.

But it had grated. She'd begun to like Matthew Cooper enormously, wanting very much to please him, to impress him favorably for all the right, real reasons. So it was difficult knowing that he was alone out there somewhere, doing God-knew-what among God-knew-whom, needing help and getting none from her.

She had just finished dressing when there was a tapping, and she crossed the room to open the door. It was Auntie Lolo—small, round, blue-eyed, rosy-cheeked, and beaming.

"Good morning, Tina, dear. There is a call for you. On the telephone downstairs. A gentleman, speaking English."

"Oh, great."

She rushed into the hallway, bussing Auntie Lolo en route, and clattered down the stairway's narrow twistings to the common room, where Uncle Otto—small, round, blue-eyed, rosy-cheeked, and beaming—held the phone out to her.

"Hello?"

"I'm sorry about Frankfurt," Cooper said. "It was a bummer, and I apologize."

Despite her resolve of only moments ago, she found herself pretending again—playing cool, when she wanted to shriek. "Oh, hi. Where are you, anyhow?"

"In a phone booth outside a little roadside inn north of Frankfurt."

"What happened? There I was, waiting for you at Baggage Claim, and you walked right past me without a nod."

"I have reason to believe I'm being tailed. I don't want anybody to know that you and I are connected. I want to hold you offstage, out of sight. You're my wild card."

"Tailed? After all the trouble we went to—"

He broke in. "Did you bring your tape recorder?"

She felt a rush of annoyance. "Of course."

"Get it. Please. I'm going to play a tape at this end, and I want you to listen to it and tell me what's being said. And I want you to record the conversation so that we both have a copy."

"Just a sec." She ran to the hallway coat rack, where she'd hung her totebag. After a brief rummage, she snatched up the recorder and returned to the phone. "All set here."

"Okay, I'm going to play a cassette now. Just listen to it first, to tell me what these guys are talking about. Then I'll play it again and you can record."

"What is it?"

"A conversation between Manfred, my butler-handyman, and somebody, somewhere, named Wolfgang. Listen."

She set up the machine on the Jacobean chest below the wall phone. "Okay, let 'er roll."

After two playings of the tape and transcribing the conversation in shorthand on a memo pad taken from her purse, she said, "Bad news. A successful sneak you ain't."

"Well? So what do they say?"

She read from the pad. "The phone rings and a voice says, 'Yes?' Manfred says, 'Good evening, Wolfgang. This is Putzi.' Wolfgang says, 'Good morning, you mean.' Manfred says, 'Get this: Matthew Cooper is coming over there.' Wolfgang says, 'Really? When?' Manfred says, 'He arrives around noon on Thursday.' Wolfgang asks, 'Is he on a vacation?' Manfred says, 'No. A business trip. Possibly very dangerous business.' Wolfgang asks, 'How come?' Manfred says, 'Something's going on. I have the impression that he wants to exhume Slingshot.' Wolfgang says, 'Shithouse mouse! I thought that lousy business was deader than a doornail,' Manfred says, 'Unfortunately, no. Ramm has stirred it all up again.' Wolfgang says, 'Ramm's a nut. He always was a nut. So what can I do to help?' Manfred says, 'You can see the problem we've got. Do what's possible. Only be very careful. Sharks are swimming in the vicinity.' Wolfgang says, 'Okay. But since I've never met Matthew, I'll need a photo of him.' Manfred says, 'A fax is on the way.' Wolfgang asks, 'Anything else?' And Manfred closes off with, 'Just keep me informed.' "

Cooper said nothing for a time, and she could hear his breathing.

"Obviously Manfred called somebody in Germany, Coop. 'Matthew is coming over there,' he said."

Cooper made a sound of agreement. "The overseas operator told me it wasn't direct-dialed, it wasn't reversed, and it wasn't charged to my line. Which means he must have charged it to somebody else's line, and that's what the phone people are digging out. They'll find the call and tell Mrs. Farman who it was billed to.''

"Why did he say, 'This is Putzi'? Is that his nickname or something?''

"Beats me. I've never heard him use it.''

They returned to their silent thoughtfulness.

Somewhere in the distance a cowbell clanged.

"So what's your plan, Coop?''

"We split up the chores. Since I'm not hiding my presence from anyone, I'll need some smoke screen now and then. Some shell-game stuff. What's an expensive, high-profile hotel in Munich?''

"My dad's agency favors the Vier Jahreszeiten.''

"All right, that'll do.''

"Like how?''

"You're going to make like my personal secretary. Call for reservations. Make a big deal out of it. Payment in full, in advance, my credit card, for the next two weeks; letter of credit, faxed before noon today. Mr. Cooper's arrival time is uncertain, but the suite must be continually ready. He'll want this, he'll want that. Be sure the bath has his favorite soap. The kitchen must be advised as to how he likes his eggs in the morning. A Mercedes limo must be available at all times. That kind of gaudy crap.''

"But what really happens?''

"It sets up an area that requires a stakeout, which soaks up the opposition's personnel and improves my edge while I'm running around, chasing down information on Slingshot and the Martin's Six-Twenty thing. I'll start by talking to Chuck Coleman at the USP bureau here in Frankfurt. I'm not sure where that'll lead me, or for how long it'll keep me on the road. But whatever it takes, you and I will make daily phone contact.''

"So where will I be? What will I be doing?''

"I want you to case the home of Siegfried Ramm, the dude who's suing me. I gave you his Munich address. Remember, he's reputed to be a son of a bitch on wheels, so I want you to be very careful. I don't want any dented Mennens on my conscience.''

''Not to worry. How about that daily phone contact?''

''If you have to get me, call Chuck Coleman's phone and leave a message. I'll check for messages every day at noon. If I have to get you, I'll call your aunt's house in Himmelsdorf, and you check there for messages every evening at six. Okay?''

''Okay.'' A pause. Then: ''Coop?''

''Well?''

''Be careful, hear? I mean, you don't speak German, and I'm not there to help you with it, and you could get in a jam, sort of.''

''I'm learning that a lot of Germans speak English. Damned good English.''

''Oh.''

There was a momentary silence in which she struggled with a nameless sensation, the kind of inner falling she felt the night of the sophomore hop, when she'd waited on the porch, crisp in her best dress and fragrant with a snitched dash of Mom's perfume, and realized that Bertie Rademacher had stood her up.

''What I mean, Tina, is that I need you more for the reconnaissance right now than I do for the German. Okay?''

''Sure.''

''What I really mean is, I need you bad.''

''Well, you know where to get me.''

The man in the pale blue parka had left the Pension Adler and crunched through the caked snow to his car, a dark green Volvo, which had been garaged in the livery barn at the end of Hochstrasse, behind the village church. There, in a musty twilight redolent of hay and manure, he had opened the car trunk and withdrawn the carrying case, a masterpiece in cordovan leather and brass fittings.

He'd stood for a moment, reviewing a mental list: chamois gloves, tinted glasses, lens wiper, nylon bandolier. Then he'd closed the trunk lid, a dull sound in the dankness, and, after making sure it was locked, had stepped into the morning mists and made for the narrow alley which, after leaving the village, coursed along a line of arbor vitae, curved upward through the meadow, past an abandoned shepherd's hut, and then to a cul-de-sac formed in the snow-drifted slope by a wedge of low, wind-twisted cedars. He'd paused here—puffing softly from the exertion of the climb, his breath forming wisps of steam— to uncase his binoculars and examine the village below.

The church there, with the black-cloaked cleric at its side door, tossing crumbs to a clutch of sad little birds. Right, to the town's central square, cold and forlorn, and its ice-glazed fountain. Right again, along the lane with the prim, gabled houses, to the *Konditorei*. Four more houses, with high, dormered roofs and ornately painted facades, to the *Gasthof*, there. And, next to the inn, silhouetted against the open, snowy field beyond, the phone booth and its occupant, the big man in the expensive overcoat.

On his knees, he opened the case and, in moments, had assembled the rifle and affixed the scope sight to its mounting atop the receiver. An interval given to little fussings with the leather sling, and then he sank to the prone and leveled the dully glinting piece so that the booth came into sharp focus. Satisfied, he slid a copper-jacketed round into the rifle's breech and closed the bolt. The oiled metal made a soft, clacking sound in the still air.

The phone box showed briefly in the lens; then, with a small, gentle traverse to the right, he picked up, first, the man's turtleneck sweater, and, at last, his face and the smooth band of forehead below his hairline.

The silence was broken by a soft rustling in the snow behind him.

He turned to stare directly into the black bore of a tube silencer.

"Naughty-naughty," a man said softly in German-inflected English. "One mustn't play with guns."

The black hole, the world around it, vanished in the flaring of the greatest, most brilliant flashbulb of all time.

Twenty-eight

Hi, Stan. Glad I caught you in your office.''

"Hello, Eli. How are things in Miami?"

"Hectic, as usual."

"What's on your mind?"

"You've filed an objection to my request for documents under Rule Thirty-four."

"So what did you expect me to do—roll over on my back and hand them to you on a platter? The rule allows me thirty days to file an objection and that's what I did—on the thirtieth day."

"You knew damn well I was having trouble getting an interpreter for the German depositions. And now you've thrown a block against my getting testimony on what documents are believed to exist and where they're located."

"As we used to say in the U.S. Army: Tough tit."

"So we go into a preliminary hearing—"

"At which I'll establish that Ramm, a notorious Nazi who has done time under German law, is a public figure, and that

regardless of whether the material in the Cooper novel is true
or false, it was written and published without actual malice.''

"How the hell can you prove that? Cooper is dead. You
won't get any affidavits out of him, pal.''

"So if the case isn't resolved by motion, it will go to a trial
by jury. The jury will decide whether or not Cooper was writing out of malice.''

"Well, maybe it would be beneficial to all concerned if we
sort of got together and had a general conference on where we
are in all this mess, and like that.''

"You're asking for a settlement?''

"Hey, whoa. Not so fast. I didn't say that at all. All I'm saying is that maybe we can find areas of mutual convenience and
advantage. The case promises to be a sticky wicket, and I think
there ought to be a discussion.''

"I think I get it now, Eli. You've heard that my client plans
a countersuit, and you want out.''

"What? A countersuit? That's the craziest thing I've heard
yet, for chrissake. What means countersuit?''

"My client deems the Ramm libel action to be unvarnished
extortion. A review of all available records has convinced my
client that there has been no libel and that Ramm, even though
he, too, knows there's been no libel, is nonetheless criminally
seeking to use his suit as a means by which to frighten the
Cooper estate into a cash money settlement.''

"Oh, come on, Stan. Criminally suing? Frightening an estate? That's one big pile of horseshit, and you know it.''

"Don't tell me. Tell the court.''

"Now just a damn minute. You say the documents show no
evidence of libel. I haven't even seen those documents yet.
And we're still—''

"I have to take a meeting now. Good-bye, Eli.''

"Tremaine? Hey, Tremaine—you can't hang up on me!''

"What is it, Gladys?''

"Mr. Ludwig is calling from Munich, Mr. Tremaine. He's
been on hold while you—''

"How come he isn't on my personal line?''

"I really can't say, sir. I—''

"Put him on four."

"Stanley?"

"I'm so sorry, Edmund. I didn't realize you've been waiting. You should have rung me on my—"

"This is an official Rettung call. I want it on the foundation's log."

"Oh. What's up?"

"I'm calling a special board meeting."

"So soon? You just had one a few weeks ago."

"There is a pressing matter that must be considered by the full board."

"Well, what can I do to help? Since I'm not a board member, I—"

"I want you to make the arrangements. We'll be meeting on the fourteenth in Jacksonville."

"Jacksonville?"

"I'll be the only one coming from Europe. Tataglia and Doubet will be in Washington that week. Allison-Dutton will be in Atlanta. Andrelou will be involved with some shipping things at Newport News. Takai will be in Miami. With Goodman in Los Angeles, that puts six members in the States at the same time. The board will have some questions about the Cooper membership problem, of course, and after the meeting Takai especially wants to chat with you about his proposed ancillary foundation. So Jacksonville seems as likely a place to meet as any."

"I see."

"Do you have any problems with this?"

"No. None at all. I'll get right at the arrangements. That'll be the fourteenth, you say?"

"The meeting will be on the fourteenth. Arrivals will—well, you know these people. Set up the accommodations to blanket the week."

"All right."

"By the way: Takai would also like to meet with Congressman Quigg."

"In Washington?"

"No. In Jacksonville."

"It won't be easy to get Quigg to leave The Hill."

"See to it anyhow. Tell Quigg nothing's more important than his chat with Takai. Nothing."

"Well, okay. Anything else?"

"Call me as soon as the arrangements are complete."

"Of course."

"And make sure Matthew Cooper is back from Europe by then. It's important that he be on standby if the board should want to question him."

"Europe? He isn't in Europe. He's sailing off Baja with an old service buddy."

"Not so. He was seen renting a car in Frankfurt the day before yesterday."

"Frankfurt? Seen by whom?"

"One of Takai's people."

"My God. He's been putting me on. He's been calling every day, ship-to-shore—"

"He may have been calling. But who can say from where?"

"Why would he put me on?"

"My guess is that he's identified you as—what do you Americans say?—one of the bad guys. He's probably found that elusive letter of Frank's which you and all your legal minions have been unable to locate."

"You don't have to be so goddammed sarcastic—"

"I'll be anything I wish. And you'll be dealing with the problem. Immediately and forcefully. Good-bye."

Twenty-nine

They would have dinner at Der Goldene Ritter, which, Coleman said, was a favorite of Frankfurt's upscale locals. But first they'd meet for a few jolts at Ziggy's, a chic watering hole nearby. Here, Cooper discovered after paying off his cab, the light was dim, the martinis were dusty, the combo was low in decibels, and the girls at the bar were glossy, leggy, and for rent by the hour or week.

"I was expecting you yesterday," Coleman said after the reunion ebullience and auld lang syne had played out.

"The schedule got screwed up. I hope I didn't louse you up too much."

Coleman, large, bald, and bespectacled, had a great grin. He displayed it now. "Not to worry. I'm quite used to the insolent eccentricities of rich people."

Cooper gave him a wry look. "Et tu, Chuck?"

"Get a lot of that, eh?"

"Do I ever. If I say good morning to the postman, he thinks I'm condescending. If I don't say good morning, he thinks I'm a haughty horse's ass. I can't win for losing."

Coleman feigned elaborate sympathy. "Poor baby."

"Up yours."

They laughed and touched glasses.

"So what's on your mind, Coop?"

"You've covered Germany for the USP since Attila the Hun, and there isn't a hell of a lot you don't know about who does what around this country. I'd like to tap into your savvy on a couple of things."

"Like what?"

"First, who in these parts is the absolute best on World War Two lore? Second, who in these parts can give me the absolute best rundown on Rettung Internationale—not the PR crap, not the 'official history' baloney, but the real scoop on who's who and who does what?"

Coleman raised an eyebrow. "Why ask me? Hell, man, from the stuff in his novels, your old man had to have had the most extensive library on the subject anywhere. And, since he was a cofounder of Rettung, ditto."

The combo shifted gears and went into a trendy treatment of Carmichael. Cooper listened for a time, chewing reflectively on the olive from his martini. "It isn't all that easy, Chuck. Having read as much as I have in my lifetime, and having written as much as I have about what seems to be going on around me, I've become pretty goddamn suspicious of all writers and what they're writing about—even my own pappy. Even myself. I've learned how easy it is to fall into a spin when I'm doing a piece, maybe to jazz it up, or to play to an editor's propensities, or get something out of my craw, or be seen as politically correct. I don't care who he is—a commercial writer or an ivory-tower academician—every writer's got a spin, an angle he's shooting, and it gets increasingly harder to see the truth behind all the spinning. History? Hell, the more of it I read the more I'm convinced that there are only two kinds of history books: the pedantic rewrites of earlier pedantry, or the glorification of assholes by their adulators. What bugs me is the awareness of all those grunts in the background. I keep thinking that for every era's hotshot there've been at least a dozen grunts who were also there—on the same spot, experiencing the same experience—and, who, because they've established no apparent rationale for adulation or any personal need for self-justification, would provide a hell of a lot more credible testimony if they could only be reached. Well, War Two and Rettung both belong to an era still ranked as contemporary, and that gives me the happy chance to talk to whatever grunts might still be around and to cut myself free of reliance on pure inkhorn bullshit.''

"Why War Two and Rettung?''

"The war, to learn what my old man really did in it and how what he did affected his life—and, bottom-line, mine. Rettung, because it's one of the mysteries surrounding my old man. How come he was a cofounder—really, I mean—when I know for a fact that he didn't have much of a flair for helping unhappy kids? Why is my dad's lawyer and pal, now my estate manager, anxious to disassociate me from Rettung? What's going on in the foundation that I'm not supposed to know?''

Coleman motioned to the waiter for a refill. "Seems to me you've got a pretty busy vacation ahead of you.''

"That's the way it is with us rich guys—always something to see to.''

Coleman failed to rise to the mild sarcasm. His brown eyes, made even larger by the lenses of his spectacles, were fixed on the backbar, as if seeking answers in the glittery forest of bottles and glasses there.

"Are you still with me, Chuck?''

"Yeah, sure. Rettung's a piece of cake. You talk with Benny Lambert, the business writer at my bureau. He's done some big-time pieces on Rettung, both for us and for *High Finance* magazine before he came with us. I'll tell him to expect your call.''

"Good. Do you have anybody like Benny I can hit on for the Nazi military stuff?''

"War Two doesn't deliver a lot of juice these days, newswise,'' Coleman said thoughtfully. "But there were some stories, way back, when the references weren't fine-scale enough and I went to see an old dude name of Feldstein. Hermann Feldstein. He lived in a big old barn of a place in Eheburg, near Oberursel, the town just up the pike from here where the Allies interrogated all the Nazi bigwigs being held for Nuremberg in the late forties. Hermann survived Auschwitz, but his family was sent to the ovens at Dachau, and he dedicated the rest of his life to searching out high-horsepower Nazis and bringing them to justice. He was a regular visitor to the Oberursel prison compound because the prosecution research teams there recognized him and his huge files as a valuable support mechanism. He's got an international rep as being one of the leading experts on the Nazis and their trivia.''

"Sounds like my kind of guy."

"You wait here. I gotta take a leak, and on the way back I'll call the night desk at the office and see if we still have Hermann's file."

Coleman pushed his bulk clear of the fake leather booth and disappeared into the lava of bibulous jocks who, with drinks held high and porcelain leers on their faces, flowed optimistically through the congregation of glossy girls.

Cooper finished his drink and craned for a glimpse of their waiter, a slim little man with a big nose and a poorly fitted toupee. The search was unsuccessful, so he sank back in the seat, discovering as he did so that one of the girls had slid into the booth beside him and was pressing a gun against his lower ribs.

"Who the hell are you, and what do you want?"

The girl, a gamin-type with her straight black hair shaped like a helmet, leaned close. She spoke quietly into his ear, her English faintly accented. "Stand up and take my arm and walk me to the check room. The girl there will give us our coats. She will hang mine over my shoulders. You will put yours on. Then we will go out the front door to the street and turn left for the river. If you do something silly, you'll be dead and I'll be gone before you hit the ground."

"I'm not the silly type."

"Good. Now move."

"I'm not alone, you know. My friend will be coming back anytime now."

"You're alone at this moment. And this moment is what we have, eh? Come on, now. Up you go."

He did as he'd been told, and they inched their way through

the gabbling crowd and, eventually, out the door and into the icy night. The street was quiet, dismal.

The girl poked him with the gun. "That way."

As they approached the corner, a wanly lit wedge of wet cobblestones, he became aware of an inner change. The initial shock and fright had undergone a metamorphosis, moving by quick stages from a sense of annoyance through anger into pure outrage—the progression he'd felt those years ago when he'd first come under fire in Bosnia. The question now, as then, was just who in hell could be so threatened by an easygoing, peace-loving dude who had no interest in them or their turf? A goddamn crime, that's what it was.

And he wasn't about to put up with it.

He swung his left arm, and the back of his fist slammed hard against the girl's face. The blow lifted her off her feet and sent her rolling across the pavement, the pistol clattering along behind her. He spun and leaped, following the sound, clawing for the weapon.

But there was a rapid motion of shadows against the shadows, and big hands seized his coat and hurled him to the ground, and something heavy crashed against his head. He was determined not to lose consciousness, but the darkness swirled, and he felt himself drifting off.

Somehow, though, the mists began to lift. He was on the pavement, lying faceup, and his eyes, focusing, showed him the girl and a man standing above him, each with a pistol pointed at his forehead.

The girl's nose and lips were a bloody smear, and her voice made liquid sounds. "He's mine. Back off. He's mine, and I'll finish him here on the spot."

"Be my guest," the man said.

Two wheezing snaps sounded, and Cooper, eyes wide, unbelieving, found it possible to be surprised that there had been no flashes of light from the girl's pistol, no awareness of shock or pain in his head. Only the snapping sound.

But even more astonishing was the result. The girl and her companion staggered, and their pistols fell to the cobblestones, and they went to their knees, side by side, as if in grotesque obeisance, to roll sideways and become inert bundles in the dank gutter.

Hands helped him to his feet, and another man's voice, close, whispered, "You are safe for now. A cab waits at the corner for you. Take it directly to your hotel."

"Who—what—those people there—"

"They will be disposed of. Now go."

He went, head aching, legs unsteady.

"United States Press. Coleman."

"Hey, Chuck, this is Coop."

"Well, what the hell happened to you last night?"

"You wouldn't believe it if I told you."

"Try me."

"One of the B-girls rousted me. Walked me out of the place at gunpoint."

"You're right. I don't believe you."

"No matter. I just want to apologize for, ah, walking out on you."

"So what happened, for chrissake? Did you really run into trouble, or was last night merely another version of the rich-guy-getting-bored-and-just-walking-out arrogance kind of thing?"

"I'll tell you about it sometime. But bored I wasn't, and grateful I am. And I still owe you a dinner."

BULLETIN   BULLETIN   BULLETIN

(Attn Desk Eds: These incidents, presented in the order of occurrence, took place within a span of two hours. This fact, plus the masks, suggests a linkage. Watch A wire for major treatment of the linkage premise, now in prep.)

RANDALLTOWN, MA (USP) —Four councilmen, a state legislator, and the county sheriff were slain here tonight when a band of hooded men swept into the town hall and machine-gunned their table in a packed meeting room.

Four in the audience, including a pregnant woman, were seriously wounded. Three others were released after treatment for minor wounds at a local clinic.

(MORE TO KUM)

NEWARK, NJ (USP) — U.S. Rep. William B. Dunn (R–Calif) was shot to death here tonight as he waited in a crowded station to board a train for Washington.

The congressman, in Newark to address a Kiwanis Club meeting, was hit by three shots while chatting with a group of club members, at the station to see him off. No one else was hurt in the attack.

Police say the gunman, whose face was hidden by a ski mask, vanished during the resulting panic.

(MORE TO KUM)

COLUMBUS, GA (USP) — Six members of an Army special assault squad were slain in an ambush tonight while preparing to raid a farm suspected to be a training site for revolutionaries.

Reports were sketchy, but a sheriff's deputy accompanying the raiders said he saw what looked to be "a dozen guys wearing hoods" open fire from a wooded hill near the Army unit's assembly point.

Other casualties have not been reported, but two military vehicles are known to have been destroyed.

(MORE TO KUM)

NEW YORK (USP) —Raymond Newell, internationally renowned host of the long-running, award-winning TV talk show "The Newell Post" died on-camera here tonight when three hooded gunmen penetrated studio security and sprayed his set with machine-gun fire.

(MORE TO KUM)

BULLETIN   BULLETIN   BULLETIN

Thirty

Their covert meeting was held at one of the city's most overt sites—a conference suite off the poolside mezzanine of Tokyo's largest hotel. They had arrived in limousines, and they were dressed in faultlessly tailored business suits and sedate silk neckties and glistening shoes; they carried slim Italian attaché cases and English umbrellas, rolled and sheathed pencil-thin, and copies of *International Business Week* were tucked in the side pockets of their Bond Street topcoats. To the workaday world they could have been simply one more segment in the hotel's seemingly endless parade of conventioneers—industrialists, financiers, entertainment titans, political scientists, academicians, bureaucrats—meeting to further organize and legitimize their multifarious greeds. But to the cognoscenti, those precious few sophisticates who could read the subtle hues and patterns in the Japanese underworld's power mosaic, they were the Council of Brothers, met to determine the economic and political fate of millions.

Takai, as chairman, had called the meeting to brief Yamaka,

leader of the Honshu Good Fellows Society and last of the Brothers to accept Yankee Doodle as a viable investment. Yamaka, a notorious skeptic, had held out until the last. But he and his chain of highly disciplined gangsters were critical to the scheme's success and therefore warranted this kind of special attention.

To establish a facade of innocence, the session was carried on the hotel bulletin boards as the Annual Conference of the Greater Japan Benevolent Society. Even so, Takai had left nothing to chance; the lobby and meeting area were under the scrutiny of two dozen young men whose dark suits hid enough firepower and blade steel to equip a commando platoon. And now, confident that all had been seen to, he settled into his seat at the head of the lozenge-shaped conference table—serene with the understanding that simply by having persuaded these men to gather on such short notice he had certified his reputation as the most powerful and feared individual in the Japanese archipelago.

"Gentlemen," he said, his voice soft, cool, "the purpose of this session is to welcome our colleague, Yamaka, and bring him up to date on the American project. It is an informational meeting, with no actions to vote on, no amendments to consider. The plan is hard, it is in motion, it is on schedule, and the progress to date is significant."

Yamaka, a haughty man, filled with self-importance, raised a hand. "All due respect, but are we to understand that the seven of us are to sit here, like students at a lecture, with no opportunity to comment or contribute?"

To show he was not offended, Takai sipped some tea, then returned the elegant cup to the mat on the table before him. "Your comments and questions are most welcome, of course. I am simply pointing out that the project has gone into the operational phase and is beyond policy alterations. This is, after all, the Brotherhood's policy-establishing body, and daily tactical operations are not within its province."

"Well," Yamaka grumped, "one can't help get the idea that we are being asked to sit quietly, like good little boys, and listen to the teacher."

Hasegawa, chieftain of the Golden Daggers and, next to

Takai, the ranking board member by virtue of his age and wisdom, stirred on his chair and broke in, his reedy voice suggesting annoyance. "Please, Yamaka, let our chairman continue."

Yamaka was not so easily deterred. "One can't help being alarmed by the fact that operations, under the direction of our chairman, have already cost the lives of six of the Brothers' soldiers, with no appreciable gain."

Takai was about to speak but old Hasegawa interrupted. "Hold on, Yamaka. Aside from the fact that those six men died willingly, enthusiastically, we must remember that our chairman is not chairman by virtue of popularity and riches alone. He is our chairman because he has served longer, and more energetically and unstintingly, than any of us here. In his youth he was tutored by such greats as Kodama Koshio, Akao Bin, Tsukui Tatsuo, and Inoue. He has served as a fighter in the Kokka-Shakaishugi Rodo To under the leadership of the renowned Higo Toru. As we've seen in the baths, his body carries many scars earned in the clandestine battles against those who oppose our aims."

Yamaka apparently saw that it was the wiser course to ease up. "No offense was intended, of course. Our chairman is indeed an honored and experienced veteran of the secret wars. But those of us here—you, Akto, Yoshimitsu, Tokygawa, Hayato, Otoya, myself—have also contributed heavily in the past, and to expect us to refrain from debate is, at best, shortsighted."

Takai, holding up a hand, moved to quiet the uneasiness. "As I say, debate is welcome. We must always be willing to exchange ideas, give our opinions. My sole point, Yamaka, old friend, is that in this particular operation things have moved beyond basic revision, reorganization, redirection."

Face having been saved, and thin ice having been recognized, Yamaka subsided. "I understand, Mr. Chairman. Thank you for your forbearance."

Takai nodded and got on with the briefing. "The basic premise of this operation, which the Americans call 'Yankee Doodle' and amongst ourselves we call 'The Plan,' is that the United States is no longer governable, thanks to its archaic governmental structure and to the general deterioration brought about by moral laxity, abandonment of ideals and fundamental tenets, runaway racism, and other forms of internal rupture. Japan itself has long conducted open and active lobbying in Washington, entirely legal and socially acceptable from the American point of view. And we eight have benefited by gaining personal control of massive assets in the United States. But the moral vacuum in American social, economic, and political sectors is growing with such astonishing speed the Brotherhood would be remiss if it were not to exploit this opportunity. Yankee Doodle moves us beyond lobbying into the next dimension; with this operation, we are able, secretly and privately, to build on the gains Japan has long since won openly, publicly. But by any measure or comparison, The Plan is the most aggressive, large-scale, and sophisticated sedition ever undertaken—by any organization, in any nation, at any time." He paused, seeming to listen to the hilarity rising faintly from the patio bar. Then:

"Progress has been swift and encouraging. Our American network expands almost daily. Many friends and allies have been acquired, either by direct money deals or by promises of hierarchical or social empowerment. The Americans are showing that they are willing to sell anything—even their personal pride—if the price or reward is right. And, since they are often naive and quickly mesmerized by the sight of quite modest sums, it is proving possible in many cases to win their enthusiastic support on promises alone."

Yamaka waved his hand again. "Could you give us some specifics, please? Some examples?"

"Of course." Takai consulted his notes. "We have, for instance, made additional penetrations of the media. Anderson Quimby, assistant director of news operations for the Alliance Network, a rapidly growing cable service headquartered in Washington, has agreed to collaborate. Quimby is very influential in deciding the content of the network's prime-time news shows. And he is the heir apparent to Will Keitel, director of operations."

"If he is so well situated," Yamaka asked, "why has he agreed to do our work? What was his inducement?"

"Beyond providing him with an estate in St. Croix, we have

suggested that he will be named chairman and chief executive officer when we acquire the network.''

''Do we plan to acquire the network?''

''No. If we already control the news flow, there will be little incentive to make such an investment. Quimby is a vain, shallow man, readily swayed by praise and promises.''

''Thank you. Please go on.''

Takai poured another cup of tea, which he sampled, lips pursed delicately. ''We have already made some key media acquisitions: three daily newspapers in California and Oregon; a leading supermarket tabloid; seven network-affiliated radio stations in the Midwest; two independent television stations, one in Massachussetts, the other in Ohio; a major motion picture and recording studio in Florida; and a nationwide chain of small-town weekly newspapers headquartered in Chicago. These information outlets, operating under a trial program designed by Yoshimitsu''—he nodded at the sleepy-eyed, porcine oldster at midtable—''are already dovetailing nicely with our gathering forces in the American outback. The Yoshimitsu plan is being orchestrated by three public relations firms, and our grassroots political movement is being sold to top-level media opinion leaders by Roland Ankoff, who for years has personified American show business and television special-event fabrications. And remember, gentlemen: All of these things I've cited are in addition to the ongoing official Japanese government lobbying campaign. The three billion the Council has budgeted for the support of Yankee Doodle is entirely apart from the government-coordinated norm, which itself has reached extraordinary proportions, if you consider as a small example the fact that five hundred million dollars a year are being spent simply to persuade grassroots America that it's perfectly reasonable to keep U.S. markets open to Japanese imports and investments while Japan closes its markets to U.S. products and investments.''

Yamaka resettled his bulk in his chair. ''How are we doing with that congressman—what's his name? Quigg?''

''He shows considerable enthusiasm for our program—that part of it we have chosen to reveal to him. I have scheduled a personal meeting with him on the fourteenth in Jacksonville. I plan to send each of you a special written report on the results of that session.''

Hasegawa had a question. ''It's not clear to me exactly how we lost our soldiers. Was Quigg involved there?''

Takai shrugged. ''Only in a peripheral sense. The main problem seems to derive from Frank Cooper's son, Matthew, who shows a dangerous curiosity about his father's involvement with Rettung, our base cover organization. I've issued orders to have young Cooper, ah, negated. However, even in his ignorance of the events transpiring around him, Cooper demonstrates a remarkable talent for survival. Three of our fighters died in direct confrontations with him. The other three were lost for reasons that aren't quite clear as yet. Cooper seems to have gathered a security system about him, but its nature is still to be defined.''

Akto, blunt as usual, said it outright. ''He must be killed at once.''

A lull followed, with the only sounds those faint ones emanating from the urban life beyond the elegant walls.

It was broken when Akto sniffed. Never renowned for his intellectual prowess, Akto, the street warrior par excellence, asked, ''Why are the Americans so stupid?''

Takai smiled dimly. ''The Americans, as a rule, aren't stupid. But they are very hedonistic. Lazy. Greedy. Their sybaritic nature overwhelms their will to create and win.''

''That makes them stupid,'' Akto said irritably.

No one disagreed.

Thirty-one

Kroger Luftverkehr, from whom the jet was leased, had made a BMW sedan available as part of the package. The car had been waiting at Kroger's Rhine-Main hangar, and Cooper had driven it directly to his hotel, from where he'd taken a cab to the many-splendored almost-meeting with Coleman. This morning, since there was no further need to slink about—the whole world seemed to know where he was—he defiantly treated himself to breakfast in the Gipfelpalast's main dining room. Later, scanning the news racks in the lobby, he discovered that, despite Stan's assurances to the contrary, the Ramm libel suit had been made blatantly public and occupied several acres of headlines and text in direct adjacency to the tons of material on what the Establishment media were calling "the incipient Second American Revolution and its bloody prologue." Exasperated, he had stomped out of the hotel and driven his fancy car openly, insolently, the eighteen miles to Eheberg.

A nasty drizzle had settled in, cold and persistent, and his head still throbbed, and his back still ached, so the going was slow. He gave much thought while driving to the frightening confrontation with the bar girl and the inexplicable, honest-to-God wonderful intervention of the stranger with the low voice and the big gun. Matthew Cooper, bless his li'l hort, had unwittingly acquired some hard-nosed enemies, some in the States, some here in Germany; but with equal innocence he had also taken on a guardian angel, and it was this puzzle that preoccupied him. Who? Why? What had he done, or not done, that would move somebody to kill to keep him alive? He was now truly an orphan; with his father gone, there was no one left in the world who had any logical or emotional reason to care about him that much. He'd made many friends of all sizes and sexes, but there were none among them he could imagine being willing to watch over him, and, in the end, aim a pistol and blow away a threat to him.

He could understand the possibility of his having bumbled into some terrible, secret war. Yet as chilling as that idea was, it was nothing compared to the growing, dreadful suspicion that it was he the war was about.

Eheberg proved to be no more than a clot on a secondary rural artery, a gaggle of medieval farm buildings so drab and so utterly melancholy in the misty afternoon it suggested a Dürer etching of Hell.

He had kept an eye on the rearview mirror, expecting a tail but eventually deciding that if there was one he couldn't spot it. Irked with this continuing distraction, he made a defiant gesture of parking directly at the dark brown front door of Leostrasse 12, a forlorn, half-timbered, gabled monstrosity that smelled of five hundred years' worth of boiled cabbage and barnyard manure. It had electricity, though. Pressing the bell button, he could hear a ringing.

The door creaked open, revealing a tall, reed-thin man whose face was framed by an explosion of white hair.

"You are Miss Smathers's friend, Mr. Cooper, obviously," the man said, pulling his worn cardigan closer about him against the cold.

"I appreciate your willingness to see me, Mr. Feldstein."

"Come in—before we both freeze."

The ceiling beams were low and black with age, the walls were out of plumb, the wooden floors were so old they had traffic ruts. But at the end of the central corridor French doors opened onto an inner courtyard, a kind of atrium with winter-cropped fruit trees, a grape arbor, and matched paving stones. Across this was a large outbuilding, newer, whitewashed, and showing signs of regular maintenance.

"I inherited the old house from an uncle, many years ago," Feldstein said, pausing on the courtyard, pointing like a tour guide. "I had this addition built in the 1950s with some money received from a grant. It's my office, my home, and, I suppose, someday my tomb."

"You have lots of room."

"I need it. So many files, references. But it's to be expected. In a lifetime of searching, watching, questioning, threatening, and weeping, one gathers things. Although conditions improved somewhat a few years ago when I acquired a computer. I've been able to transfer a lot of material onto disks."

"Your crusade against the Nazis has been extraordinary."

"Not a crusade against the Nazis. Not really. A determined search for thugs and murderers who have eluded justice. All Nazis weren't thugs and murderers, in the direct, felonious, indictable sense. They were accomplices, collaborators, accessories before and after the fact, and, in many cases, ignorant dupes. So my, ah, crusade, as you call it, has never been directed against the Nazis as a sect. That would be like trying to stamp on feathers, so to speak. My effort's been against individuals who, on a calculated, premeditated basis, used Nazism's absurd doctrines as the rationale for high crimes that have as yet gone unpunished."

Cooper's smile was skeptical. "That's a bit like eating soup with a fork, isn't it? I mean, it'll take forever—"

"And I'm using whatever 'forever' God allows me. One does what one can."

The smile became a grin. "Which makes you a standout these days, when the prevailing attitude is that one does as little as one can get away with."

Feldstein shrugged, his dark eyes following a swirling of pigeons. "Those who classically have defined civilization and made it work—the thinkers, the doers, the originators and implementers of ideas and goals that ennoble society—don't exist today, to all practical purposes. Their contemporary counterparts, those in today's catbird seats, are posturers, play-actors, who have forsaken idealism, guts, and achievement for the sybaritic life. They have become dedicated voluptuaries whose ideas and goals degrade society. Their recompense will be a world that eventually doesn't function. Happily, I'll be long gone by that time." He swept a hand toward the new building. "But come—let's get out of this cold."

The office was pleasant. Strategically placed lamps gave it a soft glow, the windows presented a view of rolling open country, and the banks of file cabinets glistened under paint recently applied. The computer blinked noncommittally on a credenza to the rear of a huge desk. Feldstein sat in a leather-backed swivel chair between the two and motioned to the over-stuffed chair that faced the lot. "Have a seat."

After they had settled and traded amiable appraisals, Feldstein said, "Miss Smathers tells me you have some questions about Nazi activities in World War Two and thought I might help."

Cooper nodded. "She did some major bragging about you. But in my work, it doesn't pay to go with a single opinion. So I phoned some old friends last night—yesterday afternoon, New York time." His fingers made quote marks in the air. " 'Of all experts on the Nazi phenomenon, Hermann Feldstein is one of the most knowledgeable, and anyone with serious questions concerning it is inevitably led to him.' " He repeated the gesture. " 'As far as Nazis are concerned, if Hermann Feldstein doesn't know about it, it didn't happen.' "

The old man smiled dimly. "Well, that's somewhat hyperbolic, of course."

"Uh-huh. My pals at the *Times* and the *Journal* don't deal in hyperbole."

"It's true that I've collected a good bit of lore—along with quite a few scholarly visitors—over the years. But that was then. What can I do for you now?"

Cooper got to the point. "My father was a member of American intelligence in World War Two. He was case officer on a probe into a Nazi operation that seemed to involve a plan by Martin Bormann to keep the Nazi Party alive on a postwar clandestine basis. And—''

''Slingshot,'' Feldstein said.

Cooper gave him a surprised glance. ''You're familiar with it, then?''

''Of course. I also recognized your paternal connection with the matter when Miss Smathers called about your visit. The name Cooper has a kind of prominence, not only in Slingshot but in several German intelligence files I've resurrected. Your father was quite a fellow.''

''So I'm finding out.''

''What specifically is it you'd like to know?''

Cooper drew a paper from his jacket pocket and slid it across the cluttered desktop. ''That's a list of some of the principals of Slingshot. I'd like to know if any of them are still living. And, if so, where I can find them.''

Feldstein took the paper in his bony hands, unfolded it, and studied the list, his wrinkled face impassive. He said then, almost as if he were talking to himself, ''Lorelei Altmann, Max Dietz, and Adalbert Klug. A rotten trio that heads your list. Where did you get these names?''

''From Helen Smathers and the Military Archives Repository in Falls Church, Virginia. The archives coughed up a rather extensive list of German personnel and a few fat dossiers. But there was no indication as to the status of those people today.''

Feldstein made a steeple with his fingers and sent a thoughtful stare out the window. ''I can give you addresses. But only that for Lori Altmann is current.''

In the small pause that followed, Cooper read a signal. Feldstein had addresses all right, perhaps other information as well. But he also had his hand out. ''I will, naturally, pay for such information.''

''How much?''

''Whatever you require.''

Feldstein's gaze returned from the view to fix on Cooper. ''That was the correct answer,'' he said.

"How so?"

"By expressing your willingness to pay my price, you will not have to pay anything. It's my little test of your, ah, sincerity. Your authenticity. You have no idea how many dilettantes, curiosity-seekers, morbid dirt-pokers have sought me out over the years. I detest such people. They are kin to those you see standing around accident scenes, salivating over the blood and ruin. They want to rummage through my years of work, but they don't want to pay for the—dare I use the word?—privilege."

Cooper shrugged. "I never got to know my father properly while he lived. Now that he's dead, I'm trying to discover what I missed. His role in the Big War seems to offer some important clues—answers. I'll pay anybody's price to get them."

There was another silent interval in which their gazes met and held.

Feldstein said finally, "I'm afraid that the addresses I have are hopelessly outdated. There is a man who, for a very high price, will tell you how to find these people. But you must be careful. He's a very dangerous fellow, tricky, violent, and filled with angers."

"What's his name?"

"Kurt Dorn, a former SS Standartenführer, who served ten years in Spandau prison alongside Rudolf Hess and the other infamous Nazi war criminals. He is said to be spending his old age with relatives in the Schwabing section of Munich. But that's mere rumor, and since I have no further interest in him I've not bothered to confirm it."

The old man turned in his chair and fingered the computer keyboard. The soft clacking moved things about on the screen, and there appeared finally what seemed to be a directory which, under the scrolling, seemed to be endless.

"Ah, here we are." Feldstein scribbled on a notepad, tore off the top sheet, and handed it across the desk. "This is the village where Altmann was last known to reside. If you can find her there—or anywhere—she can locate Dorn for you. I'm sorry I can't be more precise."

Cooper glanced at the note, then folded the paper and slipped it into his coat pocket.

"Tell me, Mr. Cooper," the old man asked after another pause, "just how much do you know about Slingshot?"

"Not much. My father's notes and the military archives deal mainly with operational detail: agent itineraries, supply problems, safe houses, short, jargon-filled memos. Which reminds me: Do you recognize, or have any information about, the American agents code-named Bacon, Eggs, and Pancake?"

Feldstein smiled. "You Yanks have such a gift for drollery. Those were the code names for your father's team members in Slingshot, as I recall."

"Do you know their real names?"

"They were never revealed in the documents I've seen. Have you asked the U.S. authorities?"

"Sure. But if anybody knows, he isn't saying so."

"Ah, well, bureaucracies are rarely noted for their helpfulness."

"One thing was obvious. There's a strange overlapping of structure and incidents between my father's novel *The Götterdämmerung Machine* and the archives."

"Which, apparently, has given Siegfried Ramm his excuse for a suit against your father's estate."

"You know about that, too, eh?"

Feldstein shrugged. "Ramm's libel charges have been given heavy play in the media."

Cooper nodded ruefully. "Another question, Herr Feldstein: Have you ever heard, in connection with Slingshot—or any other case, for that matter—the term 'Martin's Six-Twenty,' or maybe 'The Six-Two-Oh'?"

Something akin to a shadow passed across the old man's face, an indefinable alteration in which the eyes took on a peculiar indirection and the pallor seemed to intensify. It was there, then it was gone. "The term appeared several times in Wehrmacht documents regarding Operation Sunrise, which, as you probably know, was the name the Germans gave their side of Slingshot. But I have no idea as to what it meant." Feldstein examined the darkening afternoon again. His face, Cooper thought in a kind of irrelevance, suggested the stylized Uncle Sam on antique recruiting posters.

"Do any of your studies throw any light at all on what specifically happened in the war that moved my father to establish Rettung Internationale?''

Feldstein shook his snowy head. ''I've never seen any papers pertaining to the Rettung Foundation.''

''Have you ever heard of a Japanese named''—Cooper checked his notes—''Oko Takai?''

Feldstein shrugged. ''Certainly. He's very high on my list of people to watch.''

Cooper sat forward in his chair. ''Oh? How come?''

''Takai is a billionaire Kyoto industrialist. His fortune began with electronics and has since spilled into variegated enterprises all over the world. But that is his surface, and can be studied at length in any social registry or financial directory. He has my attention because he is reputed to be closely associated with the international neo-Fascist movement, the word being that as a youngster in post-Hiroshima Japan, he joined the notorious Kokka-Shakaishugi Rodo To or National Socialist Workers' Party—Japan's equivalent of Germany's Nazi Party. As a youth, rumor has it, he became a particularly effective perpetrator of terrorist attacks against U.S. occupation forces and, later, against Japanese politicians and entrepreneurs who embraced Western ideas and methods. As he grew older he apparently made an easy shift into Western ways himself, and eventually took over a central portion of the burgeoning microchip industry. But for all his public benevolences, my underground sources place him as chairman of the Council of Brothers, a cabal of very rich and ruthless Japanese gang lords—each the sponsor of one or more terrorist groups dedicated to the return of the samurai, or warrior, class that once ruled feudal Japan.''

Cooper, writing rapidly on his notepad, asked, ''If you and I know about Takai's dark side, the Japanese authorities must know. So why don't they move on him? And how can a man like that be named to the Rettung board, for God's sake?''

''Why,'' Feldstein countered, ''don't the American authorities round up and punish the Mafia overlords? How can someone like Angelo 'The Faker' Cellini, said to be the don of dons in New York, sit on the boards of Titanic Chemicals and Charities United?''

Cooper looked up from his notes. "You tell me."

"Because Cellini has never been arrested. He has no police record. His paper trail is spotless. More important, he's the benefactor of many powerful people in all branches of government and commerce. So it is with Takai."

Cooper sighed. "I'm due to take a seat on the Rettung board myself. I'm not sure I'll be able to work with an international gangster, spotless paper trail or no."

"Maybe. But an irony is at work. In their attempts to maintain a respectable facade, men like Takai—erudite, courteous, earnestly interested in the world's impoverished—do many good works. Takai is probably a very effective administrator of Rettung's charities."

"Well," Cooper said, rising from his chair and pocketing his notes, "I'm grateful for your time and counsel."

The old man's watery eyes came around from their study of the rain-washed meadows to stare directly into Cooper's. "May I offer you one last piece of advice?"

"Of course."

"Stay away from Dorn—the others. Go back to your home in the States and learn about your father some other, safer way. To ask about those people, to probe their lives, to give them the tiniest offense, is to invite serious injury or death. Go home, please. Let sleeping dogs lie."

Cooper smiled and went to the door. "I hear about those dogs a lot these days, Herr Feldstein. And while I appreciate your concern, I can't really give up on all this."

"You'll never get away with bothering those people. You'll be killed."

"You've been bothering those people for almost fifty years now, Herr Feldstein. You've gotten away with it. Why shouldn't I? Good-bye, and thanks again."

Thirty-two

Tina placed her call at twelve-thirty, Jacksonville time, because that was when Mrs. Farman would be finishing lunch. Mrs. Farman was a woman of tidy, entirely predictable ways, and a clock could be set at the moment of each workday when, desktop cleared, she would unfold her napkin, pick up her fork, and begin pecking fastidiously at the salad (she favored cottage cheese and pineapple), prepared at home and brought to the office in her plastic ice chest. The process was completed in thirty minutes, give or take a minute, depending on how long it took her to rinse things and return the desk to its business mode.

Today's connection was excellent. "Mr. Cooper's office. Mrs. Farman speaking."

"At the sound of the Alpenhorn, it'll be the Tina Mennen Show, coming to you direct from the very heart of downtown Himmelsdorf, Bavaria, Cowplop Capital of the World."

"Tina, dear! How nice! How's the weather over there?"

"Quite mild. Only forty inches of snow since breakfast."

Mrs. Farman chuckled. "How you do go on. It can't be that bad."

"Oh, yeah? I know now why there's so much yodeling in the Alps. Anybody'd yodel when the john seat registers thirty-five below zero."

"I really miss having you here in the office. You've been gone less than a week and it seems like a year. Are your relatives doing well?"

"Yep. Uncle Otto's retired from schoolteaching now, and Auntie Lolo tyrannizes him, first with affection, then with an errand list. They're a real piece of work."

"How do you spend your time over there?"

"Explaining America to little ladies with pink faces days, getting felt up by the local *Bierstube* dudes nights."

"Sounds like you have your hands full."

"No, it's the dudes who have their hands full."

"I mean—oh, Tina, you are the limit."

"Have you heard anything from Coop yet?"

"Not a peep."

"So what's going on in the office?"

"I've had better weeks, actually. It's this darned mail. It keeps building. You wouldn't believe what came in just today. Tons of it, from two kinds of people. One bunch butters Mr. Matt up, hoping he will finance their goofy schemes; the other bunch calls him all sorts of rotten names for having so much money. It never ceases to amaze me how so many people think that whoever has more than they do automatically owes them something. I mean, I was brought up to work hard, mind my own business, and be grateful for the good things that come my way, not to hate my neighbor because more and better things might have come his way. Just who do these obnoxious people think they are, anyhow?"

"What do you do with stuff like that?"

"The insults I throw out—except for the really vicious ones, which I send to Mr. Tremaine, who decides if they are police matters or actionable. The others I hold for Mr. Matt."

"You mean he actually reads them?"

"Sure does. He says some of them might be from people

who are in real trouble and need help, or from people who represent an idea or an organization that merits help. Mr. Matt is a very kind and generous man.''

Tina humphed. ''Also stupid. That's exactly what the angle-shooters and grifters count on.''

''I told him that, Tina. But he just laughed and said the money was a gift to him, so what's wrong with giving some of it to somebody who needs it more than he does?''

''Ah, yes. The Rich Heir's Disease: terminal guilt over unearned, unmerited wealth.''

''Well, if there is such a disease, he's got it. I think that's why he's all of a sudden so all-fired interested in Rettung Internationale. He really wants to replace his dad on the board there.''

''Nothing wrong with that.''

''He sees things so strangely sometimes. He'll spend hundreds and hundreds on getting rid of termites in that rotten little house in Jacksonville—can you believe it took the pest control company three days to kill the bugs in a six-room house?—but he won't spend a penny on a new suit. I mean, I practically had to turn mother and order him to buy a new overcoat for his trip. Yet he didn't hesitate a moment to spend the thousands needed for the trip itself. You know what he says? He says, 'Well, the trip is to take care of some things that are important. A coat is for me, and I don't really need a coat.' Can you imagine?''

''The hell he doesn't need a coat. Everything he wears looks like a Salvation Army reject.''

''Except that tweed-jacket-and-slacks outfit he puts on for important occasions.''

''I'll admit that looks pretty nice.''

There was a pause in which they both considered that truth. Then Tina said, ''Well, we've done up Coop. Back to you: Are you really okay? You sound tired. Hassled.''

''I've been out of sorts since Mr. Tremaine called yesterday. He was very upset with me for not telling him that Mr. Matt had gone to Europe. Very upset. He said if I worked for him I wouldn't be working for him. He'd fire me.''

''So what did you say to that?''

"Well, he really got my goat, lecturing me like that. I told him that if I worked for him I wouldn't be working for him. I'd quit before he even hired me."

"Cool."

"I hate scenes. But he forced the issue. When my boss tells me not to mention that he's gone to Europe, I don't mention that he's gone to Europe. Whether Mr. Tremaine likes it or not."

"Way to go, kid."

"I'm sort of worried about Manfred, too."

"Oh? Why?"

"I think he's had words with Mr. Nickerson."

"Really?"

"Mm. For some reason, Mr. Nickerson seems, ah, rather tense the last couple of days. There's been a lot of publicity about some killings locally—one up in Bayard, an Asian in a car sunk in a pond or something—and what with all the rich and powerful people being murdered around the country he thinks we ought to beef up the security systems around here. As a matter of fact, he's in Jacksonville right now, talking to some electronic warning systems people."

"Where's Manfred?"

"It's his day off and he's with his friend in Daytona, as usual."

"He has a friend in Daytona?"

"Mm. They've kept company for years. She's the widow of one of Manfred's wartime buddies, or something. I never really understood their relationship, and since it's none of my business, I don't ask. At any rate, I hope she can cheer him up. I don't know what Mr. Nickerson said to Manfred, but Manfred has been noticeably different."

"In what way?"

"Well, he's always been—uneasy—in the presence of Mr. Nickerson. Ever since the first, when Mr. Nickerson was a cop, checking to see if Mr. Frank was okay in the wee hours. But now that Mr. Nickerson is on the payroll, the atmosphere has become pretty darn sticky, and I have the distinct impression that Manfred is anxious."

"Anxious?"

''Well, frightened, actually. I've known Manfred for many years, and while he's a silent, aloof old coot as a rule, he's also very slow to get ruffled about things, and he's been a big help to me in many ways. So I know Manfred, and I say something's got him plain old scared. Whatever it is, it seems to have a lot to do with Mr. Nickerson.''

''Maybe they simply don't like each other. It happens.''

''This is different. This is something—specific.''

''Well, dear, for your own welfare, remember the old Chinese proverb: 'He who would stay dry stays out of middle in pissing contest.' ''

Mrs. Farman laughed. ''Oh, Tina, you say the darndest things. Is that really an old Chinese proverb?''

''I ought to know. I made it up when I was a sophomore at Haverford High.''

''Uh-oh, my other line's blinking. I hope it isn't Mr. Tremaine again.''

''Well, I'll get out of your ear. Just called to say hi.''

''You're a dear to do that. As busy as I get around here, it's really sort of lonely.''

''I've watched you work, and you're a good soldier, Mrs. F. Coop's very lucky to have you there. Bye.''

Even as she hung up, Tina was nagged by the feeling that something had been said in the conversation—something murky, obscure, fleeting—that held special significance. But what? Significant in what way? To whom?

She felt a compulsion to call back, to ask more questions. But what would she ask? About what?

''Tina,'' she said aloud, ''you need a keeper.''

There were no messages from Coop to change the assignment he had given her, so, after springing Uncle Otto and Auntie Lolo to a dinner at the Bergsteiger, an upscale eatery on the Kufsteinerlandstrasse, she dropped them off at the house, then drove to Munich in her rented Audi, arriving close to midnight. She had reserved a room and bath at the Sommerhaus, a small hotel in the Schwabing section, where she registered as Tina Mennen, foreign correspondent, *St. Augustine Record,*

USA. Dog-tired, she showered, then hit the sack for seven hours of unconsciousness.

The address for Ramm, which she had obtained from Coop's copy of the legal document packet given him by Tremaine, was Moellerstrasse 12, in the Ritterhausen section, which proved to be an area of substantial houses, well tended, liberally landscaped, and showing pricey, late-model cars on their parking pads. Number 12 was a large, severe house, with a mansard roof, an array of dormers, a pair of formidable chimneys, ranks of shuttered windows, and an arc of patterned-brick driveway. A mammoth Mercedes sedan hulked in the shadows of the porte cochere—a glistening black monster, lurking and ready to pounce.

Lacking a strategy, Tina took the direct approach, walking up the flagstone path to the front door and ringing the bell. After a protracted wait, the door was opened by a man in a white coat who was only a few inches taller than the Washington monument and who had a face Godzilla would love.

The voice matched the face. "What is it?"

"Hello. Is this the home of Herr Siegfried Ramm?"

"Who are you?"

"I'm Tina Mennen, a reporter for the *St. Augustine Record,* and I'd like very much to ask Herr Ramm a few questions regarding his suit against the American author, Frank Cooper. Is he in?"

The door slammed.

"Obviously Herr Ramm is not granting interviews," she told the satin-finished wood panel inches from her nose.

She returned to her car and drove slowly around the block, talking into her tape recorder. "The house is on a deep lot that seems to run from street to street. There is what looks to be a three- or four-car garage and a pool house shaded by large trees to the rear. While the front of the house is quite open and formally landscaped, the rear garden can't be seen from the street because a tall hedge, at least six feet high, makes an effective wall around the perimeter. I'm not sure, but there appears to be a mesh-metal fence inside the hedge, providing an additional barrier. I also hear the barking of a large dog, but

I'm not sure it comes from the Ramm property.''

As she approached the intersection at the southwest corner, her eye was caught by a small sign in the window of the house that sat on a rise to her right. FURNISHED GARAGE APARTMENT AVAILABLE, it said.

She pulled the car to the curb and sat for a time, her gaze moving back and forth between this property and Ramm's.

''Tina,'' she said aloud, ''you're a genius.''

She locked the car, then strode up the trellised walk and rang the bell. The sun was warm for early February, and water dripped from the icicles on the eaves.

''Yes?'' a tiny old woman asked from the half-open door.

''Good morning. I saw the sign in your window, and I'd like to inquire about it.''

''And you are?''

''Oh, pardon. Here's my card. I'm Tina Mennen, a reporter for the *St. Augustine Record,* an American daily newspaper. I've been assigned to do a series of stories here in Munich and I need some digs for a month, maybe two.''

The white-haired woman stepped into full view, her blue eyes friendly, her smile regretful. She held the card as if it might break. ''I'm so sorry, Fräulein, but the apartment is available only on a lease basis—six months minimum.''

''Hm. That's too bad, Frau—''

''Schneider. Offizierwitwe Schneider.''

''It looks to be just what I was hoping to find—quiet, pretty. I live a fairly reclusive life—entertain a friend or two now and then—but I like my privacy, and this has it in bundles.''

''Too bad indeed, dear. You look like the kind of tenant I was hoping to find.'' Frau Schneider smiled amiably. ''And for an American, you speak beautiful German.''

''How much is the rent for six months?''

''Well, as you can see, this is a very fine neighborhood and rental accommodations are virtually nonexistent, due to zoning restrictions and the like. But my deed, which dates from the time when this was all open, undeveloped country, permits me, as a military officer's widow, to make space available, provided I myself don't serve food or drink—that is, operate a pension or boardinghouse. So with all that windy explanation,

I must tell you the rent in American dollars is'' —her eyes considered the sky as if the monetary conversion table were written there—''a thousand dollars a month, for a minimum of six thousand dollars.''

Frau Schneider was not above the old tourist-ripoff game, Tina thought wryly. But, what the hell, Coop hadn't said anything about going on the cheap.

''That's pretty steep for a working newspaperwoman, Frau Schneider. But tell you what: If you let me look at the apartment and I like what I see, I'll give you sixty dollars—a nonreturnable one percent—as a binder to hold the apartment until noon tomorrow while I get clearance from my boss in the States to pay the full six thousand. Okay?''

Frau Schneider, for all her little-old-lady cutes, was no dummy. It took her about two milliseconds to see that sixty nonreturnable dollars for a ten-minute tour and an overnight hold of her garage apartment was not exactly a bum deal. ''Oh, I'm sure you'll love it, my dear. It has its own kitchenette and bath, a large bedroom, especially fine furniture, a private entrance, and, because it's on a rise and faces southeast, a lovely view of the distant Alps.''

It was all that Frau Schneider claimed and more—a cozy, surgically clean place, redolent of wood polish, fresh paint, and soap. Tina made all the appropriate noises as Frau Schneider pointed out the various features, then paused for a protracted interval at the large living room window as if admiring the view.

''The Alps are beautiful from here, wouldn't you say, Fräulein?''

''They certainly are,'' Tina enthused, examining the rear garden of the Ramm place down the hill and across the street. Then, as if seeing it for the first time, she added, ''And that's a gorgeous garden down there. So large and well kept. Somebody very important must live there.''

Frau Schneider sniffed, and her merriness was slightly shadowed. ''Important isn't the word I'd use. 'Arrogant' is more like it. That's the home of the architect Alois Ramm, who became very rich in the reconstruction that followed the Hitler war.''

"Is that he there? The old man seated on the sun deck, bundled up in blankets?"

Frau Schneider shook her head, and Tina sensed the little woman's sudden bitterness. "No, Alois died ten years ago. That's his father, Siegfried Ramm, a big shot under Hitler, who inherited the place and is now spending his senile eighties alone and friendless, being spoon-fed by a household staff made up of neo-Nazi goons. Although none of that should bother you as a renter, it represents the one blot on my own little paradise here."

"You don't like Nazis, then, eh?"

"I despise them. They accused my husband of complicity in the plot against Hitler's life, and although he was entirely innocent of the charges, they executed him anyhow. I tell you, Fräulein, I look at that old man down there and I truly want to vomit."

"Is he really senile? Or were you just using the word?"

"He's been dotty for some time. The word is, his mind has turned to mush from syphilis, contracted during his heroic invasion of all the crotches in Paris."

"Ugh."

"Yes. Thank God he's the last of the Ramm line."

Impulsively, Tina patted the bony little shoulder. "Well, Frau Schneider, neither of us should let that miserable rat ruin our day. We don't have to look at him, and we won't, eh?"

"You're absolutely right, my dear. So right."

"I love the apartment. Will you take the sixty in traveler's checks?"

"Of course."

"I'll let you know tomorrow what my boss says. And I'm willing to bet that he'll okay the deal."

"That would be wonderful. It would be so nice to have a lovely young woman like you close by."

The answering machine in Chuck Coleman's office beeped.

"Hey, Coop: Tina. There's good news and there's bad news.

"The good news is that your libel suit should be a cinch to defend. I reconnoitered the Ramm place today and learned that he's living in nursing-home conditions in a big house inherited from his late son. He's said to be hopelessly out of plumb, thanks to tertiary syphilis. So if he's incapable of filing a lawsuit, a member of his family, feeling subsidiary dents and bruises, must have filed it for him. Right? But he ain't got no family, being the last of his line—this according to my source, a wispy little anti-Nazi grandma who's crazy about me because I'm a lovely young woman. So that means somebody, an impostor, maybe, who has no direct or obvious or logical involvement, has filed the suit in the name of a convicted Nazi who can no longer read, let alone feel dented and bruised by your daddy's naughty writings. That's sort of like me filing a libel suit against Arnold Toynbee in the name of the Emperor Caligula. Right? Well, almost.

"The bad news is that you owe me sixty bucks."

Thirty-three

It was raining when Cooper awoke, and he lay unmoving under the huge feather quilt, watching the beads of water as they zigzagged down the windowpanes, tiny rivers flowing to some eventual sea. The street below sent up the soft hissing of tires on wet pavement, an occasional taxi horn, the gabbling of children off to school. He listened to these sounds, striving to fix his mind on their prosaic normality, the reassurance they represented. He'd emerged from sleep on the rim of a dream, a swirl of images—fleeting, imprecise—in which he struggled in a deep, luminous pool to escape from what seemed to be a large metal box. Surfacing at last, gagging and gulping air, he had been drubbed by a shower of projectiles thrown by murky figures on a nearby shore. Now, curled in his downy cocoon, staring at the sodden sky beyond the window, he recognized the images as ragged playbacks of his car's plunge off the Riddle Creek bridge, the shots and confusion and terror of the incident at Ziggy's, the hardening sense of his being used as the nexus between hidden wars. And once again there came the awareness—not the impression, not the suggestion, but the awareness—of impending disaster. He knew with a bizarre, infuriating certainty that deep, invisible currents were swirling him toward some fearful cataract, and escape, if there was to be one, depended on whatever resistance he alone could mount.

Exasperated, he swung from the bed and went to the washstand, where he made a deliberate, stolid business of shaving. But his mind insisted on breaking away into a disjointed recital of the who, what, when, where, and how of his presence in this second-rate pension on a side street in a rain-washed German city. His father's murder, the resultant uncomfortable wealth, the rejection by longtime fellow toilers in the journalistic vineyard, the abandonment of a job he loved, the implacable, irrational forces that pressed in, the puzzling behavior of Stan and Quigg and Manfred—they scrolled like flashbacks in a surrealistic film.

Then there was Tina, the compelling amalgam of little girl and resourceful woman. She, too, had appeared in his life, unexpected, uninvited—pretty flotsam on the tides of coincidence. Which was she being at this moment? Smart-mouth kid? Or the cool, level-headed linguist who could turn Katzenjammer hieroglyphics into a fascinating read?

Where was she now?

Why did he miss her—feel so uneasy about her?

He was still mulling these unanswerable questions when he arrived at the checkout desk in the main foyer. As he fished in his wallet for a credit card, the old handlebar phone on the desk rang. The concierge, a dour woman whose red hair obviously had come from a bottle, listened for a moment, then held out the phone. "For you, Mr. Cooper."

"Hello?"

"Coop, for God's sake. Do you have any idea how much effort it's taken for me to find you? I've called everybody I could think of and it wasn't until I got to Chuck Coleman at the USP that I had any luck."

Damn. Chuck should have been told not to be so helpful. "What is it, Stan?"

"I simply can't understand why you told me you were going

to the West Coast and went to Germany instead. I mean, it's very, very difficult for me to manage your affairs when you play games.''

"Well, first off, Stan, it was your great big passionate idea that I take a vacation, and so I'm taking one. It doesn't really make diddly-squat just where the hell I am if I'm not in Jacksonville, right? Second, I didn't tell anybody I was going to Germany, because I'm tracking down some stuff about my dad, and it's a little tricky, and I don't want to be distracted or hassled by irrelevancies.''

"Irrelevancies? Since when is somebody suing you for twenty-two million dollars irrelevant, for chrissake? Have you lost your mind?''

"So what do you want of me, Stan?''

"I want you to return to Jacksonville on the earliest plane. All hell is popping on the Ramm suit. Ramm himself called me—he plans to represent himself and to use Eli in Miami as his adviser, along with an interpreter because his English, while good, is short on legalese. He says Eli's getting a court order that will require us to present documents and depositions at ten A.M. next Monday.''

"How in hell can he be his own lawyer if he's banned from entering the United States?''

"Closed-circuit TV. He plans to rent a satellite and cable connection to communicate during the proceedings.''

"That's the nuttiest thing I've heard today. And I've heard some beauts. He's going to spend more trying to collect than the amount he hopes to collect.''

"You exaggerate, of course. Even so, Ramm has never been famous for his brilliance.''

"I can't imagine a U.S. court going along with that kind of crap. I—''

"Just come the hell home, will you? You're needed here.''

"I'll be back in time for the Rettung board meeting.''

"That's not soon enough, Matt. No way is it soon enough. You're needed now.''

Cooper's voice took on an edge. "I'll be there as soon as possible. That's all I can promise. Meanwhile, you're the lawyer. So figure a way to stall things.''

He returned the phone to the unhappy redhead, who, after hanging up, gave Cooper his bill. Handing her his credit card, he nodded at the phone. "May I use your phone for a moment, Frau Keil?"

Her glance, opaque with a lifetime of unrequited needs and stifled resentments, let him know that, in her mind, anybody who took rooms at her place simply had to be a loser. "I'd rather you wouldn't. It's my business line, and I want to keep it open. There's a pay phone down the street, in the little park beside the creek, next to the millinery."

Cooper remembered Stan Tremaine's tale of the Texas oil man who bought a hotel just to fire its unpleasant help. In Houston, maybe, but what the hell would Matthew L. Cooper do with this pile of bricks and boards after he canned Frau Keil? Besides, she'd probably be delighted.

Despite his annoyance, he laughed softly.

Down by the millinery he dialed Coleman's office and got the answering machine. "Chuck, this is Coop, checking to see if there are any messages from Tina Mennen. I've left the Pension Keil and am heading south to Heidelberg and the Neckartal. I'll be doing a lot of driving for the next day or so, so if you do hear from Tina, just tell her that I'll be needing her as an interpreter and to stay at her aunt's and uncle's place until I call tomorrow at noon and make arrangements to meet her. Thanks."

He was about to hang up when a click brought on Coleman's voice. "Hey, Coop—sorry. I was just coming in the door and I heard you speechifying. I have this new verschlugginer answering machine and I'm always punching the wrong buttons. So it took me a while to come on the air. Everything okay?"

"Yep. Did you hear what I said?"

"Sure. You've checked out of that garden of delights on Diestlstrasse and are headed for points unkown south of Heidelberg. And no, I haven't heard from Mennen. At least I don't think I did."

"What's that mean?"

"When I came back from lunch yesterday this goddamn thing was blinking at me in that smug, smart-ass way it has, announcing that I'd received three calls. I pressed what I thought was the play button and when I didn't hear anything I checked again and saw my finger on the freaking erase button. Those calls are now drifting atoms in the uncharted cosmos, or wherever the hell tape erasures go.''

"Well, if one of them was Tina and it was something important, she'd have called again by now.''

"Speaking of the garden of delights, a question's been bothering me: Just why in hell did you pick that crappy place? I mean, really, with all the gorgeous plastic hotels around this burg, you gotta pick that rotten little boardinghouse. How come?''

"It was central to the things I have to do. It didn't have elevators I had to stand around all day waiting for. It was low profile.''

"You know what? I think that's bullshit. And I'll tell you why. Back a few years, when I was on a midsize daily in Ohio, the paper hired a young J-school grad whose old man was super rich. I mean, big-time, household-word rich. The kid, just to show everybody he was a regular guy, rented a second-floor flat in a marginal neighborhood and drove to work in a beat-up, ten-year-old Plymouth. Trouble was, everybody knew he spent weekends at the hundred-acre horse farm he'd bought outside of town and had two Caddies, a Mercedes, and an MG in the garage. The staff resented him a hell of a lot more for being a phony than they would have if he'd driven to work in a Rolls.''

"You're saying that I'm a phony for staying in the Keil Pension?''

"No. I'm saying you're having trouble being rich. Why don't you just relax and enjoy it? Okay, so you're rich. So then act rich. Know what I mean?''

I know what you mean, Chuck. You mean it's you *who are having trouble with my being rich.*

"By the way, did that guy Tremaine ever get you?''

"Mm.''

"He seemed awful hot to talk to you. It was okay to tell him where you were, wasn't it?''

"Sure.''

"I can see from your breathless enthusiasm that it was a bum idea."

"Not really, Chuck. He's my lawyer, and it was important that I talk to him. But he just ain't a barrel of laughs sometimes."

There was a pause.

"Anything else I can screw up for you, Coop?"

"No. Just continue the middleman scene. And you can wish me luck."

He rang off, then stood for a time, listening to the rain drumming on the booth's tin roof and dealing with a sudden attack of loneliness and anxiety.

Impulsively, and with the help of an English-speaking operator, he paid for and put through a call to Tina's uncle's house in Himmelsdorf.

There was no answer, and the attack intensified.

It stayed with him throughout the drive to Heidelberg and his target town of Weissberg, a few miles beyond.

Thirty-four

"Nickerson, Chief."

"I told you not to call unless you have something definitive, concrete."

"That's right, sir. And that's what I have."

"Like what?"

"Thanks to the paper you set up for me, I was able to rummage through Cooper's house yesterday morning. I found a weapon."

"What kind of weapon?"

"A thirty-eight Taurus revolver. It was stashed in an empty, lidded, one-gallon paint can in the attic. One of the five soft-nose cartridges in its cylinder had been fired. The piece has been around, from the looks of it."

"Was Cooper there?"

"No. He's in Europe, doing something on that libel suit he's been socked with."

"So bring the sucker to me—with the ammo just as you

found it in the cylinder—and I'll send it off to the FDLE lab toot sweet.''

"Only one thing bothers me, Chief.''

"Like what?''

"Cooper's too smart to stash a hot piece. My guess is that, if he did ice his old man, the last thing he'd do would be to hide the iron on the premises. He'd make the hit, then deep-six the tool in the ocean, or someplace.''

"Don't count on it. Passion hitters do some very strange things.''

"I know that, sure. But it just doesn't fit Cooper. He's a thinker, and he's used to nervous heat, from Bosnia to newspapering. I don't see him putting an incriminating thirty-eight in a paint can in his goddamn attic.''

"Bring me the piece and we'll let the lab tell us just how good he thinks.''

"Yes, sir.''

"You don't sound very jubilant about these developments, Nickerson. Something wrong?''

"No, sir, nothing wrong. It's just that I find myself hoping somebody else stashed that Taurus. I've been spending a lot of time with him lately. I'm his personal protection adviser.''

"How'd you pull that off?''

"I told him I'd turned in my badge, being as how I was so pissed off by Santos's string-pulling, and like that.''

"Interesting.''

"It's just that—well, if he's a killer, he's a pretty damned likable one.''

"Come off it, Nickerson. Act your age. You're a two-hundred-year-old cop, and you don't like anybody.''

"Yeah, I know, Chief.''

"Put the Taurus in a shoe box, with a note on date, time, and place found, and drop it off at my house. Tell my wife to put it in the bedroom cedar chest. I'll enter your notations on a department form and get the whole thing off to the lab in the morning.''

"Yes, sir.''

"And cheer up. Ya done good, like the man says.''

* * *

Manfred waited until the dial tone, then carefully returned the phone to its cradle. He had been sitting in for Mrs. Farman, off to keep an appointment with her dentist, and when Nickerson's extension lit up he had tuned in, almost in Pavlovian reflex. As he listened, the depression and anxiety, those lifelong burdens that hung to him like demonic familiars, had escalated into raw anger and fear.

His ancient heart thumping, he immediately went to work on a connection with Wolfgang through Daytona.

"Yes?"

"Putzi here. I'm very glad I found you by your phone."

"I was about to go to supper. What's up? Have you done that fellow Nickerson?"

"Not yet. It's tricky business."

"Tricky? For an old hand like you? Come on."

"That's much of the problem—I'm old. The reflexes aren't there, I'm slow. I tried to do him the other evening, and it didn't work very well, so I had to put it off."

"Do you want me to send help?"

"That's what I called about. One of our two major concerns about Nickerson has proved to be valid. He's working as a cop, and he's presented some very incriminating evidence to his chief. I've just overheard a conversation between the two, and things look bad. Nickerson has produced a revolver found in Matthew's Jacksonville house, and the chief has a laboratory report on the bullet recovered from Mr. Frank's body. There will be a test to see if the gun and bullet match, and it seems that if they do, Matthew will be arrested on suspicion of his father's murder—probably the moment he arrives home from Europe."

"We can't have that."

"That's why I called—to get your opinion as to what we ought to do."

"Matthew still takes priority. But the Six-Twenty is key. We can't do our duty by Matthew if we don't first do our duty by the Six-Twenty."

"One of life's little ironies, eh?"

"So back to Nickerson. Do you want me to send Bolko to give you a hand? Bolko's very good at staging accidents."

"We don't have time for that. It takes too long to find Bolko, then to persuade him to take the job. I've worked with Bolko, and he's a wart."

"So it appears to be up to you, then, eh?"

"I'll work out something."

"I hope you make it quick—"

"I have to ring off now. Mrs. Farman is pulling into the driveway."

They say that once you've learned how to ride a bicycle you never forget, an old saw that was directly applicable to the science—or was it an art?—of surreptitious entry. As he worked, marveling at his recollection of the niceties of breaking and entering after a half-century's hiatus, Manfred pondered the question, eventually giving the edge to art over science.

First was the need to be sure the place was unoccupied. To accomplish this, Manfred used the bag phone to call Chief Nolan at his office, hanging up as soon as the chief came on the line. Then, watching the house, he made sure that Mrs. Nolan drove off to the downtown post office in response to his call advising her she must personally claim a registered letter from a publisher's sweepstakes headquarters.

Then there was the matter of proper costuming, especially for daylight breaks such as this. Coveralls, a bubba hat, a tool kit, and a carpenter's belt, and the neighbors—if they noticed at all—would assume the Nolans were having a balky window repaired.

And, finally, the entry itself, with the surgeon's gloves, the Gestapo lock jimmy set (a memento of the bad old days), the tweezers and cutting pliers, the jeweler's loupe and magnifying glass, the bag of dust to cover clean spots left by objects inadvertently moved, the sketch pad and the Polaroid to "freeze" the place's look and placements at the time of entry, and, of course, the cool bravado requisite to any successfully felonious act.

None of the equipment was needed, as it turned out. Mrs. Nolan, in her haste to haul treasure from the postal sea, had forgotten to lock the back door. So he simply walked into the utility room, passed through the kitchen and dining room, and went directly to the master bedroom. There, sitting in polished glory at the foot of the bed, was a magnificent cedar chest packed with blankets, two pillows and cases, and, as expected, a shoe box containing a partially loaded .38-caliber Taurus revolver and a sealed envelope addressed, "To Chief Nolan."

As he left, tool kit in hand, shoe box under his arm, Manfred decided to mystify the Nolans. He turned the back door's inside knob button to the lock position, closed the door from the outside, and then with the Model 1943 Riegel-pinzette threw the keylock bolt, thus laying on the police chief the classic tease: How, with no signs of forced entry and with all doors and windows locked from the inside, had the burglar come and gone?

"Hello."

"The Taurus is missing, Nickerson."

"What?"

"I said the handgun you brought to my house is missing. Somebody must have stolen it."

"What the hell do you mean? I personally handed the shoe box to your wife at your front door. I told her that you wanted her to put it in the cedar chest."

"Don't yell at me, goddammit."

"Sorry, Chief, but, I mean, holy hell, how can the sumbish be missing?"

"I don't know. My wife put it in the cedar chest as soon as you left. When I got home tonight it wasn't there."

"What does your wife say?"

"Not a hell of a lot that makes sense. She's very upset. Something about going around and around with the post office people about a letter they couldn't find."

"I don't get it."

"I don't either. But this much is clear: She left the house to go to the post office and she was there for a couple of hours. Somebody must have snatched the gun while she was gone."

"Any signs of B and E?"

"No. Gilda says she had to unlock the back door to get in. Nothing else was missing, and all the other doors and windows were locked, too. We lock up everything as a matter of course.

Never know when the crazies might pay a visit.''

"Well, all I know is that without that piece we don't have a case against Cooper.''

"And without a case against Cooper, you don't have a very happy career ahead on my police force, Sergeant. Good-bye.''

"Sir?''

"Sir?''

"Shee-it.''

Thirty-five

The dossiers, sent by Helen Smathers to Mrs. Farman, who relayed them to Chuck Coleman's office via fax, had arrived under a handwritten note:

Dear Face:
I attach herewith the dossier material on Lori Altmann, Max Dietz, and Adalbert Klug. I could find no trace anywhere of "Ham," "Eggs," and "Pancake." Unhappily, there wasn't too much to attach on the others, either, but what we got, you got. Give me a call now and then to let me know how you're doing. Meanwhile, good hunting.

Yr. obt. svt.
Helen

He'd studied the documents for most of his last night at Frau Keil's home for wayward zillionaires, and Helen had proved to be right. Everything was routine, sanitary, and as useful as an

1897 almanac. The men offered standard profiles in Nazi Party upward mobility: membership dating from 1933, when Dietz was a student at Heidelberg and Klug was an apprentice locomotive engineer; subsequent transition to full-time political activism; appointment to the SS; military training and eventual promotion to officer rank; service on both Eastern and Western fronts after the outbreak of War Two; Dietz's transfer to Hitler's SS honor guard in Berlin, Klug's discharge after suffering severe wounds at Stalingrad; the assignment of both to special duty with the Reichssicherheitshauptamt, reporting to the deputy Führer, Martin Bormann. A brief paragraph in each bio summarized their activity in Operation Sunrise without revealing any rewarding detail.

Only Lori Altmann offered an opening wedge: The daughter of a Neckar Valley couple who had worked many years in England as a professional butler-cook team, she had been fluent in English and employed as a maid and waitress at the U.S. embassy in Berlin in 1938. She left there in 1939 to take a minor leadership post in the Bund Deutscher Maedel. After becoming a Kreisleiter's mistress in 1940, she rose rapidly through the ranks to become national deputy leader of the BDM. Bormann assigned her to ''Sunrise'' in the winter of 1944–45 because of, first, her ability to read and interpret American military documents and, second, her renown as a woman who ruthlessly reduced formidable adversaries—men and women alike—into glazed-eyed slaves via her sexual virtuosity. (One of her postwar jobs, according to an unwitting double entendre in the notes of her G-2 biographer, was to ''befriend American intelligence officials and screw them into Bormann's communications machinery.'') Her birthplace was Weissberg, a small castle town in the Neckar valley east of Heidelberg, and she had maintained family ties there throughout her Nazi career.

Finding her was a reporter's duck soup.

He drove up to a roadside phone booth just outside Weissberg and checked the local directory. Seven Altmanns were listed, none with her initials. So he compared the seven with the relatives listed in her G-2 bio, finding only two that came close: G. Altmann (Georg Altmann, her nephew?), and K.F. Altmann (Karle Altmann, her father?). Hardly the latter. Since Lori herself was now seventy-eight years old, her father would have to be a hundred and nine—unlikely, even for a member of the master race.

He opened his tourist's handbook of German idioms and dialed Georg.

The phone at the other end lifted and a man said, *"Ja?"*

Slowly, painfully, Cooper asked, "Ist vee-liked Frawlein Lori Altmann zoo spretch-en?"

"Wahle wieder, Kamerad."

The dial tone sounded.

Cooper muttered, "Well, Georg, I don't know what the hell you said, but I get your message."

Weissberg was too small to have a city hall or a records office of any consequence, so he drove to the central square and parked in front of the church with the golden steeple.

The wind had freshened, bringing low, dark clouds and a spittle of snow, and except for a few shawled *Hausfrauen* hurrying homeward with their shopping bags, the square was deserted. Cooper stood for a moment on the bottom step of the church entrance, aware of the ice-clogged river, the barren streets, the graying steeps of the flanking hills, the far-off panting of a locomotive on the freight siding down at the depot, and he judged that, if ever there were a tour guide rating for melancholy tank towns, Weissberg would most certainly earn five stars.

He went up the steps and into the building. It was dark inside, and he waited for his eyes to adjust. A small sign hung on the carved-panel walls, and he judged from its arrow and discreet Gothic letters that the pastor's office was down there on the left, beyond the sanctuary.

The office door was open, but he tapped anyhow, and a young woman whose sad eyes were made huge by a pair of enormous spectacles glanced up from her work on the desk. "May I help you?"

Cooper smiled, relieved. "Ah. You speak English."

"Of course."

"How did you know I speak English?"

"With those clothes you could not possibly be anything but an American tourist."

"You mean Germans don't wear camel's-hair topcoats?"

"Certainly they do. But rarely with a *Wall Street Journal* sticking out of a pocket."

They both laughed, and it was a pleasant moment.

"Are you the pastor?"

"No. Pastor Hermann is making his rounds this afternoon. I'm Lisa Zimmer. I help out in the office now and then."

"My name is Cooper. I'm trying to locate an elderly Weissberg woman. I thought maybe the church records—births, deaths, baptisms, marriages, that kind of thing—might tell me if she's still living and where I might find her."

The young woman nodded, impressed, as if she had just received a sign of intelligent life in America. "A good way to start. What's her name?" She turned in her chair and reached for a card catalog on the credenza behind her. "This might take a minute or two, so have a seat, Mr. Cooper."

He sat and read from his notebook. "Lorelei Dreher Altmann, better known as Lori Altmann, born in Weissberg on four June, 1917, daughter of Karle Franz Altmann and Annamarie Altmann, nee Henkel."

The young woman closed the card drawer and laughed briefly. "Your search is over, Mr. Cooper. She's in the manse, next door."

"What?"

"Lori's been cook and housekeeper for all three of this church's pastors since 1951. She's now too old for such work, of course, but the church has given her a small lifetime pension and an apartment in the medieval ell of the manse. She is a humble and loving servant of God, and we are all very fond of her."

Cooper blinked. "I'm not sure we have the right Lori Altmann here."

"Oh?"

"It seems our big coincidence has been capped by another coincidence. I find the only Lori Altmann in town, but she's not the Lori Altmann I'm looking for."

"You mean Lori's lurid youth? You mean you can't match yesterday's Nazi harlot with today's servant of God?"

Cooper made no attempt to hide his surprise. "Hoo-boy. This Lori has a past?"

"It's what our church calls a Magdalenic conversion. The individual is so unhappy, so filled with self-disgust, and so hungry for redemption, there is eventually a kind of spiritual eruption, a volcanic outpouring of all the inner filth, which, when completed, leaves the individual drained clean and ready for a new life. Lori became so utterly sickened by her years of depravity she virtually exploded. The old Lori was dead, and the new Lori was free to find a new route to fulfillment and serenity."

"I hate to sound like an insensitive clod, but I have trouble believing that."

Fräulein Zimmer nodded reasonably. "Most people, knowing Lori's past, have trouble accepting what happened to her. It rather threatens them somehow. That's the human way—to be threatened by things we don't understand. But Lori could not possibly care less whether you, other people, believe it or don't believe it. She's healed and happy, and that's all that matters to her."

"Was she ever, ah, legally punished for her Third Reich activities?"

"Of course. Four years in prison."

"When did she experience this 'volcanic conversion'? Before jail, or after?"

"During. Halfway through her sentence."

"I see."

"You are disappointed, aren't you, Mr. Cooper. You were rather hoping to hear that Lori's healing took place at a convenient, self-serving moment, say, the week before her trial, or before her sentencing, perhaps. It would justify your skepticism."

Cooper felt his cheeks grow suddenly warm. "Hey, I'm not here for psychoanalysis. And I can't really get all torn up over the turnaround of a bimbo who used civil-service sex to climb from waitress to Nazi Party luminary. Especially when, at the end, she was working directly, personally, to search out and kill my own father.''

It was Fräulein Zimmer's turn to blush. Her green-eyed stare broke, then turned to the window and the snow falling across the valley. "I'm truly sorry, Mr. Cooper. I didn't mean to sound like an accuser. It's simply that I'm among the hundreds who care about Lori, and having never directly felt the anguish caused by the Nazis, I tend to rationalize, or even minimize that part of her life. It's wrong, and I apologize.''

"No apology necessary, Miss Zimmer. We were both doing a little pushing there.''

"You'd like to chat with Lori, I'm sure.''

"A few questions about things she might remember from the days when she and my father were, ah, antagonists.''

Fräulein Zimmer pushed back her chair, stood up, and made for the door. "Please make yourself comfortable here, Mr. Cooper. I'll go next door and see if she's available.''

"Thanks. By the way, where did you learn to speak English so well?''

"In Albany, New York, where I was born and raised.''

"You're an American? What—''

"—am I doing in this funky little town? I teach at the Osborne Theological Institute in Pittsburgh. I'm on sabbatical, doing a book on Lori.''

Thirty-six

Cooper had to admit that it was difficult to see the Machiavellian courtesan—the calculating, switch-hitting, sexual guerrilla—in this little old woman. There were traces of a once-stunning beauty, to be sure: large blue eyes that suggested an underlying wry humor; a small, straight nose; a quaint, pouting quality in the generous lips; a soft luminescence in the wrinkled skin. But the thin, yellowed hair, the withered frame, the cane and the halting walk, the shawl and Mother Hubbard dominated, and Lisa Zimmer's slowness to fasten onto the "Nazi thing" was understandable.

They sat at a little table in the pocket formed by an oriel, and the rustling of the snow at the panes beside them provided a kind of meteorological Muzak, impassive, neutral, soothing. She had offered chocolate, and he had declined.

"So what do you wish to know, Mr. Cooper?" Her voice had a throaty quality; her English had obviously been learned in England.

"You were a member of a quasi-military operation at the

end of the war. It was dubbed 'Operation Sunrise' and was led by an SS Obersturmführer named Siegfried Ramm. It had to do with the disposition of something your team called 'Götter-dämmerung,' or 'Martin's Six-Two-Oh,' or, simply, the 'Six-Twenty.' Do you remember that, Miss Altmann?''

''Who can forget something like that? I can't remember what happened an hour ago these days, but I can still see Ramm, posing like a tin god in his uniform and boots and jingling trappings. He was an ugly man, and I despised him. He always smelled like old sweat.''

''What was your job on the team?''

''Radio operator and documents interpreter.''

''Precisely what kind of device was Götterdämmerung, or Martin's Six-Two-Oh?''

The old woman dabbed delicately at her delicate nose with a delicate handkerchief. ''The team—that is, we working team members, exclusive of Ramm and that toady of his, Max Dietz—were never told.''

''Nothing at all?''

''All we knew was that it had the highest national priority and was being overseen directly by Martin Bormann himself. Knowing Bormann as I did, knowing that he was a ruthless, single-minded survivor of any unpleasantness, I dubbed the thing 'Martin's Six-Twenty' as a little joke.''

''Explain the joke, please.''

''Well, today it seems a bit convoluted and strained, of course, but in the context of the times, inside the team, it was considered hilarious. I was somewhat of a wag in those days, irreverent, iconoclastic. I would imitate Hitler, Goebbels, Ramm—other Nazi stuffed shirts—and this seemed to endear me to the men, who by then had had it with the Third Reich and were looking for ways simply to survive the war. That's why I reached down and came up with 'Six-Twenty.' ''

''I don't understand.''

''My father, Karle Altmann, was a professional butler who often took employment in England, usually with super-rich families. My mother, Annamarie Henkel, was a native of this town, and she met my father during her service as a maid for a London financier. They married, and she returned here to have me. I grew up in one mansion after another around Britain, because my parents were in high demand as a butler-maid combination. The problem was that Father was an absolutely fanatical religionist, always, when we were in-family, spouting Bible verses and threatening Mama and me with 'God's punishment' if we didn't read at least a chapter of the New Testament every day. I came to loathe him and the Bible, with which, nonetheless, I became extremely familiar. That's why, when I was introduced to Götterdämmerung and Bormann's oversight of it, I made my joke by dredging up the King James Version of Matthew, chapter six, verse twenty: 'But lay up for yourselves treasures in heaven, where neither moth nor rust corrupt, and where thieves do not break through nor steal.' Because I knew, and the team suspected that, whatever Götterdämmerung was, it had to be treasure that Bormann was planning to store up in his own private little heaven somewhere.''

''The jokes must lose something in the telling. How about the name 'Martin's lunch'?''

'' 'Götterdämmerung' was being transported in seven sealed pails.''

''Pails?''

''Mm. Sealed, and with handles.''

''Any guess as to what was in them?''

''I don't have to guess. I know.''

''Well?''

''Dietz had a passion for me. One night I shut the gate and said there'd be no more until I knew the whole story.'' She sniffed. ''Men make such fools of themselves over sex.''

''So what was in the *pails*?''

The old woman smiled wryly. ''One billion dollars' worth of cut, polished, premium jewelry-quality diamonds. Found by the SS in the secret vault of a Rotterdam import house and taken to Berlin as loot in the fall of 1944.''

''*Billion*? With a *b*?''

''Mm.''

''Good God.''

''Yes.''

''So what happened then?''

''Dietz obviously regretted his, ah, lapse with me. He was

afraid Ramm might learn of this breach of security and have him executed. Yet he simply couldn't control his randiness. So I suggested that he could have the best of both worlds if he were to kill Ramm, assume command of the team, and, at the right moment, take off with me and the diamonds.

"But Ramm must have suspected our little plot. He had always detested me and had worried all along about my power over Dietz, and so, both to remove me as a problem and to test Dietz's loyalty, he ordered Dietz to kill me. But I overheard, and so I killed Dietz before he could kill me. I—"

"Dietz is dead?"

"Yes. For all these years. Didn't you know?"

"U.S. intelligence archives have him living in Munich."

"Then the archives are wrong."

"How did you kill Dietz?"

"You shouldn't ask. As a man, it would offend you."

"As a researcher, I must know."

"Dietz's plan was to bed me and, at the crucial moment, knife me."

"How did you know this?"

"He'd often philosophized on the perfect orgasm. His belief was that it could occur only as a component of a mortal agony. He said he'd experimented along those lines several times, but the women were of inferior races and died too quickly. He was a very sick man. It didn't take too much imagination to see what he planned for me."

"So how did you kill him?"

"Appropriately."

"Come on—"

"You insist on being offended, I see."

"I insist on the truth."

The watery blue eyes considered him directly, and he could see that she was taking some kind of measure. Eventually she sighed and shook her head. "No, Mr. Cooper, I think I'll not answer your question. God and certain others know the details, and I have confessed where confession is due. For you to know the details would accomplish nothing but your total repugnance. You would see nothing but my loathsomeness." She laughed softly. "Besides, by not knowing, you must inevitably put your imagination to work, and human nature is such that your imagination could very well produce images that far exceed actuality in abomination. Your uneasiness will be the payment I exact for this interview, eh?'' She laughed again.

Annoyed, Cooper asked, ''Will you be giving Miss Zimmer the details for her book?''

''I already have. She thinks what I did to Dietz is marvelously symbolic in the modern context—'a metaphor,' as she puts it, 'that is guaranteed to satisfy the liberated woman.' ''

''But you'll be admitting to murder, and there isn't any statute of limitations for murder.''

She shook her head. ''Manslaughter at the worst. Self-defense at the best. Whichever, the act of confession will complete the purification of my soul.''

''I dare say.'' Still fighting his indignation, Cooper pretended to study his notes. ''Didn't Ramm wonder what happened to Dietz?''

''I'm sure he did. But I didn't—how do you Americans say it? 'hang around?'—to find out. I went into hiding, and it wasn't until my second year in prison under the Denazification Law that he sought vengeance via a paid assassin, a prisoner in my cellblock. I dodged the woman's knife, disarmed her, and pushed her over a third-story railing. The subsequent inquiry ruled that the woman had died an apparent suicide. Ramm presumably gave up his search for revenge, because I've never heard more from him.''

''So you don't know for sure, then, what happened to the diamonds.''

''I've heard the stories. But I don't have any direct knowledge.'' She shrugged, adding, ''I don't really care what happened to them.''

''How about Adalbert Klug? He lives in Stuttgart. Right?''

''Klug was killed in a car crash on the autobahn four years ago. I read about it in the Heidelberg newspaper.''

''Do you know Kurt Dorn?''

''The Standartenführer?''

''The ex-con. Ten years in Spandau.''

''He's been living with relatives in Schwabing, I hear. I only knew him slightly.''

''How about the American team that opposed you? Do you have any idea who was in it, how it was organized?''

''I did at the time. But there were so many code names, so many ruses, feints, counterfeints. I don't remember much of it today. Is it important that I do?''

''I guess not.'' Cooper made a note. ''Do you recall ever hearing the code names Ham, Eggs, and Pancake?''

''In English, or German?''

''Either.''

She gave that some thought, dabbing with her handkerchief again. ''No,'' she said finally. ''The names are meaningless.''

''So it would seem, then, that you and Ramm are the only survivors of Operation Sunrise.''

''Two men, the armament officer and a driver-gunner, died in the shoot-out on the day the American team tried to take us prisoners and shut down our operation. The other two, the documents forger and the line tapper, were captured and, I understand, finished out the war in an Ami detention center outside Oberursel.''

Cooper nodded. ''The archives have them. Grunwald, the documents man, died of pneumonia in a Pforzheim hospital in 1960. Boltz, the lineman, died in a commercial plane crash in Australia in 1967. So, as I say, it's down to you and Ramm.''

''There was one other man—a motor vehicle mechanic drawn from the Wehrmacht to maintain the Sunrise cars and trucks. A sergeant named Kohlmann, as I recall. I have no idea what happened to him. But he wasn't privy to the unit's secrets, so it doesn't matter, actually.''

Cooper, making notes, halted, pen suspended. He looked up. ''Kohlmann? K-O-H-L-M-A-N-N?''

''I believe that's how he spelled it, yes.''

''Can you remember what he looked like?''

She laughed again, that small, soft sound. ''I have trouble with names, Mr. Cooper, but I have yet to forget a man's eyes—or his rump. Eyes speak of character, the rump of vitality. I measure all men by eyes and rump.''

''So?''

''This man—Kohlmann—was quite tall, angular, spare. A low voice, a measured way of speaking. His eyes were blue, deep-set under heavy brows. His face was rectangular, squarish in the jaw, rather. Roman nose; blondish hair, close-cropped; ears flat against his head; longish neck with a prominent Adam's apple. His rump was an athlete's. Another place, another time, I could have been interested in him.''

''Could his first name have been Manfred?''

She laughed once more. ''Not could have been. Was. That was indeed his name. This is significant to you?''

''I know an old man by that name, that's all.''

''This Kohlmann would be an old man by now. And I'm an old woman by now, eh? You might not believe this, Mr. Cooper, but I was once a handsome woman.''

''I have no trouble believing that at all,'' he said neutrally. ''You are still a handsome woman.''

''But that no longer matters to me. Because I am, again whether you believe it or not, a greatly changed woman. I have different values now.''

''I'm sure.'' He closed his notebook and stood up, and she watched with interest as he pulled on his topcoat.

''I have to move along now, Miss Altmann. Would you mind if I contact you again—a phone call, a note, maybe—if I have more questions?''

''Not at all.'' She managed to rise and, leaning on her cane, accompanied him haltingly across the room. She opened the door to the street, where she stood, face raised and eyes blinking, regarding the darkening sky. ''This will stop soon and it'll be clear by dawn. Do you have far to drive?''

''I'm headed for Munich.''

She held out her hand. ''That could be risky in a snow like this. You should take a room in town here and leave in the morning. I understand they have some lovely rooms in the castle on the hill. Quite economical, too.''

Cooper shook her hand and was about to speak when a vicious swarming filled the air about him and incredible forces tore at his topcoat sleeve. In a crazy detachment, a bizarre apartness from reality, he watched as Lori Altmann's Mother Hubbard first fluttered, then erupted in a mad scattering of tiny red fountains.

Mindlessly, in the never-forgotten reflex of the infantryman coming under fire, he dropped and rolled off the steps and into the small canyon of a winter-empty planter box, half blinded by cascading snow and shouting insanely amidst the whirring of ricochets and splintered masonry. In the instant when his sight cleared and panic gave way to the old combat commander's objectivity, he was aware of a black car, yawing and rocking in a slithering race for the open road. As he strained for a glimpse of the license plate, there came a second racketing of a machine gun, this from a gray Citroen parked at the intersection of the town's main street and the riverside state highway.

The black car, almost like a toy hurled away by a vexed child, spun through three full revolutions, slid sideways into a curb-high concrete traffic divider, then overturned, bouncing and slamming, showering wheels and sheet metal and glass. The wreckage came to a halt in a steaming pile against the flanks of an advertising kiosk.

The Citroen hummed into life and, kicking up a wake of snow, sped up an alley and disappeared in a wild left turn onto the street beyond the Aral gas station.

Cooper, remembering, scrabbled back to the doorway, where Lori Altmann sprawled, a bundle of rags on the snowy steps. He sank down beside her, turned her face to the sky, feeling for a neck pulse.

Her blue eyes widened, staring into infinity, and her mouth opened and closed like that of a beached fish.

He held his ear close. "What is it, Lori? What are you saying?"

She was whispering.

"What? What are you saying, Lori?"

This time the words were clear: "You have great eyes. And a marvelous rump. Just like your father."

And then he saw that there would be no more whispers from her, ever.

Thirty-seven

The detective was lean, hard, and hatchet-faced, and his English was accented and unfriendly. He seemed to be personally offended by the littering of his jurisdiction with the remains of an old woman, two professional assassins, and a badly abused automobile. Worse, he appeared to be especially vexed by the survivor, an American tourist who, his waspish interrogation suggested, should have known better than to associate with an old woman whose notorious past made her eminently shootable.

First there were the routine biographical questions asked by all cops of all nations for all investigations anywhere, followed by queries regarding Cooper's passport and his itinerary as a tourist—all of these asked several times in different shades of petulance. Then there followed questions on Cooper's profession, his manner of making a living from it, his solvency. And finally, exasperatingly, a number of variations on the same core theme:

Q. Why were you calling on Lori Altmann, Mr. Cooper?

A. My father was in World War Two. I'm planning to write a history of his experiences as an American soldier in Germany. Miss Altmann was mentioned in some of the documents covering his tour of duty.

Q. Did you know that she was an ex-convict?

A. Yes, I did.

Q. Can you think of any reason someone might have wanted her dead?

A. She was a heavy-duty Nazi. A lot of people are sure to resent that. And convicts make enemies in prison. Who knows what grudge was at work here?

Q. And you were merely a bystander at the shooting?

A. I'd like to think so.

Q. What do you mean by that?

A. Many people would like to see me dead.

Q. Why?

A. Because I won't give them my money.

Q. Can we be serious, please?

A. I am being serious. You should see my mail.

Q. The two dead men in the wrecked Audi have been identified as members of the Red Front, a worldwide terrorist organization centered in Tokyo. Do you have any idea why such an organization might want to kill you or Miss Altmann?

A. Inspector, you have no idea how many times I've asked myself that question. And every time I come up with the same answer: No. I don't even know anybody in the Red Front—or in Tokyo, for that matter.

Q. Witnesses say there was a second car—a gray Citroen. They say the gunfire that killed the two terrorists came from that car. Do you have any idea as to who was in it?

A. No.

Q. I find that hard to believe, Mr. Cooper.

A. So do I.

Q. Smart-aleck remarks won't help your situation, Mr. Cooper.

A. Tell me, Inspector: Just what in hell *would* help my situation? I came to Germany to research a personal matter, and in less than a week I am kidnapped in Frankfurt by an armed woman who leads me to a hood, and when they prepare to shoot me they are instead killed by un-identified gunmen, who then order me to cab to my hotel. I seem to be followed everywhere by spooks who, my hunch tells me, have saved my ass from other spooks more times than I actually know about. And then in this charming piece of nowhere I have a thousand dollar camel's-hair topcoat torn to shreds by bullets en route to blowing away a woman I've been interviewing. Not only that, but I have the distinct impression that Lori Altmann was not the target here—I was. Will you please tell me which department I complain to about that?

Q. What is this personal business you came to research?

A. It's personal.

Q. Let's go back to the beginning, eh? Why—

A. No, Inspector, I've had enough. Either you arrest me on specific charges or I walk out that door.

It went on like this for almost an hour. It ended only when Cooper at last divined the source of the inspector's discontent: The man wanted to be stroked, sympathized with, for having had such rotten events conspire to break the tranquility of his bucolic fief. A riff (''You know, Inspector, it just occurred to me how difficult your job must be, what with all these irratio-nal assaults on the general peace''), followed by regrets (''I'm sure sorry to have contributed to your burden—the last thing in the world I had any intention of doing''), and he was on his way with a grumpy, put-upon request: ''While I see no reason to detain you further, I want you to be available to answer other questions, both here and when you return home.''

''Of course. I want to be as helpful as possible.''

''You are now going where?''

''To Munich. I keep a suite at the Vier Jahreszeiten.''

The name, coupled with the slight stretching of the facts, brought its predictable reaction—a raised brow, slightly wid-ened eyes, and the discernible fluttering of the born fawner. ''Well, now. That's a respectable address, I'd say.''

''Buzz me there. Anytime. If I'm not there my secretary will take the message and I'll get back to you."

"Drive carefully. These flurries can turn serious." The inspector walked Cooper to his BMW, then, while watching him buckle in, crooned, "I'm glad you weren't seriously hurt in the attack."

"And I hope you find the attackers soon. Their arrest should bring you some fine headlines, eh?"

"I'll admit I could use a little favorable publicity."

"Tell the news people to call me at the Vier Jahreszeiten. I'll give you a nice plug."

"Thanks very much."

In Munich, Copper sent out for a new overcoat, then took a twenty-minute shower followed by a comparably languid shave. Since it's true that a man has to think about something when he's shaving, Cooper found himself thinking heavily, partly astonished, partly sad, about Lori Altmann's dying words. And then the irritable questions: Why should he be so surprised that she'd known his father? Why should he be so surprised that she saw in him things she'd seen in his father? Why should he be so surprised that she'd chosen to hide that fact until the last moment, when nothing mattered any longer? Why should he be surprised that he felt so very, well, *blue* about it? Unable to answer, he gave himself to the busy-ness of dressing.

Thanks to Tina's enthusiastic interpretation of his instructions, the closets suggested that he planned to stay for two decades. Three sport-coat-and-slacks combinations, two three-button suits, and even a tuxedo were backed up with a full stock of staples—underwear, socks, shirts, ties, accessories—but he opted for the jeans and huge pullover he found in the stock neatly arrayed in the dresser drawers. Half amused, half annoyed, he put in a call to Himmelsdorf. Uncle Otto answered on the third ring.

"This is Matt Cooper. Is Tina there, Herr Mennen?"

"Ah, Mr. Cooper," the old man said in his labored school English, "it is good once again your voice to hear. Tina, I regret to say, is at the moment still in Munich. Since two days we have not received word from her."

"Do you have a phone number for her—the address where she's staying, maybe?"

"Yes. On the evening before the past one, she rang us up with the informations that she had taken apartments in a dwelling by Moellerstrasse fifteen, which is in the Ritterhausen section of the city. Unfortunately, she has no availability of a telephone at that place."

"Well, I'm in Munich myself, so I'll look her up this evening. Take her to dinner."

"I am certain that such would delight her. Please give to her our most friendly greetings."

"Are you and Frau Mennen doing well?"

"Indeed. All is good here."

"Best regards to you both. We should be seeing you in a day or so."

It was twilight when Cooper drove past the house in Ritterhausen, and everything was pink—the sky and its majestic towers of cumulus, the sweeps of snowy lawns, the great slants of expensive roofing—and yet for all the rosiness, the neighborhood was steeped in that inexpressible melancholy which overhangs housing developments whose primary purpose is to showcase the totems of the borderline rich. Even the bevy of kids, snowballing and sledding at the far end of the block, failed to cheer things. It seemed hugely unlikely that there would be rooms to let in all this slate and pastel brick and sliding glass; but, then, Tina was proving to be a master of the unlikely, and if there had indeed been no rentable space she would have found a way to manufacture it.

He smiled.

The jackets and suits: How had she known the size to order, the waist, the sleeve length? The trouser inseam?

And which side he "dressed on," for God's sake?

He laughed and shook his head. "Now I know your secret sin, Tina baby. You're a crotch watcher."

Truly amused, he laughed again.

Moellerstrasse 15 was, like the others, a very nice house indeed. But it seemed older, and there was an air of need about it, with traces of rust on the wrought-iron fencing, finely cracked paint on the trim. And the little woman who responded to the doorbell was very definitely older than the other sleek women he'd seen in his cruise about the neighborhood.

"Good evening," he said. "My name is Cooper, and I'm looking for Tina Mennen. I understand she has leased an apartment here."

The woman's luminous eyes narrowed, and he could see sudden anxiety in them. No. Not anxiety. Fear. And they avoided his, seeming instead to focus on something in the middle distance, beyond his right shoulder.

"Tut mir leid," she said softly, just above a whisper, *"aber ich kann kein Englisch."*

Cooper pulled out his tourist book and leafed through to the section "Asking Directions." "Ik sooke Fraw-line Mennen. Won't zee here?"

The snowy head shook in an elaborate display of the negative. *"Nein. Ich kenne Fräulein Mennen nicht."*

He nodded, catching the sense of her gibberish. "I see. I must have been given the wrong directions. Sorry to have bothered you. Ent-shooldig-en Zee, bitte."

The woman, her gaze still fixed on something behind him shut the door quickly.

And in that instant, his inherited hunch machine slid into maximum overdrive. First, it told him that the old woman very definitely knew who Tina was, and that meant that Uncle Otto's directions had been on the money. And further, while he couldn't see into the house, and there had been no more than a passing shadow behind one of the windows, he sensed that the frightened little woman was making speed for a telephone. She could have been hurrying to save a meal on the stove, or maybe to go to the bathroom, or something equally mundane. But he simply knew that, for her, at this moment, there was a greater urgency.

He *knew* she was going to call somebody.

Which meant his visit had triggered some kind of alarm system.

Alarm?

What kind of alarm? For what reason?

Lacking better ways to find answers, he returned to his car and drove off, turned the corner, and at the far end of the next block made a U and returned to Moellerstrasse, where he parked behind a large, winter-brittle bush and settled in to watch number 15 and what might happen there.

What happened there was nothing.

In fact, nothing happened anywhere in that stretch of the street. The kids had disappeared, no cars passed by. It was suppertime, and, obviously, everybody was home, doing supper, like good little Germans everywhere.

The twilight deepened into night, and, feeling useless and slightly stupid, he reached for the ignition key.

Wait.

The little old woman's gaze had been over his right shoulder. Unblinking, almost fixed on something.

What?

That big house there, across the street and slightly down the block?

Where else? All else was landscaping.

A frightened woman would not be likely to fix her gaze on a line of elms, or a hedge of night-blooming dyspepsia, or whatever. She might, however, look at something—a house, say—containing whatever it was that frightened her.

Right, Coop?

Right.

He opened the glove compartment and consulted the wanly lit basic cellular references there. Lifting the phone, he punched the indicated buttons.

"*Guten Aben,*" the friendly man's voice said. "*Hier Auto-fon Netz. Womit kann ich dienen?*"

"I speak English."

"Yes, sir. What can I do for you?"

"I need the number for the United States Press office in Munich, and I'm not near a booth. Can you find it for me?"

"Certainly. One moment, please."

He got the number and punched up the USP.

"USP."

"Hi. This is Matt Cooper, reporter for the *Times-Union* in

Jacksonville. I'm doing a thing here in Munich and need access to a city directory, or whatever it is they have here that tells you who lives at what address."

"One moment, please. I'll give you the news desk."

He talked with a man named Evans, who sounded tired and not too happy to be called into duty as a page-turner. "Corner of Moellerstrasse and Baumer Allee?"

"That's right."

"Says here in this thing that the whole damned block there is occupied by a Ramm. R-A-M-M. Siegfried Ramm."

Cooper blinked. "You got to be kidding."

"Hey, man. You want an affidavit?"

"No. Sorry. Really. I'm just surprised."

"Well, that's what I got. Now you got."

"Okay. Much obliged."

He hung up and sighed. "You need a keeper, Cooper. Ramm's address is in your goddamn notebook in your goddamn jacket pocket. Maybe you ought to look at that sucker now and then, eh?"

The night was less benign than nightfall had been. It had turned very cold, and with no overcast to reflect the city's distant glow, the darkness seemed especially deep and forbidding.

Cooper assembled the guidebooks and tourist brochures that stocked the BMW's map pockets and stuffed them in the side pockets of his new cashmere overcoat. Then he locked the car and followed the neatly shoveled Moellerstrasse sidewalk to the corner, where he stood for a moment, studying the Ramm house approaches and layout.

"All right. Let's give it a whirl. It can only get you arrested."

Skirting the privet hedge that defined the property's street perimeter, he stepped into the black shadows of an azalea bed encircling the bole of a towering oak. He considered the setup again, confirming that the bed could be readily seen from the front door of the house. Then he stooped, crumpled the brochures into a pile of paper balls, and lit them with the hotel matches he'd kept as souvenirs.

When he was sure that the blaze was bright and self-sustaining, he scurried up the shoveled driveway to the front door and rang the bell.

Sinking into the shadows of a decorative column, he whispered, ''Correction. It can only get you killed.''

The door opened and a large man with a face that was the stuff of gangster movies peered about. Spotting the glittering blaze at the corner of the yard, he rumbled some angry words, sounding like an elephant burping, then trotted off to investigate.

Cooper stepped out of the shadows and through the door.

He found himself in a dimly lit foyer whose ceiling was two stories up and whose floor was an expanse of polished marble reminiscent of an Olympic skating rink. The only obvious place to hide in a hurry was a cluster of potted palms adjacent to the stairway, which rose in a majestic curve to a wraparound balcony. He went quickly, tiptoeing like a tardy freshman evading the house mother, and had just taken cover behind the plants when the big man returned, muttering about *''verdammte Kinder''* and stamping snow from his shoes.

A tense interval followed, in which the man looked about, checked the lock on the door, emitted another rumble, and further dimmed the entry lights. Then he went down the corridor of the right-hand ell and disappeared behind one of the ornately carved doors there.

Cooper waited a full two minutes, listening, studying his surroundings. The place was silent, oppressively so, in the manner of a municipal library after hours. No squeaks, no muted music sounding, no rattlings of a far-off kitchen— nothing.

The ells seemed dicey, so he opted for the balcony. Going slowly, deliberately, stealthily, he climbed the stairs and, when he had reached the top, he stood again in the dusk, assessing the silence.

Take it from left to right, Cooper.

He went to the door to his immediate front. He held his ear to the paneling, listening for sounds beyond. Nothing.

He turned the knob slowly, then eased open the door and peered into what appeared to be a large, spartanly furnished bedroom.

There was motion to his right front, and he started.

"For God's sake, Cooper," an old man in a wheelchair rasped in accented English, "where in hell have you been? I've been waiting hours. Bormann has been on the phone, yelling questions about the goddamn diamonds and making speeches about how the Führer is getting suspicious, and you're nowhere to be found. Damn you. I thought I could rely on you, you Yankee asshole."

Thirty-eight

Cooper had literally learned how to handle surprise and anxiety at his mother's knee. The lessons dated from his reluctance to toddle off to school because he might come home and find that his mother had left forever, or had died of loneliness and boredom, as she had often warned she would. Through his childhood and teens, her unspecific melancholy and, later, her very specific alcoholism had made it impossible for him to have a consistent relationship with her. She was lavish in her claims of love and concern for him, but he was never really sure it made a difference, because those times when he'd been sore hurt and deep afraid—when he had needed her absolutely the most—she was either soddenly asleep or gazing out the sitting room window, mute, teary-eyed, and beyond approach. And Frank wasn't much better; granted, he was willing to listen and offer awkward sympathy when he was available, but crises seemed to have a way of showing up precisely when Frank was locked in his room, writing, or off on one of those research trips to Europe. The upshot: a lonely and anxiety-ridden tad who by the time he had become a college boy had devised the Matthew Cooper Worst-Scenario Therapy for Surviving the Unexpected and Scary.

The Cooper Therapy was to expect the worst. When the worst happened, there was no surprise. With no surprise, there was little time given to fright. With fright thus minimized, both short-term panic and long-term, hand-wringing worry had difficulty taking over. And, conversely, when the worse did not happen, the relief—synergistic, intense—amounted almost to pleasure.

It had worked to his great advantage in the military, that most scary of lifestyles.

It worked now, when, stepping blindly through a door that could have led to doom, he found only a senile old man—bald, shrunken frame, skin like chamois, eyes like oysters—who mistook him for his father.

His immediate, almost giddy reaction was to hold a finger to his lips and whisper, "Shh. Not so loud, Siegfried. They might be listening."

Ramm, his liquid gray eyes narrowing conspiratorially, nodded vigorously. "Yes. Of course. I forgot we weren't alone."

Cooper's mind leafed quickly through his options. He decided on taking things from the top.

"What have they done with the woman, Siegfried?"

"Woman?"

"The young American woman."

"The one they put in the cellar?"

"That's the one. Is she still there?"

"I believe so. Bormann wants to interrogate her."

"Where? When?"

"In the *Reichskanzlerei*. Tonight, I understand. Nobody ever really tells me anything anymore."

"I don't know why not. You're a brilliant leader. Look how well Sunrise is going, eh?"

"Precisely. How can they ignore such success?"

"The woman: How do I find her?"

"I'm not sure they want you Americans talking to her."

"Who is 'they'?"

"Ludwig. Takai. The other Bormann people."

"Why don't they want us talking to her?"

"Bormann doesn't like or trust that pompous assistant of yours. The natty dresser. What do you call him? Ham?"

"I'm the only one who wants to see her. I'm here alone."

"Well, then. I suppose that would be all right. Ask Bolko to take you to her."

"Bolko? He's the big man in charge of this house?"

"He's in charge of nothing. This is my headquarters. I'm in charge here. As I am in charge of Sunrise. You, Ham, Eggs, Pancake, might think you have the upper hand, but I don't mind telling you, you're dreaming. All of you. From Eisenhower down."

"How do I get to the cellar?"

"What cellar? The Führer would be furious if he heard you calling his bunker a cellar."

"I mean the cellar in your headquarters here. The one where they're holding the girl."

"Oh, that. I can't remember. Why don't you ask Bolko?"

"In a moment. Tell me, Siegfried, do you remember anything about Ham, Eggs, and Pancake?"

"Remember? Why shouldn't I? They were just here a couple of days ago. Or was it today? I'm not so good with time anymore."

"No matter when they were here. Tell me what you know about them. Ham's a fancy dresser, you say. Anything else about him?"

"He's always fingering his lapels, running his hands over fabric. Like a woman. It's very annoying."

"How about Eggs? What don't you like about him?"

"He's a Jew. You Amis think that's all right, but I certainly don't. The Führer is very much against Jews, you know. I find it offensive that you have one on your team."

"And Pancake? What about him?"

"I'm hungry. Where is Bolko with my supper?"

"Pancake: What about him?"

"Leave me now. I'm tired of your questions. Americans are always asking questions—always looking for supper. I hope there's ham."

Cooper saw that Ramm had slipped out of his spasm of semirationality. He turned and, after another moment of listening at the door, returned to the balcony.

The main staircase was too exposed and the huge foyer below offered too many choices of hallways, doors, and potential disasters. Since a house this size was bound to have a back stairway, he went in search of one, following a runner of deep-nap carpeting that led past the inscrutable doors of a bedroom wing to a kind of cul-de-sac, lit softly by a single lamp. This area gave him two choices: a closed door right, a closed door left. Which to open? The Lady and the Tiger. Heads or Tails.

His luck held, sort of.

The door to the left opened on a flight of narrow stairs leading downward to a landing, where it turned back on itself. Descending slowly, stealthily, he made it to what appeared to be a ground-floor butler's pantry, beyond which, at a table in the brightly lit kitchen, Bolko the Terrible gnawed at a sandwich that seemed to be made of two loaves of bread separated by a side of beef.

Cooper waited in the shadows, trying to work up the nerve for a move to the door directly opposite, which, ajar, revealed what was obviously a cellar stairway. Bolko helped things along by finishing his sandwich and then, with considerable clatter, clearing the table. Exploiting the clamor and Bolko's preoccupation, Cooper took three fast steps and made it to the stairway unnoticed.

The cellar was huge and faintly illuminated by a scattering of low-wattage ceiling lights. Moving as quickly and quietly as possible, he made his way through a maze of workbenches, garden tools, ladders, a stack of tires, a snowmobile, skis— even, of all things, a suit of armor and a plaster statue of Bismarck—searching for signs of Tina. There were two doors, one leading to a large room filled with wine racks, the other opening on a furnace room. At the far end of this was a small padlocked door.

He tiptoed back to the workbenches, picked up a large screwdriver, and, returning, went to work on the lock hasp screws. It was slow going; the need for silence and the years of corrosion and paint collaborated in a major balk. But he finally worked the hasp free of the wood and managed to get the door open.

It was a cubicle, brightly lit and painted a sterile white. In its center a metal military cot had been bolted to the floor. Atop this was a dirty mattress, and atop the mattress—on her back, wrists and ankles bound to the cot with ship-gauge rope, mouth sealed by a band of tape, eyes wild, hair matted—was Tina Mennen.

Except for the tape, she was nude.

Cooper went to her side, pulled off his overcoat and covered her with it. Then he knelt, and with careful, gentle fingering, eased the tape free.

She sighed, her mouth swollen.

"Coop."

"Easy," he whispered. "Try not to make a sound while I get these goddamn ropes off."

Her face contorted and her eyes filled with tears. "They took my clothes away."

"Shh. We'll get you some new ones."

"I look awful."

"Not to me."

"Take me out of here, please."

"That's my project for the night. To see how quick I can make that happen."

He loosened the last rope and lifted her from the cot. She clung to him fiercely, breathing in the little gasps that preface sobs.

"I will not cry."

"Of course you won't. It makes too much noise."

Slinging her into a modified fireman's carry, he moved out of the cubicle, across the cellar, and to the foot of the stairs. There he put his lips to her ear and whispered, "Can you stand? If you think so, nod."

She nodded.

He lowered her to her feet. Into her ear again he said, "I'm

going to the top of the stairs. When I give you the nod, I want
you to yell as loud as you can.''

She shook her head. ''No. That big—''

''Shhh. Just do as I say.''

He climbed the stairs, step by slow step, and when he
reached the landing peered gingerly through the open door.
Bolko, he saw, was at the sink, rinsing dishes.

He nodded, Tina yelled, and Bolko came running. As the big
German dashed through the door, Cooper stuck out his right
foot.

Tripped, Bolko executed a wild, arm-waving swan dive,
which in midflight became a kind of half-gainer. He landed,
head-first and with a sickening crunch, on the concrete cellar
floor at the foot of the stairs, and Tina, leaning over his unconscious form, yelled again, a stadium shriek that ended in a sentence: ''I hope you broke your goddamn filthy neck, you son of
a bitch of a blue-balled bastard!''

''Such language.''

''Get me out of here, Cooper.''

''Hang on.''

He carried her through the kitchen, along a corridor, across
the foyer, out the door, down the driveway, and over the snow-
banks to the BMW. There he buckled her into the front passenger seat, pulled the cashmere overcoat close about her, and
wrapped her bare legs and feet in the lap robe supplied by the
car rental people. Then he went around the car, climbed into
the driver's seat, fired up the motor, and had them under way,
heater blasting.

''Do you need a hospital, Tina?''

''I need a bath and a shampoo.''

''Did that big bastard—''

''Nothing like that. I wasn't raped or anything. He must
have seen me surveying the Ramm place with my binoculars
from the apartment window. He and some other guy just came
through my door, punched me around a bit, then dragged me
across the street, stuck me in that closet, and took my clothes
away. 'So you not only can't run, but wouldn't run even if you
could,' they said. You know something? I never felt so vulnerable.''

"It's SOP in hardball interrogations. Make them naked and they sing like canaries. Did they question you?"

"No. They seemed to be waiting for somebody."

"Who was the other guy?"

"Beats me. Middle-agey. German. Where are we going?"

"To the Vier Jahreszeiten. To get you decent and scrubbed. Why?

"We have a lot of talking to do."

Thirty-nine

"G ilchrist speaking."

"This is Milano."

"Hi, Al. What's up?"

"Did you get a call from Brad Willoughby?"

"He's on my list of call-backs. I haven't got to him yet. Why?"

"Well, I guess he didn't want to wait. He called me to tell me that Quigg has left for Jacksonville. He's supposed to meet with Takai at Tremaine's beach house."

"This is definite?"

"Quigg's already on the plane."

"A very interesting development. They weren't supposed to meet until the Rettung board meeting, when Takai could slip in for a bona fide business reason. He's arrived early. Rather arrogantly early. Which means they're getting more open about things, more confident."

"Why shouldn't they, for chrissake? Half the country's shooting the other half, everybody's so mad. Half the country's yelling for the president's impeachment, the recall of Congress, new elections by April. Who's going to notice—or care—who some goddamn Japanese gangster's talking to or what he's doing?''

"It's a bad time, sure enough. The Russian thing, with an American twist. All the more reason to keep with this Yankee Doodle caper. With the government unraveling, we don't need that kind of aiding and abetting.''

"I sometimes wonder what the hell good it will do. Why we bother.''

"We bother because we're paid to bother.''

"We won't be paid very long, at this rate.''

"Can you think of any alternatives?''

"I guess not.''

"What steps are you taking about this meeting?''

"I have the beach house pretty well bugged. What they say, we'll hear.''

"Good. Send me tapes as soon as.''

"I have a few other bits and pieces.''

"Like?''

"For one, there's hard evidence that young Cooper killed his old man. Nickerson, the city detective, found a thirty-eight stashed in young Cooper's house in Jax. The chief says the piece, as soon as he gets hold of it, will be sent to the FDLE lab for ballistics.''

"Gets hold of it? What the hell does that mean?''

"Apparently the piece was misplaced after tagging and bagging. They're tracking it down.''

"God. What a rinky-dink operation.''

"The St. Augie cops are good. So something's a little weird about this.''

"What I think is weird is that Frank Cooper was more than likely shot by the Yankee Doodler—maybe even Hefflefinger himself—who then planted the piece in the kid's house, and Nickerson is simply ignoring that idea because he has the hots for a gaudy scalp and a promotion.''

"If he has a piece and the tests show a match, it's Doodlers-Schmoodlers. The country may be coming apart, but plain old murder marches on. Besides, there's no way Nickerson can know about Yankee Doodle. He wouldn't be so avid if he did know about it. And there *was* a lot of bad blood between Cooper and his boy.''

"Well, there's no skin off our asses either way.''

"Seems to me there is.''

"How so?''

"With young Cooper inside on a murder rap, he gets out of our way on the Hefflefinger thing. That may make it good for the Doodlers, but it also makes it nice for us.''

"You mean one of our guys might have planted the piece?''

"I wouldn't go that far. But you'll have to admit that it would be nice. And you'll also have to admit our top guys aren't too bashful about stacking the deck. So just about anybody could have planted that shootin'-arn in Cooper's house. Even us.''

"Jesus. What a rotten mind you have, Milano.''

"I'll say. I live in a rotten world.''

"Well, keep me informed on the matter.''

"Another thing: The Mennen woman has disappeared.''

"What?''

"We had her pretty well in our sights after she tumbled to that Middiot, Abernathy. She went from him to Hefflefinger and from Hefflefinger to Tremaine. I don't know how much she got out of them at this point, but the fact that she saw the linkage could get in our way, big-time, especially on top of what young Cooper was digging up on Hefflefinger for the *Times-Union*. The Middiots obviously saw it the same way, because she went to visit her family in Philly, and *poof*. Our people there say she's not around.''

"Did they query the parents?''

"Her old man, guy owns a travel agency. He said she popped in, said hello, then took off somewhere with friends— where, he wasn't sure. We were afraid it would shake the pudding too much to get more hardball at this time. So—''

"Well, no big deal. She's probably at the bottom of the Delaware River about now, if Frank Cooper offers a pattern.''

"Could be. But we'll keep looking. We can't afford to have her bumbling around in our kitchen.''

"Anything else?''

"One thing: I need some more travel voucher forms."

"All right, Al. You got 'em."

"Bye."

"Good morning, Mrs. Beatty."

"Well, if it ain't Manfred von Schnitzelfritzel. What the hell you doin' here, ya ole goose-stepper? Have a seat."

"Thank you, but I must hurry along. I have come to look in on Mr. Matt's house across the street and make sure it has been tented and treated for termites. I saw you here on the porch, and so I have the great pleasure to stop by and give you my greetings."

"Good to see ya, man. Ya been okay? Ya look pale-ish, matter a fact. But then you Krauts allus look the color of mushrooms, to my mind. Ha ha."

"I have been extra busy because Mr. Matt is in Europe and has given me things to do."

"Europe, eh? His pappy used ta spend a lotta time over there. Now him. Yore a Europe kinda guy—how come ya ain't with him?"

"It is my responsibility to keep his properties in good order. Even that old place over there."

"The debuggers was there for three days. Put the whole house under a tarp and gassed the hell outa the termites. What a production. Sheesh."

"Do you remember exactly what days those were, Mrs. Beatty?"

"Shore do. The tenth, eleventh, and twelfth. I remember because Nellie had to go to the vet's on the eleventh, and those guys were over there the day afore and the day after Maude Maxwell, the Elderly Aid helper, came to pick her up. Nellie raised holy hell, I'll tell you. She's one cat hates them tote boxes."

"Do you also remember everybody who went in and out of the house at that time?"

"Well, ain't nobody to remember. The buggers stayed outside, havin' no need to do elsewise. An' the only people came and went over there I already told Matt about. Guys an' a woman with limos, and things like that."

"So, nobody else, then?"

"Hey, man, I watch everything in this here neighborhood, and somebody comes and goes, I know it. And if I don't like what I see, I make a note on this here pad. Like the note I made for Matt when them weirdos went inta his house, lookin' like burglars."

"Did anyone enter the house after the tenting?"

"Nope. Only you, t'day. Why? Sumpin' wrong?"

"No, no. Being a mushroom-colored Kraut, I am most methodical in my record-keeping for Mr. Matt."

"Ha ha. Ya gotta sense a yumor. An' I like that."

"As for you, Mrs. Beatty, have things been going well for you?"

"Shore. Nuthin' ta complain about. Was a mite worried about Nellie there fer a while, but she's okay now."

"Do you need anything? Is there anything at all I can do for you?"

"Nah. But thanks anyhow. 'Preciate yore askin'."

"My pleasure. You have the St. Augustine number. Call me if anything needs to be done."

"Thanks, Manfred. Yore a good ole soul."

"Good day, Mrs. Beatty."

"S'long, pal. Come again."

Forty

Quigg had been both cheered and depressed by the trip to Jacksonville. It was uplifting, exciting, to hear the applause and the shouts of approval from the crowds at both terminals. Airport police had actually been compelled to clear paths for him, and at the Jacksonville end they had been briefly overwhelmed by the crush of those who wanted to shake his hand or pat him on the back. Yesterday's speech at Valley Forge had been virtually ignored by the Leet networks and print media, which were content with severely edited versions of the wire service coverage; but live cable and the fiercely pro-Middie "maverick press" had been there in force, and the national reaction had been immediate and stupendous. Fen Quigg was becoming a phenomenon, pure and simple. He recognized that his incredibly rapid rise to political stardom was the precise cause of his dejection: He was a source of hope for millions, but to be so brought the hatred of additional millions, who viewed him as a rabble-rousing malcontent. In sum, the old saloon rhetoric—expanded, polished, and sophisticated—had elevated him to a politician's paradise, but now he wasn't so sure it had been worth the price.

He'd been finally squeezed into the limo driven by Al Milano and escorted by motorcycle police to his hotel, where, after running a gauntlet of local media types and autograph seekers, he managed to get in a shower, a jolt of bourbon, and a two-hour nap.

And then there was the glittering, candlelit dinner in the monumental seaside home of Stanley M. Tremaine, where he made fatuous small talk with a dozen Southeast barons and their fragrant spouses whose names were synonymous with glamour and riches but whose eyes bespoke boredom and a poverty of spirit. There was not a name that failed to impress him, not a face he managed to recognize. Tremaine was at the table's head, of course, but the black-tied flankers and their bejeweled consorts were strangers, all come to be seen and fawned over in return for their generous checks.

Oko Takai, the underlying cause of all of it, was nowhere to be seen until midnight, in the library, after the dinner party had dispersed and the great house was silent.

"I was disappointed when you weren't at dinner with us," Quigg said. "I've heard so much about you over the years."

Takai, seated in one of the huge leather easy chairs, nodded politely and tipped his brandy glass in a casual salute. "I likewise have been looking forward to our getting together, Congressman. And so now here we are, just the two of us. Brandy?"

"No, thanks." Quigg sat on the sofa.

A pause, slightly strained, was broken when Takai, presumably in some nuance of his native courtesy, felt it advisable to explain. "I was not at dinner because my presence would have been too difficult for the guests to deal with comfortably. Mr. Tremaine had invited them in the interest of your presidential campaign, and since they were all of the same stripe—bound inextricably to each other by economic, social, and cultural factors that give them a cookie-cutter sameness—a notorious Japanese in their midst could have confused and embarrassed them. And believe me, Mr. Quigg, I have seen often enough how quickly a confused and embarrassed rich man snaps shut his purse."

"I'm sure Stan appreciates your sensitivity. I know I certainly do."

Takai nodded again and sipped some brandy. "Your speech at Valley Forge was a huge success, obviously."

Quigg smiled. "And no one was more surprised than I was. I'd been giving variations on that speech for years."

"Ah, but the audience itself has changed. What you said years ago has taken on new breadth, a new urgency, eh?"

"So it seems. My country is in desperate straits, and its people are looking for a leader with answers. I appear to be pressing some of the right buttons."

"And that is why we are here, eh?"

Quigg, because he had no idea of what else to do, stopped fencing. "Just why are we here, Mr. Takai? Why did you ask me to come to Jacksonville?"

The small man showed a small smile and peered into his glass. "Because I think it is time we have an understanding— a clearly stated agreement, simply between the two of us—as to our obligations to each other."

"I'm not sure we have any obligations to each other."

"At times I become so involved in my various affairs I'm led to somewhat mistaken assumptions. In this case, obviously, I have wrongly assumed that Stanley Tremaine has briefed you on my interest in the United States and what is taking place here. First, let me make it clear that I am not acting solely alone. A consortium of very rich, very powerful, and very determined men has asked me to serve as leader and spokesman in this matter. I do so gladly, because I believe that their vision will ultimately serve the best interests of your nation as well as the more narrow, ah, esoteric interests of the consortium."

Quigg, uneasiness gathering, asked, "What interests does the consortium have in my nation?"

"Your nation is rapidly becoming no nation at all. Like the Soviet Union before you, the government establishment— aging, inept, autocratic, indifferent, and, worst of all, self-perpetuating—has finally aroused the focused anger of the populace. There has been much talk in the media lately of the Boston Tea Party, of Lexington and Concord, as proper responses to a foreign ruler who, in those days, was delivering the kind of government to the American colonies that your government is delivering to the states and localities today. This is hyperbolic, to be sure, but in emotional terms, it strikes precisely the right note for the growing mass of outraged Americans. How else could your fiery speech at Valley Forge have met with such instantaneous, spontaneous approval? 'Our government acts as if it's on another planet,' you said. 'Our government is nothing but a group of wealthy elite who view you and me as mere money machines that feed their selfish indulgences,' you said. 'The only way to fix our government,' you said, 'is to throw it out and start over.' You were being wildly demagogic, of course, as you most always have been since your arrival on the political scene—playing to people's angers and fears and prejudices for your own gain. But in this instance your timing was superb, and the results show it. If the election were tomorrow, you would probably win it—not only because of what you say but also because you are the only national politician who is saying it so openly and bluntly at a time when so many citizens are literally up in arms.''

Quigg persisted. ''So what are these 'obligations' you're talking about?''

''Putting it simply, my obligation is to see that you are elected to serve as president of the United States—to provide the large sums that will assure your, ah, victory. Your obligation is to see that, once you assume office, my personal interests are served. You get the job and all that goes with it; I get special attention.''

Quigg leaned forward in his wing chair. ''You are, in other words, buying the presidency.''

''I, and the consortium.''

''Who makes up this consortium?''

''I'm not at liberty to discuss that.''

Quigg experienced a sudden and uncharacteristic rush of annoyance. ''They are like you? Japanese gangsters?''

Takai shrugged. ''One man's gangster is another man's entrepreneur, Mr. Quigg. You are a politician, and you deal in labels. I am a businessman, and I deal in reality. And in this case, the reality is that the United States is up for grabs, and my associates and I are in a position to grab. This makes you, personally, very fortunate. By having been selected to serve our ends, you will become enormously wealthy and powerful.''

"Selected? What means selected?"

"You were chosen after an exhaustive study of the American political spectrum. We had developed a computer profile of the man most suitable to our needs, and you'll no doubt be pleased to learn that, of the nearly eleven hundred political figures examined, you were a standout. No one came closer to the model.''

"What were the criteria?"

Takai laughed softly and finished his drink. "You can best answer that question by first, looking in a mirror, and second, reading your own resume.''

"Am I to take that as an insult?"

Takai waved an apologetic hand. "Not at all, Mr. Quigg. Certainly not. You are to take it as a tribute. You are an exceptional man. You are an extraordinary admixture of physical presence, charm, intelligence, political savvy, and self-serving pragmatism. You are a master diplomat, capable of acting in such a way that each of two diametrically opposed forces can be persuaded that you are firmly in its camp. Yet with all this, money and power transcend; you will do anything to acquire both. And that, my friend, makes you precisely like me and the other members of the consortium. You are not only 'our boy,' as the American slang has it—you are one of us. Eh?'' He laughed again.

"The president doesn't rule the United States, you know. He and his Cabinet administer the measures established by Congress. And when either or both get out of line, the courts call them to heel.''

"A tidy, succinct description of the system, to be sure. But irrelevant. We will—and the procedures are already under way—purge those who populate the existing government, including a majority of Congress and those jurists deemed pivotal, and replace them with our own people.''

"These 'procedures' that are under way: you mean the assassinations, the raids, the rebellious acts so evident in the media?"

"Those are mostly window dressing, initiated by us, but window dressing nonetheless. Our primary mechanism is the clandestine purchase of key personalities in all branches of the federal government, in the political party hierarchies, and in the mainstream media."

In a kind of mad aberration, Quigg thought of the old gag in which a distraught man, groaning, "Oh, God, I wish I was dead," is hit on the head by a flowerpot falling from a highrise windowsill. Staggering, he gazes blearily aloft, whining, "Hey, come on—can't you take a joke?"

He saw the irony at once. For years, good old demagogic Congressman Quigg had been calling for just this—a summary cleansing of government, a cathartic ouster of the rascals and the installation of legions committed to reform and a return to basic values. And now here it was, the flowerpot on the head, the stinging realization that it could really happen. Only the reform was being worked by a new set of rascals and the basic values were to be those of a barbaric tribe.

To his surprise, he felt a simultaneous rush of anger, shame, contrition, frustration, and, of all things, sorrow—and in the struggle to deal with this, to evince Uptown Cool while battling Downtown Heat, he could come up with no more than an inane statement of the obvious:

"You must be spending billions."

"Indeed. But look at what we're buying. We're buying control of the world's premier nation. Actually, it's long been for sale. We're simply the first to have amassed the resources and guile required to—how do you Americans put it? To 'pull it off'?"

"What about the nation itself? What will the consortium have it be?"

"Ah, yes. The most logical question of all. And the most easily answered. It will be what you, the president, and your Congress and judiciary make of it. All the consortium asks is that you follow its recommendations on trade and regulatory systems. Private monopolies, cartels, will, as you say, be in again.''

The emotion Quigg had been working so hard to contain finally broke through. ''Ah, yes,'' he grated, ''the culmination of Japan's single-minded, ages-long trade war against the United States. The ultimate trade barrier: The American market becomes an exclusive, formally controlled offshore extension of the Japanese market.''

Takai waved his small hand again, this time dismissively. ''Hold on, Mr. Quigg. There's something you don't quite understand. The consortium is in no way working in the interest of the government or people of Japan. If the truth were known, the Japanese people would like nothing better than to have free trade—unimpeded access to American goods and services. The Japanese people are, in the main, kindly, decent, energetic, and honest, and are much more benign toward the United States than Americans seem to realize. But historically their governments, out of fear that foreign groups—'gangster consortiums' like ours, if you will—were waiting to plunder their vulnerable island economy, have long maintained formidable trade barriers. Seen from their point of view, that makes sense. But, you see, our consortium has no brief for any of this. We are entirely apolitical. We care no more for the Japanese government than we care for yours. And the only American politics that interest us are those that will make it easy for us to accumulate more money and power than we now enjoy. So in all candor I say, 'Make of your nation what you will—so long as its laws and actions aid and abet my consortium's ambitions.' ''

Quigg thought about this for a time, and the only sound in the room was the ticking of the grandfather clock. When the clock chimed twelve-thirty, he stirred in his chair and spoke. ''It seems to me you're overlooking a major vulnerability.''

''What is that, Congressman?''

''What if this new government takes on a life of its own and refuses to do what pleases your consortium?''

''Mm. A good point. In such an event, Mr. Quigg, the process would begin again. With your assassination, I might add.

Followed by liquidation of those key appointees who have reneged on our deal with them. In this sense, we—the consortium—are indeed gangsters. Eh?'' Takai's soft laugh sounded once again.

"So, Congressman: What do you say? We make you king of the world and you make us happy plunderers. Is it a deal?"

"Do I have a choice?"

"I see no other choice. Do you?"

Quigg, for one of the few times in his life, found himself stammering. "I—it's—it's difficult for me to talk so openly about becoming a whore—"

"Correction, Congressman. You have long been a whore. And if you are uncomfortable talking about it, you can relax. There is no one to listen but me and my personal tape recorder. The bugs that someone placed so liberally about this house and its adjacencies were surreptitiously removed before my arrival by the consortium's technicians. We are thorough in our security measures, you see."

Forty-one

The morning was wretched, full of recollections of the grubby scene in the Ramm cellar. She was not unaware of the fact that, on a scale of one to ten, her figure was an eleven. Or that the texture and tone of her skin was about as good as could be expected this side of a cosmetics ad. Nor was she a prude in matters of sexuality, except for the barbaric or sicko kinky. What she was, was a neat-freak—uncompromising in tidiness and personal hygiene. And this part of her nature had been thoroughly traumatized by the incident. Tethered under the harsh light, spread-eagled on the filthy mattress, tousled and begrimed and naked, her mortification was then, and remained still, absolute. She had not been raped in the sexual sense. Moreover, she'd long ago learned to expect lewdness from boys and men—even some women; she'd been peeked at in shower stalls and locker rooms—so Bolko's leering and his pal's goggling had been not so much an offense as it was a kind of brutish certification that her centerfold potential had outlasted her teens. What rankled was that Cooper had seen her at her very worst. No matter his polite obtuseness, the Victorian averting of his eyes as he had covered her with his coat; being a man he had sure as hell taken a good look, and she simply had to have presented a disgusting sight.

Damn it.

"You're being awfully quiet today," Cooper said as he steered the BMW onto the Autobahn-West ramp.

"I don't feel so hot today."

"Well, you've had a bad time, all right."

"I don't need your sympathy, so back off."

"Excuse me all to hell. You were the one who said we had to talk. Now that you've had a good sleep and a gigantic breakfast, I thought maybe we'd get into the process."

"I'm just not in the mood yet."

"Right. Neither am I."

Nothing more was said until they had cleared Munich and were halfway to Fürstenfeldbruck.

"You're upset because I saw you without your clothes on, aren't you."

"Come again?"

"You heard me."

"Lots of people have seen me without my clothes on."

"So then why are you upset because I saw you?"

"You're saying I'm upset. I didn't say I'm upset."

"Well, if you aren't upset you're sure giving a great imitation of somebody who is."

"Why don't we just drop the subject?"

"Because I'm more upset than you are. Sure as hell a naked woman isn't anything to get in an uproar about these days. But it's different when you see somebody you like a real hootin' bunch being humiliated. You take it personally."

She gave him a sidelong glance. "You do?"

"I'm sorry that I had to be part of your humiliation, Tina. I mean that."

"You really like me a real hootin' bunch?"

"If I didn't, we wouldn't be having this silly goddamn conversation."

"It's not so silly to me."

They rode in silence for a long time. Outside Augsburg, she

said, "You're ten years older than I am, you know."

"I didn't mean to be."

"When I'm eighty, you'll be ninety."

"If you get bored then and want to do a little playing around, I won't mind. Just don't bring your boyfriends home, is all I ask."

This time the silence between them was even longer, deeper. Then:

"I can't make any kind of commitment, Coop. You know that, don't you?"

He shrugged, elaborately nonchalant. "Who said anything about commitment? I was just kidding around."

"I simply must run as fast and far as I can. I can't afford to get entangled with guys right now. It would confuse me, make me—falter. I can't allow that to happen."

"Makes sense. Who are these guys?"

"What guys?"

"The ones you can't get entangled with."

"There aren't any. It was just a figure of speech."

"Oh."

She gave him another glance. "You aren't mad at me, are you?"

"Hell, no. Why should I be mad at you?"

"I mean, you look sort of—ticked off."

"No way. I can't afford any entanglements either. That's why I've been a bachelor ever since I was a little kid."

"I want us to be friends. Real much."

"No problem."

Later, as they followed the bend north at Darmstadt, she cleared her throat and said, "Up to now, I've had a lot of trouble trying to decide if I should clue you in on the story I've got running."

"Oh?"

"But the sharp way you picked up on my tip about Ramm, the way you popped down and saved my bod, shows me that you're a top-gun sort of dude. But now that we understand each other, and like that, I've made my decision. I don't think you'll scoop me."

''We journalists never use that word anymore. 'Scoop' is a barbarism, a cliché of the first magnitude. I forbid you to use it.''

''Our new understanding is only an hour old and already you're forbidding me to do things.''

''That's because, like all men, I am intimidated by women, and to compensate—reassure myself—I indulge in macho posturing. I bluster. I swagger. I even refuse to put the john seat down.''

''With sarcasm, you are mainline weird.''

''What tip about Ramm?''

''Say what?''

''You said you tipped me about Ramm. What tip? When?''

She gave him a look. ''You didn't get the message I left on Chuck's answering machine?''

''What message?''

''How Ramm's fuses are blown. How he couldn't possibly have initiated a lawsuit against you. How that means somebody is using Ramm as a device to get at you. How you owe me sixty bucks.''

''Chuck was having trouble with his answerer. He must have erased your call.''

.''So how did you know where to look for me?''

''By brilliant detective work. By calling Uncle Otto for your Munich address. By not finding you at said address. By looking elsewhere.''

She stared out the window, struggling to dispel a renewed vision of the grubby cellar.

''So what's this big story you've got, Tina?''

''Hard evidence of an armed rebellion. The Second American Revolution against a callous, exploitive government.''

''For God's sake, Tina, that kind of speculation has been all over the papers and the talk shows for weeks now. You're reinventing the wheel.''

''It's no speculation. A militia is being formed. Actually, it's like a damned guerrilla army, and it's being paid for by foreign interests that want to hassle our government like France hassled England back in 17-umpteen.''

"Tina, you're not listening to me. It's all rumor, a puff of wind blown up by the media."

"And you're not listening to me, damn it. It's no rumor—it's real."

"So how do you know that?"

"That district judge you were after—Hefflefinger—well, he's not running guns for the mob, he's part of a network in Miami, New Orleans, El Paso, and L.A. that imports illegal guns and sneaks them to the militia. Which is being formed and led nationally by ex-General Harry Allen and drilled by local and regional commanders. St. Augustine's leading realtor, for instance, Claude Abernathy, is one of hundreds nationwide. And—"

He broke in, and she felt his surprise. "How did you know I was after Hefflefinger?"

"I interviewed Abernathy and the judge, too. I tried to interview Tremaine, but it was like trying to get an audience with the pope. He was always out to lunch. The other two sang like divas, though, I'm glad to say."

"You interviewed them. Just like that."

"Yep."

"And they talked. Just like that."

"It was like pulling teeth, actually. But I used all the techniques you listed in your Orlando seminar."

"My God. People actually *listen* to the speakers at seminars?"

"This people did."

"Like what techniques?"

"You said the best one—the one that works most—is the old 'Have you stopped beating you wife?' bit, backed up by, 'If you won't answer my questions I'll just have to write the story based on what others have told me.' The first technique flusters them; the second scares them into thinking their confederates are ratting on them, so they start talking, to be sure their side of the story gets told. And I'm here to tell you, Herr Berichterstatter, that it works like a freaking charm."

"But only if one of the crew is a weak link—if he's unsure

of himself, or guilt-stricken, or resentful, or suspicious of his pals. It only works those times.''

''My guys were a bit of all those. Abernathy was like on the end of the limb, bouncing in the wind and feeling all alone. So he got more chatty than he intended, I think. Then Hefflefinger, who obviously doesn't think much of Abernathy, went up in a hot, tight spiral when he heard what Abernathy told me. He got so mad he dropped Tremaine's name as a kind of god who would fix Abernathy's crock but good. I'll admit I didn't get too far with Tremaine, but his refusal to see me was negative confirmation, like you said in Orlando. A man who has nothing to be ashamed of loves to spout off to the press—especially a pol—but a man who clams up has just got to have muddy shoes.''

''So, all right. So what did these guys tell you?''

''Abernathy is pretty low on the totem pole—there are lots just like him around the country. He's the equivalent of a battalion commander in the army. It's his job to recruit and have in basic military training at all times at least two companies of a hundred men and women each who are between eighteen and thirty-five. He takes his orders direct from Allen, whose main dodge is CEO of a sporting goods company in St. Louis. Abernathy showed me—let me take pictures of it—an arms stash in a tunnel hidden under a field house at a private school. Machine guns, bazookas, assault rifles, sidearms, grenade launchers, shoulder-fired missiles, radios, radar, night-vision stuff— it's big-time. The recruits train on these in a huge tract behind the school, all of it owned by Abernathy. I've taken a look at this ground, and they go to great trouble to erase vehicle tracks, spent ammo, the traces of combat maneuvers. I mean these guys are huge on security and secrecy. Even recruitment is hush-hush, conducted through the grapevine, a word-of-mouth sort of thing with emphasis on adventure and vengeance, and—''

''Vengeance?''

She nodded. ''Yep. The likeliest recruits are those who have been hurt by the government—or who think they have been hurt by the government. A daddy who's been laid off due to tax-induced down-sizing in industry, or a mom whose kid has been shafted by the school system, or a dude whose old folks have been screwed by the federal health care program, or a teacher who's been canned for political incorrectness—that kind of thing. The bottom line: They're mad as hell and want to widen some Elite nasal passages.''

Cooper humphed. ''You have to be awful mad to be willing to put up with military training. Mads very seldom last long, and when the mad peters out, there goes your recruit.''

''I suggested that. Abernathy says they don't recruit people who are just mad. Their recruits are filled with rage that approximates vendetta, or a holy war against infidels.''

''How do they determine that?''

She laughed softly. ''He says earlier recruits, who are now in the officer corps, are trained psychologists who recognize real fury because they're real furious.''

''Sheesh.''

''He says you wouldn't believe how many Americans are really furious these days.''

''The hell I wouldn't. I invented furious.''

He steered the car off the autobahn at Heidelberg and picked up the two-lane blacktop leading through the Odenwald northeast to the Main River basin.

''What's this road do, Coop?''

''It's the back door to Eheburg.''

''Which is?''

''Where I begin to nail down my contribution to your story.''

She gave him a quick glance. ''Say what?''

''I've been picking up on a lot of things that didn't seem to make sense—to hang together—until your little soliloquy. The stuff you've dug out is the stickum for the stuff I've dug out. Without your story, I'd still be nowhere.''

''That makes it our story, doesn't it?''

''No. All I'm doing—all I've done—has had one rationale. And that's to find out who killed my father. To punch that individual's ticket. What you're doing is mainline. What I'm doing is sidebar.''

She sighed. ''Are you just being nice to me? Condescending?''

His face suddenly incandescent, he pounded the steering wheel with his fist. "Goddammit, Tina, will you *ever* get off that tiresome bullshit? You're a grown goddamn reporter and you've got a line on the story of the sonofabitchin' century and when you pop it you'll never have to worry about condescension again. Now get off that crap and give me a frigging break, will you?"

They rode in taut silence for a full minute.

Then Tina said, "You've got to stop using language like that."

"Say it isn't so."

"Refined men never say 'condescension.' "

They exchanged glares, which transmuted into fierce, grudging grins, followed by explosive laughter—loud, hard, and on the rim of hysteria.

"You're a real piece of work," he said eventually.

"In your face, buddy."

Herr Feldstein, the tiny old housekeeper informed them, was at the synagogue and wouldn't return until two o'clock, so they found a *Konditerei* down the road where they treated themselves to mountainous eclairs and pots of strong, black coffee. Their conversation was spare, partly because it was hard to talk around mouthfuls of cream and gummy chocolate, but mainly because they each were dealing with, first, their ticklish new emotional-professional alliance, and, second, meditations on how to handle and where to take the volatile compound their separate investigations had produced.

Feldstein was all smiles and apologies when they finally took seats in his cluttered office.

"Life gets so full. I need a forty-hour day."

"We'll try not to take too much of your time," Cooper said. "But we've run into some interesting developments as a result of questioning Lori Altmann and Siegfried Ramm, and it would be—"

Feldstein broke in, surprise on his seamed face. "You talked to Altmann before she was assassinated?"

Cooper nodded. "Just before. I almost went with her."

"So, then, you were the 'bystander' who—The press reports were not quite clear—"

"I'm the man."

Politely, Feldstein regarded Tina. "Were you there also, Miss Mennen?"

"No. I was investigating another matter in Munich at the time."

"I'm glad. You both might have been killed. Such a dreadful experience."

There was an interval, a moment suspended, while this truth was given thought. It was broken when Cooper said quickly, bluntly, "I know who Ham and Eggs were."

The room took on a new, special tension while Feldstein, his gaze fixed on Cooper, dealt with this. Then:

"I don't follow you, Mr. Cooper. That seems to me to be a non sequitur—"

"Let's stop fooling around, shall we? Stan Tremaine was Ham and you were Eggs. Who was Pancake?"

"Where—how did you get this, ah, peculiar idea?"

"First of all, nobody, no source, not even the official World War Two archives of the United States Government, has the specific knowledge, the, well, intimacy, I guess it's called, that you showed when I questioned you about Slingshot the other day. I was impressed by that at the time, but a long double-take made it pretty obvious that you had to have been there—you had to have been one of the participants. And that suspicion has since been confirmed by others."

"What others?"

"I began with Altmann, as you suggested."

"And? Who else?"

Cooper ignored the question. "I ask you again, Herr Feldstein: Who was Pancake?"

"That's a difficult question to answer."

"Why?"

"It forces me to choose between two unpleasant alternatives. If I tell you, I'll be compelled to put a longtime friend in jeopardy. If I don't tell you, I'll be reneging on a promise to another even dearer friend."

"As my mother used to say, 'Stay with the truth. It hurts only once. A lie hurts for a lifetime.' "

"Ah, yes. Poor, dear Mary Jane, the tormented psychic who liked to be called M.J."

Cooper stared, incredulous, almost unable to speak. "You knew my mother?"

"I never met her. I knew her through your father. He loved her deeply and spoke of her often." Feldstein turned in his chair to face the window, his faded blue eyes regarding the meadows beyond. The drizzle had become a slow, steady rain that drummed on the roof and sent runnels down the panes. "I was a member of his team on Operation Slingshot. Our friendship began during the war and continued through all the years since. We met every time he came to Europe."

Cooper leaned forward in his chair, waiting.

Feldstein sighed, and it was clear that he was carrying a load of unhappiness. "Frank said it might come to this."

"Meaning what?"

Feldstein's voice was full of that mixture of weariness and affection an old man brings to recollections of hard years endured. "You represented a great ambivalence in Frank's life. He was simultaneously proud of you and fearful of you. In our phone conversations of the past several years, he would speak glowingly of your professional accomplishments, your tenacity, your awareness, your reporting skills, and so on. And yet he also agonized over them—feared them. He was afraid that you might someday bring them to bear on him, that you might look into who he was and how he got that way. 'If Coop shows up on your doorstep,' he said once, 'it means he already knows too much about me and deserves to know the rest. If he doesn't show up, let the fiction live on.' "

"Fiction? What did he mean by that?"

"Operation Slingshot was a fraud. Your father and I—all of the others—were pulling a scam."

Forty-two

Y ou mean the diamonds?'' Cooper asked.
"So you've learned about those, then.''
"They were the root of your scam?''
Feldstein nodded slowly. "Would you like me to take it in rough chronology?''
"Whatever pleasures you.''
"It began in mid-February, 1945, when those close to Hitler were becoming uneasy over his apparently worsening dementia. The Führer was adamant: There would be no deviating from the scorched-earth policy, under which all loyal Germans would fight to eventual extinction on the ashes of the Fatherland. Martin Bormann, not one to enthuse over a suicide edict that included him, began to look for a way out—an exit that would enable him to keep control of whatever elements of the Nazi structure might survive Hitler's nationally mandated death wish. He called in Ramm, a longtime, trusted friend, swore him to secrecy, and asked him to lay out an escape route that would get them—Bormann and Ramm and some crates of

documents—to a rendezvous with a submarine off the Spanish
coast on or about April seventh, from where they would sail to
sanctuary in South America. Ramm got right to it, selecting as
an assembly point a farmhouse near Starnberg. From there, the
Bormann party would be driven on back roads leading west
through the south of France—still heavily populated by
Vichy-French Nazi collaborators—to a deserted beach near
the French-Spanish border. Bormann approved the plan and
told Ramm to take up residence at the farmhouse and await the
small party, handpicked by Bormann, reporting for duty as
security guards, weapons and radio specialists, and driver-
mechanics. Ramm was also told to expect what Bormann
called his 'portfolio of plans for a postwar Nazi revival.' These
plans would be delivered by courier on or about March fifteenth, and they were to be held for Bormann's arrival on or
about March thirtieth. This, because Bormann feared these
treasonous documents might, if they were kept in Berlin, be
discovered by Hitler's agents, who by then were spying on all
top members of the Nazis' capital hierarchy.''

Feldstein paused, his eyes thoughtful, his fingers toying
with a pencil. Then: ''While all this was going on, an American counterintelligence team, led by your father, was working
with me in France on the exploitation of a captured war criminal who, for amnesty, was giving us the lowdown on the German concentration camp hierarchy. One day in early March we
were tipped off to the Bormann-Ramm plot by one of the
members of Ramm's team, a Wehrmacht automotive sergeant
who had been assigned to Ramm as a driver. This fellow was
up to here with Nazis and Nazism and, seeing that here was
just more of the same, he decided to turncoat. We—''

Cooper interrupted. ''How did he know how and where to
find you and my dad?''

Feldstein smiled appreciatively. ''A very perceptive question, Mr. Cooper. The man was not a Wehrmacht sergeant. He
was really a Gestapo agent who had become thoroughly sickened by the Nazis and their system. He was well acquainted
with me because I was one of the very few to organize a successful escape to England from Menzing, that lovely little Nazi
death camp for Jewish intellectuals in Holland. He was serving

there at the time. Since my escape had made me somewhat of a celebrity on both sides of the line, it was no trick for him to keep informed of my whereabouts. There was even a story in *Stars and Stripes* when I returned to liberated France as a Military Government adviser—which, of course, was a cover for my real duty, which was to track down war criminals.''

Cooper held up the pen with which he'd been making notes. ''Hold here. Why had this man been assigned to Ramm? Why this one, of all the automotive noncoms available?''

''Another good question. Bormann liked to keep tabs on those he gave delicate tasks, so he asked Heinrich Himmler, the Gestapo chief, for a capable agent who was far out of the inner circle of Berlin's palace intriguers and could serve as a personal informant 'on a sensitive matter,' as he put it. Himmler gave him this agent who was, at the time, infiltrating a prisoner-of-war camp near Mannheim, spying on Allied PW's who were suspected of planning escapes. The agent was extremely intelligent, Himmler said, and, because he was trying to work out a minor punishment, would more than likely deliver a thousand percent on such an assignment.

''The man was flown to Berlin, and charged by Bormann to report to Ramm's team as chief driver and make periodic reports to Bormann on the team's comings and goings. As a kind of reward, the man was given a one-week furlough before reporting to Ramm. However, he used this interval to 'visit a friend at the front,' where he allowed himself to be captured by advancing American troops. An IPW officer brought him into my office in Epinal, saying that this prisoner had asked specifically to talk to me about a very important Nazi plot. I listened to the man's story about Ramm and the Bormann thing, and, convinced that there might be something to it, I asked the IPW officer to give me custody of the prisoner.''

''And this was when the Gestapo agent became 'Pancake.' Right?''

Again Feldstein showed a weary, surrendering smile.

''And Pancake's real name was—is—Manfred Kohlmann. Right?''

''Yes. Of course,'' Feldstein said. ''Manfred had been an attorney with a private practice in Berlin, and in the early days of Hitler's regime he was enlisted by the Gestapo to investigate and prosecute nonpolitical crimes, such as bank robberies, embezzlements, kidnappings—the kind of thing your FBI does. Later he was pressed into service with the Gestapo's political wing, but he showed such open distaste for the duty he was punished. His assignment: to serve undercover as an inmate of various concentration camps, spying on those who planned escapes. It was filthy, lonely, detestable work for anyone, let alone a sensitive, highly ethical lawyer, and Manfred developed a real hatred for the Nazis.''

Cooper put it together then. "Even so, if Manfred's former Gestapo affiliation were discovered by the authorities in the States, his citizenship would be withdrawn and he'd be deported as an undesirable. This is the 'jeopardy' you mentioned. Right?''

"I'm astonished at how much information you pulled from Lori Altmann. She was notoriously tight-lipped.''

"She got religion. She was in a repentant mood.''

Feldstein shrugged. "It happens. And it was she who told you about me?''

"Let's just say I found out about you.''

The old man resettled in his chair and his gaze went to the window again. "I had Manfred repeat his story for your father and Stan Tremaine, the team's second-in-command. They agreed that the story was worth looking into and arranged to have Manfred parachuted into Bavaria the day before he was to report to Ramm. His instructions were to carry out whatever duties were assigned by Ramm and to stand by for further instructions from Frank, once Frank and his team parachuted into the area.''

Cooper, writing rapidly in his notepad, asked, "How could you trust Manfred? I mean, he was a Gestapo agent, giving you some kind of story about how sick he was of the Nazis. What made you believe him then—and accept the reports he was supposed to give you later?''

"In the business we were in, Mr. Cooper, we never believed anybody. We always checked, and we checked out Manfred, and his biography was confirmed by G-Two, whose central registry kept dossiers on all known Gestapo personnel. Moreover, we always made certain that we had a very large carrot to dangle before an informant. In Manfred's case, he understood that, as a concentration camp control officer, he would be an automatic arrest after the war and would unquestionably do time as a human rights violator. But, we told him, as long as he cooperated with us, as long as his reports held water and his performance stacked up, he would enjoy amnesty—even after the war."

"What were Stan Tremaine's duties?"

"He was, as I say, Frank's assistant. He was in charge of logistics, supplies, radio communications, and the administration of confidential funds. I never liked him much."

"Why?"

Feldstein waved his thin right hand in dismissal. "He was out of his depth in our kind of work. He was pedantic, coldly indifferent, and had little apparent enthusiasm for risk. Frank was audacious, quick, inventive, keen for search and discovery; he was warm, witty, and kind. Yet they liked each other, obviously, and seemed to complement one another, not only on the job but also as human beings." He blinked, turned in his swivel chair and regarded Tina amiably. "Speaking of indifference, Miss Mennen, you must think I'm entirely thoughtless. Would you like a cup of tea, or coffee, perhaps?"

Tina shook her head. "No thanks. I'm still dealing with a ton of chocolate eclair."

"You're being very patient, as well."

"I don't know one end of a war from the other. But the people you're talking about are wide-screen."

Cooper was annoyed by this digression, which, he suspected, derived not so much from Feldstein's courtesy as from the old man's effort to interrupt the rhythm of the questioning. An interview put off-pace was an interview likely to miss some important points.

"All right, Herr Feldstein, so where do the diamonds come in?"

The old man obviously heard the impatience in Cooper's voice. He answered quickly: "Frank passed the story on to Eisenhower's G-Two, who, after consultation with Ike, sent us to the OSS center at Dijon for parachute training, after which

Frank, Stan, and I dropped into Bavaria just north of Bad Tölz.
We were carrying meticulously prepared documents showing
us to be Gestapo agents on a special, top-secret mission. After
the drop we made our way to Starnberg, where we comman-
deered a house and a car. Our plan was, with Manfred's help,
to keep a secret watch on the Ramm people. When and if the
Bormann documents arrived, Manfred would help us make
surreptitious photos of them. And then, when Bormann himself showed up, we would tail him into Allied territory and arrest him as a war criminal.''

Cooper said, ''Sort of dicey, wasn't it? I mean with neither
Frank nor Stan able to speak German, they'd have been up the
creek if you'd come under questioning.''

Feldstein looked slightly surprised. ''What makes you think
Frank and Stan didn't speak German?''

''You mean they did?''

''You really don't know much about your father, do you.''

''Less and less every minute. Stan, too.''

''You didn't know Frank had spent eight years as a boy with
his maternal grandparents in Wiesbaden?''

''I guess I didn't even know he had grandparents. It was
never discussed, and it never occurred to me to ask.''

''Why? Were you really that uninterested in your own father? He often said you never seemed to—''

Cooper broke in. ''I'm not here to explain my complicated
relations with my father, Herr Feldstein. I'm here to find out
who murdered him. Now you just let me ask the damned questions.''

Feldstein made an apologetic gesture. ''I'm sorry. It was a
presumptuous question, asked spontaneously. Please forgive
me.''

''So go on.''

''Frank was very fluent, of course. Stan spoke schoolbook
German, with an accent. But Germany was overrun by dis-
placed persons who spoke poor German with strange accents.
Even the Waffen SS had units composed of foreigners. Stan's
cover was that he was a Lithuanian Nazi who had been appointed to the Gestapo for duty in the Eastern Zones and was
now working on this special case.''

Tina, presumably in an attempt to ease the tension, laughed softly. "How did you dudes keep all this straight? You had wall charts and name tags, maybe?"

Cooper was unamused. "Butt out, Tina."

"Hey, guy, lighten up. We're all on your side."

The silence that followed was brief, but strained. In the moment, Cooper saw the quick glances exchanged by Tina and the old man, and they told him that they feared he might be losing his cool. And perhaps he was. Perhaps it was getting beyond what he could handle. His father: a sometime international scam artist who spoke German and hung out with all-time champion sickos. His lawyer: ditto.

God.

"Go on," Cooper said.

"One day Bormann's 'portfolio' showed up at Ramm's house, which was about a mile from our villa. Manfred told us it had come in seven sealed pails delivered by a Storch liaison plane that had landed in a meadow to the rear of the Ramm place. It wasn't more than a day later that Manfred reported the pails contained not documents, but a huge fortune in diamonds, and Ramm had placed them under maximum security. The next day Frank and Stan and I walked in on Ramm and proposed the scam."

"Let's have some detail on that, please."

"Frank announced to Ramm that he and Stan were American agents who had been following the Bormann-Ramm thing since its inception. Their job, he said, was to wait until Bormann showed up in Starnberg, where he would be seized along with his 'portfolio.' Ramm and his people would then be summarily executed and Bormann would be held until an American plane picked him up and flew him and his portfolio to Eisenhower's headquarters."

Cooper looked up from his note-taking. "Why was he telling Ramm all this? Why didn't my dad's team just wipe out the Ramm group and take all the diamonds for themselves? Why all this palaver?"

"Those were the very questions asked by Ramm. And Frank answered with the unvarnished truth, as the saying goes. 'Because,' he said, 'my people and I are merely looters, not mur-

derers. We want only half of the diamonds—themselves
looted by the Nazi government from a conquered nation. We
do not want to kill anybody to acquire them. And we want to
be able to tell our headquarters that we carried out our mission
by capturing Bormann and found that there were, in fact, no
plans—no portfolios—just Bormann. But to do this, we need
the German team's cooperation. And for your cooperation, you
will be rewarded with your lives, an unhindered escape, and a
half-share in the diamonds.' "

"In other words, Ramm was given an offer he couldn't refuse: 'Give us Bormann and half the diamonds or die here on
the spot.' Right?"

Feldstein nodded. "That is correct. Ramm understood that,
even as they spoke, hidden guns were trained on him and his
party."

"What if he had refused? Would he and his team have been
killed on the spot?"

Feldstein shook his head. "No, it was all bluff. We were indeed not murderers. But even if we had been, with only three
of us, we were badly outnumbered and outgunned. We would
have done the dying."

"So what did Ramm agree to do?"

"He would continue to operate in the normal fashion, making preparations and sending reports to Bormann. This would
enable us to report to Eisenhower's G-Two that our case was
progressing as planned and that Bormann's capture was im-
minent. To corroborate, we would send G-Two copies of
Ramm's messages and other Sunrise documents, ostensibly
filmed surreptitiously by Pancake."

"Did Ramm know that Manfred—Pancake—was a turncoat collaborating with you Americans?"

"He never found out, I'm happy to say. Ramm would photograph his own documents, then hand the film roll to us, and
we would forward it to G-Two as Pancake's work."

Cooper was puzzled. "How did you keep a wretch like
Ramm in line? I mean—"

"He had no choice but to stay in line. As soon as he deviated
from his duties to Bormann, he'd be shot summarily if found
out. If he deviated from his agreement with us, he would like-

wise die. We had given him a chance to survive and live as a wealthy man—so long as he played our game and hid that fact from his own bosses.'' Feldstein cleared his throat. ''Needless to say, Ramm and his people accepted the deal.''

So Cooper's father was a criminal conspirator. Applying his Worst-Scenario Therapy, Cooper sought to roll with the blow; it had been increasingly apparent that Frank Cooper had been living with a secret unhappiness, and to discover nothing more serious than the sharing of a villain's booty with another set of villains, was, in a way, a relief. No murders lurked, no heinous crimes against humanity or the state. There hadn't been even a dereliction of duty: Frank's duty had been to intercept Bormann's plans for postwar Germany, and, since he had determined—at great personal risk—that there were no such plans, duty had been met. At least in Cooper's opinion.

Still, there was this—what?

Grubbiness?

Shame?

Tina sought to ease the strain. ''I'll have that coffee now,'' she said brightly.

Cooper shook his head. ''We're just getting to the juicy part, aren't we, Herr Feldstein.''

''By 'juicy,' I assume you mean the plot's resolution.''

''Something like that.''

Feldstein sighed. ''As you've probably guessed, Ramm had no intention of going along with Frank's proposal. He ordered Manfred to service the team's fastest car, a Mercedes phaeton, and to arm it for a long, fast combat run. He instructed his deputy, Max Dietz, to organize a raid on Frank's house and kill the American team. But Dietz, who was sleeping with Lori Altmann, told Lori of the scheme, and Lori told Manfred, who told Frank, of course.''

''Why would Lori tell Manfred? She barely remembered Manfred's name when I questioned her.''

Feldstein smiled wanly. ''That's Lori for you. She and Manfred were lovers from the day he reported for duty with Ramm's team. It was Lori who told Manfred about the diamonds. She wanted him to help her kill Ramm and Dietz and the others and then run off with the gems.''

"Sheesh."

"God," Tina said, "you people were almost as sneaky as my high school sorority sisters."

"Frank's team launched a preemptive raid on Ramm's place, but in the shooting Ramm and Dietz and Altmann escaped. We, however, had the diamonds."

"And you did what?"

"Frank messaged G-Two that the mission was blown, that Bormann and his portfolio never showed up, and that the Slingshot team, now the target of enemy posses, would have to go into hiding in a safe house in Mannheim and wait until the American army passed through. During that long wait we each began to suffer conscience pangs. Heavy pangs. But how could we return the diamonds to their owners when it was impossible to determine whose they were? So we made a pact. We swore that we would use our shares of the untraceable, unreturnable Nazi loot for some form of reparation, relief among innocents of whatever nationality who suffered under the Nazi terror— mainly women and children. Each of us could do it his way— do what he felt was proper. But none of us would deviate from the pact's primary purpose, which was philanthropy and justice."

"So my father eventually set up Rettung Internationale with Nazi loot. Right?"

"Mm. And I used my share to finance the search for, and the indictment of, all Nazi war criminals—not the top dogs, who were already being tried at Nuremberg, but the Ramms and the Dorns and the Altmanns and the Dietzes, and so on and on."

"How about Stan? Manfred? What have they done with their shares?"

"I am not at liberty to say. Confidentiality was part of the pact. But even if I were not bound by the pact I wouldn't tell you. That's a question to be answered by Stan and Manfred."

"These shares: We're talking about two hundred and fifty million dollars each. That's a bunch of diamonds, and it's no easy job to deal with a collection that big. Hard to smuggle, and hard to fence. You stayed in Europe, so all you had to do was bury your stones and fence them piecemeal. But how did my father and Stan get their shares home?"

Feldstein shook his head slowly, and his face took on an odd grimness. "That," he said, "is something I absolutely refuse to tell you, Mr. Cooper. You have no need to know that. As you have no need to know where those gems that remain are located. To tell you would be to tempt you."

"Diamonds are a man's best fiend, eh?"

"Cut it out, Tina."

"Hell, Coop, don't take yourself so seriously. You're already an uneasy, vaguely guilty rich man, and guess where your riches came from. Nazi loot."

"That doesn't mean I have to keep the money."

"Who are you going to give it back to, for cripes sake?"

"That," Feldstein said, "is precisely the dilemma faced by Frank and Stan and me. So, my dear, unhappy Mr. Cooper, welcome to the club."

Ignoring the gentle needle, Cooper said, "Well, then, tell me this: Are you the guy Manfred calls 'Wolfgang'?"

"Yes. That's his code name for me. And he is 'Putzi.' We've used those tags during the years we've been keeping the wolves at bay."

"What wolves?"

Feldstein smiled wryly. "You don't think for a moment that Ramm never tried to find us after the war and claim his share of the loot, do you, Mr. Cooper? He tried, but he never succeeded."

"How did he try?"

"He sent thugs here to Eheburg to force me to cough up. He sent thugs to the United States as 'tourists'—to force Manfred to do likewise."

"And?"

"The thugs were, shall we say, out-thugged."

"By you, personally?"

"Heavens, no."

"By the guys who saved my neck outside the Frankfurt night club? On Lori Altmann's doorstep?"

"And several other times you are not aware of."

"So who were the people who tried to kill me?"

"We are not sure. We recognized none of them. We simply had you under protective surveillance—at Manfred's re-

quest—and when there was rough stuff, my people inter-
vened.''

"Why?"

"Because Manfred and I promised your father that we
would protect his wife and son from Ramm's continuing attempts at vengeance. That is precisely why Frank arranged
Manfred's emigration to America. Manfred would be a lifelong, live-in bodyguard, so to speak. Much of your mother's
unhappiness came from her knowledge of why Manfred was in
her house. But, thanks to him, she survived several attacks by
Ramm's hired killers.''

"What happened to the hired killers?"

"You really don't want to know, Mr. Cooper. In any event,
I'm not about to tell you.''

"Could the people who killed my dad, and who have tried to
kill me, have been working for Ramm?''

"No. And that, frankly, is what confuses us. Ramm is no
longer competent. He is, in fact, insane. No one but nursing
personnel work for him now. And he's obviously beyond
memory of Slingshot and Sunrise and all those long-ago events
that have led us to this melancholy day.''

"So how could he be suing me?"

"He's not. He can't. He's a front for somebody else.''

"Who?"

"I have no idea.''

Cooper thought about that for a moment, then snapped shut
his notebook and stood up. "Well, thank you, Herr Feldstein.
You've been a very real help, and we appreciate it." Turning
for the door, he said, "Come on, Tina. We're out of here.''

"Where are we going?"

"To Munich and our last two interviews. And then, pal,
we're going the hell home.''

They stopped at the Vier Jahreszeiten to freshen up and use
the phone for making appointments. The lawyer could see him
the next morning at ten, but by the time Cooper had made the
second call it was after hours—compelling another wait until
tomorrow. While Tina took a shower, he checked the day's
messages, and, surprise of surprises, there was a desk clerk's

note that Manfred had called and wished to speak with him at his earliest opportunity.

"Hi, Manfred. You called?"

Manfred's voice was full of sleep. "Oh, yes. Yes, Mr. Matt, I have some information which I feel is of extreme importance to you."

"What's that?"

"The detective, Nickerson, has found a gun in your Jacksonville house. He was attempting to have it tested for ballistics, with a view toward comparing it with the bullet recovered from Mr. Frank's body. He believes you killed your father and that such a comparison would prove his case against you."

Cooper gave that some thought. Then: " 'Attempting to have it tested'? Is that what you said?"

"Yes, sir. But, I'm happy to say, the attempt has been unsuccessful so far."

"How come?"

"I stole the revolver and its evidence transfer receipt before it could be sent to the laboratory."

"You *stole* it? Who from? Where? When?"

"I'd rather not say, sir."

"Well, *why,* for chrissake?"

"Without the gun, Nickerson has no case against you."

"Oh, my aching ass. Manfred, that's interfering with the police, for God's sake. That's not only theft—it's obstruction of justice."

"I know, sir. But I am sending you a fax of the transfer receipt and a note from Mrs. Farman. I think you'll find it most interesting. As a matter of fact, the fax should be waiting for you in the hotel office."

"All right. I'll read the fax. But this is what *you're* going to do: You're going to return that gun and its papers immediately. I don't care how you get them back, but I want you to get them back. Understand?"

"That would defeat my attempt to help you, sir."

"Manfred, will you listen to me, for God's sake? Get that gun back as sneakily as you got hold of it. And just hope that the police don't realize it's missing. Because if its theft is traced to you—my employee—it nails down my coffin lid.

Didn't they teach that kind of thing in the Gestapo, damn it?''

A moment of shocked silence followed. Then Manfred, his voice far away and weak, said, ''Oh. You have discovered about me.''

''You're damned right. I've discovered a hell of a lot of things, now that I've had a talk with Hermann Feldstein.''

''Oh.''

''Are you there? I can hardly hear you.''

''I suppose that this means I'm terminated from your employ. Isn't that right, sir?''

''No, goddammit, it does not mean you are terminated from my employ. But it does mean that I want you to answer some hundred-watt questions. Where are you right now?''

''I'm in bed, sir.''

''All right. You stay right there until I get the hotel office on the intercom. And, until the fax gets here, you and I are going into the answers.''

''Very well, sir.''

Forty-three

M r. Mueller, I appreciate your willingness to let me break into your busy day. I'm Matthew Cooper."

They shook hands, and the lawyer, a tall, meticulously groomed man in his fifties, waved to what was obviously the visiting client's chair. "Please, Mr. Cooper, have a seat."

Cooper settled into the chair, Mueller returned to his behind the glass-topped desk, and they traded sparring smiles.

"What can I do for you, sir?"

"I'm not sure this is ethical, or whether I'm violating whatever protocols you attorneys live by, but I'd like to discuss the Ramm libel suit."

Mueller's craggy features changed not at all. "The Ramm libel suit?"

"Yes. I'm Matthew Cooper, the defendant."

"I must admit I'm somewhat confused, Mr. Cooper. I'm not familiar with the subject."

Cooper blinked. "You are Ramm's lawyer, aren't you?"

Mueller shook his noble head. "I have no client named—what is it? Ramm?"

"Would there be another attorney in Munich whose name is Max Mueller?"

"Not that I know of. And I've been practicing here for more than twenty years."

Cooper sank back in the chair. "Why am I not surprised?"

"Sir?"

"Sorry. I've just confirmed a suspicion I've been carrying around with me lately. I'm the son and only heir of Frank Cooper, the American novelist. A German national, name of Siegfried Ramm, is suing the estate for a considerable sum. The suit was filed in Ramm's behalf in Munich by an attorney named Max Mueller, but Mueller has since been dismissed by Ramm, who has taken on a lawyer in Miami. There has always seemed to be something fishy about the Mueller connection, and that's why I'm here. To see why it is I'm so uneasy about it."

For the first time, Mueller showed genuine interest. "It seems we share an impostor between us, eh?"

"So it seems."

"Would you happen to have any of this Max Mueller's correspondence with you, Mr. Cooper?"

"A photocopy. No original."

"That should do. May I see it?"

Cooper opened his briefcase and, after a bit of rummaging, drew out a copy of the initial contact letter. He passed it across the desk, and Mueller gave it a prolonged scrutiny.

"It's my stationery, all right," Mueller said finally.

"Could somebody have stolen some from you?"

"Of course. They had to have. I simply can't imagine when or how."

"How about service people? Phones, computers, plumbing, that kind of thing?"

"We engage those services under contract. We know all those people."

"Well, one of them might have been paid to steal some stationery while passing through—"

"Ah. The watercooler."

"Watercooler?"

"I remember now. Several months ago. A man came to check the condition of our office watercoolers. He said he was a technician, and his services were apart from those of the man who brings the water bottles."

"How come a busy man like you remembers a minor incident like that?"

"A good question, Mr. Cooper. But one readily answered. I remember it because the man was so ugly. Not hideous, or anything abnormal. He simply looked like a thug, a movie gangster. A very large man, with a very mean face."

"You're saying that he might have posed as a watercooler technician simply to steal stationery?"

"That's precisely what I'm saying."

Cooper nodded. "Well, it's pretty clear somebody in Munich was using your name to lay a phony lawsuit on me. And then, after things got in motion, they 'fired' you and 'hired' the Miami lawyer."

"No doubt about it."

"Any suggestions, Mr. Mueller?"

The tall German smiled wanly and shrugged. "Well, for one thing, I suggest you inform your own lawyer of this immediately. And for another thing, I will suggest to my office supervisor that he insist on checking the credentials of all—I stress 'all'—service people who visit our offices."

Cooper returned the smile. "Sounds like good advice. How much do I owe you?"

"I owe you, Mr Cooper. I owe you my thanks for exposing this weakness in our systems around here."

Cooper stood and prepared to leave. "Let's say we're even, eh? Thanks a lot, Mr. Mueller. Nice meeting you."

They had an early lunch at a café near the Rathaus in the Old City Ring, one of those places with low ceilings and high prices and waitresses who looked like storm troopers in drag. A little old man in lederhosen sat in a far corner, squeezing *Volkslieder* out of a concertina that had to have been made when Beethoven was learning scales.

"You haven't touched your food," Tina said, "and I've had

more stimulating conversations with fire hydrants.''

"Sorry. I've been doing some mega-thinking.''

"Anything I can help with?''

He heard the concern in her voice, and he regarded her with sudden affection. Seeing her now, her expression soft and guileless, he perceived the child that lingered in her womanhood. She was emerging as a true friend, and he felt ashamed once again over his inability to tell her how much that meant to him. But there was certainly no reason to be surprised. He came by it honestly. Frank's unfinished letter to him was proof enough of that. "No, Tina. It's something I've got to work through, and it's so hard to get hold of I can't even talk intelligently about it. Thanks, though.''

"Sure.''

He began to eat, but in a moment put down his fork, dabbed at his lips with the napkin, then stood up. "Hold the fort here, will you, please? I have to find a phone.''

"Will you be long? Or do I get stiffed for the bill?''

"Ten minutes, at the most. Okay?''

"Sure.''

He found a phone booth in the corridor leading to the twin doors marked *Damen* and *Herren* and dialed Stan's Ponte Vedra number. There was no answer, so he gave the international operator his credit card number and called the FBI in Jacksonville.

"Is Special Agent Milano in?''

"One moment, please.''

After a silent interval, he came on the line. "Milano speaking.''

"Ah. I'm lucky. You're in your office for a change.''

"Who's this?''

"Coop. We need to talk.''

The big man didn't bother to hide his surprise. "How did you know to call me here?''

"I've known you're FBI since the first, when I remembered seeing your name on an FOI trace slip.''

"Sheesh. You've let me do all this playacting for nothing? Without saying something?''

"I checked with your chief, and he asked me not to get in your way."

"Damn. We've got to change the way we handle those damned trace slips. Where are you now?"

"I'm still in Munich. But I need your help."

"Munich's out of my jurisdiction."

"But national security isn't."

"So what's on your mind?"

"I've got a real problem. That St. Augustine detective, Ed Nickerson, is waiting for my return so he can arrest me for my father's murder. He's found a gun in my house in Jax. It isn't mine, but I'm going to have to prove that. But in the meantime, I've made some rather astonishing discoveries over here, and I think you ought to follow up on them no matter how tied up I get when I land back there."

"This is the national security you're talking about?"

"Right. What's your fax number there?"

Milano gave it to him.

"I'm going to send you a rundown of what I've learned. I'll dictate it to Tina Mennen, who's here with me, and she'll find a public steno and shoot it off to you this afternoon. Okay?"

"Sure." There was a pause. "Are you sure about Nickerson? I mean, he's waiting to pinch you for real?"

"That's the word I get. And I'll include a fax of the evidence he's got against me—just for the hell of it, because I know you can't mess around with local matters. But Dad's murder is directly involved in the other stuff I'm sending you—which is big, international, and directed at the United States."

"Okay, get it over here, pronto. I've put it at the top of my list."

"Fine. Thanks."

"Coop?"

"Well?"

"I'd help you with the Nickerson thing if I could. You know that, don't you?"

"Thanks, Al."

"The law's the law."

"And a man's got to do what a man's got to do, according to John Wayne. Or Clint Eastwood. Or was it Julius Caesar? I can never remember which."

"And thanks for not blowing my cover."

"You're welcome. I think what I'm sending you will contribute very effectively to what I think you're working on."

"All that thinking could get you in trouble."

Cooper laughed. "Come visit me in the pokey. You can do that, can't you?"

"I'll bring you a cake with a file in it. But, since the law's the law, the file will be made of rubber."

"So long, Al."

"Good luck."

BOSTON   (USP)—Thousands of antigovernment protesters stormed the Patriot Convention Hall here tonight, forcing the governors of 11 states—meeting with federal officials on means of coping with civil unrest—to flee to safety in a convoy of armored cars.

Seven protesters are known to have been killed in the violence, which included bursts of machine-gun fire from the military vehicles and exploding grenades hurled by army units deployed around the meeting site.

An army spokesperson said, "We haven't been able to get a count yet, but the casualties on our side are heavy, too. We're pretty sure that a squad of infantry, ambushed by Middies wearing hoods, was wiped out."

President Fogarty, entertaining Congressional friends at Camp David, has not yet issued a statement. However, the White House chief of staff, William "Boots" Milliken, has confirmed that the governors have asked Fogarty to declare a national emergency and activate the National Guard in their states.

"They feel that they have been singled out by the Middies as bad guys," Milliken said, "because they support the president's proposed federal retail tax on coffee."

The protesters did, in fact, have a permit to hold what was touted as a "Boston Coffee Party" near the waterfront site where, over two centuries ago, irate colonists raided British ships and dumped bales of tea into the harbor as a protest against a British government tax.

But, according to Boston police spokesperson Gladys Marelli, last night's protesters "spilled out of the authorized meeting area and started running wild." Marelli estimated that "more than 20,000 people converged on the convention center."

Samuel Sorenson, Altoona, PA, hardware merchant and one of the rally's organizers, said, "We've had it with a government of elite know-it-alls who don't know the first thing about earning a living in this craphouse world telling us how to live and how much we got to pay for the privilege.''

Matilda Connell, used car salesperson from Raleigh, NC, was even more blunt. ''We're not going to stop until we tear every lousy, conniving, self-serving rat out of our statehouses and Congress. If we can't deselect them, we'll recall them, and if we can't recall them, we'll march into their offices, pick them up, and throw them out the goddamn windows.''

The media came in for similar treatment. Said Jason Murray, an Illinois farmer, ''We're calling a boycott. We're not going to watch another minute of TV or read another newspaper put out by bastards like you, who give us only the news you think we ought to have instead of the news we need to survive. News reporters? You aren't news reporters. You are flacks—propaganda artists,

sucking up to the Leets.''

Meanwhile, Gov. Dwight Ramsey is consulting with state and municipal law enforcement leaders on how to quell the rioting that has already destroyed many shops, overturned dozens of cars, set serious fires in downtown Boston and seems likely to continue through the night.

The White House and Department of Justice officials are also keeping an eye on outbreaks of disorder in Chicago, St. Louis, Memphis, and Atlanta. FBI spokesperson Laura O'Neill said, ''Reports we're receiving indicate the violence is not as intense as in Boston, but they seem to involve large numbers of so-called Middies rampaging through governmental centers. Also, TV stations and newspaper offices in Toledo, Omaha, and Fresno are under assault by armed gangs and have suspended operations. There are no reports of casualties.''

(MORE TO KUM)

(Note to desk eds: It is assumed that you will delete the taboo words in paragraphs quoting protesters' denunciations of the media. Words have been included for your info only.)

BULLETIN   BULLETIN   BULLETIN

Forty-four

Milano's Jacksonville office was furnished in the antiseptic manner common to minor federal buildings. The desk, the three-shelf bookcase, the visitor's chair, the computer stand, the coat rack, even the window blinds were fashioned of metal; those fabrics in evidence were of a low-grade nylon, and the entire lot was gray, some dark, some light, all uninspired. Only the swivel chair, a gag going-away gift from his office when he had been transferred from Denver to Buffalo years ago, departed from this monochromatic dullness. It had a wide red leather seat that accommodated his bulk, a tall red leather back that eased the chronic ache between his shoulder blades, solid mahogany arms that gave him a place to put his elbows, and base legs with hard rubber casters that rolled easily about on the time-stained, commercial-grade gray carpeting. The chair had moved with him in every subsequent base change, and, because it was uniquely his and because he had logged so much time in it, it had become a retreat, a place of recovery and reassurance. He sat in it now, feet propped on the aluminum windowsill, head bowed over a sheet of fax paper in his lap. He was so motionless and lost in thought he suggested a mountainous Uncle Fred dozing over the Sunday funnies. After a time, he sighed deeply and reached for the phone.

"Records."

"Milano here, Alice. I would like to access a Freedom of Information file initiated by a Matthew L. Cooper, a reporter for the *Florida Times-Union*. It's got quite a few entries, but I can't remember when it began. Can you lend a hand?"

"Sure. Give me a few minutes and I'll put it on your screen. Anything else?"

"No. I just want to look over the trace slips. I want to see the ones I might have signed off on. Okay?"

"Coming up, Al."

He flipped the switch on his PC and watched the swarming of amber. When the file settled in, he scrolled slowly from "Day One" to "Current." He paused three times to make notes on a yellow pad. When he was finished, he turned off the computer and rested back in the chair, his eyes fixed on the ceiling fan.

Taking up the phone again, he punched in the direct line number.

"Nickerson."

"Hi, Nick. Milano here."

"Well, well. God's gift to Congress."

"It's time for me to make a confession, Nick."

"Oh? What's that?"

"I know that you haven't really left the police force. That you're undercover, trying to nail the Frank Cooper murder on Matt Cooper."

"Oh? How the hell did you find that out?"

"I can't tell you that. It would compromise a friend."

"Hell, the only other guy who knew about this was Chief Nolan himself."

"Well, you didn't hear it from me."

"You mean the chief's the friend you don't want to compromise?"

"I'll give you A for being quick."

"I didn't know you know the chief."

"You do now, and I'd like to keep that confidential, if it's all the same to you."

"Sure, why not?"

"Another reason I called, Nick, is to tell you about a federal operation that's about to take place on your turf. We're moving in on a sedition case."

"*Sedition?* In St. *Augustine?*"

"Yeah. And nearby St. Johns County."

"What's up?"

"I've been assigned to get something on some of your locals suspected of gunrunning and seditious plotting."

"Like who?"

"There's about thirty of them. The most prominent one is Claude Abernathy."

"The real estate guy?"

"He and the Duval district judge, Abner Hefflefinger. Next Tuesday we're going to raid Abernathy's school and pick up him and some of his people and a bunch of weapons. Your chief and my chief have already met on it."

"Well, I haven't heard about it."

"Our people in Duval are already holding Hefflefinger. Sedition is the main charge. Conspiracy next, then firearms violations."

"I'll be go to hell. Whatever happened to prior notification to local enforcement agencies?"

"We take maximum advantage of the Lewis-Meacham Fed Priority law. Notification chief-to-chief only."

"You sure as hell do take advantage of it."

"By-the-book-wise, my chief has done what's called for. It should be on your police network about now. The Bureau and various military intelligence agencies have been working on this for months. We're having nationwide raids between now and three P.M. Tuesday, eastern time. We'll be knocking the ass off the Middies."

"Don't sound so goddamn pleased about it. My sympathies are with the Middies."

"So are mine, Nick. But, like you said when we met that time, law's law. I'd arrest my own mama, she broke the law. If the Middies want to throw out the government, they got to do it legal. Smuggling guns and blowing away those Leets just ain't the way to go.''

''Well, they've sure blown away a lot of them.''

''Have they ever. And a lot of them I'm not so upset about, between us girls. But I got a lot of regrets over Congressman Quigg. He's my kind of guy, and it's a goddamn shame he's so ID'ed with the Middie thing. He hasn't got a chance in hell of being elected street sweeper after today's shit hits the fan.''

''Don't worry about Quigg. Guys like him always bob to the surface again.''

''There's one more thing I have for you. Word from abroad that might be helpful.''

''What's the word?''

''Cooper will be coming back to the States next Tuesday. He will be flying into Jax, where he'll attend a special meeting of the board of Rettung Internationale.''

''What time? Where?''

''The meeting's at one-thirty P.M. in the Jackson Club. I don't know when or how Cooper'll be arriving in the city, but I know he will be at that meeting. You might want to set up something with the Duval County sheriff to make the pinch yourself.''

''You bet your ass I will.''

''Okay. I knew you'd want to know.''

''Why are you telling me this?''

''Like I told you, way back when: With me, the law's the law. If the bastard offed his old man, he's got to pay.''

Forty-five

As was his custom, Ludwig arrived at the office precisely at noon. After hanging his overcoat in the closet and positioning his briefcase in the knee well of his desk, he consulted the day book, which lay open in the exact center of the credenza and confirmed with its white space that today's schedule was empty.

He sat in his high-backed leather desk chair and exulted in the sun-washed brilliance of a winter day that expected nothing of him. But the pleasure diminished subtly as he considered the view beyond the windows. The blue Alpine cornice along the distant Bavarian heights, the medieval steeples of the old city and the glistening spires of the new, the nimbus from the sea of chimney pots, the prairie of masonry and slate and timbers sparkling under a layer of settled snow: Together and separately they stirred him strangely, and uneasiness gathered, becoming gradually a sense of waiting for some cosmic shoe to drop.

Odd. What was there to be uneasy about?

Analyzing it, he recognized ambivalence in its purest form—a simultaneous euphoria and anxiety—and a repeat of the feeling he'd had the day Anton Rettung had suffered his fatal heart attack, when he'd known, with a combined headiness and gloom, that someone important to his life and times would most surely die today. Now, as it had then, an ancient Tyrolean folk admonition, so fearfully respected by his forebears, sounded in his mind: *When sun beams and cross gleams, when mind is glad but heart is sad, ere the next cock's cry, your idol will die.*

Drivel, to be sure, but a weird, irritating memory to have at this specific moment.

Idol? The only individual anywhere to be remotely evocative of that designation was Emma, his wife of twenty-nine years, who had stopped being his idol on their wedding night, when she wept and literally became nauseated during foreplay. Still, he was fond of the old icicle, and he'd hate to see anything bad happen to her.

His gaze moved to the glittering cross on the cathedral, the totem of a churchy childhood in which good and bad had been distinct, when he'd been continually and pleasantly haunted by—how had that English poet, What's-His-Name, put it? Intimations of immortality? Now, after the years of his growing away, the simplicity had been obscured, and suddenly, in this moment, the emblem became a personal condemnation, a fervid reminder of love spurned. And he felt lostness, melancholy, inexpressible guilt.

He started, breaking away from his morose ruminations. The agreement was that he would call Takai at 12:05 hours for instructions regarding Bolko's prisoner, and a glance at the desk clock told him that he was already two minutes late. As he reached for the phone, the intercom trilled, and he jumped again.

"What is it, Gerda?"

"You have a visitor, sir. Mr. Matthew Cooper, of Jacksonville, Florida. Are you available?"

Ludwig sought to offset surprise with analysis.
So here was the controversial Matt Cooper.

Like his father, a sinewy man, with the same level eyes, the same firmness around the mouth, the same standard haircut, the same ignorance in matters of dress. A man Frau Emma von Ludwig would dismiss—as she had once dismissed Cooper's father—as "a flophouse reject." A man Herr Dr. Edmund von Ludwig would, if he were into theatricals, cast as "an almost-bearable American tourist."

Still, the man had a presence of sorts. He came into the office as if completely unawed by its size and opulence. He did not seek to shake hands in that insufferable American way, offering instead a polite nod. His overall manner, while not cordial, was diplomatically correct. Given time and the proper clothes, he might even take on the air of the hugely rich man he was.

"Please, Mr. Cooper, take the chair by the fire. It's a beautiful day, but the cold stays with one. Coffee?"

"No, thanks."

"This is indeed a splendid surprise. I had no idea you were in Munich. In Germany, for that matter."

"It's just a quick trip. I'm looking into some personal things. Family things. And while I was here, I thought I'd drop in to ask a few questions."

"Ah, yes. I can't tell you how sorrowfully we received the news of your father's death. Such a despicable tragedy."

"It was that."

Ludwig settled in the chair behind the desk and gave Cooper the amiable smile—practiced for hours before a mirror so as to remove all traces of condescension—that he reserved for visitors of marginal importance. While young Cooper had ambitions to assume his father's seat on the Rettung board, he represented no clear threat, no power center to be reckoned with, because his only asset was money. More than that: Even if Cooper could somehow persuade the board that his name and money were enough, even if he could influence a return to the original bylaws requiring his presence on the board, the whole would be trumped by Oko Takai, whose objectives had become, at this point, virtually inscribed in stone.

Making conversation, he said, "Dreadful news out of Washington this morning, eh?"

Cooper, leafing through the notepad on his lap, did not look up. "Dreadful, but not surprising."

"Much like Russia in the nineties, wouldn't you say?"

"Not really. For one thing, the Russians were arguing over how to replace a government they'd already deposed, while the Americans are blowing their stacks over oppressive taxation by an imperial government they want to depose."

"Well—"

"But there's a larger difference. The Russian rioting was touched off by a long-term buildup of internal heat—a kind of spontaneous combustion. Last night's American explosion was planted and exploded, like a remote-controlled land mine."

"What a curious idea. My sources in the States have been telling me that the American people, like the Russians, have been simmering for years—"

"Your sources are right as rain. But last night's attack on the meeting of governors was an artificial event—a happening extraneous to the simmer. It was pure sedition, planned, financed, and triggered by you and Takai and choreographed by the Americans who've enrolled in your Operation Yankee Doodle. For some reason, you've considered me a threat to all of this and so you've tried consistently to get me out of the way—filing phony lawsuits against me, having me run off the road, planting evidence that would make me guilty of my father's murder, and having me shot at. But I have a great sense of humor, and so I'm not going to go into all that. I'm just going to ask you how in hell you and Takai expect to get away with the diversion of Rettung Internationale funds to support the overthrow of the United States government."

So here it was.

The ultimate revelation, so long feared, so minutely planned against.

So unexpected on a beautiful, bright winter afternoon.

So grotesquely laid on him by—of all people—an insignificant alien squirt who had yet to learn that one never wears blazer and slacks when making a business call on the CEO of a multibillion-dollar foundation.

His mind, dealing with shock and surprise, shunted into replay, showing him an excerpt from the day on which his father had confronted him with the pornographic magazine he had hidden in the barn. Now, as then, he felt a burning in his cheeks, a shortness of breath, a constriction behind his belt buckle, a panicky inability to find words that might, in some magical way, make it all go away.

Today, though, he would apply the lesson learned on that long-ago evening. Today he would admit nothing. Deny everything. Lay the blame on someone else. There would be no admissions, no confessions, which, having been given in good faith—in the spirit of churchy absolution—could be turned against him in churchy, hellfire condemnation.

"Have you lost your senses, Mr. Cooper?"

The Tourist ignored the question and asked one of his own. "When Takai was being considered for membership on the Rettung board, were you aware that he was an international gangster, hated and feared even in his native Japan?"

"I was aware of no such thing. His credentials are impeccable."

The Tourist made a note. Then: "How is it, if that's the case, that the investigative files of the Joint Committee on International Trusts of the American Congress carry a confidential Rettung interoffice memo, signed by you and addressed to Stanley Tremaine, which reads: 'Stan—At this stage, should anyone, from Anton Rettung to the janitor, attempt to bring the name of Oko Takai into the conversation, you are hereby directed to claim no knowledge of the man. None. I dislike laying out rules for your comportment in any situation, since you are a most intelligent and responsible member of our team. But I can't put it strongly enough: For now, Takai's sordid background must be shared by you and me alone.' So, Herr Ludwig, the operating word in that memo is 'sordid.' If something 'sordid' had been shared by you and Tremaine, then surely you had knowledge of something less than 'impeccable' in Takai's credentials. Right?"

Ludwig pushed back his chair and stood up. "I think I've had enough of this conversation, Mr. Cooper. I'd been looking forward to meeting you and making you my friend, but obviously that's not possible now. It's my policy not to associate with ignorant louts.''

The Tourist, apparently unfazed, continued to study his notes. ''Louts. Louts. Let's see what we have on louts. Ah, yes. Herr Ludwig, these same files indicate that you employ as chauffeur and 'personal escort' one Heinz Rudel—aka 'Bolko' Rudel. Would you like me to read off *his* credentials? The part about his difficulty in passing the tests for a driver's license, maybe? Or his rather lengthy rap sheet with Interpol? I mean, is that an ignorant lout or what?''

''How did you get those documents?''

''Documents? You want documents? Wait until you see the documents I have, pal. I've got documents that are going to put you in jail for fourteen eons.''

''Are you here in a police capacity, Mr. Cooper? Or as a journalist, perhaps? Just what role are you playing in this absurd fantasy?''

''I'm here in the interests of my father, who was set up and killed by you and Takai. I'm here to let you know that documents in my possession show you both conspired to kill him to keep him from reporting your Yankee Doodle sedition to the FBI. I am here to let you know personally that I am going to fix your wagon for that.''

Ah.

Ludwig felt his panic subsiding.

The Tourist was bluffing.

There could be no such documents because there had never been any such documents.

Takai had made a very large thing of this. No paper. Not a scrap on the delicate matter of Frank Cooper. And garble phones were mandatory when discussing the subject with Tremaine, obviating the threat of bugs.

Smiling, Ludwig pulled together his authoritarian pose. ''You are quite contemptible, you know. These documents you say you have simply don't exist. Forgery is possible, of course, but there are no real documents that could possibly link me with these preposterous charges. This is because I have had nothing to do with Yankee Doodle—whatever that is—or

with anyone involved with it. Nor have I had anything to do
with anything involving your father, outside his membership
on the Rettung board. Nothing. Absolutely nothing. And there
is nothing you can produce that would indicate otherwise.''

Cooper nodded in mock seriousness. "Have you talked with
Bolko in the last day or so?''

"Bolko? I know no Bolko.''

"Excuse me. Heinz. Heinz Rudel. Have you talked to
Heinz?''

"I have not. Heinz is away on an errand for me.''

"How do you get around, then?''

"I can drive my own car, Mr. Cooper.''

"Well, hold on a second. I've got somebody waiting in that
sexy anteroom of yours who can throw a little light on what
Heinz has been up to.'' Cooper called over his shoulder. "Yo,
Tina. Come on in.''

There it was again.

The hot cheeks. The shortness of breath. The tightness in
the belly. The inability to speak. The instant transition from
elaborate innocence to inarticulate panic. Cooper, standing,
notebook in hand, glaring accusingly, even looked like the
Hans-Christian Ludwig—up-country dairy farmer, father of
five, Bible-thumper, beloved husband of Irmgard Anna Ludwig—of fifty years ago.

"I'm sorry, Herr Ludwig,'' Gerda, the shaken unshakable
secretary whined. "She came in before I could—I mean, the
man called, and she just stood up and—''

Ludwig waved Gerda away, his stare fastened on the pretty
face of the young American woman.

Cooper was saying, "Do you recognize this man, Tina?''

"He was the dude with Bolko. He salivated while Bolko
took off my clothes and tied me to the bed. This is Ludwig?
The big breeze himself?''

"This is Ludwig.''

"Creep.''

Ludwig pressed the button under the lip of his desk, and
after a time—it could have been seconds, it could have been
an hour—the two day security men materialized in the door-

way, coming through briskly and with determined frowns on their brutish faces.

"Yes, Herr Ludwig?" the larger one—what was his name? Schmidt?—barked in his former-policeman's way. "Is this man giving you trouble?"

He found his voice. "I don't want a scene. Just hold these two in the conference room while I make a call."

"Come on—out," Schmidt grated, throwing an armlock on Cooper and pushing him through the door to the adjacent conference room. The other guard placed a hand under the young woman's arm and literally lifted her off her feet as he followed after and slammed the door behind him.

Ludwig picked up the private line and got Takai on the second ring.

"Well?"

"I'm sorry I'm late calling you, but I've been held up by a dreadful development."

"And what is that, please?"

"Matthew Cooper is here in my office. He knows everything. And the woman got away from Bolko—God knows how—and is here with Cooper. She—"

"Calm down, and stop talking so fast. You say they are there—you mean they are secured?"

"My guards are holding them in the conference room as we speak. I've called to see what you'd have me do."

"What do you mean, Cooper knows everything?"

"He has documents. He is talking knowledgeably about Yankee Doodle, about his father's death—oh, Lord, I don't know what else. But he's angry and he's accusing you and me, and he's out for revenge. And—"

"Will you please calm *down*?"

"Sorry. I—"

"You're quite right. This is most serious. Now here's what I want you to do. Instruct the guards to take Cooper and the woman down your private elevator to your car. I assume it's parked in the basement garage."

"Yes, yes."

"Have one guard, you, and the other two locked in the backseat compartment, then have the other guard drive all of you to my place here. When——''

''Me, too? You want me in the backseat with them?''

''Of course. Along with one of the guards. Locked from the driver's seat so Cooper and the woman can't possibly escape, even if they managed to overpower you and the guard. During the ride you can question them——find out how much they really know——so that you can help me in my examining of them when they arrive here. Understand?''

''Yes, yes. Oh, this is terrible. I never wanted it to come to this——''

''Easy, old friend. We're still very much in charge. These things happen, and the important thing is not to be carried away by excitement or surprise. Just get those two down here and I'll take over. All right?''

''Yes. Certainly. It's just that——''

''Easy. If you leave now you should be here in an hour. I'll be waiting at the main house. You'll be staying for dinner, of course.''

Dinner. What a beautiful, mundane, marvelously reassuring word. To plan dinner in the midst of the apocalypse——how extraordinarily cool and in command. A wonderful word, used at the precise time, with the precise tone, to give heart to faltering troops. No wonder Takai had risen to the pinnacle. What a privilege to work with a man who could teach so much about leadership.

''Thank you. That's very kind of you.''

The man behind the wheel of the gray Citroen sat up in his seat and pointed. ''That Mercedes——the big black one coming out of the garage. It's Ludwig's.''

''So?'' The man beside him let the question become a yawn.

''So do we follow it?''

''Why?''

''Ludwig is the only one in that building Cooper can have any possible interest in. If Ludwig's leaving, where's Cooper?''

''He could be coming out the front door any minute now and heading for that cute little BMW parked over there.''

"But what if he's in the Mercedes with Ludwig?"

"How do we know Ludwig himself is in the car, for God's sake? Maybe Ludwig's chauffeur is taking the damned thing downtown for servicing or something. With those dark-tinted windows, who can tell?"

"We'd better make up our minds. The car's heading for the boulevard. If we don't get on it now, we can lose it very quickly in all this snow coming down."

The man in the passenger seat made an irritable sound and shifted the weight of the machine-pistol on his lap. "Feldstein's paying us to follow Cooper—not big black Mercedes sedans, damn it."

"I still say you should have gone into the building behind Cooper."

"And where would that have gotten us? There's a reception desk and a guard. What would I have told those people, eh? 'No, I don't have an appointment with anybody. I'm just here to keep an eye on that guy in the cashmere overcoat.' I'd have had my ass out the door in two seconds flat."

"Well, what do we do, Herr Know-It-All? Follow the Mercedes or sit here in this goddamn blizzard?"

"We sit here and watch the BMW, that's what we do."

The driver sank back in his seat. "I hope you're right. If we lose Cooper at this late stage, Feldstein will have our heads flattened and bronzed and tacked to his garden wall, believe you me."

"Relax. We're doing what we've been told to do."

"Well, it's too late anyhow. The Mercedes has turned onto the boulevard and already I can't see it anymore."

"Hey, pal, *relax.*" The gunner reached for the cooler in the backseat. "How about another sandwich?"

The afternoon sky had surrendered to low, fast-moving clouds with gray bellies and cargoes of wet snow, which fell in large flakes and lathered the world with a surrealistic opaqueness. Schmidt, who was at the wheel, directed the Mercedes to the traffic circle at the Prinzregenten Bridge over the Isar, then along Maria Theresa Strasse to the intersection where the signs pointed southwest to Starnberg. The traffic, impeded by the snow, moved sluggishly, and Schmidt was unable to free their car from the wake of a two-trailer truck rig and an Audi driven by a woman and filled to the sunroof with hell-raising kids and a joyfully barking cocker spaniel. Near Starnberg, Schmidt finally broke away at a feeder strip and picked up a secondary road to the Ammersee's western shore, which seemed to be relatively open. Ludwig watched all this from his central seat in the rear, paying great attention to detail out there as a means of avoiding the need to start asking questions in here. Cooper, to his left, and the girl, to his right, were likewise silent, probably deep in assessments of their problem and schemes to escape. The other guard, whose name was Romer, sat on the jump seat, stoic, pretending to be above all this.

There would have to be something for Takai, some piece of information that would help in the questioning to come, so Ludwig considered Cooper gravely and asked, "Does anyone know that you came to my offices this morning?"

"Tell Schmidt to turn the car around and drive us to the Vier Jahreszeiten. We can go up to my suite, have some drinks, and chat."

Ludwig sighed. "You know, I'm truly sorry that things have come to this. I truly don't understand a lot of your accusations—lawsuits, planted evidence, shootings, whatever. I know nothing of those things. But more importantly, I am not a man given to physical force. My whole life has been centered on altruism and benefactions, so to compel you and Miss Mennen to do anything against your will is quite unnatural to me."

"You lying son of a bitch," the woman snarled.

Ludwig ignored her. "I honestly wish that we could come to some kind of compromise—some sort of agreement in which each of us gets most of what he wants. Perhaps then we could dispense with these, ah, cinematic high jinks and permit ourselves to go our own ways in peace."

"Ludwig," Cooper said, "you are truly a piece of work. A gold-plated, ermine-lined, music-playing armadillo's anus. You sit on top of stolen billions and pretend to feed the hungry and tend the sick and enlighten the ignorant. But what do you really do? You slide the stolen money into a plan to steal the system that enabled you to steal the money in the first place.

Compromise? Agreement? How could I make any kind of a deal with a thief who craps that hugely in his own swag?''

"You're not making any sense—''

"You think *you're* making sense? You? An altruist? A benefactor? Get real. You're a cheap crook. A thief. A kidnapper. A seditionist. An oily toady for a Japanese Jack-the-goddamn-Ripper.''

The Mennen woman glared at him, furious. "Where does a guy like you come from? I mean, what happened to make a do-gooder like you were into a side-winding do-badder like you are?''

Ludwig heard his own voice as if it were coming from someone else, from somewhere else. "You have no idea how many times I've asked myself that same question.'' He paused for a moment, seeking a handle on the elusive thought. "I think it began with my understanding that the world's disadvantaged, those people and nations I wanted to help, would rather play vengeance politics—stick it to the haves—than feed their starving fellow have-nots. My moral code, my concern over the world's inequities, were no longer relevant in a world where getting even was much more important than getting well and productive. I saw finally that I had become a ridiculous anachronism—a man with a nineteenth-century sense of charity in the start of the twenty-first century's malevolence and greed. So, when Takai came along with his blandishments, his talk of world reform, I was very receptive. How do you Americans put it? 'If you can't beat them, join them'?''

Cooper asked, "What were Takai's 'blandishments'?''

"I would be elevated to chairman of the Rettung board and given virtual autonomy in the day-to-day operations of the foundation and its ancillaries. I would become a very powerful man in the world reorganization he envisioned. Isn't that amusing? I already had everything a reasonable man could want, but I was moved to play my own little game of vengeance politics. Stick it to the have-nots for not appreciating my altruism. How's that for hypocrisy, eh?''

His own question jarred, and Ludwig returned to the reality of the situation. "I've said enough. I'm supposed to be asking the questions here.''

"You're the one who seems to need to talk," Cooper said.

"That's enough. I suggest that we all keep quiet awhile."

"I don't want to keep quiet," the woman snapped. "You're a very interesting case: The Repentant Horse's Ass."

Ludwig glanced at Romer. "Make her be quiet."

The guard drew an automatic from his shoulder holster and, leaning, placed the muzzle at the tip of the woman's nose. "One more word, and it's the mother of all sneezes."

For the rest of the ride, the only sounds were the rushing of the tires and the soft thumping of the wipers.

Schmidt pulled the Mercedes under the main house porte cochere, but a doorman appeared and told him to take the car around the loop and down to the boathouse area. It was snowing quite heavily now, and, with the evening's dimness deepened by the forest of towering evergreens, they needed headlights to negotiate the winding slope to the lake. With its bow rising and falling like a boat's in waves, the car passed through the forming drifts and came to an eventual halt in the lee of the boathouse, a frame structure that hulked on pilings at the edge of the frozen lake like a huge, winter-numbed insect. Two large men in black overcoats stepped out of the shadows and motioned to Schmidt to unlock the car.

"Everybody out, please," one of the men said. "Mr. Takai will be here in a moment."

Ludwig waited until Cooper and the girl were clear of the backseat and then climbed out to stand beside them in the gloom. Schmidt and Romer stood to one side, lighting cigarettes. No one said anything.

A door opened and Takai came out of the boathouse. He was wearing a parka and galoshes, and he was smiling. "So," he said, "you got here despite the storm, eh?"

Ludwig, pulling his coat closer against the cold, tried to match Takai's heartiness. "It wasn't too bad on the way down, but the trip back promises to be wicked."

"Oh, you won't have to worry about that," Takai said reassuringly. "You won't be going back."

"I don't understand."

"I'm sure you don't, Ludwig. You are such an ass."

Takai nodded to the men in the overcoats, and they drew out pistols, and without the slightest pause put two bullets each through the heads of Schmidt and Romer. The shots sounded like the clapping of hands.

Ludwig watched, immobilized by shock, as the two guards collapsed in the snow. There was a roaring in his ears, and it was impossible for him to breathe.

"Takai—what are you doing—"

As from a distance he heard Cooper's voice: "He's erasing traces, you dumb shit. The guards, your secretary—"

"Takai—not me—"

"Especially you, my dear, stupid, conscience-stricken Ludwig. You and the Americans are going to have a terrible accident."

Ludwig felt hands seizing him and thrusting him into the backseat of the Mercedes. He heard the slamming of doors and the clicking of locks. As if watching through gauze, he was aware of Cooper and the girl falling under blows from the pistols swung by the overcoated men. Of their unconscious forms being slid into the front seat, and of more locks falling to. Of hearing Takai's voice: "Turn on the motor and put the gear selector in drive, Henzel. It must look like driver's error."

The car lurched and then picked up speed as it slewed down the slant of a boat-launching ramp. Ludwig saw the ice part in a beautiful spray of glistening shards, like fireworks in a twilight sky. The three-pointed star and circle on the car's nose plunged into the dark green swirling, and he was aware of the car's buoyant sinking, its sliding down the steep slime, and there was an inrushing.

"Oh, Mother of God—"

He kicked and pulled at the doors, pounded on the windows, but the roiling blackish-green, as cold as ether, rose about him, so insistent, so numbing, it seized his body and struck him mute.

How did it go? Please—how did it go?

"Father, I have sinned—"

No. That wasn't it.

One more breath, one more sound: "Father, forgive me, for I have sinned—"

The green was all around him now, and, oddly, the cold had diminished, and he could see—quite clearly—Cooper and the girl rolling about in the eddies rising beyond the glass partition. And beyond them, the headlight beams, pointing the way into the deep, black abyss.

A thought: *I am the idol who is dying this day.*

Father, my greatest sin was love of self.

I'm so alone, and lonely.

Father—

Oh, please: how did that go?

Father—

BULLETIN   BULLETIN   BULLETIN

STARNBERG, Germany (USP) —Multimillionaire Matthew L. Cooper and Edmund von Ludwig, chief executive officer of the worldwide Rettung Foundation, died tonight when their limousine skidded out of control in a snowstorm and plunged into an icy Bavarian lake.

Also lost in the accident was Tina Mennen, a reporter for the St. Augustine Record, a Florida newspaper. She had been interviewing the two men and had accompanied them on their drive from Munich to visit Oko Takai, Japanese industrialist who maintains a vacation home on the Ammersee, a lake southwest of here.

Takai, who told police that he had witnessed the mishap, said the car was moving fast along a driveway on his estate and the driver, who was thought to be Cooper, "obviously became disoriented in the snowy woods and made a wrong turn."

The limousine, according to Takai's report, "went into a bad skid near the boathouse and slid down an ice-covered launching ramp and into the lake."

Efforts to retrieve the car and its occupants have been unsuccessful. Police Inspector Otto Keitel said, "The water is very cold and deep at that location, since the lake is actually a water-filled canyon formed by many centuries of Alpine runoff, and heavy currents cloud the depths with silt. Our divers are continuing the search, however, even though the conditions are so difficult and dangerous it could take days, even weeks, before the car is found."

(MORE TO KUM)

(Note to desk eds: Deep-dish bios for Cooper and Ludwig are in prep for a.m. traffic on A Wire. Also sidebar on Takai and

his lavish lifestyle, along with maps and photo art of accident site. Jacksonville bureau is readying material on Mennen. New York and London bureaus are getting reaction stuff from the financial world.)

BULLETIN   BULLETIN   BULLETIN

Forty-six

Tremaine and Quigg had breakfast together in Tremaine's penthouse suite, dabbling with eggs and toast and pretending to be blasé in face of the television set's hysterical, leapfrogging coverage of the Boston riots. The pretense called for a major effort, because positive, cool conversation was difficult against a backdrop in which historic buildings collapsed in flames, once-tidy streets were strewn with rubble and corpses, combat troops trotted through the smoke from incandescent automobile hulks, and airhead anchors traded off-camera pseudoprofundities on the meaning of it all.

They had met primarily to go over the basic themes to be introduced and exploited in Quigg's presidential campaign. The Rettung board meeting was scheduled for one-thirty in the Jackson Club penthouse suite several floors above, and would be preceded by a luncheon at noon. Both of them had been invited to attend the lunch and be prepared to discuss, at least informally, what Quigg stood for philosophically and how he would translate the theories into programs that would return

the United States to the economic and political stability needed
to lead the world out of its present torment. Of the six current
members, only Sam Goodman was an American and therefore
eligible to vote in the U.S. election; but the other five were
very much aware of the stakes and had already slid enormous
personal contributions under the various tables occupied by the
kingpins of Quigg's rapidly growing national machine. Still,
Takai had been most firm: Do not, under any circumstance,
infer that the members were being hit for additional gifts, because, in the final analysis, they were not. What was critical
was the board's authorization to commit five hundred million
of Rettung's cash reserve to the George Washington Fund, established by a like-sum grant from their fellow board member
Oko Takai. And it was up to Takai alone to introduce the
proposal at today's meeting. Again, under no circumstances
were members to have the slightest clue that, with Takai as
chairman of GW, the practical result would be the clandestine
diversion of Rettung money to the support of (1) the Middie
revolution, and (2) Quigg's candidacy for U.S. president.
Moreover, since the GW Fund was new business yet to be introduced, neither Quigg nor Tremaine, as outsiders, could be
expected to know anything about it.

The CNN camera panned across a littered street, then held
and closed in on the dead body of a handsome young woman
whose stylish clothes had been shredded by a grenade blast.

Quigg put down his coffee cup, and it clattered in its saucer.
"Godamighty—that's just plain goddamn awful—"

"Shall I turn it off?"

"Hell, yes. I can't think with stuff like that floating through
the room."

Tremaine punched the remote and the screen darkened.
"They're just repeating themselves anyhow. That's the third
time I've seen that shot."

"Awful. Just awful."

"Those things happen in wars."

"I've never seen anything like it."

"I have. In war, you get accustomed to outrageous sights."

"Well, goddamnit, this is one war I don't think we should
be having. There's got to be a better way than killing young

secretaries on their way home from work—''

Tremaine gave the congressman a narrow-eyed glance. ''Steady, Fen. Steady. You've been calling for this kind of war, remember?''

''The hell I have. I've been calling for the removal of a corrupt and tyrannical government. By peaceful means, I might very well goddamn add.''

Tremaine smiled wryly. ''There is no way a corrupt tyranny can be removed by peaceful means, Congressman.''

Quigg threw down his napkin, pushed back his chair, and stood up. ''Well, then, count me out. I simply won't lend myself to a scheme that murders people in the streets as the way to achieve political ends.''

Tremaine's smile faded and his eyes glittered. ''I knew you were naive, Fen, but I had no idea how abysmally naive you really are. What do you think we've been running here—a high school pep rally? We're trying to overthrow a bloated, inefficient tyranny so that we can replace it with our own tyranny. So that we can dominate the world's economy and influence its political future. Murder bothers you? My God, man, every major government in the history of humankind has derived from murder—socially acceptable murder, called 'war' or 'revolution.' How would you have us do it? By winning two out of three volleyball matches?''

Quigg began to pace, his face clouded with anger. At the far end of the room he spun about and rasped, ''You know what? That's exactly what I started this game with—high school kind of pep rallies, held in bus stations and saloons and Grange halls. And it was damn well agreed that the reason the country had gone to hell was because the upper class—the elite sons of bitches with all the important money and all the important jobs in commerce and finance and government—had become immoral, lying, angle-shooting, self-indulgent, plundering exploiters of the working stiffs of America, the middle-class yahoos who make the country run. And we agreed that the way to fix that was to call their hands, show them we know what they're doing to us and let them know that we're going to throw their elite asses out the door. Nobody said anything about armed insurrection, or blowing up buildings and killing pretty women in the streets. Nobody said anything about setting up our own tyranny. What we said was that we were going to put the country back where it was in the first place—where honorable dudes like Washington and Jefferson and Adams and all those cats put it—by unelecting, and unappointing, and restoring the machinery to its original condition.''

Tremaine clapped his hands lazily. ''Bravo. How very touching. But I must remind you that Washington and Jefferson and Adams and all those cats got where they were by killing Englishmen—and a lot of their own countrymen as well. You can't make an omelet without breaking eggs, and you can't make a country without breaking heads.''

Quigg sneered. ''And I remind you, Tremaine, that nobody would've been hurt if the Englishmen's king had stopped doing to the colonists exactly what's being done to us by those limp-wristed bastards in Washington and the statehouses and the corporate headquarters and wherever else the Elite meet to cheat. And now you and Takai and the others want to do the same thing—your way. Well, I'm buying out. Hook some other naive jerk for your president.''

As Quigg turned and made for the door, Tremaine called angrily after him. ''A very noble speech for someone who solicits bribes. Your speech might have been more convincing if its audience didn't know, as I do, what a truly grubby grifter you are.''

From the foyer, his hand on the doorknob, Quigg said, ''Right. I am everything you say. But I am not a willing accomplice to murder. So this is one grubby grifter you're going to have to get along without.''

Tremaine sat on the sofa and stared out at the skyline for a long time, surprised and puzzled by his calmness in face of this, the climactic failure in a lifetime of failures. He had worked months to find Fen Quigg, to package and sell him, to play kingmaker by elevating a nobody to the supreme somebody. He had thought of everything but the possibility that Quigg's greed and ambition had limits. It had been totally illogical to expect that there could be too much loot for a master looter.

The question now was precisely when and how he should inform Takai of the disaster.

Should he just ring him up? ("Sorry, Mr. Takai, but our carefully selected candidate for president has just given us the middle finger. I thought you ought to know before the luncheon and the meeting and all.")

Or should he send a handwritten note? ("Dear Mr. Takai: I regret to inform you that Congressman Quigg has taken quite ill and has decided to retire. Have a nice lunch.")

However he broke the news, he knew, he was a dead man.

So, then, that being the case, he would simply toddle on up to the Jackson Room and tell the little bastard flat out. ("Hey, Takai: We both got a be-e-e-eg prob.")

Alone in the silence, he laughed.

Takai had spent much of the morning in the Jacuzzi with Nikki and Tikki, highly skilled, golden-haired, eighteen-year-old twins flown in from Copenhagen. As he climbed out of the swirling water and took up a towel, he said, "You are darlings, and I am much impressed."

Nikki made her most attractive moue. "You are leaving so soon?"

"I must dress for a meeting. Take the day and shop. I'm having dinner with my wife and some others, but I'll see you girls here at about ten o'clock."

Tikki made *her* most attractive moue. "Perhaps your wife will join us. Does she like to play?"

Takai smiled. "No, dear. She's quite conservative. But it was nice of you to suggest it."

Vibrations told Nickerson that something special was afoot. The house—meaning Mrs. Farman and Manfred—had been plunged into the darkest melancholy with the news of Cooper's death in the Bavarian lake. Nickerson had just left the shower and was dressing for the day when the TV morning show had been interrupted by a bulletin. His first reaction had been shock, closely followed by disappointment and anger. He had been working very hard for weeks now, and to have his main suspect suddenly evaporate in a blink of whimsical fate was unsettling, the source of a huge and unspecific resentment. He'd gone to bed still gloating over Chief Nolan's miraculous discovery of the Taurus thirty-eight under the bed, behind the cedar chest, where, apparently, Mrs. Nolan—frazzled over her call from the post office—had shoved it. And he had arisen to the news that it counted for nothing. His promotion to lieutenant would have to wait for another case, another day, and the knowledge of this was cause for instant despair. He had been trying to handle this when, in the apartment next door, he heard Manfred's anguished cry, which meant the old man had just caught the news himself, and from there everything had been downhill. Mrs. Farman, completely shattered, had called in a day off, leaving no one to answer the phones. There was no hot water in his apartment ell, thanks to a tank that chose now to break down, and the meeting of his security staff had to be called off because Stan Tremaine had phoned instructions to put a tight ring around the house against the TV crews, reporters, curiosity seekers, and vandals who sure as hell would be descending on the property. There would be no statements from anybody but him, Tremaine reminded Nickerson, and he would be down to go over things in the next several days.

But then something strange happened.

Manfred, who had wandered the house and grounds like a dejected ghost for most of the weekend, seemed suddenly to brighten. It was indefinable, but the old man's forlorn strolling through the gardens, hands clasped behind his back, face drawn and pasty, gave way to an oddly purposeful stowing of a suitcase in the Jeep.

The old man had long bothered Nickerson. There was a discord there, a falseness, a story unperceived and untold. Manfred had been something special to Frank Cooper, and there had to be a reason beyond all the reasons given. He had seen Manfred drive off a number of times, a suitcase in the backseat, to visit his lady friend in Daytona. And, while this was Monday, the day for it, Manfred was wearing his best suit and shiniest shoes—another discord to add to all the others—and so Nickerson's detective's juices began to flow.

He climbed into the Ford and followed the old man all the way to Jacksonville, where, much to his astonishment, Manfred checked into the Omni, a posh hotel on the Southbank. He called Arnie Kratzer, the man on duty at the Water Street house, to report his whereabouts and the fact that he, too, would be overnighting at the Omni.

The question nagged: Tomorrow being the day of the Rettung board meeting, why was the butler of the late great Matt Cooper all duded up and visiting the city where the meeting was to be held? Was he a messenger, taking documents to the meeting? If so, why? Tremaine, the Cooper lawyer, had long since gathered all of Frank Cooper's files. So what was Manfred taking to Jacksonville? Nickerson shook his head. That Manfred had more angles than a kaleidoscope, and he had to be watched like a freaking slide specimen.

So Nickerson subsequently haunted the hotel lobby and adjacent restaurants, keeping an eye out for Manfred, but he saw him only once, the next morning, at breakfast in the snack bar, where the old man alternated his attention to eggs and toast with frequent glances at the wall clock.

An interesting development was the announcement on the electronic board in the hotel's lobby that limousines for those attending the board meeting of Rettung Internationale would be waiting at the hotel's entrance at eleven-thirty.

Manfred, the sneaky Kraut, in the same hotel with people heavily ID'ed with Frank Cooper's past? Manfred had to be up to no good, and Nickerson was damn well going to find out what it was.

Maybe the butler did it after all, eh?

Forty-seven

Rudy was in his element, of course. By twelve-thirty, his beloved Magnolia Room, the most exclusive of the exclusive Jackson Club's exclusive penthouse private dining rooms, was banked with flowers, aglow under dimmed chandeliers, and thrumming with the muted piano ramblings of Charlie Lang. The parquet floor was waxed to blinding; the linen and silver were brilliant; the bar was a perishing wonderland of polished ebony, mirrors, and backlit crystal; the buffet was witchery for guests who preferred to stroll, ponder, pick, and choose, and the table wait staff was at maximum fawning-alert for those who didn't. The guests themselves, the board members of Rettung Internationale, were garden-variety jillionaires, each with a special way of showing how to be a pluperfect horse's ass. In Rudy's secret heart of hearts, the room, the setting, and the service were altogether too good for these dorks, who, owning so many good things, hadn't the slightest appreciation of good things.

Allison-Dutton, the Englishman, was a drunken slob who

placed wet glasses on polished wood; Tataglia, the Milano industrialist, trimmed his nails at the table; Doubet, the Pari-
sienne, raked away the meringue and ignored the crust of the
exquisitely delicate banana cream pie; Andrelou, the Greek,
left the spoon in her coffee cup; Goodman, the New Yorker
and grossest of them all, poured catsup over his cottage cheese
and belched frequently and noisily. Takai, the tiny Japanese,
had a tendency to bully the help. Only the attorney, Stanley
Tremaine, showed signs of urbanity, and even he had a tendency to strike haughty poses.

Why were wealth and power given to such squids?

If there was a God, She surely wasn't paying attention to her
Department of Fair Shakes.

Tremaine tapped his spoon on the rim of a water glass. The
sound was festive, but his face was grave. "Ladies and gentlemen, may I have your attention please?"

The piano fell silent, but Goodman finished telling his joke
about the man who came home to find his wife in bed with her
bridge club, and, although the board members hadn't the
slightest understanding of the American sense of humor, they
rewarded Goodman's leering punch line with feigned amusement.

" 'It was a grand slam-dunk,' " Allison-Dutton echoed,
chuckling. "Oh, I say, that's rich. Rich."

"Please. Silence, please, ladies and gentlemen. Mr. Takai
has an announcement."

The gabbling eventually ceased and Takai, like a wax figurine whose round, impassive face had melted into the suggestion of a frown, came to the center of the room and stood,
regarding the group with a smoldering gaze. "I'm sure," he
said softly, "you all will share my disappointment to learn that
Congressman Quigg has been called back to Washington and
will not be available to answer our questions today. It had been
my hope that he would share with us his personal point of view
on some of the recent developments in the American Congress
and thus we would be able, both individually and as a board, to
sharpen our vision of the future. Since he can't be with us, I
suggest that we leave the luncheon area and take seats at the

large table by the windows and move directly into our board meeting." He gestured. "Mr. Rudy, will you please have the room cleared?"

Rudy raised his hand and whirled it in a parody of the military's signal to assemble, adding emphasis with little snappings of his fingers. The waiters and busboys scurried about, Charlie Lang abandoned the piano bench, and the Rettung group made its way across the waxed parquet to the designated area.

"May I have coffee at the table?" Madame Doubet asked in her pouting way.

"No, madame," Takai said. "That would require service, and since we will be discussing some confidential matters, it would be inadvisable to have the wait staff—other outsiders—standing by. Sorry."

They took seats at the polished table, which was aglow from the reflected light of the faultless Florida afternoon outside the plate-glass wall. After the settling-in had subsided, the irrepressible Goodman asked, "Tell me something, Takai. How come you, the newest member of this board, seem to be taking over as the honcho? I mean, even I have more seniority than you."

Takai was ready for that one. He opened the folder before him and, without so much as a glance Goodman's way, said, "This is a special meeting, called at the request of our late CEO, Edmund von Ludwig, to consider a special matter—the establishment of a new fund under the Rettung aegis. Edmund asked me, and I have a memo to that effect in my folder here, to serve as discussion leader at this one session for this one purpose. So, even with Edmund's, ah, absence, I believe the members will agree that I should carry out my assignment. Are there any formal objections?"

"Yes, as a matter of fact there are."

Like coordinated puppets, the board members turned quizzical faces toward the source of this disruption.

Cooper stood, briefcase in hand, at the kitchen service entrance, near the bar and to one side of the piano. His face was solemn. "This meeting is a setup, and you're all being played for patsies. Takai plans to rip you off—to use your foundation's money to bankroll an organized attempt by foreign gangsters to usurp the leadership of the United States government. Such as it is.''

For Rudy, the surprise of the day—perhaps of the century—was the transformation of Matthew Cooper.

Cooper's sunrise materialization in the doorway of the restaurant management offices had been astonishing enough, what with the news about his having died in a freak automobile accident in Germany and all. And it had been a major struggle to keep from gaping while Cooper strode quickly down the hall, peering in each door. *Are you the only one here, Rudy? Yes—I'm always the first to arrive in the morning. The others won't be in until eight. Is there a room I can use without being bothered between now and lunchtime? Certainly, but I don't understand. I'll explain later, but right now I need absolute privacy and a phone, and these five hundred dollars are for your trouble.*

Five hundred dollars! Unlock the vacationing Fred Delaney's office at the end of the corridor, hand Cooper the key, and walk away with five pretty bills in a snowy white envelope. A lovely morning indeed.

But what was truly, incredibly surprising was the change in Cooper's physical appearance. No longer did he suggest something you see under a cardboard box in a dead-end alley. Gone were the unpressed bargain-basement slacks, the two-hundred-year-old sport coat, the frayed shirt and run-over shoes. The hair was neatly trimmed, the eyes clear and direct, the manicure professional. But the clothes! God, what lovely clothes. A perfectly fitted Chesterfield, a suit of British cut that had to have cost two thousand dollars, oxfords polished to glassiness, a Bond Street shirt whose French cuffs were garnished by solid gold links and whose natty collar sported—wonder of wonders—a perfectly knotted Italian silk necktie. All of which made Cooper gorgeous and Rudy once again awed by the power of money. Money can do anything. It can even make an ink-stained wretch look like the CEO of Stayne & Rech, Inc.

But if Rudy had been shocked, it was nothing compared to the reaction of those at the conference table.

The silence was tangible, as if a layer of cotton batting had been lowered from the ceiling to envelop each man, each woman, each object and particular. The soundlessness persisted until Stanley Tremaine made a strangled sound. "Coop. My God—Coop."

There was another interval of absolute quiet. Then Madame Doubet stirred and asked, "What is this—usurp?"

Surprisingly, it was the uncouth Goodman who answered. "It means to take over by shoving the legal guys aside and putting their own guys in command."

"Who are you, young man?" Allison-Dutton demanded.

"Matthew Cooper," Melissa Andrelou said, amused, beguiled. "Look at his face, you idiot. It is Frank Cooper, with improvements."

Cooper strode to the center of the room—tall, somber, classy, like the emcee at an undertakers' trade show. "This won't take too much of your time, ladies and gentlemen. I'll speed things up a bit with a copyrighted news story that will appear exclusively in the *St. Augustine Record* this evening, then sent out under a special agreement on the USP A Wire for the papers and TV news shows of tomorrow morning." He called, "Tina, will you come in now, please?"

The group turned its collective stare to the service entrance, from which Tina came striding with an armful of papers. She was wearing a tailored red suit and heels, and the jaded Madame Doubet was moved to murmur, "Nice ensemble."

"Tina," Cooper explained, "is a journalist—an investigative reporter. She will distribute among you copies of the article so that you can follow along as she reads."

The papers were passed about and Cooper said, "Okay, Tina. Have at it."

Tina, her voice full, throaty, began to read:

"Special to the St. Augustine Record. By Tina Mennen, Staff Writer (Copyright).

"Jacksonville, Florida—Killer riots in five cities and the assassinations of scores of prominent Americans have been traced to an international criminal conspiracy to foster civil unrest and take over the topmost levels of the U.S. government.

"The scheme, devised and led by a ring of rich and powerful

Far East gang lords, involves hundreds of U.S. political and business leaders and is heavily funded by one of the world's wealthiest and most reputable philanthropic foundations—itself established on an enormous cache of World War II Nazi treasure.

"The conspirators' aim is first to intensify the pressures on the existing government—middle-class anger over oppressive taxation and government inertia, widespread ethnic and cultural hostilities, severe economic dislocations—then to finance and arm an actual insurrection.

"The recent riots in Boston, Washington, Chicago, Denver, and Los Angeles were triggered by terrorists employed by the gang lords led by Oko Takai, a billionaire described by Interpol and the FBI as 'the most powerful and dangerous criminal in the Far East.'

"The murders of presidential advisers, media and financial personalities, and municipal government figures were also carried out by Takai's terrorists and—along with the riots—represented the opening acts of the conspiracy's armed-rebellion phase. The subsequent and ongoing insurrection involves guerrilla units of so-called 'Middies,' initially equipped and financed by Takai's 'Council of Brothers' and soon to be enriched by monies provided by the George Washington Fund. The GWF is planned as a wing of Rettung Internationale, a philanthropic group often described as the 'Ford Foundation of Europe.'

"In the course of this reporter's investigation, it was learned that Rettung Internationale had been founded in 1952 by the late Frank J. Cooper, renowned author and resident of St. Augustine, with money derived from a cache of diamonds looted from Dutch enterprises by Adolf Hitler's SS and then appropriated by Cooper while serving as an American secret agent in Germany at the close of World War II.

"Cooper's intelligence team included Stanley M. Tremaine, now a prominent Jacksonville lawyer who serves as an adviser to the Rettung Foundation. According to sources in Germany, Cooper, Tremaine, and other team members 'had conscience pangs' and, instead of keeping the diamonds for themselves, pooled the gems and agreed that they would be used only for humanitarian purposes. It was from this source that Rettung and its far-flung charities sprang.

"Takai was named to the Rettung board last year on the voucher of Edmund von Ludwig, CEO of Rettung and a Takai collaborator. Ludwig did not inform the board of Takai's terrorist and gangland backgrounds, instead touting him as a respectable, highly regarded businessman.

"The next move of—"

Takai pounded a fist on the table, pushed back his chair, and stood, his face flushed and angry. "The next move is that I stop listening to this libelous drivel. Then I will call the security guards and have you both taken down to the street and thrown out of the building."

"I'm afraid the guards won't be of much help to you. They no longer come with your Jackson Room rental fee. I bought their little company, Ajax Security Service, three days ago, and all eight of them are now working for me."

"Cool," Goodman said, grinning.

Madame Doubet complained, "Will somebody please explain what's really going on here?"

"What's going here," Takai said, his angry voice actually seeming to hiss, "is that Cooper is seeking to, using his word, 'usurp' the Rettung organization. He wants to replace his father as president and eventually remove us all from the board. To do this he must sow dissension, and he has begun by lying about me and my intentions. I assure you, ladies and gentlemen, he has no proof, and you will be my witnesses when I bring suit against him for this vile defamation."

Cooper was reasonable. "Proof? It's proof you want?" He opened his briefcase and drew out a sheaf of papers. "For one thing: a profile of Takai and his criminal associations as compiled by the FBI and Interpol and summarized by investigators of the House Select Committee on International Commerce, provided me personally by Congressman Quigg." He put the first set of papers down. "A Spengler Business Research report on Takai's known American acquisitions and their linkage via lobbying groups with the White House and key federal departments and agencies—bought for fifty dollars from the Spengler organization." He dropped the Spengler report on top of the profile. "A committee report tracing Takai's relationships with media kingpins, industrialists, supply and distribution magnates, and known transnational money launderers—also provided by Quigg; Takai's connection with American revolutionary groups via Edmund von Ludwig, Stanley Tremaine, District Judge Abner Hefflefinger, and realtor Claude Abernathy—all established via interviews and photos taken by Tina Mennen. There's more—but maybe you'd like a bit of eyewitness testimony. Word from the inside, eh?"

Cooper lowered the papers and called out again, "Okay, Ludwig. Come on in."

The German appeared in the doorway, gaunt, subdued. He peered about, warily, nervously, like a cat deciding whether to enter a room.

"You heard what's been said here, Ludwig?"

"Yes. I was in the pantry, listening."

"Is Tina Mennen's article correct—accurate?"

"Entirely."

"Why are you so sure?"

"I was CEO of Rettung Internationale. She interviewed me the day before yesterday. She has presented my answers accurately."

"Why were you so ready to give such candid answers to such self-condemning questions?"

Ludwig hesitated, blinking, in the manner of an old man distracted by memory. "Because," he said eventually, "I was never fully in agreement with what Takai expected me to do. Because I was not yet ready to die. Because I felt remorse, a need to repent. Because you and the young woman could have left me to die. But you saved me, and by saving me, have given me a chance to atone."

This silence was even deeper, longer.

Goodman suddenly pushed back his chair, took up his attaché case, and stood, glancing about the table. "All this makes me nervous," he said to no one in particular. "And when I get nervous, I walk out."

"I haven't finished reading yet," Tina snapped.

"You don't need to read any more to me, sister. I know a

disaster when I see one. I resign, here and now.''

''And so do I,'' said Madame Doubet, gathering her purse and following Goodman to the exit.

''Say 'Interpol' to me, and I'm gone,'' said Allison-Dutton. He, too, made his way out.

As did Tattaglia and Andrelou.

And, finally, Takai strode stolidly, wordlessly, to the foyer and its elevator bay, where he was suddenly surrounded by large men in dark suits, one of whom flashed a badge.

''Yo, Al,'' Cooper called, ''did you hear all that?''

Milano's husky voice answered from the pantry. ''Bet your ass. Every word, and it's all on the tape. And my guys have Takai in custody.''

Tremaine, a solitary figure at the glossy table, asked quietly, ''Do you want me to leave, too, Coop?''

''No. Sit still. I want to talk to you.'' Cooper turned to Tina. ''Would you go into the pantry and ask the others to come in?''

''All of them?''

''Al, Manfred, Ludwig, you. I want you four to sit in on this conversation.''

Forty-eight

How much easier it would be, Cooper thought, if he could tell Stanley Tremaine simply to go away—to get out of his life and never reappear, ever. But there were too many loose ends, too many involvements, too many sad duties, and he had a sense of bleeding that could not be stopped without a resolution of this matter between them. There had been many times in the past two weeks when images of the old, terrible war days drifted through his mind—his father and Stan, huddling over some table in some dreary German warren, spellbound, an array of diamonds before them, struggling against the Lorelei of greed. Staring across the table at Stan now, he tried to picture him as he might have looked in those times, but the reality of snowy hair, defeated eyes, and sardonic smile made the transposition impossible. *Ah, well.*

Cooper glanced at Milano. "Is your recorder running?"

"Check."

"Okay, Stan, can we talk?"

Tremaine sent a slow gaze around the table, considering

those sitting there in the manner of a lawyer evaluating the temper of a jury. Returning to Cooper, he said, "So, then, you have come back from the dead after having followed the trail of crumbs to Feldstein and the truth."

"Crumbs is the word."

"Ah, yes. A harsh word. But I, the others—Frank, Feldstein, even Manfred—have used harsher ones on ourselves. Hijackers, thieves, perjurers, to name a few."

"You're not going to ask us to feel sorry for you, I hope."

Tremaine smiled. "Hardly. I was just reminding you that at first we saw ourselves as Robin Hoods, stealing from the bad guys to give to the poor. But that wore pretty thin, because, believe it or not, we each had a code, a private sense of morality, and our guilt buttons had been pressed. And compounding the sorry mess was the fact that each of us was also the kind who, no matter how well intentioned, seems always to end up in deep dung."

"Soft cello music here," Tina put in sarcastically.

Tremaine ignored her. Giving Cooper an especially close inspection, he said softly. "You know, I can't quite handle your being here. If it's not a miracle it's got to be the damnedest surprise I've ever had. Takai was so positive. He said the car sank out of sight under the ice with you and the girl and Ludwig locked in. There was doubt that you would ever be found, he said. Just how in hell did you manage to escape?"

"Icy water and German engineering. The car's ignition was on and its electrical system kept working for a time. The cold water woke me up—Tina, too—but we swallowed a lot of the lake before I put it together: if the ignition was still on, the door locks and sunroof were probably still working. I punched the buttons, and we were out of there."

"And you took Ludwig with you?"

"He was pretty well done in, but Tina helped me to pull him out and get him to the surface, where we worked our way ashore through the broken ice. You know something? I could see those taillights, still glowing, even after the car was below us, sinking through a cloud of silt. No wonder those cars are so frigging expensive, eh?"

Tremaine said nothing, waiting.

"Takai and his people had gone up to the main house to call and wait for the police, so we crawled up a dock ladder into the heated boathouse. The supply locker had some brandy and towels and work clothes, and that combination got us through the night. We hid in the dark, drying and thawing out, watching the cops and divers search for us. Before dawn we made our way to the highway and hitched a ride to Munich, and all three of us were on the plane to Jacksonville that night."

"Why did you hide from the police?"

Cooper shrugged. "We didn't want you and Takai and the others to know we were still around. We all had scores to settle, and the cops would only stand in the way."

Tremaine nodded. "And so today you're settling the scores. Takai first, now me."

"You set up that phony libel suit, didn't you."

"Of course. With some help from Ludwig and that creep, Bolko What's-His-Face."

"Why?"

"We had to have a logical reason to search Frank's papers and records."

"Why did you want to do that?"

"When Frank figured out what we were up to he threatened to contact the FBI—even though it would incriminate himself for having illegally appropriated Nazi contraband, and having sponsored Manfred, an immigrant he knew to be a former Gestapo official, and all. He'd never got over his one big lapse into big-time crime, and on a kind of rebound, he had turned into a card-carrying Righteous Richard, wearing a size extra-large hair shirt. So when he saw that Rettung, the thing that had given him back some self-respect, was to serve as the root for an even bigger crime, he went into intergalactic warp, shaking his word processor at me. So after he was killed, I had to find out if he'd written and sent such a letter, because we hadn't had too much success buying up the FBI, and the Bureau would be all over us like a ton of wet noodles if they tumbled to Yankee Doodle, which was what we called our plan. Obviously I couldn't just ask you, 'Hey, Coop, mind if I root through your daddy's house for a while?' without your getting curious. And, believe me, I learned long ago that there's nothing more bothersome than a curious news reporter.''

''And when I kept being curious anyhow, you tried to have me killed.''

Tremaine shook his head emphatically. ''Wrong. I had nothing to do with those attempts. In fact, they really upset me, because I like you and saw no need for it. And, as you've seen for yourself, Ludwig doesn't have any stomach for rough stuff. No doubt about it: It was Takai who put a contract on Frank and it had to be Takai who put out a job order on you. It's his SOP to torpedo people who crowd him.''

''What really happened to the diamonds, Stan?''

''We—the team members—decided to pool them and give custody to Feldstein. We envisioned a bad, maybe impossible time taking shares and smuggling them back to the States, and, since we all trusted Feldstein and knew of his plan to remain in Germany and spend his life nailing war criminals, we agreed on a split, to be drawn on, as each of us saw fit, from the cache—its location was known only to Feldstein—for our various projects. And Feldstein would serve as fence, banker, and records-keeper.''

''What did you do with your share?''

One of those moments followed, a time of noisy silence in which somewhere far off a phone rang and there was the faint sound of a vacuum cleaner. Tremaine folded his hands and placed them on the table, and the others watched, as if something marvelous would spring from them. ''Ah, yes, the big one. The question that will reveal the depth of my greed and the extent of my treachery. I'm not sure you're ready for this, Coop.''

''Try anyhow.''

''My share, after Feldstein had fenced the diamonds, was worth close to three hundred million dollars. All of which, except for one million dollars, remains in the Swiss bank account supervised by Feldstein. The million was spent partly on putting Frank Cooper, the author, on the best-seller lists and partly on making Frank Cooper wealthy.''

Cooper let his astonishment show. "What the hell does that mean?"

"Frank's first novel, *A Job for Despair,* is, to my mind, one of literature's best, most moving portrayals of the awfulness of war and those few politicians—whatever the time in history—who decide to have them. But it was going nowhere. As a first novel, it had no promotion to speak of, got virtually no important reviews, and was obviously on a fast trip to total obscurity. I thought it should be widely read. So I took five hundred thousand of my diamond share and paid friends in key cities to buy Frank's book in great numbers. In those days, such a sum could buy a hell of a lot of books, grease the palms of a hell of a lot of book critics, buy a hell of a lot of radio and newspaper commentary. And, of course, in cases like that, the process feeds on itself; the more the talky-talk, the more books are sold, and the more the sales, the more the talky-talk. Frank was famous almost overnight, and his subsequent book contracts and royalty advances ballooned out of sight. I—"

Cooper broke in. "Did my father know what you'd done?"

"Of course not. It would have killed him to know that his popularity initially had nothing to do with his talent. Later on, of course, he became truly popular and sought after by publishers because his work was indeed excellent. So, no—he never knew how I triggered things, thank God."

"What about the other five hundred thou?" Milano asked.

"Here's where we get around to my self-serving scene. Frank was complaining one day about his inability to handle the money that was pouring in. I, a run-of-the-mill lawyer with an expensive wife and snooty, judgmental in-laws, was having trouble finding ways to make money pour in. So I bet Frank that if he let me manage his money I could, with smart investments, make him a half-million-dollar profit in the first year. He agreed, and, while I did indeed make him some money, it was nowhere near the half-million I'd promised. So that's where the other half-million went."

"And," Cooper said, "you continued to manage his money and continued to make him a nice profit each year."

Tremaine nodded, not without satisfaction. "I turned out to

be very good at that kind of thing. I made us both very well-to-do. And, I might add, I did it honestly.''

"Then why—what made you play footsies with Takai and his bummers, Stan? Hell, you didn't need them.''

"They promised to make me an important man. Takai mentioned the attorney general slot after Quigg's election. And that had a special appeal, because all my life people had thought of me as a professional mediocrity who had nothing but lots of luck and influential friends going for him. My father thought I was a jerk, my colleagues thought I was a jerk, my wife and her parents thought I was a jerk, and now, after all those rotten years, I had a chance to shove it all up their rosy rectums. That, Coop, is why I threw in with Takai.''

"But you're one hell of a good lawyer—''

"Certainly I am. But I'm trapped in a perception. Everything is perceptions. If people perceive you as a jerk, they treat you as a jerk, rarely seeing the good stuff you might be doing. Our whole goddamn civilization today rests on perceptions. And our dependence on perceptions is going to kill our civilization, buddy, because we're so busy perceiving the rotten stuff we have little or no time and emotion for the good stuff. Civilization is already into a bad wobble, and I was determined to build myself an escape capsule for use when the ship goes entirely out of orbit.''

"Hell, man, you're seventy-something—''

"And I'm ready to bet that I'll still outlive this rotten civilization we've got. You don't seem to understand, Coop: Everything's in the toilet, and the chain's been pulled.''

Milano sneered. "Well, no matter how much time you've got left, it looks like you'll be spending it in the slammer.''

Tremaine gave him a jaded glance. "Don't count on it. I'm a very good lawyer. And I still have a lot of friends in high places, as the saying goes. Especially those I've bought who don't want it known that they've been bought. Including some of your own colleagues, I might add.''

Cooper looked up from his notes, feeling a sense of futility. He wished it could be anger—undiluted rage over the injustice of humanity's being so villainous when it could have been so majestic, so righteous. But why should he care at all? He glanced about him, and it was as if these people were unlikable strangers, because they had somehow taken something from him, leaving him with this lousy empty hole in his chest.

"Does anybody have questions? Something to say?"

"I do."

It was Nickerson, standing in the doorway, inscrutable.

Cooper looked at Milano. The FBI man's heavy face was impassive, unresponsive.

"What's on your mind, Nick?"

"I'm here to place you under arrest for the murder of Frank J. Cooper. Your father."

"Get serious."

"Oh, I am, man. Very serious. And I've been waiting very patiently for you to come back from the dead. I didn't buy that phony accident bit for a minute."

"This is the thanks I get for giving you a job when you needed one so bad?"

"I never needed a job. I was a cop all along. Assigned to nail you to the wall. And now I've got the hammer: a thirty-eight caliber Taurus I found in a shoe box in your attic whose ballistics match the slug recovered from said Frank J. Cooper. And, incidentally, from the body of William Logue, whose murder I'm also arresting you for."

"Manfred, would you get that briefcase in the pantry? The one with the combo lock."

The gaunt German left his chair and was striding across the room when Nickerson snapped, "Hold it right there, Manfred. And that goes for you, too, Tina. Just keep your hands away from your purse and on the table." The detective glanced at Milano. "You want in on this, Al?"

"No. You're doing fine. It's all local. But don't forget your Miranda."

Cooper sighed. "Well, the briefcase isn't all that important right now. I have a photocopy of a paper in it. The original is in a safe downtown. I was going to give the copy to you, Nick. It's the paper that proves you killed my father."

Forty-nine

Once again Tina seemed to see things with an extraordinary clarity, as if powerful lenses had come between her and the slice of the world she happened to be confronting at the moment. The phenomenon had occurred the first time in the water, a universe of dark gurgling in which she awakened, gagging, suffocating, unable to choke or cry out, rolling and careening and colliding cruelly with the surfaces of the car. She had seen with a terrible lucidity the churning ice, the silt-clouded water, eerily backlit by the headlights; Cooper's face, faint and strangling and wide-eyed in his struggle with the doors; the upward passage of flotsam as the car sank, down and down, like some grotesque elevator leading to Hell. It was as if she had been given special sight, an ability to see the entire reach of the beginning, the present, and the ending—the brackets of the finite. And for all the fearfulness, she had known with an absolute certainty that they would not die, not there in that car and that time. So a calmness just this side

of serenity had settled in, and she had worked quickly, precisely, to help Coop to clear the sunroof and then to follow and
to pull open the rear door and retrieve Ludwig, ghostlike in the
diminishing light, eyes closed, lips seeming to be set in a sad
smile.

The second time had been the next morning in the hotel,
when Coop had materialized in her room, beside her bed, shaking her awake. Opening her eyes, she had looked into his, and
there was an unconditional acceptance of the truth she had refused to acknowledge since the beginning: He was, and would
be, the only person—thing, presence, entity, force—that mattered. His eyes, calm, amused, were the lenses through which
she gained this larger vision of herself, and it was then, with his
good-natured scolding about her sacking out when he was
fully dressed, filled with breakfast and ready to charge, she
knew that she was hopelessly, irrevocably tied to him for the
length of whatever life was to be granted her.

And now, again, in the golden light of the afternoon's glare
and profiled against the urban reaches, his face—cool, determined—manifested the infinite potentialities that their union
promised her. It was more than a face. It was a holographic
representation of her destiny.

Easily, almost dreamily, she watched the developing confrontation.

As expected, Nickerson scoffed.

"If you're trying out for comic, you aren't going to make it,
Cooper."

"Manfred tells me you've been blackmailing him. You saw
his picture in in a public library book, *The Pictorial History of
Hitler's SS*. The same picture as the one I found in my father's
records. You've been charging him five hundred dollars a
week to keep his secret, which, if it became known to Immigration, would have him deported overnight. My father found
out about it, accused you, and said he was going to bring
charges against you. You shot him, and then, when you got a
load of me and my confusion, decided to pin the murder on me.
When that didn't seem to be working out, and when I showed
signs of getting too close to your blackmail gig, you hired Billy

Logue to kill me. And when that fizzled, you killed Billy to cover your tracks. You're a real hairball, and I'm having you pinched.''

The squat man sneered. ''What the hell have you been smoking? You can't prove any of that.''

''I've got a notarized copy of a police department evidence transfer form you filled out for a thirty-eight-caliber Taurus revolver. You certified on the form that you discovered the weapon in a shoe box in the attic of my Jacksonville house. You certified that the date of discovery was January eleventh, this year. I also have a bill from the Collins Pest Control Company of Jax, marked Paid in Full, that shows the house was fully tented and filled with cyanide gas for three days—January tenth, eleventh, and twelfth. And Manfred has given me an affidavit from Mrs. Alice Beatty, my Jax neighbor, that she watched the house those three days and nobody—not even a squirrel—got into that house. So it just wasn't possible for you to recover anything from my house on January eleventh, Nick. Which means the gun, whose ballistics check out with the murder slugs, was in your possession on and before that date. You're not only a killer and a blackmailer—you're a documented liar.''

Tina felt a smile forming as Cooper turned to Milano, saying, ''Thanks for believing me, and for helping me out with that phone call to this creep. Between you and Manfred's sucking him in, I thought it was iron-strap sure that he'd find this meeting. I was right, right?''

''You couldn't have been righter, man.''

''I'm making a citizen's arrest, Al. I know it's out of your jurisdiction, but would you do me a favor and put cuffs on this dude and pop him into some kind of jail somewhere?''

Milano stood up, huge and formidable, and reached to unclip the cuffs from his belt. ''My pleasure.''

''No. Leave that pleasure to me.'' It was Chief Nolan, striding in from the foyer, brandishing a set of handcuffs. He grinned at Milano. ''I owe you, Al. I didn't want you to be right, but the documents have it. And so you're right.''

Milano grinned back. ''I'm always right, you tank town flatfoot.''

From there things began to come apart, but the clarity was still with her, and she saw it all, almost as if she were reviewing frames from a stop-action film.

Nickerson spun about, a black pistol in his right hand, and fired once. She saw the tiny flash, heard the thunderous, contained boom, felt the stunning concussion. And she saw the fabric of Milano's shirt flutter, the instant red stain, the staggering and collapsing. A second shot, directed at Nolan, snapped nastily, but by then the chief and everybody but Coop were diving for cover, and so the slug's only accomplishment was a long white slash in the bar's dark wood.

Above the clamor, she heard Nickerson's voice: "Nobody but nobody threatens me." Leveling the pistol on Coop, who stood, seemingly frozen, he grated, "You're next, hotshot. Bon voyage."

There was a peculiar howling behind her, part growl, part shriek, and a soft rumbling.

She turned her head to see Manfred, crouching, his eyes wild, his mouth a raw gash in the ancient pastiness of his face, pushing Charlie Lang's roll-around studio piano ahead of him like an ebony battering ram. It moved with incredible ease and swiftness, but Nickerson managed to get off three quick shots.

Manfred's battle cry became a cry of pain, and he staggered, blood gushing from his mouth. But the piano continued on its own momentum, gliding with an insensate purpose, striking Nickerson full on, lifting him off his feet and carrying him inexorably through a glittering explosion of plate glass and into the void beyond.

Wind howled as the warm air of the room rushed to mix with the winter cool outside, and papers flew from the table, and unoccupied chairs actually inched toward the gaping hole in the high glass wall.

She was beside Cooper then, holding him, together they dropped to the floor and peered over its edge.

The piano, a tiny shower of black splinters, was in its final ricochet off the second-floor set-back, and as they watched, it crashed conclusively into the courtyard fountain. Beside it, in a separate splashing, landed something resembling a clump of rags.

* * *

Milano was all right—sitting up, pale and dabbing at his shoulder with a napkin.

There was no helping Manfred. She and Cooper knelt beside him, holding his hands. He smiled up at them briefly, then died without a word.

From his place at the table, Tremaine said, "It's just as well. Deportation would have killed him more slowly."

Cooper said, "He never intended to be deported. He intended to ride the piano all the way down."

"You know that, eh?"

Tina bristled. "Yes, he knows that. And so do you."

Tremaine laughed softly.

She went to the wall phone and dialed 911. Coop watched her, his face showing shock and sorrow. As she listened to the ringing, she formed her lips in a reassuring kiss, and his eyes softened.

"Nine-One-One Emergency. How might we help you?"

"Let me count the ways," Tina said.

WASHINGTON (USP)—J. Fenimore Quigg was elected president of the United States today in a landslide that confounded the experts, purged Congress of hundreds of incumbents, and set the stage for a massive reformation of the federal government.

Riding atop a huge wave of voter dissatisfaction with what he derided in his campaign as "government of the elite, by the elite, and for the elite," Quigg swept every state, took every electoral vote, and saw his organization win all but three House and Senate races.

Quigg, a self-styled "anti-Establishment renegade whose mission is to give America back to the Americans," prevailed against odds deemed by most political sages to be "insurmountable."

With the country torn by guerrilla warfare and violent protests, and in face of opponents' charges that he had been bribed by foreign interests, Quigg's triumph came in one of the most tumultuous periods in the nation's history and was seen as a smashing repudiation of mud-slinging as a political technique.

From the moment he announced his intention to run, Quigg came under attack by powerful political action committees and media luminaries as "the candidate made in Japan." Fighting back, Quigg turned the tide in September when, during a widely televised speech, he admitted that he had been offered—and had rejected—"great sums of Japanese gang money to subvert the will of the American people."

Today's voters, by giving him a plurality close to unanimity, obviously accepted his assurances that he's "not for sale to anyone—especially a bunch of foreign hoodlums—because [he considers himself] already under contract to the great American middle class," which expects him "to deliver it from the social and economic dungeons of the Beltway oppressors."

(MORE TO KUM)

(Attn Desk Eds: Suggest transition from this lead into balloting specifics, localized where possible. A major roundup is in prep and will be ready on A line for use in a.m.'s of tomorrow. National, international reaction sidebars will accompany. Stand by.)

BULLETIN   BULLETIN   BULLETIN

Fifty

Cooper was parked in a no-parking zone in front of the newspaper building. The car's top was down, and he was awash in the sunglow and jasmine that make early spring in St. Augustine a cause for desertions in Duluth.

He dialed around the radio, found nothing but gabble and dairn-dairn-dairn. He slipped a disk of Vivaldi into the player, but in a few moments even that proved to be too tzee-tzee-tzee-tzee tzeeee for a nice day like this. So he turned everything off and sat, eyes half closed, smelling the smells and listening to the calls of the gulls that wheeled in the deep blue above the city's spires.

She came out of the building, laden as always with cameras, sling-bags, and mysterious lumps in that thing with all the pockets she wore to everything but bed. Maybe even there, for all he knew.

She saw him at once, because it's hard to miss a red Mercedes convertible in brilliant Florida sunlight.

"Well, hi there," she said, her face brightening. "My, look at you: Rodeo Drive East."

"I decided that if I've got to be a rich dude I might as well start looking like one."

"Well, you certainly do."

"And you look like a successful paparazzo. I heard you were in St. Augie to visit your old buds. I took potluck and came by."

"I'm glad. You're a sight for sore contacts."

"What are you working on? With all that gear it has to be the sequel to 'On the Seventh Day He Rested.'"

"Something of a somewhat smaller scale. A Federal Historical Commission task force is in town to study the feasibility of moving St. Augustine to Buffalo Dung, Nebraska, where the tourists will find easier parking."

"What will they put where St. Augustine was?"

"Buffalo Dung, Nebraska."

"Makes sense."

They laughed, enjoying the blarney and using the interval for memories.

She had matured in the passage of a year, he saw, and in that short time the pretty girl's face had become a beautiful woman's face, the kid's lope had been replaced by the assured stride of The Professional on the Go. But the dark eyes were still merrily quizzical, the grin impish.

"I hate to say this," he said, "but obviously your experiment with the freelance life has been successful. You look absolutely super."

"I'm a pig in mud, Coop. No better way to go."

"Got time for lunch?"

"I've got to be at the airport by two to catch the commuter plane to Jax."

"Where you going from there?"

"Seattle."

"My God. That's still a combat zone—"

"*Chronos* magazine wants me to do a piece that explores why the Middie revolt is so stubborn in the West. Seattle is synonymous with stubborn fighting, so I'm starting there."

"That doesn't take any exploration. Everybody knows that

the farther west a place is the less connected it feels with Washington. The secession talk gets heavier than hell west of the Mississippi.''

"Well, President Quigg is working on that. I think he might even get results with that Denver conference he's laid on. Who knows?''

"Get in the car. There's a mom-and-pop eatery near the airport that has great chili.''

"I have a rental car—''

He tapped the phone on the console beside him. "I'll call and have the rental people pick it up. Even bring it to you, if you want.''

"Well—''

"Come on. In the car. Right now.''

The mom-and-pop place was closed on Mondays, so they went to a ferny place near the World Golf Center and took a table beside the windows in a quiet, ferny corner. They ordered sandwiches which, when they arrived, proved to be mercifully fern-free.

She glanced at her watch. "I don't mean to be rude, but I don't want to miss that plane.''

"Relax. If you miss it, I'll fly you to Seattle, if you'd like.''

"Oh? You have a plane now?''

"Sopwith Camel. You'll have to sit on the lower wing and hold on to the struts, but, hell, you can't beat the price.''

"Come on.''

"It's really a jet that goes from here to there in seven milliseconds. I run back and forth between here and Munich like a Long Island commuter, so it made sense to get my own flying machine.''

"You're spending most of your time on the Rettung job?''

"No. Not most. All my time. This lunch is my vacation this year.''

"How's it going?''

"All right. I've got a board that's real gung-ho, and we're trying hard to remove the stain left by the Takai thing and all the rotten publicity it generated.''

"Ironic about Takai. He puts up ten million dollars' bail just so he can fly back to Kyoto and commit hara-kiri.''

"It was a samurai thing, I'm told. Everybody has some kind of code, some higher power he believes in.''

"What's with the others? I've been on the Third World beat so long I've lost touch with the other two worlds.''

"Tremaine's still in court, and will probably be there for another hundred years. But he still lives in that Ponte Vedra sand castle and is still interviewed by media people who dote on charismatic crooks. Ludwig has become a monk in Italy. Al Milano has been named something huge in the Bureau, but don't ask me what. Ramm died last November. Feldstein is still nagging Nazis from Eheburg and is still sitting on a mega-fortune nobody's left to claim. He's offered it to Rettung, but I've refused, naturally. Rettung has enough trouble living down the Nazi money it has, without taking on another fresh load of it.''

"The media sure gave Rettung the biz, all right.''

"God, I thought they'd never let up. One good thing came out of it, though. All of my old man's books are back in print and selling like you wouldn't believe.''

She sipped her coffee thoughtfully. He studied the shine of her dark hair, the long lashes and deep, downcast eyes, the delicate curve of her lips. It was hopeless, he thought, but he still wanted her, sought explanations for her determination to keep her distance, waited absurdly and forlornly for her to prove whatever it was she was trying to prove. Almost as though she had somehow tapped into his thoughts, she returned the cup carefully to its saucer and said, more serious than he'd ever seen her, "All that seems like another lifetime. Yet I still wake up in the middle of the night, holding my breath and, well, swimming, like. I see the car around me and feel the cold, and I see you banging on that window, and we're sinking. It's worse than it was when it was actually happening. Want to know something? I have this strong hunch mechanism—intuition, or something—and I knew we weren't going to die in that car. I just plain knew it.''

"You're infected, too, eh? Premonitions are my main mental health problem. They're different from yours. Yours can come up with positive things, obviously. Mine are always doom and gloom.''

She smiled, her eyes still averted. ''Opposites attract, they say.''

He had nothing to add to this platitude.

She gave him one of her quizzical looks. ''Do you ever miss the news business, Coop?''

''Only when I'm awake or asleep.''

''That bad, huh?''

''I miss it almost as much as I miss you.''

Despite his most earnest promise to himself that he would remain objective and keep the conversation friendly and debonair, rather just this side of aloof, the damned admission had simply popped out, like a hiccup. He looked at her quickly, with alarm. Had she been offended? Annoyed at this fleeting, spontaneous violation of their pact, agreed upon eleven months, three days, and ten hours ago? *What's with you, Cooper? Can't you keep your freaking mouth shut?*

Something akin to heat lightning had flickered across her features, the suggestion of turbulence, far off.

''Sorry,'' he said. ''That just came out.''

''I'll tell you something else about those moments in the car. As calm as I was, I was, well, aware, I guess you'd call it, of this terrible sadness—a regret, kind of. And it was about you and me, about how whatever this is between us had never been worked through—resolved.''

He looked at her, startled.

''I miss you, Coop, every hour on the hour and every minute between.''

Steady, boy. She's just being sociable. ''Well, now. That's good.''

''There is absolutely no reason why I should miss you so much. You're not all that great looking, you're sort of dumb lots of times, you don't know a damned thing about clothes, you know even less about women. But your greatest defect is your wealth. You're stinking rich, and everything I ever did, no matter how much on my own, no matter how remote I was from you, no matter how singularly ingenious I might be, I could never stop suspecting that somewhere somebody was pulling strings for me just because I sleep with a dude who's loaded.''

"Sleep? Hell, I don't want to sleep with you. I want to marry you.'' He coughed. "Let me rephrase that—''

Her shoulders began to shake. A soft snickering at first, then a chuckling, a burst of laughter, and, finally, a guffaw. "God, you really are a klutz, aren't you.''

"Are you laughing at me, or what?''

"I'm laughing because I think you are the weirdest, straightest, dumbest, smartest, funniest-looking, most handsome son of a bitch I've ever known, and I absolutely adore you. There is no reason I should give you a second glance, but what happens? I get the hots just hearing your name, that's what happens. But tell me—please tell me: How can I become the world's greatest journalist if I'm married to the world's richest ex-journalist?''

He reached across the table and clasped her hand. "Tina, listen to me. It's what you look like to yourself that matters. If you know that, by way of guts and ingenuity and persistence and talent, you've really earned the title of the world's greatest journalist, what difference does it make what others think about how you got the title? And if you don't marry me only because I'm rich, you'll be letting others—mean, envious, judgmental people we don't even know—take away your greatest chance for fulfillment as a human being. That I guaran-damn-tee you.''

"Yeah? What do you know about it?''

"I don't know anything but this: When you're not with me, all I can think of is you; when you are with me, all I can think of is how lousy I'll feel when you're not with me. Is that sick or what?''

She looked out the window and sighed. "That's sick, all right. I should know. I've got the same disease.''

There was an interval in which the restaurant made its muted clatter and the canned music drifted tinnily through the ferns. She sighed again and brought her gaze back to him. "You're not kidding? You do have a jet that can make it all the way to Seattle?"

"One phone call, and it'll be warming up on the line."

"At Jax airport?"

"Yep."

They traded stares for a full minute.

"I have an idea," Cooper said finally. "What if I become sort of your camp follower? You go roaring off to Kenya, or Australia, or Spitzbergen—wherever—and I follow in my Little Alice Blue Airplane, available at any moment when you have need of a hand-squeeze or a pat on the shoulder or a low-interest loan. That will let you keep working on your quest for the world champ title, and it will let me be miserable where I can see you once in a while instead of being miserable where all I have is memories."

"No involvement in my work? No string-pulling behind my back? No bribing of editors, or like that?"

"None."

"No marriage?"

"No marriage. I will be a kept man. Your concubine. And if you're still worried about image, I will even change my name—'Mr. Matthew L. Mennen'—so people who see us together will think I am your no-good, freeloading brother, hanging around you because he can't get a job."

"With a red Mercedes convertible and an Alice blue jet, that'll be sort of hard to sell."

He thought about that. "Yeah, I guess you're right. So I'll be Mr. Matthew L. Mennen, your no-good brother, scrounging from you because he can't afford gas for his tan Yugo sedan and his Sopwith Camel."

"I've got a better idea," she said. "Let's get married and then use that jet to take both of us around the world, freelancing as we go. You do your stories, I do mine, and we make he-and-she betweeners."

"What happens if your story is in Nome and mine is in Tierra del Fuego?"

"I get the jet and you get the Sopwith. We'll meet weekends in Panama."

"Makes sense."

She reached out, seized his shirtfront, pulled him across the tiny table, and kissed him hugely.

"Please, dear," he murmured finally, "not here. The ferns will see us—"

THE BEST OF FORGE

☐ 53441-7   CAT ON A BLUE MONDAY $4.99
                Carole Nelson Douglas   Canada $5.99

☐ 53538-3   CITY OF WIDOWS $4.99
                Loren Estleman   Canada $5.99

☐ 51092-5   THE CUTTING HOURS $4.99
                Julia Grice   Canada $5.99

☐ 55043-9   FALSE PROMISES $5.99
                Ralph Arnote   Canada $6.99

☐ 52074-2   GRASS KINGDOM $5.99
                Jory Sherman   Canada $6.99

☐ 51703-2   IRENE'S LAST WALTZ $4.99
                Carole Nelson Douglas   Canada $6.99

Buy them at your local bookstore or use this handy coupon:
Clip and mail this page with your order.

Publishers Book and Audio Mailing Service
P.O. Box 120159, Staten Island, NY 10312-0004

Please send me the book(s) I have checked above. I am enclosing $ _____
(Please add $1.50 for the first book, and $.50 for each additional book to cover
postage and handling. Send check or money order only—no CODs.)

Name _____

Address _____

City _____ State / Zip _____

Please allow six weeks for delivery. Prices subject to change without notice.

THE BEST OF FORGE

❑ 55052-8   LITERARY REFLECTIONS $5.99
        James Michener   Canada $6.99

❑ 52046-7   A MEMBER OF THE FAMILY $5.99
        Nick Vasile   Canada $6.99

❑ 52288-5   WINNER TAKE ALL $5.99
        Sean Flannery   Canada $6.99

❑ 58193-8   PATH OF THE SUN $4.99
        Al Dempsey   Canada $5.99

❑ 51380-0   WHEN SHE WAS BAD $5.99
        Ron Faust   Canada $6.99

❑ 52145-5   ZERO COUPON $5.99
        Paul Erdman   Canada $6.99

Buy them at your local bookstore or use this handy coupon:
Clip and mail this page with your order.

Publishers Book and Audio Mailing Service
P.O. Box 120159, Staten Island, NY 10312-0004

Please send me the book(s) I have checked above. I am enclosing $ _____
(Please add $1.50 for the first book, and $.50 for each additional book to cover
postage and handling. Send check or money order only— no CODs.)

Name_____

Address_____

City _____ State / Zip _____

Please allow six weeks for delivery. Prices subject to change without notice.